MW00653599

RIDGE

S.L. SCOTT

To keep up to date with her writing and more, her website is
www.slscottauthor.com

To receive the Scott Scoop about all of her publishing
adventures, free books, giveaways, steals and more, sign up
here: http://bit.ly/2TheScoop

Audiobooks are on major retailer sites.

To receive a free book now, TEXT "slscott" to 77948

New York Times Bestselling Author
S.L. SCOTT

PROLOGUE

Dave "Ridge" Carson

Somewhere between El Paso and Tucson, I found my soul under the bright stars of the Southwest.

Looking up, I drink her in. Meadow hates when I stare at her, but beauty like hers is rare. Her chin dips down, and she kisses my cheek, trailing more toward my ear where she whispers, "You feel so good inside me."

"You have it all wrong. You make me feel good inside you." I capture her lips on the edge of a laugh and kiss her while she continues to rock on top of my lap.

The sound of our bodies, our skin slick against each other becomes part of the hum of the desert outside the car. A night wind whistles through the cracked open window as the temperatures continue to fall well after sunset. We couldn't wait—not for a hotel or a rest stop. When her hand dipped to my pants and she rubbed over me, causing my body to react, I pulled over.

Time is our enemy. There's never enough of it when I'm with her. Every time I'm with her, I want to drain every ounce of life from the seconds, minutes, few short hours we get to be with each other.

My gaze rolls over the bottom of her jaw as her head tilts back, her mouth open, her bare breasts in front of me. I want to hold her still, hold her here, right the fuck here on top of me.

I run my hands over her body as I make love to the woman who's become an addiction of mine. I breathe better, easier when I'm with her. The music of our bodies together is the only melody I hear. She's become my friend.

My lover.

My muse.

Lifting up, she eases back down and then lifts again, gripping my shoulders and digging her nails into my skin. The pain is pleasure when doled out in provocative ways. "Dave," she whispers on the end of a purr. No other name has been uttered in pure ecstasy like the way she says mine.

I hold her by the hips in the back seat of the SUV taking in the full view. "Hey," I say.

She comes back to me, her eyes open, her soul exposed in such a vulnerable way, setting my heart on fire. "Hey." She smiles, and I hold her still again, wanting this to last forever while equally wanting to rush the release.

A few sips of the wine we've been drinking straight from the bottle make her eyes sparkle. Caught between want and need, her smile is even until the corners, which curve up. It's a smile that both hurts and heals my heart when it appears. "Don't leave."

Leaning down, she kisses my forehead, my nose, my mouth. With her lips against mine, she whispers, "I have to go."

I've been careful about making plans with her for so long that the words feel foreign to me even now when this feels more intimate than any other time before. Every time with her is like this—better than the last. "I want you to stay."

I fell for the free-spirited beauty long before we left Austin. But like all who are meant to soar, she can't be caged by antiquated notions of romance. Meadow Fellowes has been clear about what we are or ever could be—*nothing serious*. But sometimes, when she looks at me, I see more hidden in the emerald pools of her eyes. I understand the yearning. She says, "My flight is tomorrow night."

We've been so good at keeping it casual, but *nothing serious* means we're fucking because we want to have sex. This isn't fucking, just like we're not casual, not to me. "Can you change it? Give us another week. Another day. Give us a chance."

Leaning down, she kisses me and then sits back up. With her palms on my chest, she holds her smile. "I am. By leaving." Her eyes close, and she starts moving on top of me again.

So I grip her a little tighter, holding her while I can. I meet every one of her pushes with a thrust of my own. As she comes back to me, the lids are half-mast, but her gaze is fixed on me. She whispers, "Tell me what you're thinking."

"I'm thinking how good this feels. Just us. Alone. In the desert, making love, having sex, fucking. All of it. All of you. You feel so good to me. Maybe we should be more to each other."

"You're more than you know," she purrs softly and then leans back as if our connection is too much before she starts a slow gyrate. *God, she feels amazing.* A hand rubs over my chest, and this time, my eyes meet hers, coming back from the hazy edge of release. "We're not those people."

"What people are those?"

"The kind of people who make plans."

Our bodies glide together as I say, "We've made plans before."

"Spur-of-the-moment plans. Those don't count."

"They count." *They fucking count.* I want to argue, but my mind clouds as our bodies move of their own volition. My eyes dip closed, and I swim in the moment, buried deep inside her.

We fall, tipping over that line that keeps us safe and the one that will end us—heart, body, and soul. It's where I prefer to be with her. If only we could stay in this place longer than it takes for our breathing to recover.

My heart calms, and my breathing steadies. Meadow slides down with me still inside her and rests her head on my shoulder. Her fingers toy with the hairs on my chest before a kiss is placed on my neck. "Six months," she says. "I'll be back in six months."

I tighten my arms around her. I don't care that my body's too big for this back seat or that we're covered in sweat. All that matters is that I have her in my arms for a short time, and I intend to savor every second until she boards that plane.

1

Meadow Fellowes

Six Months Later . . .

Act surprised.

They've gone to a lot of trouble for "the American," the nickname I've been called on a daily basis since I started my internship last January. Working in London has changed me. My look. My attitude. My future. My gratitude for this experience at Brown and Davies can't be summed up in a simple thank you.

I hate surprises. I hate surprise parties even more, but they've gone to a lot of trouble to make me feel like a part of the team while I've been here. And from the french fries and burgers I smell wafting over the cubicle walls, I've made an impact on them, even if it's just the fine art of appreciating junk food.

Opening the blush compact, I use the mirror to apply my favorite shade of red lipstick, Tom & Cherry. I never wore red lips before moving here. It's bold, like I've become the past six months. And apparently makes my green eyes sparkle like emeralds. *So I've been told.* My flatmate's compliment came after a drunken night out, but I'll take it.

When I snap the compact closed, I pick up the burgundy Mont Blanc pen and read the engraving—*Well done, Miss Fellowes.*

Carrig Davies set the gift down on the table at lunch earlier in the week. *My gaze flicks back and forth between the classic white paper and gold bow and his ice blue eyes for an uncomfortable beat too long.* "What's this?"

"Open it."

I don't know why I hesitate. Unsure if this is a last-ditch effort to date me or if it's work related, I hold the oblong box in my hand and study it. I'm not sure why he gave me this present. "You shouldn't have."

"It's not a big deal. A parting gift to remember me . . . the company by."

Although he's a Davies, as in Brown and Davies, and his father is the founder and CEO, it will be his company to run one day. The contracts are already in place. He's been groomed for this since he was born. Basically, a dream come true—handsome, successful, loaded. But I have dreams of my own, and they're starting to come true. This internship is prestigious, and I'm returning to America with not only experience working for a global marketing firm, but also a recommendation that holds weight wherever I apply after graduation next year.

I have no intention of insulting a friend. He has shown me nothing but support at the office, so I slowly pull the bow and rip the paper away from the leather box. When I lift the lid, the light hits the pen. I must look confused because he says, "For all those deals you'll sign one day."

It actually is very kind. I smile, taking it out of the box. "Thank you. It's very nice."

"Like you."

. . . I use the expensive pen to sign my exit interview and then stand, adjusting my black pencil skirt and straightening my white silk blouse. I'm going to miss this place. Miss London. My flat, and my flatmate, Darcy. But I miss my sister so much, and every once in a while, when I'm home alone, I allow myself to think about a road trip I once took from Austin to LA, and I miss the man who looked at me like I hung the moon.

When I look down, the curled ends of my blond hair shine from the rays sneaking in through the window. I click my red-soled heels and silently remind myself—there's no place like home. Until I land back in the States, I put on my best straight face and pretend to know nothing regarding this party and start walking toward the conference room. I open the door, and it's showtime.

The pub is packed, which is typical for a Thursday night. Darcy is chatting up two guys from Australia who wandered into Punch and Judy a little while ago. Revelers needing a drink after work overflow onto Covent Garden.

Several pitchers in, my work mates are drunk fools. They claim they're celebrating as part of my going away party that started in the office and flowed down to the pubs shortly after. They'll use any excuse to have a pint. I guess I'm theirs tonight.

". . . Meadow." I usually leave Darcy to her own devices, but without fail, she eventually involves me in her shenanigans. "American . . ." I pick up bits and pieces of her conversation, still hoping she's not trying to set me up again, especially considering it's my last night here. "To Texas tomorrow."

Holding my hand up, I correct her with a slightly embarrassing slur. "LA actually."

I shouldn't have said anything. Darcy has stars in her eyes when it comes to celebrities, whether British or American, or any other. She loves the gossip, and here it comes. She clears her throat. "Meadow's sister is getting married to one of The Crow Brothers," she half-whispers but makes sure to speak loud enough to have everyone in the vicinity's attention. "You know, the band?"

They nod enthusiastically, and then I feel the heat of all eyes on me. I swivel in the other direction on my barstool until my knees bump into Carrig. "Oops. Sorry."

His hand braces my knee to keep from slipping another few inches and endangering another part of him. But he leaves it there. "Are you having a good time?"

"I am. Too good. I should have gone home an hour ago to finish packing."

"I'm closing out the tab for our group. May I see you home?"

The offer is tempting, considering the state I'm in, but I worry that a kiss is coming under the pressure of this last goodbye. "Thank you, but Darcy and I can manage," I say, slipping off the stool but wobbling on the high heels.

Carrig helps to steady me. "Let me hire a car for you then."

Surely there's no harm in that. "Darcy," I say, nodding toward the door. "Time to go."

She's dramatic and over the top with her arms in the air and a big disappointed sigh. She'll thank me later, though. We walk out with Carrig, and she elbows me, clearly more drunk than she realizes since that hurt like hell. I rub my arm and stand on the sidewalk as Carrig steps to the curb, looking in either direction and then back down at his phone. "The car's down here."

We walk down a bit and around the corner. When he sees it, he opens the door, and Darcy slides in like the princess she acts like she is. I stand, clutching my purse with both hands. "Guess this is it."

"Yes, I suppose so. You're off to America and back to your life."

He makes it sound more exciting than the reality. Not sure what to do, I say, "I should go."

As I duck into the back of the car, he says, "Take care of yourself, sunshine." He shuts the door, and I roll down the window.

"I will. You too." Guilt overcomes me. "If you're ever in the States—"

"I'll look you up."

"Yes." I smile and lean forward to give the address to the driver. Looking back, I wave. "Bye."

As soon as the car pulls away, Darcy says, "I will never understand how you can pass up that man. Whoever kept you from moving on with Carrig Davies must be one hell of a great lay."

This time I elbow her lightly. "Darcy." My face heats when the driver's eyes meet mine in the mirror.

Dave. It's a name I don't ever say and I think about too much—the man more than the name. Out of habit, I take my lipstick out of my purse and pull the cap off.

Darcy swipes it away and glides it over her full lips without a mirror and to perfection. She's the one who got me into makeup—to play with it and use it to my advantage. I don't wear as much as she does, and I'm not as colorful, but I've learned a trick or two since my Austin days.

She says, "It's true, and I cannot wait to meet him."

"There's no him to meet. I'm single. I was single when I left the States, and I'll be single when I return."

"Speaking of single, am I going to be your plus-one to

the wedding? Don't forget, you promised me over cider and biscuits last month."

"We may have been drinking, but I didn't forget. Don't worry, my sister already knows you're coming."

We wake up early to catch the tube to the Square Mile, work our derrieres off all day, and then hit Covent Garden five out of seven nights. I never tasted freedom until this move. With no friends or family to rely on, I made my own way.

Darcy never needed a roommate but moved me in before I could pay another month's rent at the other place. We just became instant best friends. She became someone I could rely on.

But she can drink. Returning to the States will give my liver a much-needed break, but it's been a blast. "I'm going to miss you."

Her curly tendrils cover my neck when she leans her head on my shoulder. "You've come a long way, Fellowes, and I'm not referring to the miles. Whoever shall I party with now?"

"You have a billion friends. I'm sure someone will happily take my place."

"You're going to have an amazing time back in Texas, but I still get full credit for bringing you out of your shell."

"I know it's hard to imagine," I say sarcastically, "but I had a life before meeting you." Patting her leg, we both laugh.

She leans against the window and looks at me. "Until I see it with my own eyes, I refuse to believe it."

"I can't wait to show you around Austin and then Los Angeles when we're there for the wedding."

"You know, you've never shared how your sister snagged a famous rock star."

"Because, my dear Darcy, he is the lucky one who snagged her."

While laughing, she leans over and hugs me. "If she's anything like you, he is most definitely the lucky one." Slumping back in the seat, she closes her eyes. "Wake me when we arrive."

"Okay."

It's not much longer until we reach our row of flats, but just enough time for her to doze off.

Before heading to the airport the next morning, I jump on Darcy's bed and smother her with a hug. "I'll see you in two weeks."

She pushes me off with a smile on her face and an eye mask crooked across her forehead. "I need peace and quiet, noisy American."

"I'm going. I'm going."

I make it to the door before she sits up, and says, "I'm going to miss you."

Tears well in her eyes. She's usually great about having a stiff upper lip, but now that we're saying goodbye, I'm glad to see her give up some of the pride.

Running back over, I flop onto the side of the bed and hug her silly. "You too. Only a couple of weeks."

There's no time to waste. The car's waiting downstairs for me, so I hop off the bed and walk to the door again. She pulls her eye mask down and waves me away. "Go. I can't handle this much emotion early in the morning."

"It's almost eleven."

"Still before noon," she singsongs. "Anyway, you need to get back to whoever has preoccupied your sexual mind for the past six months."

I roll my eyes. "For the last time . . ." I realize it is for the last time, and the thought makes me sad, but I take a page from her book and raise my chin. "For fuck's sake, Darce, there's no one preoccupying anything of mine. That's why you gave me that toy. So I appreciate your constant concern for my sexual satisfaction, but I'm good."

"But you'll tell me if you meet someone, right?" Flipping her mask up, she eyes me.

"Yes. You'll be the third or fourth to know."

"Wow, Fellowes. And here I thought we were besties."

"We are." She stretches her arm toward me and then her pinky pops out. I wrap mine in a pinky promise. "Besties."

"Besties." As soon as our hands fall away, she says, "You're still prettier than Angelina Jolie."

"You're still drunk. Go to sleep and I'll call you later tonight when I'm settled in."

"Cheerio."

I laugh because I've been here for all this time and never heard one English person use that term until now. "Now you're just showing off your fancy accent and English-isms."

She laughs as I drag my suitcase to the door. Stopping, I take one last look before I go. "It's been good, flat, but it's time to go. Cheerio."

2

Meadow

THE FIRST WEEK back in the States is spent acclimating at my sister's new house in the Hollywood Hills. I lounge by the pool most days, and we go shopping for new furniture and décor on the other days.

We've gone sightseeing, to the beach, and I've napped a few afternoons away. "Basically, I'm living my best life," I brag-joke to Darcy on the phone.

"Sounds like it. Any new details about the wedding I should be aware of? Which celebrities will be in attendance, and is there a way to get a copy of the list of single men who will be there?"

"No new details. Yes to musicians. And no to the list. Does that answer all your questions?"

"For now." She laughs, then says, "I need to go. My boss is being a real wanker today."

Her boss, Carrig, laughs in the background. "Is that Meadow on the phone? May I speak with her?"

"Yes," she replies, but her voice is muffled as if she's covering the phone with her hand, "but she's off in the City of Lost Angels and can't be bothered with us lot."

"Are you speaking with her on company time? That's against policy, you know."

Next thing I know, his voice fills the line. "Hi."

"Hi." I lie in my bed with the phone to my ear, not wanting to get up to start the day.

"How are you getting along across the pond?"

"Fine and dandy. It is where I'm from," I say as if he'd forgotten. "The transition back is much easier than when I arrived in London."

"I imagine. Darcy was telling me that you're in LA. I have business there in two days. I was thinking we could have a meal together."

"How long will you be here?"

"One night and then I'm off to New York for meetings there."

"Quick trip."

Not shy to put on the pressure, he adds, "Seeing a friendly face will ease it."

"Two days? I've already made plans, so—"

"I'm only there for one night, and I was really hoping to see you."

I'm sucker for the guilt. "Well, whether I go or not, we can at least meet for a drink."

"Yes, at least," he says. "Text me the details and I'll see you then."

He hangs up so fast that I don't even get a chance to say goodbye to Darcy.

"Which one?" I ask, flipping between the two dresses. "The green or the red?"

My sister glances from one dress to the other and then scrunches her nose. "They're so dressy. It's just a bonfire."

"But I'm getting drinks beforehand." Swinging the green dress in front of my body, I study my reflection in the full-length mirror in her master bathroom. "I want to look nice."

"You always look beautiful whether you're in cutoffs or fancy dresses, but you can't wear heels on the beach." She sits on the vanity chair, and asks, "When did you become such a fashionista anyway? You didn't used to pay much mind to labels."

"The dresses look expensive, but Darcy gave them to me. So, you see, I got an amazing deal." We didn't grow up with money to blow. Stella still drives her aging beige sedan she's had for years, so she tends to be frugal. But her fiancé, Rivers Crow, is like my big brother. I've known him since I was eleven, so when they got engaged last year, he offered to help pay my living expenses and college tuition. This included my internship in London.

I saved in other ways to afford a few nice things, which allowed me to be a whole new me in England. It was a gratifying change, but overall, I'm still the same girl I always was. I don't mind a broken-in pair of jeans and cozy tee. Darcy, who has money to burn and seems to be working for fun, gave me a few of her hand-me-downs, like last season's runway hits. But according to her, they're out this season. I happily took those off her hands and bought her a few cocktails in payment for the others.

"Can't beat that good deal."

Stella comes up behind me and messes my hair up. "What are you doing?" I gripe, ducking out of the way.

"Trying to find Meadow."

"I'm right here."

Although she's being a brat, her smile is still kind as she looks at me. "You're the fancy version. If you don't mind slumming it, I have a new sundress that would look perfect on you and fits tonight's occasion."

I drape the dresses over my arm, and say, "Lead the way." I haven't changed that much. But being around Darcy for six months helped me realize I like to dress up occasionally. Before I leave the bathroom, though, I dab the corner of my mouth where my lipstick has smudged.

Standing in the middle of the bedroom, I wait for Stella to appear from her immense closet. Hollywood homes have the best closets I've ever seen. She walks out holding a white dress on a hanger with tags still hanging from the side of the dress. I move closer to inspect it. "It's actually very pretty."

"Gee thanks. You say that as if I wear ugly clothes."

Touching the bottom of the skirt, I say, "No. I didn't mean it that way. I just didn't expect you to like something so sweet. It reminds me of what I used to wear in Austin."

"Me too." I'm not sure if she's referring to me or her, but either way, she's right. I'm the spitting image of my older sister. Her hair is a little darker and her green eyes a shade softer, but there's no denying from our features that we're closely related.

"The tags are still on. Are you sure you don't mind me borrowing it?"

"Not at all. I think it's perfect for you and tonight." She hands me the dress, and asks, "So your date tonight—"

"It's not a date."

She looks at me, analyzing me. "Then what is it?"

"It's two friends getting together."

"Ah," she hums as if she doesn't believe me. "I thought he was your old boss?"

"He's not old, but he is a friend."

Sitting on the bed, she rests her weight on her hands. "There were never any sparks?"

For him. *Maybe.* For me. *No.* "I told you—"

"Yeah. Yeah. Yeah. You're just friends. I get it."

Cocking an eyebrow up at her, I ask, "You sure?"

That makes her laugh. "I'm sure."

"I'm going to wear dressy shoes for drinks, but I'm bringing flip-flops in my bag for the party so I don't have to come home first." With the three dresses in hand, I turn to go to the room I'm staying in while I'm here. "Thanks for the dress."

I should have known better. Carrig somehow managed to wrangle himself an invite to the bonfire. The reality is I was a sucker for his poor me sitting in a hotel story. One day, I hope to grow a backbone.

Having drinks was fun, but I was hoping to catch up with everyone without having to entertain someone else.

As soon as we got our first drinks, he had to take a call from Tokyo, so we headed out front to get away from the crowds. He's since wandered down the driveway.

With a red Solo cup in hand, I sit on the porch under the light collecting flies. The wood bench is hard, so I begin to pace until I hear voices coming up the path. "Carrig?" Looking around the wide column, I freeze.

And so does he.

Dave stands on the pavers looking at me as though he's seen a ghost. The woman on his right stares at me, but then her gaze drifts to her date. "Ridge?"

The name brings him out of the state I seem to have caused, and he says, "Meadow."

My heart beats faster from the sound of his voice.

My heart beats.

It's the first time I've felt that organ come alive after so many months. "Dav—Ridge."

I don't need a man to make me feel whole, I remind myself.

I definitely do not need Ridge Carson trying to woo me into his bed.

All he ever had to do was give me that smirk, and I'd be two steps ahead. Seeing him now, it's clear I need more time to build up a tolerance so I don't fall under his seductive spell again.

Too late.

He shoves his hands in the front pockets of his jeans. "It's good to see you." *You feel so good to me. Maybe we should be more to each other.*

Dressed in a body glove of a revealing red dress, the woman with long and wild strawberry hair wraps her hand around his arm. I suddenly feel like a child in this white dress. I straighten a spaghetti strap that's fallen down. "You too."

The woman doubles down and adds her other hand to his arm. "Should we go inside?"

I take a sip and hope they're gone by the time I lower the plastic cup. His gaze finds its way to the pathway, and he nods. Just as he passes me, he says, "I'll see you inside?"

"Yeah."

His words from another time suddenly feel meaningless. When the door closes behind them, I'm left feeling like an idiot. I finish off the wine I've been nursing and set the cup down just as Carrig comes back. "Did I tell you how ravishing you look?"

"Ravishing. No. I would have remembered that."

The smile slips up the right side of his mouth. "Ravishing indeed."

Unlike what I just experienced with Dave . . . well . . .

Ridge, I guess here . . . Carrig is excited to see me. *And it's only been ten minutes and not six months.*

"Thank you. You look . . . beachy." He's nailed 1990 with his rolled-at-the-ankles khakis and white-and-pink-striped button up. All he needs is a sweater wrapped around his shoulders. He's always in a suit or a more casual version of it when I've seen him. I'm curious if he always tries to hit the theme of a party or if tonight's just special.

His elbow pivots out, and he says, "Shall we go in?"

"Absolutely."

When we walk inside, the house is fairly empty. "Most people are at the beach already. Want to grab a drink and head down?"

I get another cup of wine, and he fills his cup with beer from the keg. We then make our way across the patio and down the steps to the sand, my eyes immediately landing on Dave despite the dark.

The fire roars to life to a thrill of happy hoots and hollers. Carrig takes a few steps back, but I stay. Teasing him, I ask, "You afraid of a little fire?"

He points at the bonfire. "That's not little."

"Don't worry, I'll protect you." I laugh and take a sip.

At least he has a sense of humor and laughs. Within minutes, I've run out of things to say. I never had this problem in London, but here, with my sister, friends, two of three of the Crow brothers, and Dave, my mind's gone blank. I could blame it on the wine or the company, but deep down, I know.

It's him. "The one" Darcy loved to tease me about.

I've caught Dave's eyes on me a few times just as he's caught mine on him. We've orbited around the fire as if our paths have never crossed and never will.

It's probably best I accept that our short *time of fun* was just that. I don't know if the woman on his arm is his girl-friend, but he hasn't left her side.

Because he is a gentleman, Mead. You know this.

I sigh. She doesn't seem like his type, but what do I know these days. For a while, I knew him and thought I knew him well, but he hasn't been in my life for six months, and I've not been in his.

We've been leading entirely different lives. Even though he seems like the same man, I'm not the same little girl he once knew.

I introduce Carrig to Stella and Rivers when they're free from chatting with others, then say, "You do a mean big brother stare, Rivers."

Rivers half smiles before crossing his arms over his chest and keeping his eyes on Carrig. "Mission accomplished." Carrig doesn't come off as intimidated, but I know him well enough to know he won't push back.

Stella finally elbows Rivers, and says, "Leave him alone."

She turns to Carrig and smiles. It's not as genuine as most of hers, but she still manages to make him feel at ease. He leans closer to me. "Would you like another drink?"

"Let me get you another beer."

"Okay." I dash off before he decides to come with me.

Tonight feels weird. I knew it was a bad idea to bring him. I can't relax, too worried he's not having a good time instead of only worrying about myself. Between him and the jet lag that I can't seem to fully shake, a tension hangs around my shoulders.

And I'm still surprised Dave didn't know I was back in LA. Hadn't Rivers said anything to him? Or did he really not actually care? *Gah.* Overthinking much? Just go to the loo already—*the bathroom. Leftover British influence.*

Inside the navy blue powder room, I pull my lipstick from between my boobs and carefully apply a new coat. I

don't rub my lips together to spread the temporary paint. It
messes up the smoothness.

I tug a few strands of hair back in place and then open
the door.

Standing there with his back to the wall of the hall and a
leg kicked up while his arms are crossed, Dave says, "Hello
again."

3

Ridge

God, she's gorgeous.

Meadow was before, but wow, she's changed. Gone is the girl I met last year in Austin and standing here is a woman. *A sexy, stunning, and fucking incredible woman.* Every part of her from those emerald-green eyes to those full cherry-red lips causes a guttural reaction in the rawest form.

"Hi," she says, shifting out of the doorway as we exchange places. We've been doing this dance all night. I move to the left, she moves to the left. Our positions around the bonfire are always changing, but the distance never lessening.

I'm starting to take things personally.

"How are you?" Fuck, this is awkward. Standing alone with her in this hallway, there's no hiding how I feel, and every hard swallow is heard. But it seems she's forgotten how to read me. Her expression is one of curiosity, but shyness is winning out.

"I'm fine. Good. You?"

"Yeah. Fine. Good." This is fucking painful. *Kill me now.*

Maybe I've also forgotten how to read the nuances that make up the myriad of Meadow Soleil Fellowes's emotions. Even now, she looks down the long hall, her discomfort obvious, but why? It's me. Me, the man who offered to lasso the moon that night in the desert. And her, the girl who managed to lasso my heart with just three words—*I'll miss you.*

"I should go," she says, glancing down the hall for like the billionth time. I'm tempted to ask if she actually did miss me or if it was easy to forget who we once were. But that sounds bitter, and I haven't been bitter until now.

"Why?"

Her eyebrows shoot up. "Why what?"

"Why do you have to go?" I ask with nothing left to lose.

Her expression softens, and she smiles. What a glorious sight to see. The question seems to put her at ease, and she rests her shoulders against the wall. "Why is this so awkward?"

"I was just thinking the same thing. It's not like us."

"No," she agrees with a nod and a little laugh that tickles my ears. "It's not us at all." Pausing, she finally looks at me, past the hazel of my eyes and deep inside. She always had a knack for seeing the real me. *Dave* instead of *Ridge.* "How are you really?"

"I have great days." Leaning against the doorframe, the light from the bathroom behind me shines bright on her, putting me in a silhouette. "And some really shit days."

"Why do you have shit days?"

She never used to swear or maybe I just never noticed before. "Same ole. Gets lonely on the road. It's tiring to perform so many shows in a row."

"How are you lonely when you're surrounded by friends?"

"I think you just answered your own question." *Friends.* Not the more we once talked about. *Just friends.*

"First time back?"

"Yeah. I was kept busy at the firm. Made friends." Her eyes light up. "London was amazing. I didn't expect to like it as much as I did."

"That's good, right?"

"Yes, that's good." The light dims in her eyes, and she looks down. "I'm sorry I didn't call—"

"No, you were busy. You did what you needed to do. I'm sure it wasn't easy to leave. I'm proud of you."

When her eyes find mine again, she asks, "You're proud of me for leaving?"

"I'm proud of you for following your dreams."

"Oh," she replies, toeing the hardwood floor.

"There you are." The sound of Kiki's voice echoes from the other end of the hallway. "I've been looking for you everywhere."

Meadow pushes off the wall and glances at me once more before she walks away. Her head isn't lowered, and the shyness gone when she passes Kiki, and says, "You found him."

The clack of Kiki's heels on the floors as she comes toward me could wake the dead. Stopping in front of me, she crosses her arms and pushes her hair away from her face. "Did you hear what she said to me?"

"Yes."

Looking over her shoulder, clearly to make sure the coast is clear, she turns back, and rants, "She's so rude. Obviously, she wants you, and she's just jealous of me." Touching the front of my T-shirt, she puts on a fake smile and utters, "Namaste, bitch," under her breath.

We're an inch from each other. Did she really think I wouldn't hear that? "Don't call her that."

"But you heard how she talked to me—"

"Ever."

A thin, tweezed red eyebrow cocks, and her lips purse. "So you've had sex with her? If not, why would you defend her?"

"It's none of your business. You and I are friends. I don't owe you answers regarding who I do or don't sleep with."

"Friends, huh?" she asks to herself as if she's just accepted a challenge.

I knew better than to bring her. She caught me in a weak moment—lonely, drunk, and horny as fuck—and begged me to give her another shot.

She just blew it. *Again.*

Going inside the bathroom, I shut the door behind me, making sure to lock it so she doesn't think it's an invitation. I hear her hanging around outside the door, and then she says, "I'm sorry. I get jealous. You know that, Ridge."

I understand jealousy. I've fucking felt it all night, but I've been better at hiding it behind bad alibis—the wood crackling, the waves crashing. The growl that ripped through me earlier when that preppy asshole touched Meadow's lower back was explained away with a lame excuse of a piece of glass cutting my foot. It distracted Kiki enough to forget she heard my body reacting to the woman in the white dress.

There was no glass, only a bad acting job on my part. Kiki wants to hook up so badly that she'll swallow any pill of an excuse I give her. That I have to give her excuses is the exact reason I didn't want to bring her.

I take a piss and then wait her out. When the heels clack back down the hall, I open the door and decide it's time to leave. I can't be here with her. I don't want to be here with Meadow and that dick in the rolled-up dad pants. Am I giving him a fair shake? *Nope.* I sure the fuck am not. Do I care? *Nope.* I sure the fuck don't.

Kiki's out on the patio. As soon as she sees me, she wraps her arms around her body and shivers. "It's so cold."

"Sorry. I don't have a jacket." I stand near the railing and look down at the bonfire, scanning the partiers to find Meadow. When I don't see her, I say, "I'm ready to go."

"Me too." She comes to me and rubs my arm. "I'm so ready."

As soon as we go inside, Meadow's there with a red cup in hand. I'm not sure what to say, not in front of Kiki. Seconds tick and Meadow finally says, "I was getting a refill. Wine."

"Wine. Yeah." Stepping forward, I ask, "Hey, do you have quick sec to talk?" Her eyes drift over my shoulder to Kiki, so I add, "In private?"

"Sure." The answer is as awkward as we are right now, but I'll take it.

I may not be happy with Kiki, but she deserves better than I'm giving her, so I try to fix it the best I can. Turning back to Kiki, I keep my voice down. "Do you mind waiting a minute?"

Her arms are crossed over her chest, and her foot is tapping. As she searches the high-beamed ceilings for the answer, she huffs. "I guess."

"Thanks. I'll be right back."

Taking Meadow by the arm, I guide her to the back hall again, but this time, we enter one of the bedrooms. When I shut the door, she doesn't even flinch, not one worry crosses her pretty face. Because she knows me. She trusts me.

"I'm being a total asshole to her right now."

That makes her smile a little too big. "You are."

"It's worth it to talk to you."

"It is, huh?"

I replace a heavy breath, and suddenly, it feels like us

again. Without pretenses or dates, just her and I alone, we can let down our guards. "I want to see you."

Surprise colors her face. "That's unexpected."

"Not really. Let's meet and talk. Catch up. I want to hear about everything you did in London. I want to hear about where you lived and what you ate. Who you hung out with and your work. I want to hear about you."

She sits on the end of the bed and takes a sip of her drink. Knowing Kiki is waiting on us, and asshat is probably waiting on her, I dig her rebellious time-sucking ways. "Only to talk?"

"I think it's clear we aren't where we were when you left. So let's get to know each other again."

"As friends?"

The question knocks me in the gut. *Is that what we are?* "I thought we were friends."

Her smile returns. "We are. I leave for Austin next week. Maybe we can get together before then?"

I pull out my phone to get her number, realizing I already have it. She walks next to me and stands, arm to arm, looking at the phone in my hand. "You never called me either." She opens the door and looks back over her shoulder when I look at her over mine. "You've still got my number. Make sure to use it this time."

She leaves the room, and I'm left with my phone in my hand and the faint scent of her perfume lingering in the air. *Fuck.* She's amazing. *Make sure to use it this time. Feisty little thing.* I call the number I never took off speed dial.

Laughter echoes down the hall, and then she answers, "Hello?"

"Hey. It's Ridge—" I catch myself. "It's Dave. Dave Carson. I don't know if you remember me."

"I remember you. Long time, no talk."

"Too long. Sorry about that."

"We all get busy sometimes."

"Yeah, we do." I clear my throat, and then say, "So I was thinking we could get some tea or grab a beer together. Something low-key and catch up."

"You remembered I like tea."

Peeking out of the room, I spy her leaning against the wall at the far end of the hall. She's sliding one of her flip-flops back and forth and smiling as she looks down. That's the smile I remember she had just for me. "Some things are hard to forget."

Her voice is low for privacy, but light as air in emotion. "They sure are. I'd like to catch up with you. Did you have a day and time in mind?"

"Tomorrow too soon?"

"No. You're right on time."

"I'll text you tomorrow morning then."

"It's a date . . . I mean, it's a catch up."

I chuckle. "Yeah, a catch up."

Her sweet melody of a laugh follows mine, and she says, "Bye, Dave."

"Bye, Meadow."

I give her a minute to rejoin the party before I leave the room. We left it in too good a place to ruin it with my exit as I take another woman home. To her home, not mine, but still. I don't want get into all that tonight.

Anyway, she has her own situation to sort out. By her body language tonight and considering she just said yes to meeting up with me, I'm taking it that they're nothing serious. A favorite phrase of hers.

Wonder if it's what I'll hear this time around.

Fuck, I hope not.

4

Meadow

PULLING the covers up to my neck, I lie in the dark bedroom of my sister's house. It doesn't feel like home since the surroundings are still so new, but it feels homey, like her, like Rivers. Even a little like me.

I'm comfortable here, but I'll be returning to Austin soon to finish my last year of school. Not before a quick . . . I don't know what it is, but catch up feels safe to use when it comes to Dave. Ridge. *What do I call him these days*? He was Ridge when I met him and became Dave as I got to know him.

The woman in the red dress called him Ridge. It makes me wonder how well she knows him. For the public, I always called him Ridge too. He was Dave to me in private. Ugh. I've drunk too much to get caught up in this mind spin.

I close my eyes, my thoughts going back to the beach tonight.

Carrig's nowhere to be seen, so I ask Rivers, "Is he dating her?"

"Is who dating who?"

Sometimes, I wish men were more in tune to reading women's minds. I whisper, "Ridge. Is he dating the woman he was with when he was here?"

Rivers takes a drink of beer and looks around as though he hadn't noticed they left. Lowering the cup, he shrugs. "Dating's not really what they do."

"Oh." I try to act casual, but there's a weird ache in my chest. I rub it with the pad of my palm. "So they're a thing? Like you've met her before?"

It didn't seem like she had met the band by the way she was dragging him over to Rivers and Tulsa and chatting them up. Tulsa was distracted by his wife who was skinny-dipping, and Rivers doesn't play the fame game. If someone acts like a groupie, he retreats inward and goes quiet. Stella is great about taking the lead at times like those.

He shakes his head. "We haven't met her, but we've seen her around before. She's connected to the Hollywood scene. Her brother's a producer or some movie exec."

Stella joins us with a half drunk beer in her hand. "I love the ocean."

Rivers's arm wraps around her shoulders, and he pulls her close. He always keeps her close. After a five-year breakup, he's not willing to lose her again.

But what I love the most is watching Rivers come alive when Stella is near. Having watched him around Kiki, I saw the man reticent to engage. But he's so different with Stella. He's great for her, but God, she is amazing for him. Seeing them together? It almost makes me believe in fairy tales. Almost.

I'm careful not to walk that tightrope. Too many people fall and there's only one place to land—heartbreak city.

A text catches my attention, and my heart beats a little faster. This is not a good sign. I thought he was out of my system, but a simple chime has me wishing we were right back where we used to be. Dave and I may not have ended on a great note, but we always made great music.

That fast beating heart sinks to the pit of my stomach when I see the message is from Carrig. I want to tell him to fuck off, but he's not doing anything wrong. He hasn't crossed any lines since I drew them in the relationship sand.

Just because we went out a few times together and it didn't work out doesn't mean he's the enemy. He's actually a decent guy, just not "the one" for me. But when I was in London, he became a friend I appreciated.

Tonight wasn't all bad. I mean besides the good of seeing Dave again, Carrig was entertaining. By the end of the night, he managed to find his way back to his hotel in Beverly Hills despite getting lost on the beach after taking a walk. He finally found his drunken way back to the bonfire, but is lucky the neighbors didn't call the police.

He's definitely out of sorts when he's not in the city. Our goodbye was short, and though he tried to make it sweet, his lips landed on my cheek.

The text reads: *I had a good time tonight. Leaving in the morning, but would love to have a chat soon.*

Me: *Safe travels.*

I'm not sure what else to say, so I leave it at that, and apparently that's enough because he does too.

Or so I think. My phone rings. "Ugh. Really?" I answer to get it over with so I'm not the one left to have to call him back. "It's late, Carrig, and—"

"It's Dave."

I sit straight up. "Oh. Hi. Sorry, I thought it was—"

"Yeah, Carrig. I gathered that." He chuckles, and I appreciate that he's not upset. I mean, why would he be? He doesn't really have the right. Something I also don't have.

We were never a couple in the traditional sense, but we were working our way there. Life. *His.* School. *Mine.* We had so many obstacles in our way. My internship came at the right time. It allowed me not only the perspective I needed to stay on track with my own goals but also to focus on me.

Now that I've had a taste of real life beyond school, I'm more motivated than ever to graduate and finally start living.

He says, "I was lying here thinking about you."

"Something we have in common."

"You're lying in bed thinking about you too?"

I start giggling. "Something like that. So what were you thinking about me?"

"It was good to see you again. I just wanted to tell you that."

Dave was always a good guy, but it's nice to have the reminder. "It was good seeing you again too. And I'll see you tomorrow, right?"

"Yes. Good night, Meadow."

"Good night."

My smile remains long after we hang up. Something with us, the interactions and the vibe between us seems different. *Better.* I have to go back to Austin, but this time when I leave, maybe we can remain friends.

I was tempted to wear one of my fancier dresses but decided it was too much for a tea date. Anyway, he's a rock star who never cared about fashion. He used to love yoga pants and a tank top on me. So I know I can dress casually.

That doesn't mean I've given up all sense of fashion just because I left London, though. I straighten one of my flutter sleeves that has been giving me trouble since I left the Holly-wood Hills. Giving up on the impossible sleeve, I tug at the top of my capri-style jeans to make sure the bloating from all the vino last night isn't making a grand entrance.

Dave stands when I walk in. I weave my way through the tables to the one in the corner. I've been to this coffee shop before and know it's impossible to score a table. I lift to kiss him on the cheek, but he angles back not sure what I'm doing. "Oh," I say, "Sorry about the cheek kiss. Habit I picked up in England."

"I was going to say Hollywood, but what else did you pick up in England?"

I'm not sure if he's referring to people or habits, and since I set myself up for that, I let it go. "How early did you have to get here to score this table?"

"Just a few hours."

My jaw drops. "You've been here for hours?"

He sits down after I do. "No," he says, laughing. "I just walked in, and a guy was leaving. Great timing is all."

"As a guitarist, you always did have great timing."

"Maybe not so much with us."

"Your timing was perfect. It's my timing that . . ." I set my purse down on the edge of the table since the floor looks like it's in need of a good mopping. "Well, no sense living in the past."

A barista walks to our table and sets down two hot drinks and a plate of treats. "I love these biscuits . . . I mean, cookies."

"Wow, you really acclimated right into the English lifestyle."

"I went into survival mode so I wouldn't be made fun of. Over there, they called me 'the American,' but here, my sister says I picked up an accent."

"You did. It's not strong, but I hear it."

Of course he does. Musicians have great ears. But that he noticed after so few words, that . . . well, that makes me feel a little special.

"It will fade completely once I return to Texas." I spin the mug around and read the tea tag, "Your life is made of infinite possibilities."

"It's true."

"Yes," I say amused. "I'll be saying y'all before you know it."

"The part about your life and the possibilities."

I nod. "I'm starting to believe it's true." I leave the tea bag in the cup and don't use cream or sugar violating British law. Well, I'm sure it has to be a law over there by how much I was harassed by Darcy to remove the bag before drinking. The memory makes me smile. "Thank you for the tea. You remembering what I like means a lot to me."

"You're welcome."

When I look up, his eyes are trained on me, running the course of my face as if checking for other differences between who he knew me to be then and now. I say, "Stella said the band has already played fifteen shows this summer."

Wading into safer waters, he sits back and begins to relax. Like me, I can tell he's trying to figure out so much of what we were versus what we are. "We have fifteen more to go and then Europe in September."

"How many shows?"

"Four overseas and then we're back."

"You're popular in London. Sometimes I would hear the songs playing through the open windows of a passing car or speakers in the park, and my roommate listened to your albums more than a few times."

"You'd hear us played everywhere, but did you ever listen to the songs?"

Avoiding the question, I reply, "I know the songs. I know them by heart."

He sees through me, still knows how to see the truth. He chooses not to pursue that avenue, and asks, "So you're going back to Austin next week?"

"Yes, I'll be registering again, but it's mainly because I have to meet with my advisor to turn in my paper. The internship provides credits I need to graduate, but it all has to be verified as well as me writing about it. The trip will be fairly quick since I need to be back for the wedding planning." My gaze falls to the tea that's getting cold. "Are you going to drink that?"

Looking obligated, he picks up the mug. I've never seen him drink tea before, and I watch with rapt attention as he takes a sip. "Do you like it?"

"It grows on you. It's good to hear you'll be back."

"Thanks. I'm trying to help my sister as much as I can. She's always been there for me. I want to be there for her."

"You've always been close. I remember the first time I saw you . . . *two*. The Fellowes sisters."

Taking a shortbread cookie, I break it, devouring one half and savoring the other. "What do you remember?"

"I remember the jeans you were wearing."

"The jeans?" I ask, shocked by his answer. "I don't even remember what jeans I was wearing."

"They were tight in all the right places."

I burst out laughing. "Of course, you remember that."

There's no shame in his memory game. He adds, "They hugged your ass, and your legs looked a mile long."

"I need to find these jeans. They sound awesome."

He takes another sip, seeming to let it *grow on him* as he puts it. "They are."

Conversation with him smoothed out and got easier. So much so that we lose track of time until his phone buzzes across the table, stealing his attention away from me. "I'm sorry. I have to take this."

"It's okay. Go ahead."

He stands and goes outside. With one finger plugged in the opposite ear of the phone, he stops pacing on the sidewalk and looks down. It's not a pleasant call by the visual cues. I check the time and wonder how long we can honestly let this carry on.

I don't want to our time to end, but there's something to the saying—*Always leave them wanting more*. I stand when he comes in the door. When he comes back to the table, he stops in front of me. "Are you leaving?"

"I have to go."

Our eyes lock over the familiar words that were said so long ago. He laughs to himself, his gaze falling to the phone in his hand. When he looks up, he says, "I'm not sure what to say."

"You don't have to say anything. Today was nice. Really nice, but—"

The toe of his shoe bumps against the toe of my flats. "But?"

But you're still as gorgeous and genuine as I remember. But I want to work out what I should do with my life. But time with you is so easy, easy to get lost in you again. "But for now . . . that's all there is?" Why did I phrase that as a question?

He leaves some cash on the table, and we walk out silently. As soon as the door closes, though, he turns to face me. "Is that what you want, Meadow?"

"For now, it is."

"Not sure I agree with you there, beautiful. What if we could be whatever we want to be? What if we get to define our lives however we see?"

Caught up in the moment, I ask, "What do you see when you look at me?"

"Infinite possibilities."

5

Meadow

A BEAUTIFUL BACKYARD with an incredible view gives me the perfect opportunity to avoid responsibility. So does a certain rock star with soulful eyes who I can't seem to stop thinking about.

Focus, Meadow.

My inner voice has become more demanding since this morning; the reminders to concentrate became harsh since treating myself kinder didn't work. That voice has also been using a mean British accent, but that's because my head is all messed up as I transition between two countries.

A nicer voice chimes in from the other side of the pool, and I look up to see Stella with two drinks in her hands. "You've been out here for hours."

"I can't seem to wrap my head around my time in London for this paper. Twenty thousand words seems like a lot until I try to squeeze an experience that feels bigger than an *internship* on the page."

She sets a glass of iced tea in front of me and then settles in a chair across the table with her own drink in hand. "It changed you." She doesn't get into the nitty-gritty of how I'm different, but we both know.

"Yeah, it did. I don't know what it was, but I felt alive when I was there."

Although I know my sister is happy for me, she seems to be struggling to hide something that resembles pain in her eyes.

"Don't go quiet on me." I ask, "What is it?"

"I'm in LA. You're in Austin now, but I was hoping you would come out here once you graduated. Now I'm worried you'll fly off to London." Guilt weaves into her brow, and she looks down, dragging a finger through the condensation on the glass. "It's selfish, but I miss you." When her softer shade of green eyes find mine, she adds, "I thought you would come back to visit at least while you were gone, and you didn't. If you move there, will I ever see you again?"

Stella has always protected me from the uglier side of life. That includes our parents when she could. She's not been just my sister but also a best friend, a mom, and a dad. So hearing her share her feelings is something newer, something she's learned to do after the bad she went through . . . we all went through last year. I guess life-and-death situations do that to you. It taught me that my sister needed me. Prior to that, like most younger siblings, I had no clue. Particularly because of life circumstances, she was my go-to person. Now, as adults, we're closer and more . . . equals.

"I'm not moving to London. At least I don't think so. I have no reason to be there. It was an amazing experience, but it was temporary, which is why I stayed and didn't visit. I'm sorry if that hurt you. It was honestly because I was trying to live in the present and enjoy the opportunity that you and Rivers made possible."

"We only contributed money, Meadow. You earned the opportunity through your hard work." Resting back, she looks out over the yard, staring at the trees. "They're fruit trees. Lemon and orange, and we have an avocado tree over there. Imagine walking out and just plucking them right from the branch." The smile that everyone falls in love with appears. "I think I died and went to heaven."

Rivers leans out the open pocket door that divides their inside living space from the patio outside. "Hey babe, any packages come?"

"Strings?"

"That would be it."

She replies, "I put the box on top of the blue guitar case so you could find it." Glancing at me, she does a half eye-roll, teasing. They're funny together.

"That would be a good place to find it." Rivers is laughing at himself, but stops to ask, "You guys need anything?"

This time, I reply, "We're good."

Satisfied, he goes back inside.

I say, "Heaven on earth." Wanting to steer the topic away from me, I take a sip of tea. "How's the wedding planning?"

"Considering I have a planner, I'm busier than ever." She laughs lightly. "I want to get the house in order before we're married as well. When I come back from Hawaii, I'm going to look for work."

"You've been busy since moving here. It's a lot to move across country."

"And a luxury not to worry about money."

"For sure." Her gaze darts to mine before we both burst out laughing. "See? It was only a matter of time before I sounded like me again."

"Well, the Valley girl version. Eventually, you'll work

your way back to the Texan. Speaking of you, did you hear from Mom while you were gone?"

"No, but Dad called once."

We no longer speak to him for choosing booze and gambling over his daughters. The result was devastating for us since we had to pay the price, so like her, I was surprised to hear from him as well. I thought I had been clear about no contact the last time I saw him. The unannounced visit to the diner where I worked didn't bode well for him. "He did?" she asks. "What did he say?"

"That Mom had called him looking for me. He told her to try my number. Guess she didn't. Does she not love us at all?"

"No. She doesn't. She loves a man who wants her to have nothing to do with her own kids while playing stepmom to his. She doesn't even know I'm engaged. Or moved. She has no idea what I've been through or seen what a beautiful woman you've become. I don't understand how she could walk away from her children like she has, but you know what? I don't care anymore."

My sister's voice is firm and unshakeable, unlike mine. Maybe that's what age and wisdom does for you—makes you strong. There's a pause in the conversation that she doesn't seem anxious to fill. I hear her suck in a breath before she says, "I'm not sending her or Dad an invite."

Our parents have chosen to love other people or things over their daughters. The past five years have been hard on both Stella and me, but our four-year age gap never stopped us from being close as sisters or best friends. "Neither of them deserves the honor." I struggle to keep the bitterness from my tone. "Because we share the same bloodline with them doesn't make them family. Family consists of the people who show up when you need them most. I'll be there. You have Rivers by your side. Jet, Tulsa . . ." My voice softens.

"*Ridge*. Everyone you've invited is your family, Stel. This is the reward for the hell you've been through."

"When did you become the big sis?" I can hear her happiness, the lightness returning to her tone.

"I've had an amazing example." I have always idolized my sister. Still do. From pursuing her teaching career to opening her heart to the man she's always loved. Seeing how hard they fought to be together can make any cynic a little envious.

She stands. "I think the pizza should be here soon. I'll be back."

While she's gone, I take a quick break, stretching my legs and reaching for the sky. Breathe. I bend forward into down-ward dog and hold before rising into sun salutation. Just a few moves and four deep breaths later, I'm feeling more centered. *And hungry.*

The screen of my phone lights up with a message. I smile, the reaction too quick for me to hold back.

Dave: *I like your red lips.*

Me: *Is that why you're texting me? To tell me you like my lipstick?*

Dave: *I meant to tell you yesterday, but we were interrupted. Sorry about the call.*

Me: *Your openers are getting better.*

Dave: *LOL. I didn't know they needed work. #takesnote*

Me: *We all do, don't we? I'm a #workinprogress*

Dave: *Question: Why do we use hashtags in text messages?*

Me: *Question: Why do we pose questions with Question?*

Dave: *Good point. So . . . about that call I got yesterday—*

My fingers fly across the screen. Me: *You don't have to explain. You don't owe me anything.*

Dave: *I want to owe you something. I'd like to make up for it before you leave LA.*

I pause, staring at the phone. When I left for London, I checked the life I had been leading at the counter and left it at Heathrow when I arrived. It was a chance for me to have a fresh start, to live life on my own, and I did it. That wound began to heal. Am I willing to reopen it when I'm about to leave again?

Dave: *Your silence says a lot. I'm sorry if I overstepped—*
Me: *You didn't. Do you mind if I think about it?*
Dave: *I leave in the morning for two days.*
Me: *I'll let you know . . .*

I stop typing and call instead. He answers, "Hey."

"Hey. I, um, thought I should call because it will come out all wrong in text, and I don't want that."

"I don't want that either."

"It was good to catch up yesterday and easy to be with you again, but we're different. I know you feel it. Time and life have opened our eyes in new ways. I'm finally figuring out what I want in life while you're living yours."

Dave Carson is a quiet man in general. Ridge, his rock star persona, is much more vocal. I almost prefer a witty comeback or a one-liner that will make this conversation easier, but he remains quiet, listening and waiting for me to continue. I say, "What we had—"

"Was good."

"Yes, it was good. Very good, but I've changed. I know what I need right now."

"And that's not me. You don't want to date."

"I didn't know you were offering yourself up for the job."

"Sometimes it's hard to read between the lines."

I nod even though he can't see me. "It's not you I don't want to date. Time away helped me realize that I can't tie myself to anything or anyone," I add, lowering my voice to a whisper. "Not right now."

"How about friends, Meadow? Do you need friends?" *Yes. I've been so focused on work and my studies that I was lonely. I didn't realize how much until I landed in London.*

Darcy, my coworkers, and even Carrig made it apparent that I had drifted from the friends I used to have in Austin. I don't want to be alone . . . lonely once I return to school again.

Although the words themselves can be construed as a snipe, I hear the kind and open tone of his voice, and know his offer is genuine. "I do. Is that something we can be?"

"Yes."

That light as air, easy to talk to feeling seeps back in, making me smile. "I think it would be a good place to start."

"I like starts."

"A new beginning. No guilt for not calling. No hurt feelings when we can't hang out, especially since you'll be here, and I'll be there. Casual."

"Nothing serious," he says, but I detect some sarcasm.

"Are you using my words against me?"

Now he outright chuckles. "No. I'm using it for you. Saving you the trouble."

"You're prickly sometimes, rock star."

"Comes with the territory." He exhales, then says, "So maybe I'll see you around when you're in town."

"Sounds like a plan."

Laughing again, he follows up with, "The non-plan plan. We've always been great with those."

"The best."

"Thanks for calling." Him ending the call actually surprises me. He was always so honest with his emotions, never wasting time with what he called the "bullshit" that gets in the way. So I have no reason to doubt him now.

"Anytime. I meant what I said the other day. You have my number. Don't be afraid to use it."

"I won't. That goes for you too."

"Break a leg this summer."

"Kick some ass, Mead."

"I intend to."

"I have no doubt."

His words mimicking how I feel about him cause my smile to grow until my cheeks hurt. I cradle the phone close, and say, "Take care."

"You too."

6

Meadow

RIVERS WALKS in the front door with two large pizza boxes. Glancing my way, he grumbles, "I had to walk down the driveway to get the delivery."

"Why not just open the gate and let them drive up?" Standing, I trail him in the wake of the pizza, inhaling the delectable smell.

"It's stuck, and I'm hungry."

"That's fair." Settling on a barstool at the counter, I situate myself in front of the supreme.

Stella sets three beers down on the island and slaps his ass. "I'll call the company again."

"At least we're in for the night," he replies, taking a slice. We start eating. No fancy plates. Heck, not even paper plates. Hot pizza right out of the box. I haven't done this in a long time. Darcy insisted on glass as the bare minimum if I wouldn't allow her to use china. Rivers asks, "What was with the Brit at the bonfire?" He's swiftly elbowed. Stella's tensed lips and wide eyes are easy to read.

I shake my head and laugh with my mouth full. They make it hard to keep my lips sealed. When I choke down my bite, I say, "You know I can see you, right?"

As if a weight is lifted, Stella turns to me, planting her hands on the marble countertop. "Then stop making us guess and just tell us. Did you date him in London? He's cute."

"Right here, babe."

Stella just laughs. He knows he's the only guy she sees.

Leaning my hip against the counter, I shrug. "We spent time together, but more as boss and employee. I can assure you, we're friends, and that's all."

"And you and Ridge?" Rivers asks.

Rivers never liked gossip, so I wonder why he seems mildly interested. Did Dave say something while I was away? Before I can answer, he says, "Nothing serious?" He laughs. *Yeah. Knew that would come back to bite me.*

"Clearly, you know we hung out before I left for England, but there's nothing new to report. We've decided it's best to remain friends." Stella's left eye is blinking crazily. "Something in your eye?"

Rivers bursts out laughing this time. "She's winking. Every so often, she nails a good one." He wipes his hands and mouth and steps behind her. Wrapping his arms around her middle, he says, "I'm not marrying her for her winking skills."

That earns him another elbow, but when she turns in his arms and wraps hers around his neck, I feel like a third wheel. Their connection has always been palpable. It's even more so since they got engaged.

Taking a beer and a slice with me, I slip out of the kitchen and head back outside where I've been working.

I finish my pizza as I walk to the edge of the perfectly manicured green yard and stare out at the city in the distance.

My sister joins my side and takes a sip of her beer. Keeping my eyes on the horizon, I say, "The view is amazing, but we always said we wanted to be near the ocean. What changed?"

"Me." I turn her way, thinking about the answer. She adds, "We looked by the ocean, but it's quite a drive back to LA and to his brothers. Jet has a studio at his house. If I want to see Rivers most days, that means living closer. I choose him over an ocean view any day. Does that make sense?"

"It does. It's not a compromise, but something you're happy about."

"Yes. That's what it's like."

I feel the change happening, the one where my sister watches over me less and treats me more like an adult. "Your hair is a mess," I say, bumping into her side and smiling.

Shaking her head so her hair flies wild, she stops, and says, "But my life isn't anymore."

"No. It's quite magical actually."

She smiles and wraps her arm over my shoulders. "One more year and the world will be yours for the taking."

"Is that what a degree will do for me?" I ask earnestly.

"No. That's what living life on your own terms will do for you."

Wrapping my arm around her waist, we stand there and look at the world before us as the sun finally sets. "Hey?"

"What?"

"Remember that time we went out and ran into your ex-boyfriend?" *Rivers.* I had a front row seat to that show.

She waggles her eyebrows, causing me to laugh. "And his cute friend?" *Ridge.*

A million little lights dot the landscape as night takes over. "You once told me not to date a musician."

"Eh. What do I know? I fell for a musician. Twice."

"The same one, at least."

"Look at us now."

Leaning my head on her shoulder, I say, "Yeah, look at you now. Living the life."

"I meant *us*. Look how far we've come."

"All the way from Texas to Hollywood."

"Via England in the middle. I'm happy you had such an amazing time."

"I did, but now I feel lost between worlds."

With a quick kiss to the head, she says, "Yeah, I get that. I think when you get back to Austin and you find your new normal, you'll find your way. Just remember who you are, Meadow." I've always loved that Stella tells me this. It's her way of reminding me that we can weather any storm.

I always respond the same way. "Who am I?"

"My sister. My strong, beautiful, and capable sister." But this time, she adds, "But don't close off your heart. Sometimes, true love only comes around once." That's new, but it also makes perfect sense why she'd say it now.

"And in your case?"

She shrugs. "Twice with the same man."

"Now you're just showing off," I joke, pushing off her in fake annoyance.

"Have you seen my fiancé?" Wiggling her booty, she laughs. "There's a lot to brag about."

"Ew. He's like my brother."

She has a devious glint in her eyes. I roll mine because she's a goof.

For some reason, Rivers's earlier question comes back to me. *Am I good?*

I am.

Really good.

I may be back in the States and getting back in the swing of things, but I welcome the challenges ahead and look forward to seeing what comes next.

An alarm beeps on my watch, drawing my attention. It's the daily reminder I programmed to make sure I get this project done. "I need to get back to this paper. Five days left."

She meanders back around the pool toward the house. "You can do it. You've already proven you can do anything you set your mind to."

"Thanks. Love you, big sis."

"Love you, little sis. Now get back to work," she says with a laugh.

Nikki has dragged Stella and me from one boutique to the next on Melrose Avenue all afternoon. She's amazing. "How's married life?" I ask just as we're handed another glass of champagne in another fancy clothing store.

Lead singer of the popular band, Faris Wheel, designer in the making, and recently became a Crow—the blonde bombshell is a powerhouse all on her own. She's a SoCal girl who knows how to shop like a professional. Stella had said she was awesome but spending time with her lives up to the hype.

Her smile shifts to the side, as if she's debating what she wants to share. "Tulsa is . . ." Her eyes close, and she sighs dreamily. "Incredible."

I'm not sure if she's talking sex or marriage at this point, but she makes it sound awesome either way. Other than that it's with Tulsa. The youngest Crow brother is hot, I guess, but again, like Rivers and Jet, he's like a brother to me. So if she's talking about sex—Ew.

She flits from one rack to another in the small store, and says, "I don't like when they tour without our band. Opening for them last summer was a dream come true. It's been two days since they left for Tucson, and I miss him." She turns to Stella, and asks, "How are you holding up, Stella?"

Stella holds a T-shirt up, and whispers, "This is two hundred dollars. That can't be right, can it?"

Nikki laughs. "It's probably right. It's cute. You should try it on."

"It's cotton and white. I'm good with Gap or Target for the basics." When I walk over to get a closer look, I agree with Stella. I got a little lowdown before we headed out. Nikki is loaded. She was raised with money, she's made her own, and now she's married into it. Price tags are not something she checks.

Her and Darcy are going to get along like two houses on fire. I ask Stella, "What does the phrase get along like a house on fire mean? It makes no sense."

"It's get on like a house on fire. Just means quickly like a house burns."

I knock into her. "Of course the teacher knows."

"As a teacher, it's hard to pay twenty dollars for a pair of pink socks, even if they are the softest I've ever felt in my life." She rubs the socks against her cheek.

Nikki sidles up to us, rubs shoulders, and whispers, "As a soon-to-be wealthy rock star's wife, you can treat yourself to the socks."

"Oh gosh, I don't know," she replies. "Rivers and I both grew up scraping by. It's hard to spend money like it grows on trees."

Wrapping her arm around my sister, Nikki says, "I love that you guys don't waste money. It's refreshing. You do what makes you feel comfortable."

Turning to me, she adds, "As for you, I heard you own a pair of Louboutin's and a Chloe dress." She wraps her arm around me and steers me into another room full of every major name in fashion.

"The dress was a hand-me-down I happily accepted from my roommate in London. The shoes, a fancy gift from Stella and Rivers."

Nikki appears impressed as she looks back at Stella. "So her weakness is nice shoes?"

I nod. "Also, she doesn't mind buying for others. It's herself she struggles to spend a dime on. Have you seen her car?"

Nikki's shoulders sag. "God, it's a monster. I'm going to need a lot more time to work on her to get her into the car she deserves."

Stella is laughing while listening to us as we don't even try to whisper. I say, "Good luck on that front. I've failed to convince her so far."

With her phone in hand, Stella says, "Rivers just got home. Are we ready to wrap this up?"

Nikki is the first to go, thanking the sales staff and dropping her glass on the tray as we exit. I'm right behind her, having a great time, until we walk right into a paparazzi trap. Flashes are going off, and men are yelling Nikki's name when they're only a foot away.

She turns back, and the store's security guard locks the door after we re-enter. Moving to a spot away from the glass doors, she says, "The car's four blocks down."

"I'm sorry. I wanted to walk, but I didn't think about . . . you and what you need."

"Don't worry about it, Meadow. It happens all the time. I just don't want to go out there right now. How can we get the car and pull it around?"

Stella's new to the limelight and is still learning the ins and outs, but it's not something I think she'll ever get used to. By association, I've landed in pics online but am still safe when I'm back in my world. Being with a famous musician has put her front and center lately, the wedding adding an extra level of crazy interest in her. I volunteer. "No one has a reason to follow me. I can go get the car and pull around."

"I don't like that idea," Stella says, her eyes fixed on mine. "It's not safe for you."

"I'll be fine. Keys?"

"Are you sure?"

"I'm sure." Nikki hands me the keys. "They've never harassed my best friend when she's been with me or without. She'll be fine, Stella." Before I leave, Nikki adds, "Be safe."

"I will."

A sales associate leads me to the back door and instructs where to pull up when I return. "It's a private lot, so they can't cross into it."

"All right. I'll be back soon."

I start walking, glad I wore flats with my yellow dress. The wedges I had on aren't made for hiking down sidewalks or cutting through parking lots behind the stores. I hold my purse close and keep the keys in hand to use as a weapon if needed, just like Stella taught me when I was a teen.

The car is farther than I thought. I've gone at least six blocks and haven't found it. I stop to text Nikki: *I can't find the car. Is this the street we parked on?* I send her a photo of the street sign.

Nikki: *My car's not there?*

My phone rings. "It's not here."

"Shit. Was it towed?"

"Seems that way."

She grrs in irritation. "Come back and I'll call for a ride. Sorry."

"No, no worries. Sorry that happened."

"Take a photo of the towing information if you can. I'll need to call them."

"Will do."

I find a sign that we all missed earlier that says no parking during business hours and snap a pic before I start heading back. Just before I reach the final block, a black sports car comes around the corner, skidding to a stop and cutting me off.

7

Meadow

"Really, Tulsa?"

He shifts into park and pushes up through the open top of the convertible, resting against his seat. "I'm here to rescue you."

"First of all," I say, "we don't need rescuing. Secondly, it's a two-seater. There's three of us and two of you, so riddle me how you were planning on 'rescuing' us anyway."

I spied his passenger before I laid eyes on Tulsa, but I kept my focus on the driver. I finally glance at Ridge and hate that I mentally called him Ridge. It seems with our newfound friendship, I've fallen in line with everyone else. That shouldn't bother me as much as it does. *It's as though things have really been reset after all. But do I really want that? That's what I said I wanted . . .*

He seems to have mixed feelings about being here . . . or seeing me. It's hard to tell by the neutral expression, but the torrential storms in his eyes tell me more.

I give in first. "Hi."

He does what those hot guys did back in school—one confident nod with his eyes solidly on me before his gaze dips lower and back up. "Hey."

Even though I hate that I thought of him as Ridge before, it seems fitting now. Stepping closer to the beautiful car, I rest my hands on the window next to him. "What happened to the Ferrari?"

"I wanted something less flashy."

"You? Less flashy?" I lean back and eye the car up again. I'm having a hard time believing this BMW i8 with the gold rims is less flashy in his opinion. I guess he means in color—matte black. "Alrighty then. So, what's the plan?"

Tulsa drops into the seat and fastens his belt. "I'll drive my wife, but I can only fit two in the back seat."

"Holy wow. This thing has a back seat?"

"Kind of," he replies, thumbing back there. "Ridge is too big to sit back there, so I can drive you and Stella home and let Ridge catch another ride—"

Dave whacks him in the chest. "Thanks, man."

Tulsa leans forward, and says, "You'll ride with him, right, Meadow?"

What? "Sure, of course."

Gripping the wheel, Tulsa says, "Hop in and we'll go pick them up."

"Hop in where? I'm not squeezing into that tiny space."

"Ridge's lap then. Chop, chop. It's like one block. Won't be the first time you guys have shared a space."

The door lifts, and Dave steps out, coming face to face with me. "Sorry about this. I don't want you to think—"

"Don't worry. I'm not thinking anything."

He turns back over his shoulder, staring into the distance. "You take the car. I'll walk over."

We're being so kind. *So polite.* I'm not sure how I feel about it. "It's fine. We can ride together."

"You sure?"

"Yep." He gets back in the car, and I maneuver my way onto his lap, tucking my legs with his.

I lean back, so he can close the door. "There is nothing safe about this."

"There never was. That's what made it fun."

Practically snuggled to his chest, I catch his slip. "Made?"

"*Makes*. Makes it fun."

Tulsa sped away with Nikki and my sister, making a show of it for the paparazzi. If anyone ever enjoyed fame, it's them. They were made for this lifestyle. As for Stella, I'm sure she's hiding in that tiny back seat.

Dave and I hop in a car he ordered. The first few minutes are traveled in silence. I direct my attention out my window, but it feels weird between us, so I reach over and tap his hand that's on the seat. "Hey."

When he turns my way, he smiles just enough for me to see. "Hey."

"How were the shows?"

"Good."

"I heard you were in Tucson?"

"Yep. Tucson."

Okay. Yeah, I need to end this. "Do you want me to leave you alone? Because I'm getting that vibe."

"No, Meadow. I don't want you to leave me alone. You know I'm not much for small talk."

"I know, but I usually don't have to pull teeth."

He runs a hand through his hair, and I catch sight of the dark circles under his eyes. "Sorry. I've had a rough day. A lot on my mind and just tired."

"Oh." When I set my hand on the seat, the tips of our fingers touch. He looks down at the connection like I do. "I'm sorry. You probably just want to get some sleep, and here I am, making you ride all the way back to Stella and

Rivers's place. Let's have the driver drop you off first. I don't mind."

"It's okay. I don't mind either. Let's get you home. I know Rivers and your sister worry about you."

"I wish they could just enjoy their lives and stop worrying about mine. My sister means well, and I love her for it, but I hate adding to her load."

"She's your sister. She'll never stop worrying about you. You're thick as thieves because you always only had each other." His gaze glides up to my eyes. "As much as you're trying to branch out from where you've been, she knows a part of her has to let you, at least in her mind. So go easy on her. Seeing you grow up and move on is probably harder for her than you realize." He chuckles. "You sure have grown up, Meadow girl."

Leaning forward, he gives the driver an alternate route when we hit traffic.

It's then that I realize I don't even know where Dave lives. When he rests back, his attention returns outside the window. I take the time to look at him. I was so blinded by the past that I haven't seen who he is in the present.

One thing is for sure. He's still a damn good-looking man.

"Where do you live?" I blurt.

The question takes him by surprise. "Me?"

"Yeah. I have no idea where you live or if you still have your apartment in Austin. I don't know anything about you anymore."

"And you want to?" Genuine curiosity lies in his eyes.

"How can you think I wouldn't?"

When his head hits the back of the seat, he blows out a big breath. "I don't know what to think when it comes to you anymore."

I'm about to tell him I'm some of the girl he knew with a

lot more of the woman I want to be after London, but I pause. He's just not himself. Reaching over, I touch his arm. "Hey, what's going on? You can talk to me."

He rubs his eyes with one hand but doesn't move the other that's touching mine. *Until now.* When I lean back like he is, he moves hair that falls in my eyes. "Meadow Soleil." There's a rough tinge to his voice, trapping it somewhere between exhausted and exasperated.

"What is it?"

His hand slips under my hair to hold my neck. "Damn girl. You're sunshine on an otherwise shitty day."

The comfort of his hand warms my skin, and I relax into his hold. "What made it shitty?"

He just looks at me with that roguish smile I remember so well as if that's an answer. Maybe it's the only answer he's willing to give right now. I recognize the street we're on. We'll be back to the house soon. Since he doesn't say more, I do, "Whatever made your day so bad, I hope it gets better."

"It already has." He pulls his hand back to his side just as the car pulls up to the end of the driveway. *But I wasn't ready for him to pull away, to break our tenuous connection.* I want this man in my life in some form. A friend? *Yes.* Right now, he seems like he needs a friend, too.

I tell the driver, "You can stop here."

Dave asks, "Is the gate still broken?"

It's a running joke at this stage. "Yeah. Do you want to come up?"

"I'm going to take off and get some sleep."

"Okay. I leave tomorrow." I don't know why I offer up the information, but he says, "Safe travels and—"

"And you'll use that number of mine sometime?"

"I will."

I'm still not used to the platonic goodbyes when we had

steamier exchanges at one time, but I appreciate his respect for this friendship. "Take care of yourself."

Popping the door open, I don't drag it out. I move around the car and wait for it to back out before I punch in the code. When that doesn't work, I lean down to the keypad and call the house. Rivers answers, "Gate not working?"

"Nope."

"Motherfuck. The service company was just out here. I'll come down."

After a moment, Rivers opens the gate and looks out. "Meadow?"

I walk through the open door, but he keeps looking out. "Did Ridge leave?"

"Yeah. He said he needs sleep."

"Me too. Whatever could go wrong with the road crew did. Not our best show." The gate slams closed, and he walks next to me up the long driveway. "Did you have a good time?"

Thinking about Dave first, I realize Rivers means the shopping. "Your fiancée never treats herself to anything. I don't know what your actual money situation is, but I feel like you have enough for her to buy herself a twenty-dollar pair of socks that she fell in love with."

"Twenty-dollar socks?" He smirks.

I don't roll my eyes this time, but I want to. "You two are so made for each other."

His expression is thoughtful as he shoves his hands into his pockets. "So she didn't buy them?"

"No. And while we're at it, her car is hideous. Let the woman ride in style."

Rivers is tall like his brothers, but he carries his frame with ease. The least showy of the Crow brothers, he listens more than he speaks and always weighs the options. He gets that this conversation is not about socks, but something deeper. Taking in the advice, he replies, "I was going to get her a new car as a wedding gift, but she's shown no interest in car shopping."

"Do it now just because. This doesn't come from me wanting you guys to blow money. It comes from the fact that neither of you should feel guilty for the money you've earned. You get the glory. She should get the stinkin' socks."

He stops, searching my face as if he doesn't recognize me. "Where's the kid I used to know?"

"Everyone keeps saying that. I haven't changed that much."

We start walking again. He wraps his arm around me, and says, "Nah, you're still you. You're just also growing up."

"Is it that bad?"

"No." He chuckles as we part again. "It's that good." When we step onto the front porch, he asks, "Any ideas what kind of car she'd want?"

"It's Stella, so I would say practical, safe, and little sexy."

"Not just a little. I'm the luckiest fucking bastard in the universe."

He opens the door for me, but before I dash upstairs to my room, I say, "Hey, Rivers?" He stops just before he reaches the kitchen and looks back. "We're lucky to have you."

A singular nod and no words. Very Rivers—appreciative, but not needing the glory.

In my room, I pull the card I sneakily purchased out of my purse and sit at the desk Stella set up for me to study when I'm here.

Dear Stella and Rivers,

I wanted to say thank you for always being my cheerleaders and biggest supporters—emotionally and financially. I will always be grateful for the opportunity you gave me to take an internship an ocean away. You made that possible, and it's something that will stay with me forever.

Everyone is saying how much I've changed. I feel it too. Sometimes I'm able to see it in the mirror as well. I just hope if I've truly changed it's for the better. I think it is.

Anyway, thank you again for everything you do for me and have done. I hope to make you proud.

Love,
  Meadow

I put the card back in the envelope and seal it, planning to leave it behind on the bed when I leave in the morning. Getting up, I pull the gift I also bought from my bag. It's wrapped in tissue with a little sticker sealing it. I set it next to the card and get to packing.

8

Ridge

THE BELLMAN DOESN'T MAKE a move to help me as I carry my duffle bag to the front desk. I must look as bad as I feel. Being on the road will do that to a guy. Add in the lack of sleep and I'm spent.

This is Hollywood, though. A billionaire can be dressed in cargo shorts and Birkenstocks and a struggling actor dressed to the nines in a suit he bought with his last dime.

But even I'm surprised they're even letting me in this place at this point. I must not look as battered as I feel. The desk clerk summons me but immediately starts tapping on the keyboard, ignoring me when I approach. Without looking up, he asks, "Do you have a reservation?"

Dropping my bag on the floor next to me, I lean on the counter, and whisper, "No. Do you have any available rooms?"

Tapping.

More tapping.

His gaze slides up from the screen, up my dirty shirt, and

stops cold on my unshaven face. Eyes go wide, and I know what's coming next. A year ago, I couldn't get arrested in Austin if I tried. Okay, I could get arrested, but I couldn't get decent publicity out of it. Now, I'm plastered on a billboard down the street.

The clerk leans in, and a sly grin replaces his initial judgment. "We have a suite available, sir, but only one. Would you like it, Mr. Crow?"

"Carson," I'm quick to correct. It's an easy and common mistake to make. The band is called The Crow Brothers. I'm a Carson among Crows. This comes with a unique set of challenges, such as everyone assuming I'm one of the brothers. They're cool, but I can only claim them as friends and bandmates.

"Your first name is Carson?"

"No, my last name is . . ." *Shit.* I should really use an alias like Rochelle, our business manager, told us to do. To the outside world, the band is an overnight success story, recognizable, and a household name. We know the hard work we've put in. For ten years, we each paid our dues several times over. I'll take the money, the fame, and the success, but I'll never pretend that I didn't earn every fucking copper cent. Right now, though, I want a bed to pass out in and no hassles. Only one name comes to mind since the only person who I would detour my mission to sleep for did just that. I inwardly chuckle. She won't mind. "Fellowes."

He begins typing, but his fingers stop. "And your first name?"

Meadow . . . "Field?"

"Are you asking me?"

"No. Field."

"Field Fellowes?"

"That's right." I pat the counter and look around ready for him to hurry this along.

"I'll need ID, sir." Leaning forward again, he whispers, "Your information will be safe with me. We have strong policies in place to protect the privacy of our clientele."

I slap the ID and credit card down on the black counter with a chuckle. Field Fellowes. That's got to be the most ridiculous fucking alias ever. Before I check into another hotel, I really need to sort that shit out and come up with something cool. Although it makes me laugh, Field Fellowes sounds like a botanist who chases fucking butterflies. Not exactly the rugged, badass image I'd like to be remembered for.

After getting my key to the suite and being sent off with a wink, I drag my ass up to the room and toss my bag on the couch. The door closes, the lock bolting on its own behind me. Walking toward the windows, I stare out at the Hollywood sign in the distance as my phone vibrates in my back pocket.

On the screen, I see a message from Kiki: *Heard you're back in LA. Want to get together?*

No. I don't. I'm in no mood to deal with her. I'd be better off fucking a stranger than busting a nut with her. She looks good, but her psycho scent is stronger than pheromones. My life is crazy enough. I don't need to add more into the mix.

Anyway, my balls are going through their blue period, similar to Picasso's, but there's no paint involved, and it's not related to art at all. Basically, we both just need the inspiration to get us out of this funk. Someone soft and warm instead of this calloused hand would be a solid start.

But something's been holding me back . . . *Someone*. I don't know why I've hung on to memories of what might have been with a certain sexy little green-eyed blonde when I can be with anyone. Meadow is the definition of complicated, her breakfast order is as mixed up as her taste in music. She makes no apologies for listening to everything from rap to rock with a dose of classical thrown in, and she's more stunning than ever.

Fuck me.

It's as though she was brought back to test me, built with all my weaknesses in mind—dangerous curves from the waist to the hips, great tits, and full lips. A killer little body with that wild hair and sharp intellect. Her sense of humor is a huge turn-on and her independence an aphrodisiac.

I'm like an addict, carrying a token buried deep inside to represent my strength and conviction. I don't need to be tethered when my career is taking off. Things have never been better, and I'm free to do whatever I want.

Why do I still want her?

There's nothing about us that makes sense, yet, besides my career, she was the best thing I had going last year. The only one who got Dave and not Ridge.

Friends, I remind myself.

It's the only logical way to be with her. We have one thing tying us together—great chemistry—and a hundred reasons we should only be friends.

I'm here in LA.

She's there in Austin.

I'm on the road half the year.

She's in her final year of college.

I'm twenty-six.

She's twenty-one.

I like coffee.

She likes tea.

But when she looks at me, none of that matters. She's funny, a little quirky, and damn sexy.

Friends.

That's all.

If she had stayed, what would we be? I'm not sure, so I think the time away was good for both of us. Fuck buddies aren't meant to be forever. I feel shitty for calling her that, even just mentally. We both know we weren't as basic as that.

Somehow, she makes being friends feel like I'm still winning. I don't have the time or the energy right now to date anyone seriously anyway. So being *nothing serious* with her sounds just about right to me. Maybe over the past six months, time has started to smooth the rough edges of who we used to be. We were a moment in time, something tangible before sunrise.

Complicated.
Does that mean we won't have a future?
Guess we'll see.

I sit on the couch despite wanting to go to bed. Wandering around the large suite from the separate bedroom to the kitchen to the living room with the view, this place has style. I've come a long way from playing gigs on Dirty Sixth and sleeping on friends' couches. I spent too many nights on the floor of the van touring Texas back in the day with my old band.

Hollywood is now my sandbox, The Crow Brothers' playground. Sitting pretty on top of the charts, we own this city. Anything we want is ours for the taking. I have everything I could want and more than I'll ever need. I'm living the high life in this castle in the sky.

So why do I feel like something is missing?

Standing up, I walk to the bedroom, kick off my shoes, and strip off my clothes. Climbing under the white covers, I shut the blinds with the click of a button. I lie in the dark, restless in my surroundings, wondering if I actually have everything I want and need, then why does this place feel so empty?

It's this room. It's too quiet. The only noise is the white noise ringing through my ears.

I toss.

Then I turn.

Check my phone.

No messages.

Thank fuck Kiki got the message and didn't text me again.

Take over the whole mattress by spreading out. I like owning this king-size bed. I like the freedom to sleep however the fuck I please. I don't need anyone.

But . . .

It's not the room that feels empty.

It's me.

Why am I thinking about her? *Her* smile. Her curled against me. Her body in the early hours of the morning. God, it's been *months*, but after touching her today, having my hand around her neck—*how I wanted to lean in and claim those lips*—it's as though my body found what it's craving. *Her*. Beautiful Meadow Soleil.

I've missed her.

Friends.

Fuck.

Fuck this noise.

I flip the covers off, make my way into the bathroom, and flip on the shower. Looking at myself in the mirror, I'm a fucking mess—mentally and physically. It's not been twenty-four hours since I was standing on that stage in front of thousands of fans that were chanting our name.

The lights are down, and I can't see a fucking thing. My fingers find the strings I need, and I wait. The spotlight hits, and the drums kick in. Despite fifteen thousand people screaming, I hear Jet in my earpiece counting down.

The lights hit us just as we play the first chord. I don't think. I just play the song I've played a million times before and had a hand in writing. My mind drifts to the beat as it centers me as my favorite guitar vibrates against me. I feel the chords, the songs, the music. My soul bleeds through each riff, dying through each set.

I give my all, and when the show is over, I'm done. I can sleep for a week, but I'll get two nights. This time. More than one is a luxury when we tour.

. . . Figures I'd be faced with beauty when I'm at my worst. Between the show and the call in the middle of the night, I wasn't good company for anyone. But there's Meadow, put in my path to revive this tired soul with just a look in her eyes that tells me I'm not alone. "*You can talk to me.*" Maybe when I'm feeling less . . . *depleted* . . .

Getting under the warm water eases my sore neck and the muscles in my shoulders. We're only halfway through the summer tour, and I'm starting to feel it. Add the issues at home and my mind is always spinning.

I need to forget all that. Think about the release I'm desperate to have—free my mind, relax my body, and get some sleep.

Meadow standing in a white dress. The bonfire flames dancing between us. Her eyes like stars sparkling in the night. My dick stirs just thinking about that impossible woman, and the muscles in my lower belly tighten. She was a sight to fucking see in the moonlight, *but I liked it better when she was on top of me.*

I take hold of my dick and start a slow pump to warm up. It's been a while since I did this.

My body clenches as my fist does, and my dick hardens. Resting one hand on the wall, I speed up the other. *God, how I want her tits in my hands. In my mouth. I want her taste. Everywhere.* This is what this woman does to me. *Beautiful eyes. Soft-as-silk skin.* "Fuck." My grip tightens, and I pump harder. *Faster.* "Oh fuck."

The water rinses my body clean of my dirty thoughts, the

images of Meadow, her perfect, ripe tits and nipples hard from the cool desert air.

I grab the hotel soap and rip it from the package before scrubbing my body and washing my hair. Rinse. Shower over.

After toweling off, I lie back down and close my eyes again. This time, my body feels heavy, matching my thoughts. I surrender and let my mind drift back to some of the good times we've had.

"Are you really going to eat all of that?" With her hands on her hips, she tilts her head to the side.

The Cheetos fall into the shopping cart, and I wiggle the Hostess box in the air. "Yes. And you're going to help me."

"I don't think I've eaten a Ding Dong since high school." As soon as the words leave her mouth, her face scrunches, and she points at me. "Don't. I know what you're going to say."

I think she's going for menacing, but the girl's just too cute to pull it off.

I zip my lips and raise my hands from the shopping cart. "I wasn't going to say anything. I'm innocent."

She walks farther down the aisle. "Sure. Sure. Whatever."

"Although . . ." Her ponytail swings as she shakes her head. "I have a vivid recollection of you eating my D—"

"I knew you couldn't resist."

This time, I shrug as I laugh and then push the basket to catch up. "Question. How many Ding Dongs did you eat in high school?" That earns me a swift punch to the bicep.

"Damn, that's my dominant arm, woman." I rub it, but it didn't hurt.

She's too busy laughing to notice me watching her. She's fucking gorgeous. "Oh!" She snaps her fingers in the air. "I'm almost out of tea."

I follow behind her to the tea and coffee aisle. She tosses a box of coffee K-Cups into the cart, the ones she knows I like, while she treks down to stand in front of the wide selection of tea. I stop a few feet back, wanting to take her all in so when I leave, she'll still be with me.

Her toned and tan legs escape cutoff jean shorts that hang low on her, exposing the soft skin of her stomach. The tank top she threw on after sex is loose and shows the neon yellow of her bra straps and the slightest hint of side tit. I position the cart in front of me and adjust my dick.

We rolled out of bed and hit the grocery store for replenishments. After fucking for almost two days straight, all the food was gone. But now I just want to get the fuck outta here and get her back in bed . . . or maybe we'll make use of that armchair this time.

She drops a green box in the cart, and asks, "Do you like cookie dough?"

"I like cookie dough." I don't have a major sweet tooth except when I'm around her for some reason. "Can I eat you?"

Turning back, she asks, "Eat cookie dough off me?"

"No."

"You're so bad. Here I thought we would go down to Barton Springs for a swim and then watch movies all night."

I go to her because I've struggled to keep my hands off her for the last hour. We're in public, but in Austin, I can roam around a lot more freely than in LA. Paps are on every corner there. Here, I can grocery shop until I drop.

Wrapping my arms around her from behind, I kiss her neck, and whisper, "We can do whatever your heart desires."

"When's your flight?" She giggles when my scruff tickles the skin under her ear.

"I have to leave at seven a.m., or I won't get back in time to make sound check."

Spinning in my arms, she wraps hers around my neck. "What happens if you miss it?"

"I get my ass kicked."

She kisses me. "That would be a shame. It's a nice ass.'
Pulling back, she looks at the cart. "We have more than we need
for less than a day left together."

"Save it for the next time."

"When will you be back?"

"The second I'm free." And even that isn't soon enough in my
book. God, this woman consumes me.

9

Ridge

M*Y* *PHONE* *VIBRATES* on the nightstand, catching me on the edge of sleep. Vivid dreams fade, and my mind tries to grab on to something real. I lick my lips. My mouth's dry, and my head is pounding.

Not sure if it's the whiskey I drank to help me sleep or the exhaustion.

But the fucking phone keeps pulsating across the glass top. My mind finally wakes up, and I grab it before it stops. "Hey. Hello?"

"Did I catch you at a bad time?"

"No. I was sleeping, but I'm awake."

"It's three o'clock."

He forgets every damn time. I try to let it slide since he has more important things on his mind, but I still remind him, "I'm not in Texas. I'm in California. It's only one here."

"Did you have a show?"

Swinging my legs off the bed, I'm grumpy. For two days, I've paced this hotel room, gotten a massage, jacked off numerous times, ordered room service, and hibernated as if I'm in recovery from some tragic event. Traumatic seems more appropriate. I consider lying. He'll judge me either way, though, so this time, I move this along. "How's Mom?"

"She's not herself."

Understatement of the year. "What does that mean?"

"It means the meds have side effects that she's not happy about."

Happy about? Why the fuck would anyone be happy about taking all those drugs? I pull open one side of the curtains and look out. The view is standard LA. Hollywood sign, traffic, and billboards. Fortunately, I'm leaving this overly priced hotel suite today. Some sunlight will do me some good. "What can I do?"

"There's nothing we can do but wait."

"Wait for what?"

"To let your mother decide what she wants to do."

I hate even saying it, but I do. "Is she in a good place to make those kinds of decisions?"

"Yes." When he pauses, I know he's trying to figure out how he can get off this call.

I save him the trouble. "Keep me updated."

"Will you be available?" *Why is he doing this again*?

"Dad, let's not fight. I'll be available. Tell her I love her."

"I'll tell her we talked, David."

"Thanks. I'll call later." He hangs up as soon as I finish talking. Niceties like goodbyes are considered time wasters to my father. He's the opposite of my mother in almost every way, but somehow, they've made their marriage work for thirty years.

An alarm on my phone goes off, reminding me to pack up my shit. It's time to move on. In the foyer, I find my clothes washed and folded on the entry table, ready to throw in my bag. I love laundry service.

Packing doesn't take me long since I tend to travel light, so I get it done quickly and then shower and shave because I look like a fucking caveman.

I've never been one to be idle, so sitting around with little to do and on my own has always felt wrong. I've started to lose my mind, so I'm glad we're hitting the road again. At the end of each gig, I'm dying for rest, but this time, I've felt unsettled. *And I have a fair idea why. Should my mom really be making these decisions on her own? Should I be calling her to listen or talk it through? Fuck if I know.*

But right now, I know what I need. Music. It's always been there when I had nothing else. I can't believe I left my guitar with the crew. But after the call about my mom, my head was in a daze.

Next stop is Chicago and then on to Kansas City. The dark clouds of my mood start to lift, knowing I'll have guitar back in hand in a few hours and be doing what I do best: losing myself in music. *My lifeline.*

"Are we going out?" Tommy, the band's manager, asks as soon as we land in Chicago.

He's eyeing me, so I reply, "What are you thinking?"

"Beef. Booze. Babes."

"I'm not going to a strip joint." I shake my head because I can already see the shitstorm that would cause. "The paps would love that."

"Not all three all at once."

"Then I'm in. I'm starving."

"For food or fuck—"

The flight assistant comes from behind him and leans against the side of his chair. "I'd be happy to make a suggestion."

I don't know how he does it, but Tommy can get pussy when he's not even looking for it. He angles her way. "You from Chicago?"

"I live in the heart of the city. There's a great little restaurant near my apartment. I could show you around."

"The apartment or the city?"

Running a manicured nail over his shoulder, she bends down and whispers in his ear. Whatever she's offering, he's buying. "Do you have a car at the airport, or you want to ride with me?"

The woman's gorgeous, and that uniform is what fantasies are made of. She's also not shy about what she wants. "With or on?"

"You're bad," he replies with a wink. "I like it." The man is skilled, and women dig him. He gets laid, and in the media, he remains unscathed. Lucky bastard. I say, "I really wish I'd chosen a seat somewhere else." I'm not in the mood to watch him flirt. Not that I ever am, but fuck off all right already with them. The plane finally comes to a stop, and I pop my seat belt and am out of my chair.

He leans into the aisle, watching her walk away. When he turns back, he says, "I've got plans."

"Asshole. Bros before hos, man."

"Baes to get laid."

"That's lame. Don't use it." I laugh, then look around. "Anyone up for going out?"

Jet packs his headphones away, and says, "I'll go."

***

Jet being married to one of my best friends made us allies from the day we met. Being bandmates solidified our friendship. We may not have to tour in a crummy beat-up van together, but even flying on private jets and playing in stadiums are unique experiences that not many will understand.

The Crow Brothers band has a bond that can't be broken.

Except, it seems, for Tommy, who traded our company for a hookup with the fairer sex. I don't blame him. I'm not sure what's keeping me from fucking my way through a tour. I have plenty of opportunity, but no one seems to interest me. It used to be part of the routine to rid my stress from the late nights when I couldn't shut the buzzing off in my head, the adrenaline pumping through my veins, and the high from performing live. But since I met the pretty green-eyed beauty who kick-started my heart, no one else has caught my eye or tempted my libido.

Jet leans back from the table, pushing away an empty plate that once held a steak dinner. "Hannah's worried about you. Do I need to be?"

"Nope." I toss my napkin on the table and finish my beer.

"Is that what you want me to tell her?"

I shrug. "Tell her what you want."

"Cool. I'll tell her you're being an asshole."

I scoff, but it turns into a chuckle. "I'll text her."

"You don't owe me shit, brother, except a hundred and fifty percent when you're on that stage or in the studio. Other than that, it's your time to blow however you want. But you're not yourself, and everyone notices."

"Everyone needs to stop gossiping about nothing."

"Is it nothing?" The check is delivered, and Jet reaches for it. When we got our first big payday, we stopped worrying about checks at restaurants and bars. I remember walking blocks looking for change on the fucking street to buy a thirty-cent package of ramen. It's incredible that none of us bats an eye at a four-hundred-dollar dinner. When the waiter leaves, he asks, "What happened in Tucson?"

"What are you talking about? I played my fucking heart out."

He sets his card down just as the waiter returns to take it away. "Drop the defenses. I have no complaints about your performance, so this isn't an attack. I just noticed you were quiet . . . quieter than usual on the way home."

My mind is rummaging through believable excuses, anything to say other than the truth. "No one can get a word in edgewise with Tulsa around. That kid's a fucking chatterbox."

He laughs. "I've never known a happier dude. He's been like that his whole life. There's a good lesson to learn from him. Live life to the fullest. Enjoy every second. Tulsa knows loss. He was fifteen when our mother died. You know we didn't have a dad who stuck around, so . . ." He turns away, his gaze running over the wall of wine bottles. "I did the best I fucking could, but I couldn't replace her."

Thinking about my mom and how this came out of nowhere, my shoulders roll forward as I lower my head.

We're men, so Jet doesn't rush over to comfort me or push for more of what's going on inside my head. He's curious but leaves it. He knows better than anyone that sometimes we just have shit to work out in our heads.

The check is returned, and we leave. We walked the three blocks here, but word has gotten out and a crowd has gathered on the sidewalk. The restaurant calls a cab for us, and we dart for the open door. Safe inside, I'm not sure if it's the darkness of the cab or that I just need to get it off my chest. He mentioned his mother, so he'll understand. "My mom's in the hospital."

That pulls his attention from out the window over to my side of the back seat. "Sorry to hear that."

"So am I. My dad called after the show in Tucson."

He nods his head, everything making sense now. "When are you going to Austin?"

"I can't until after Chicago and Kansas City. So three days, I guess."

"Sorry. You know if you have to go—"

"I don't, but I want to. I'll go during the break."

"You'll meet us back in LA for the radio interviews?"

"Yep." I turn my attention away, not wanting to discuss it anymore.

As soon as we get back, I cover the fare, and we head upstairs. Being in a band is built for the nocturnals, but even after two straight days of being locked in that hotel room, I'm still tired. "I'm gonna have an early night."

"That's cool. I'm going to bug my brothers." Jet continues past me when I stop in front of my door to open it. Before I can slip inside, he adds, "Sorry about your mom."

"It's okay." It's not okay, but it's not his burden to bear. He has enough riding on his shoulders, so I won't add to his load.

I go inside and let the door slam closed behind. This room doesn't have a separate living room, but it has a bed, desk, and large sitting area. I sit in a chair by the window and kick my feet up on the table. I need to get my fucking mind off the sad shit. I have so much good going on, and it's getting buried.

Pulling my phone from my pocket, I get up and grab a small bottle of whiskey and a can of Coke from the mini bar. There used to be one surefire way to take my mind off things. I text: *You awake?*

Meadow: *It's only 10:30, Grandpa Carson.*

I knew she'd drag me out of my bad mood. I chuckle while mixing my drink. I take a big gulp and then settle on the chair, resuming my original position. Me: *Don't drag my grandpa into this. I don't intend for this to be appropriate.*

No dots. No reply.

Shit.

Friends.

Fuck.

Me: *Sorry. Bad habit.*

Meadow: *We were never bad, except for our timing.*

Considering how good we once were, I wonder if we can ever overcome that bad timing. Or maybe she's right, and we're how we're meant to be. Me: *What are you up to?*

Meadow: *Studying. My summer classes start tomorrow.*

Me: *School during the summer?*

Meadow: *If I want to graduate on time and I do.*

The drink sloshes against the side of the glass when I take another gulp.

Meadow: *What are you doing?*

Me: *Sitting in my room texting you.*

I smile, though I don't know why.

Meadow: *You should have called then.*

Me: *I can call now?*

Meadow: *Okay.*

Finishing the amber liquid, I hit the speed dial number. "Hello." *God, her voice. Her voice soothes my soul.*

"Why are you studying if school doesn't start until tomorrow?"

"To get ahead. Why are you sitting in your room alone at . . . where are you? LA?"

"Chicago."

"We're in the same time zone." I detect a light lilt to her tone as happiness sneaks in.

"We are."

"It makes me feel closer to you. That's weird, right?"

"A little, but I feel the same. Did you get settled back in?"

"My apartment needed a good cleaning, so I spent most of yesterday doing that. My closet is way too small for the clothes I bought while I was gone. And I had no food or drinks in the house, so I had to go grocery shopping earlier. It's kind of been a pain in the ass since I got back."

I miss this. I've missed her. Even though she's complaining, her tone is light. She still sounds happy, making me think back on the times we were together. I remember the awesome fucking, but this? I'm reminded that she's always been the light, and I liked having her light in my life.

"I was recently thinking about this one time at the store and a box of Ding Dongs."

She laughs. "I remember that too. Now I'm craving a Ding Dong."

There's so much I could say to that, but this time, I actually do let it go. "You never told me about London."

While she talks about her "flatmate," the British cadence I noticed before returns. "Sounds amazing," I chime in. "Also sounds like you got into plenty of trouble."

"We did. It was the best time ever."

Ever . . .

Her contentment in a place that became her home, at least temporarily, makes me wonder about her in the future. "Do you think you'll go back after you graduate?"

"I don't know. Guess we'll see where life is going to take me."

I don't keep her on the phone forever. This friends thing is new, so that means making new memories, but the other times we spent together are hard to forget. "Guess I should go. We have interviews in the morning and the show tomorrow night."

"Wow, we've been on the phone for almost an hour. Time just slips away when I'm—"

"With you."

There's a lingering pause before she adds, "I'm really glad we're friends, Dave."

"Me too." I'm glad I called. It's good to have a friend still here in Austin. "Good night, Meadow."

Just before I hang up, she says, "I'm glad you texted and called. It was good to hear a friendly voice."

"It was. Maybe I'll do it again sometime soon."

"I hope you do. Good night, Dave." *Dave.* That's who I needed to be tonight. Not Ridge with all that entails. Not David, the son who disappoints. Dave, the man this beautiful woman likes spending time with.

10

Meadow

ALTHOUGH I'VE KNOWN the date of Stella's big day since she set it, I still can't help but smile when I see the invitation. Holding my sister's pretty invitation in hand makes it feels more official, something tangible put out into the universe.

She deserves every celebration leading up to her nuptials. I've never known two people more made for each other than Rivers and Stella. They may have lost some years along the way, but they fought their demons and found their HEA.

The other day, she not so casually mentioned that love was worth the battle. I'm not afraid to fight. I'm just afraid to lose the war. Dad did. He loved Mom so much, and then was blindsided when she left.

Guess she didn't bother to let him in on her secret like she did me. *"You're either going to be the one who leads in life, or the one who's left behind. Which will you be, Meadow?"*

"I'll lead. I promise, Mommy."

"That's my good girl."

Regarding my love life, I sometimes wonder if I've kept

things casual because I'm afraid to be left behind. When my mom left, she was the first, but then others left me in her wake. Dad may have been physically there, but his mind drowned in a bottle of booze, taking his care of me with it.

I couldn't be happier for my sister's new life, but I wish it wasn't so far away from mine.

Sitting here alone in my apartment, I have everything I said I need—the ability to concentrate on my classes. Rivers and Stella made sure I didn't need to worry over money or work, giving me the freedom to focus. But when I look around, why do I feel like something's missing?

Clearly, the notes from class can't keep my interest. I grab my phone and go into the kitchen. After filling the electric kettle, I turn it on, waiting for the magic to happen. The sound is comforting, and when I rip open a tea packet, the smell fills me with a sense of calm.

With a moment to spare from studying, I call my sister.

She answers on the second ring, "Hello."

"Heya. I got the invitation today."

"Yay. What do you think?"

"It's pretty. I like the floral design. Classy and beautiful."

"That's what I was hoping for. Two months to go. I have so much to do. Hey, have you had a chance to look at the dresses yet?"

"I looked at them, but they're all gorgeous. You should pick your favorite."

"I want you to be happy."

"I'm happy, sis. I want you to have everything you dream of for this wedding."

"Well." With a light laugh, she replies, "I think the purple is so pretty and would look amazing on you."

"The purple it is then."

"I'll call the designer and let him know. So what are you up to?"

I dunk my tea bag in the mug, leaving it to steep while I return to my desk. Sitting down, I say, "We're three days into school, and I already feel behind. I can't seem to get my head out of London and back into academics. Is it bad that I wish I was just graduating already?"

"No. I think it's natural. You had a life-alternating experience that you'll always carry with you and has shaped your perspective."

"They should make us do the internship this year instead of junior year. The adjustment back into school life is rough. *Oh.* Before I forget, Darcy's my plus-one."

"Yes, you already told me. Can't wait to finally meet her. From her videos on Snapchat, it seems she has a large personality."

I join her laughter. "She does but a huge heart to match."

"She adores you, so I know that must true. It's time for both of us to focus on our futures. For you to live your story."

"Does mine come with a happily ever after?" I laugh as if the idea itself is preposterous.

"Of course."

Of course, she says as if it's written in the stars, destiny waiting to happen. Is that true? "I'd settle for a—Oops. Never mind."

"What? What would you settle for?"

Shit. "Um. Well."

"Well what?"

"I miss being intimate."

"Oh." The idea seems to settle in. I've partied and gone out with my sister many times. Me having sex isn't news. Me talking to her about it is. "Before Rivers came back, I was lonely. I know what you mean. Do you have . . .?"

Oh God. End this. "Yes. I have things. It's just not the same as someone being here in person."

"We don't talk about this stuff, and I guess we know each other's . . . you know about it."

"Sex life?"

"Yes. But I hadn't thought about that with you. Do you use an app?"

"Oh, good God. No. We're not doing this."

She laughs. "I know. I'm the worst. I was never with many—" She goes silent, and then I hear panicked breaths.

"Stella?" My hand tightens around the phone. "Stella? Say something." I know where her thoughts have gone. She never told me all the details of what happened last year, but I hate that sick bastard for what he did to her. *I hate him.* Come on, Stel. Please, be okay.

I hear her take a deep breath, thank God, and then she says, "I'm here."

"I'm sorry. I'm so sorry." Tears prick my eyes. "I shouldn't have said anything."

"It's okay, Meadow."

"No, it's not."

"I meant *I'm* okay. I'm not that easily broken. And we should be able to talk about things. I didn't do anything wrong, but I'm grateful I'm alive."

Is that the price of this happily ever after she talks about? Going to hell and hoping you're strong enough to survive it?

"Meadow?"

My name pulls me from the darkest part of my mind. "What?"

"Are you okay?"

How can I say anything but yes to the woman who survived the actual attack? "Yes," I say, finding no strength in my voice.

"Remember who you are?"

"Who am I?"

"You're my brave and amazing sister. The world is yours, Meadow. You can achieve anything you dream."

The words are so simple, but coming from her, I believe them. A small smile fights through the gray clouds, and I say, "I am. I'm Stella Fellowes's, soon-to-be Stella Crow's, sister." I release a heavy breath and stand. "I think I need to get some vitamin D outside. I'm going for a run."

"Sounds like a good plan."

I do yoga. I also run. I did both while in England to stay fit and healthy. But damn if the humidity and heat in Texas isn't gonna kill me right here dead on this trail.

I'm dripping from head to toe. Pushing into Coffee Bean & Tea Leaf, I feel my hair stuck to my skin, and my socks are wet. August in Austin is a real bitch.

After buying a large bottle of water, I find a table and try to cool off before running back toward campus. My phone vibrates against my leg, so I unzip the hidden pocket of my running pants and pull it out.

And smile.

"Hi," I answer.

Dave says, "Where are you?"

"Austin. Where are you?"

"Austin."

Oh. *Ohhh.* I find myself sitting up a little straighter and adjusting the waistband of my pants. "What are you doing in Austin?"

"I was thinking we could catch a movie or something?"

His response gives me pause, not because of what he asked, but because of what he avoided. "I'm a couple of miles from my apartment. I've been out running."

"I can pick you up?"

Just looking out the window makes me feel hot. It's just gone six o'clock, and I've hit the hottest part of the day. "I look like crap and probably smell worse."

Chuckling, he says, "It doesn't matter what you look like. We're friends, remember?" *He does know me well.*

"Good point." *Very good point.* Guess we'll see how good of friends we can be when I look this hideous and probably smell worse. "Okay. I'm at Coffee Bean on South Lamar between the river and Barton Springs."

"You're close. I'm downtown, so I'll be there shortly."

"I'll be the sweaty one with hairy legs."

"That sounds so hot."

"Hot is right." I snort. "Gross hot."

"Still hot."

"I think we're talking about two different hots here."

He chuckles, and I like how the sound makes me feel good inside. "I'll see you soon, Meadow."

I appreciate the air conditioning in here for another few minutes before I take my bottle and head out front. I'm not sure what car he's going to be in so when one turns in, I stick out my leg and shake my ass. "Oh God. I'm sorry." I back away from the sedan with a man driving who has kids tucked in the back.

Horrified, I turn to hide my face. "Hey! How much?"

"Screw y—" That familiar voice courses through me, and I turn back around to find Dave in a brand new looking shiny black Cadillac. "Nice car."

"Nice ass. Want a ride?"

"Sure." I shrug with an *I don't give a dang that I just humiliated myself* smile. I get in and say, "I was told never to accept a ride from strangers."

"Good thing I'm not a stranger then."

Resting my elbow on the door, I ask, "So what brings you to town, sailor?"

His smile slips, but it's back in place before he has to justify the change. "Family stuff. You're like red in the face. You know that, right?"

I hold up the bottle. "Yeah. I was more ambitious than this heat wants me to be. I can't say I'm complaining that I get a free ride home."

"That's me. Here for the free rides. Where to, sweaty moletti?"

11

Meadow

FEELING FRESH AS A DAISY—SHOWERED, shaved, and ready to go out—I enter the living room and spin for Dave who's sitting on the couch. Even though this friendship is new in the sense of not touching each other like we used to, I notice the way his lips part as he unapologetically takes me in, the way his body shifts, and how he seems to restrain himself by gripping his legs.

I ask, "Do you like?"

"I'd prefer my face on your chest," he deadpans.

Cheeky. I can't help but laugh. "I meant, how do I look?"

There's no rush to answer. Nope, he takes his sweet time looking at me, reminding me how he used to take his time appreciating every freckle on my body. His eyes finally meet mine, and he leans forward. "Incredible." Standing, he heads for the door, ready to leave. Without turning back, I hear him mumble, "Fuck me," before he says louder, "Perfect for the movies *with a friend.*"

He has a valid point about the friend thing, except when

I look down at my short skirt and Resistance band shirt that hugs the curves of my chest, I realize that I probably shouldn't have picked something so . . . fitted. Grabbing my purse, I follow him out the door and lock up. "Did you buy tickets?"

"Figured we'd risk it."

"You always did take risks," I reply, trying to keep it casual. I wasn't kidding when I told Stel I missed intimacy. Dave was the last man I slept with, which means it's been seven months since I've had sex. My run earlier tired me physically but not in *every* way.

Stopping down the hall, he glances back. "Some paid off and some didn't."

"It was worth the effort."

"Was it?"

I join his side, and as we walk to the elevator, I hook my arm around his. I'm not sure if I should, but I do it anyway. Friends do this. "You're a paid musician with the world at your feet. I say yes. It paid off."

"Ah. We're talking about music. I see."

"What else would we be talking about?"

"Nothing else, I guess."

When the elevator doors open, we walk in with me still draped around him. I get a good feel of his hard muscles before I release him, my stomach twisting in little knots as I move to the other side of the elevator.

Darcy and I often walked arm in arm, and as much as I like to tell myself that doing that with Dave is the same, it's not. It's *so* not. I know this man, and I know him intimately. His body. His touch. *Him.* And that makes something very clear—my body reacts very differently when I touch Dave Carson. With heat. With desire.

Darcy *never* made me feel like this.

Dave and I were friends before.

I don't know why I've felt as though we have to start again. We don't. We're just not supposed to have sex anymore.

My sex drive cries.

I haven't been with many, but I can imagine that no one will ever live up to Dave between the sheets . . . on the counter . . . in the shower . . . that one time in the movie theater. I look over at him in the dark theater, indulging in how strong a jaw he has and those pillowy lips that have been everywhere on my body. Remembering how I came during an eleven a.m. showing of a James Bond movie once.

He catches me eyeing him and leans over. "Not enjoying the movie?"

"The movie's fine."

Angling over, he whispers, "Remember that time we—"

"God, yes." I press my arm against his to get closer because I'm so turned on just thinking about it. "I was just thinking the same thing."

He starts laughing. "That was so fun."

"*Fun*? What?" I mean it was fun but not in a comedy way. "What are you thinking about?"

"That midnight swim at Blue Hole. What were you thinking about?"

Oh God. I slink into my seat as far down as I can go without my ass hanging off the end. "Nothing. Nothing at all." I wave him off, hoping he doesn't realize I was actually getting aroused from a memory. A different memory than the one he mentioned. "I was not thinking of anything but this movie." Holding my finger to my lips, I shush him. "Shh. We should just watch the movie. This weird, weird movie."

His hazels stay on me as if I'm the entertainment in this

theater. Without looking, I push his chin until he's facing the movie. That makes him laugh—too loud—and we draw attention. When he eyes me again, I just hold my finger to his lips this time. "Shh."

His hand slides under mine on the shared armrest, and our fingers fold together. Sliding down low enough to be equal with me, he leans over the armrest, invading my space again how I like it, even if I am the only one who remembers how I came on his hand in the middle of a movie theater. Guess it's a little harder for me to forget. With two fingers . . . two strong, hot fingers that made me—"Meadow?"

"Huh?" I ask on the verge of a panting breath.

He turns my chin in his direction. "Hey. I was just teasing. I wasn't really thinking about the skinny dipping."

"What *were* you thinking about then?"

"How wet you were when I fucked you with my fingers the last time we came to the theater together. How your body clenched around me while urging me for more. How your eyes closed and your mouth opened." His breath against my neck causes my breathing to deepen. His words in my ears make my nipples hard. "I was thinking about how I kissed you while you came and how I swallowed your moans." I bite my bottom lip and slide my gaze down to his lap. Seeing how hard he is makes me wet for him all over again. "Do you want to get out of here?"

"Yes."

He stands and with our hands still together, he leads us down the back aisle and toward the exit. As soon as the light from the lobby hits us, my hand is released, and he shoves his into his pockets, pushing them forward. "What do you want to do?"

I roll my eyes and storm toward the doors. "You're the worst friend ever." Although I'm technically teasing, I'm also being left high and . . . well, wet.

"What'd I do?"

"Yeah. Yeah. I need a stiff . . ." He cocks an eyebrow, and I burst his bubble. "Drink."

"I think I do too now."

"All's fair."

"In love and war. But how does friendship play into that?"

"You're really bad at this friend thing, Carson."

He shrugs as he chuckles while dangling the keys around his middle finger. "I was great at the friend with benefits thing, though. Why'd we give up the benefits again?"

We reach the car, standing on either side of it. The locks pop up, and I open my door. "Because 'more' got involved."

"Ah. That's right. Now I remember. Heaven forbid two people who like spending time together and have fantastic sex together want more."

"Heaven forbid." I bite my lip to keep from kissing his because it would be heaven to have that fantastic sex together again. He drives a hard bargain. Among other things, he's very skilled at driving and has me wishing I could fuck *forbid* and throw caution to the wind.

Laughing like a lunatic, I pick up my glass only to realize it's empty. "Did you drink my drink?"

"No," he says, smirking. "You did. Good thing you're not driving. By the way, I like your new apartment."

"I moved my stuff in last January, but as you know, I left right after. I haven't had time to do too much decorating, but I guess it's home."

"Do you still have your place?"

"I pay to store my shit, but I need to clean it out soon. Most of my stuff is probably garbage. Obviously, I don't need it since I've gone so long without it. It's just easier to pay rent than to go through the crap."

"I can help, if you want."

Something flashes in his eyes, and a smile settles. "I can't ask you to do that. You're busy with your own life."

Resting my chin on my hand, I lean forward. "You can ask me for anything."

"Don't offer yourself up so easily, Meadow Soleil."

I'm still so confused as to when exactly I finished my drink. I reach for the bottle, but he takes hold of the neck. "But that's what fri—"

"Don't you have classes tomorrow?"

"I do." Holding my glass between us, I say, "Fill 'er up, rock star."

He rests back on the couch, cradling the bottle to his chest. Lucky bottle. "I think you've had enough. That you don't remember the last might be a good sign to have some water."

"I think you're right." Pushing off the chair, I grab two bottles from the fridge, tossing one to him and opening the other for me.

While I swallow the cold liquid, Dave asks, "Question. Why don't you have a boyfriend?"

Maybe the water is too cold because I freeze under the question. When I lower it to the counter, I look at him as though he might know the answer. He doesn't. Staring at me, he says, "You're fun and beautiful. So fucking smart. Any guy would be lucky to get to spend time with you. You're a catch."

I don't want to be caught.

"Maybe. Maybe not." My voice cracks before I gain solid footing again. "My mother was caught, trapped in a marriage she told me she regretted. I don't want that." He has the courtesy to look away as I crash this train. "I know it's fucked up. Logically, at least when I'm more sober—"

"More sober?" He gets up and stands across the kitchen island from me. Our hands are palm down on the granite, staking claim to our sides. "You're drunk, Meadow. Emotions run rampant when we've had too much to drink. We've had a good time. I don't want to see you upset—"

"Then look away, Dave."

"You don't have to talk about anything you don't want. I'll listen if you want to share, but I know your parents are shit. You deserve better."

"I do. *I did.*" I lower my head, fucking mad that I said anything and even madder that my parents are shit, just like he said.

His hands move to my side and cover the tops of mine. He leans down so far that he looks up at me. "Hey, sunshine, don't be sad. Gray days are never meant to stay. Look for the rainbow. Look for the sun."

"Remember who you are."

"Who am I?"

Strong. Beautiful. Capable. The world is mine. I can achieve anything I dream. I feel a smile appear, hearing her voice in my head. "That sounds like something Stella would say."

Lifting up when I do, he says, "Your sister is a wise woman."

"She is." I notice his hands are still covering mine. "Thank you."

"For what?"

"For derailing that train of thought before I crashed."

One side of his mouth lifts and then the other. "My pleasure." He gives me a once-over and then turns. "I should get going."

"Already?"

Chuckling, he pulls out his phone. "It's almost two in the morning."

"Wow. Time just flew."

Glancing at me, he says, "Too fast for me too."

Coming around the counter, I take another sip of water. "Where are you staying while you're in town?"

"Why, are you going to come see me?" He winks and then says, "Five minutes until my ride's here."

I like that he's not driving because he's right. I'm drunk, and that means he probably is too. "My head feels swimmy."

"Drink this water, and then another before you go to bed. Okay?"

I follow him to the door and then salute him. "Yes, sir."

He opens it and steps out while I lean against it, wishing he was staying. "What did you mean when you talked about more?"

"In the desert?" I nod. Touching my cheek, I lean into it, and he shakes his head. "Let's not do this. It's the alcohol talking. The last thing I want is for you to ever regret something we do together."

I tug on his shirt, bringing him back to me. I wrap my arms around him and rest my head on his chest. "I won't," I whisper, listening to the thumping of his heart. "I promise." *I just need to be held, Dave. Please hold me.* As if he heard me, he strokes his hands down my arms and hooks them around my back. *God, I've missed this. Him.*

When he doesn't say anything, I look up to find his eyes searching mine. Taking me by the wrists, he lowers them to my side. "I had fun, friend."

"Friend," I repeat more for myself.

Walking backward toward the elevator, he smirks. "Good night, sunshine."

I lean against the doorframe and give him a little wave as I watch him walk away. It's a really great walk and an even better ass, but my gaze drifts north to those broad shoulders while his filthy sexy words fill my head. *"How wet you were when I fucked you with my fingers. How your body clenched around me while urging me for more. How your eyes closed and your mouth opened."*

"Good lord, that man." Shutting the door, I lock it and laugh as I lean against it. "I'm definitely going to need my toy tonight."

12

Meadow

I VAGUELY REMEMBER Dave telling me he didn't want me to regret anything we do together.

I'm filled with regret this morning.

Mostly, I regret how much I drank. Other than that, I'm pretty good with how things turned out.

Ow. Thinking hurts my brain. Rubbing my temple, I get out of bed, take two ibuprofen, and down them with some Gatorade. Sitting at my desk, I check my email while wearing my sunglasses. The screen is blinding me, and it's almost as dim as it can go.

The wedding invitation draws my eyes, and I run my finger over one of the flowers. Stella and Rivers set the standard for true love. When I'm around them, a little light shines inside me, exposing the hope that still exists in the dark.

I can talk a good game and even convince myself that love is something we were fed through fables when we were younger. But sometimes if you catch me at the right moment, usually after a drink or three, I still believe.

Dave caught me on the right night and in the perfect frame of mind to see him in a new light. Last night was fun and easy. Unexpected.

Slow.

Steady.

Perfect.

Things have changed so much in the past eight months. At least for me. But it took distancing myself from my comfort, Dave included, to really see if I could survive on my own. I didn't just survive. I thrived.

Now that I'm back in Austin, easing into my old routine, I'm not sure if this life fits who I am anymore. I've had my eyes opened. Seen a new world. Made new friends.

I couldn't have predicted anything on that road trip I took right before. It seemed easy—Rivers wanted his 4Runner in LA. Dave and I would drive it from Austin.

With each mile we covered, our relationship seemed to intensify. We'd been together maybe a dozen times total—free and easy. No expectations. Heck, I didn't even have to wear makeup around him. He told me he liked me how I was. Everything was going so well. But the energy between us was changing.

"Are you asleep?" I ask, careful to whisper in case he is.

"Kind of. Kind of not."

"What are you thinking about?"

"The way your heartbeats have synced with mine and your breathing warms my chest." He pulls me closer as if we can possibly get any closer than two naked bodies squeezed in the backseat of this 4Runner. "Coyotes are howling in the distance."

"Will they come near the SUV?"

"They shouldn't. We're safe if they do. The window is only cracked open enough to let some cool air in."

Sweat has left a fine sheen across our bodies from the heat between us and from making love. I used to think we were just rolling around in the hay, having a good time, but I don't anymore. Every time he looks my way, his hazel eyes shine with his desires, the same ones that used to be just sexual. They're not as of late.

I can't blame him. I feel it too—a pull so strong that I worry I'm already too far-gone. I've dated guys before. Another had burned me so badly that I felt as though my heart had charred since then.

I didn't expect it to start thrumming again. It became a regular occurrence that I could count on. A low, dull knock showing up every time Dave did, gathering strength and insisting I notice each time we kissed, touched, or did more.

A foolish heart won't protect me, won't feed me, or take care of me. A foolish heart is what got me hurt in the past. But in Dave's arms, it feels like the rest of the world and the problems I have are distant sounds in the wind, a lot like the howling.

Will I be able to keep them at bay until LA?

I'm leaving. That means leaving these feelings behind for the time being. Without knowing how deep Dave and I had fallen into our own secret routine, I was told to go to London and experience life to its fullest. Breathe in the cool wind. Eat crumpets and drink tea.

Expand my life.

I don't know if I will. The future is always so unpredictable, but it's best for me if I try. And he's right. Our hearts are in sync. Unfortunately, as to where we are in life at the moment? That's where I'm unsure.

I snuggle against him, wrapping my arms around him tighter, though I know it's impossible. Like him, I'm trying to hold on to something I can't.

Come sunrise, we'll return to our lives, letting our heads keep

*things casual as my heart loses its beat once again and I head to
England.*

He whispers, "What's wrong?"

"Nothing."

"You're cold."

*Reaching over, he pulls his hoodie from the front seat and
wraps it over me. I kiss his chest and then close my eyes, hoping
to get some rest while keeping my fears at bay.*

"If you could have one wish, what would it be?" he asks.

"Another night just like this."

He kisses my head, and I finally give in to sleep.

*The weight of the waking hours finally caught up to him.
Hours later, I got what I need, but now I'm awake and not
wanting to miss anything. I feel dirty from the journey, and the
sex, but he feels so good that I don't care. I've never felt better,
sexier, more beautiful than when I'm with him. But that's not
what can carry me in the future.*

*Only I can do that—only my convictions, determination,
and dreams will take me where I should be.*

*I maneuver until I wedge my way through the center of the
front seats. There's no way to move without disturbing him. He's
restless, but soon, he settles again. I slip on my clothes and pop
the door open as quietly as I can to sneak out.*

*Before the breathtaking sun that's rising, I stand at the cross-
roads of my youth and my future. Am I being selfish?*

*What would Stella say if she knew the full truth about me
and Dave? What if I told her he looks at me as though I hung
the moon, but I fear for the fall ahead? The one my parents
warned me about?*

*"Nothing good lasts," my dad said just before taking the lid
off a McDonald's soda and pouring three shots of vodka into it.
"Don't go getting knocked up or shackled down to someone who
tells you love will get you through." He stabs the straw in the
air toward me. "It won't. I loved that woman more than my*

own life and look where that got me." That woman, my mother.

I stopped asking for rides to school after that because at fifteen, I'd learned that vodka had no smell. Years later, I realized why that mattered.

The pop of the door in the distance catches my attention, and I turn back to see him naked, looking like a Greek god.

We've never lacked chemistry. We may not have had sex the first night we met, but we did shortly after. I've never had a regret when it came to him. I get to see what the world doesn't. I get Dave, and he's confident and gentle when it comes to me. Sexy with a heart any woman would be lucky to own. He's funny, wicked, and someone so easy to be around. Genuine. The world gets Ridge, the charismatic, brilliant musician with the come-hither smile. Mind you, I get that smile too, and it works . . . every dang time.

With our unfinished conversation from last night hanging in the air, I head back, knowing we need to talk.

I've got to get my personal life out of my head.

School.

Classes.

Graduation.

That's all that matters.

Focus, Meadow. Focus.

My degree is all that matters. Hoping to drown out that ping in my ears, my heart's not-so-subtle reminder to listen to her, I grab the remote and click on the TV, settling on a morning show while I get dressed.

It's strange how I can be thrust right back into my old life and fall in line. Then along comes Dave as if he never left. That both heals and hurts my heart. Conflicted, I feel my head is still elsewhere. But as soon as that first text dings, I'm smiling. Dave: *What was that movie about anyway?*

Laughing too hard to keep walking, I stop just on the

perimeter of campus to type: *It was a docu-indie via a kid from Minnesota who tracks the mating habits of cockatiels in Brazil.*

Dave: *Wow! You got all that from the forty minutes we watched it?*

Me: *No. I just copied and pasted the summary I found online. Forty minutes? You got further than me.*

Dave: *What's a docu-indie?*

Me: *Half true. Half fake, I guess.*

Dave: *I feel really lame asking these questions. Stay in school, kids. Question: Why was there a guy dressed as a T-Rex?*

Me: *He was the star.*

Dave: *The actor or the T-Rex?*

Me: *I have no idea. Should we have stayed? Should we go back and watch it?*

Dave: *No. We made the right decision. How are you feeling today?*

Moving to the side of a set of steps, I sit on a low wall. Me: *Like crap. You?*

Dave: *Not too bad.*

Me: *Braggy pants.*

Dave: *Speaking of pants, I leave late tonight. Hoping to stop by before I go.*

Me: *How do pants and you stopping by work together in this scenario?*

Dave: *They don't. How's five?*

Perfect.

Me: *See you then.*

I spend all dang day wishing the hours would tick away, but now that it's five till, I'm nervous. *Why am I nervous?* He only wants to hang out like last night until he has to catch his flight. I'll take the flattery that I'm more fun than hanging out at an airport gate.

At five on the dot, there's a rap on the door. I recognize the rhythm as Dave breaks into a Crow Bro band drum solo on the other side of it, eliciting another smile I can't hide when I swing it open.

Huh? "Dave?" He steps from around the corner and holds out a bouquet . . . of Ding Dongs.

I swoon. "Thank you. This might be one of the best gifts I've ever gotten. And you have perfect timing. I'm starving." Taking the bouquet and hurrying back to the kitchen to rip one off the stick, I devour half of it in one bite.

When he doesn't say anything, I turn back, but my mouth is too full to speak, so I wave him in. Guess he was waiting for an engraved invitation. We are way past that.

With a wolfish grin, he comes in and shuts the door. "You always did have a thing for shoving Ding Dongs in your mouth." Standing right next to me, he adds, "You should slow down and learn how to swallow."

So bad. So naughty. Sexy. Mmm. Stop, Meadow. "You're a funny guy." I take the other half and shove it in his mouth when he starts laughing. The laughter stops, but something else comes over him, something indecipherable. "What?" I manage to ask after taking his pervy advice and swallowing.

"Nothing." His eyes close tight for a second to rid his mind of whatever's on it, but the grin is still just below the surface wanting to come out. Touching my cheek, he gently runs his thumb over the corner of my mouth. "You have chocolate on you."

For a quick second, images of him licking it off flash through my head. The beat of my heart kicks up, and my breathing slows. I dip the tip of my tongue out to lick to clean it but meet his thumb instead.

My lower body tightens on contact; all those nights in

London touching myself to the memory of one night in the desert rush back. His pupils widen, watching me as I run my tongue over his skin once more.

Friends.

Stupid F-word.

"Um," I start, trying to figure out what to say as I turn back to the counter. He doesn't move, his heat emanating as his presence shadows me from behind. I scratch the back of my head. "We shouldn't be doing this. Testing boundaries will only result in them being crossed."

Would it be so bad if he touched me again?

Would it be such a sin if we kissed?

Would it be so wrong?

The only rational thing that finds its way to the forefront of my hazy thoughts makes me doubt the authenticity of what's happening—*Am I lonely or just missing intimacy?* "Why did we stop seeing each other again?" *Please remind me because I can't seem to remember.*

"School. Uncomplicated. Nothing serious." Each answer is firm in tone, methodical in delivery. I'm caged in, his hands resting on the island in front of me. The pressure of his muscular body pressed to the back of me. "We were combustible. That's why we stopped seeing each other. It was only a matter of time. You got out while you still could."

"I wasn't trying to get away from you. I was trying to find me."

"Did you find yourself? In England? In LA? Back here in Austin? Tell me you found the person you were searching for."

"I thought I had, but now . . ."

"Then what's changed?"

This time, I'm not making drunk admissions. This time, I want him to know. "Seeing you again."

My hair is brought to one side and pushed forward over my shoulder. "You never had to change for me."

"How about now?" I dare to ask as his forehead rests on my shoulder.

"I still like you just the way you are." *That's the problem. Nothing changed for me either.*

Getting a handle on my senses, I bend and slip out of his hold. I move across the room, needing the space to think more clearly. "We didn't spend time together. We slept together."

"I don't remember much sleeping."

"You know what I mean."

"Live music. Standing on Congress watching the bats. Hiking. Grocery stores. Movies. We did other things together. Normal, everyday things. And yes, we had a lot of great sex."

"All I remember is the sex, and although I will give you that it was great, it's not all that matters in a real relationship."

"We were real. Just because we didn't label it doesn't mean it wasn't real."

"I can't think clearly around you."

"Why? And why does it worry you?"

"Because I don't want to lose me." Because it would be easy to toss my future aside to be whatever you wanted.

"You don't have to. You're someone I want more of, all the fucking ti—"

"I'm not who I need to be when I'm with you." I hide so much inside, burying it beneath the surface, but even I know those words are all wrong.

"Who are you, Meadow? Tell me."

My sister's words coming back again.

"I have my own dreams and goals. I proved I could stand

on my own." My tone sours even though I didn't want it to. "I liked who I was when I was in London."

"You liked being without me."

I fold my arms over my chest. "We may not have been fucking others, but we weren't a couple."

Crossing the room in three large strides, he stops when he's next to me. Disappointment knits into his brow and reflects in his eyes as he looks into mine. "Whatever you need to tell yourself, sweetheart."

The door is opened, but I remain standing there, defiant to protect my needs and my heart.

It closes, and he's gone. And for someone who wanted the silence, wanted the quiet, his departure sounds so loud. *Damn it. How did I botch that up so quickly?*

13

Ridge

MEADOW SOLEIL FELLOWES has to be the most stubborn woman I've ever met.

Intelligent.

Funny.

Quirky.

A stunning mess of emotions.

But stubborn as fuck.

I still can't figure out why she's so stuck on this friends thing. At first, I agreed with her. She had been gone, and during that time, I wondered how much we really knew each other prior to her leaving anyway.

I knew her well enough to want more with her. But when I thought about what more meant to me, was it getting to know her more or take it to the next level more?

Beating around the bush was not something I did. I usually just hack right through it to get what I want, but Meadow's different. So as much as I want to kid myself that I didn't know exactly what I wanted when we talked in the desert, I did. I wanted a life. I wanted a life with her instead of being teased with the pieces that our limited time together doled out.

She didn't feel the same. Or if she did, she was stronger than I was.

Or was she?

I watch Meadow standing at the edge of the gas station in this one-light town. Something's on her mind, a storm of emotions brewing inside her in such contradiction to how I know her to be.

One. Two. Three. Four. Five.

She turns on the fifth step every time. Repeat. Pacing relentlessly.

The carefree smile she used to wear is gone, lost somewhere just on the other side of New Mexico.

She's unsettled, so when the gas starts filling the tank, I join her, hiking a foot up on an old, blown-out tire. While she stares across the street at a dilapidated building that once housed used furniture by the faded sign above it, she says, "I feel lost."

"We're on the right track. I just checked the route a few minutes ago."

A soft smile graces her lips when she turns to me. "I'm scared of leaving. I'm scared of going. I feel lost in between."

"Why are you scared to leave?"

Her arms slowly uncross, and a hand finds mine, her fingers weaving between my fingers. The hold is firm; though not tight, it's tighter than usual for the normally carefree spirit. "I like what's happening." She licks her lips and the sound of the light changing from red to green draws our attention back to the street. "Between us, Dave. I like this. I like you."

"I like you too." I bring her hand up and kiss it, keeping my lips pressed to the back of her hand.

"There's no one I'd rather be with right now."

"On the road trip, at a gas station on the state line, or the night before you leave to start your new life?"

A humorless laugh precedes a sigh. "All of the above."

"England's going to be great. You'll see."

"Have you been?"

"Once. The band did a promotion there. We were there for like ten hours before we were on a plane to Germany."

Her shoulders sag. "So no words of wisdom, then."

The wind picks up just as I whisper, "Come back to me."

"What?"

"Come back. The only words of wisdom I have."

Stepping up on the curb, she's eye level with me. Resting both her hands on my shoulders, she says, "You want me to come back, Dave?" I want you to come back and finally be mine.

"Yeah." This time her laugh is genuine, her cheeks a little wind-whipped pink. "Cherry cheeks."

She cups my face, her thumbs running over the scruff of my jaw but still gentle on my rough skin. "Cherry cheeks?"

"They don't remind me of apples, but of the sweetest cherries."

Her lips find mine, and she kisses me as if I'm just as sweet. When she pulls back, it's just enough to search my eyes for answers to questions she hasn't asked. "I'll come back," she says, the last part lost in another kiss.

Maybe she was never mine to ask to do a favor for my heart, but I was hers.

God, I was so hers.

Hers for the taking if she wanted. Some guys might think that's weak, but I know a good thing when I see it. And Meadow was and *is* a very great thing.

"Prepare for landing."

The announcement moves me to sit up and double-check my seat belt. The flight attendant comes by and leans over to move my seat into the upright and locked position. "For safety, sir."

"Thanks."

The blonde is pretty, every hair in place, face made up with precision. Red lips. I close my eyes, thinking of the blonde, red-lipped girl I want to see. Her lips were the palest of pinks both times I saw her while in Austin. Her hair was a mess. Casual clothes as if she has no one to impress. She just didn't see how much she impressed me.

I pull my phone from my back pocket and hold it in my hand. As soon as the wheels touch down, I turn it on. By the time we're pulling up to the gate, it's searching for service. When I walk off the plane, I call her.

"Hello?" she answers, her voice unsteady. I fucking hate that I caused that.

"I'm sorry."

"For what?"

"I don't know. I'm just sorry things were left the way they were."

"You don't owe me an apology. You did nothing wrong. You're doing everything right. I really do know I'm the one screwing up, and my screwed-up head is messing with everything else."

"How do we get back on track?" I'm bumped to the side, and a camera's shoved in my face. "What the fuck?"

"What's wrong—"

"I have to go." I hang up and shove the phone in my front pocket with my hand still wrapped around it.

I'm led to the side and told to follow a security guard in a dark blue jacket. He's a big dude who takes life seriously by the lack of laugh lines on his face. "Follow me, Mr. Crow."

Inhaling a breath to correct him, I grunt and just let the name slide. It's not worth the time it will take to explain.

Shifting my duffle bag to my other hand, I'm flanked as we near the outside. "Do you have a car?" the main guard asks.

"Yeah." The doors are opened to a line of black SUVs waiting at the curb. "Black . . . fuck."

"We'll find it."

Flashes are going off as I stand and wait back inside the doors. Even the paparazzi are kept at bay, though there's no privacy. I tug my hat down over my brow and keep my eyes lowered. The guard next to me receives a message, and she taps my arm. "Your car's here."

"Thanks."

The doors open, and my name is yelled. "Ridge? Look this way. Ridge. Over here. Ridge. Sign this. Ridge. Ridge. Ridge. Ridge. Ridge."

The door closes, their voices muffled until we pull away and I can't hear them at all. Leaning forward, I ask the driver, "You have the address?"

"Yes. We're looking at an hour if there isn't traffic on the freeway."

"Okay. Thanks."

I pull my phone back out and call Meadow back. "Are you all right?" she asks, worry getting the best of her.

"Fucking paps at LAX."

"Are you safe?"

"I'm fine, Meadow. I can handle it." When she doesn't say anything, I realize what I've done. "I didn't mean to snap at you."

"It's fine. I can imagine it's very stressful to live your life."

"What does that mean?"

"In the spotlight."

"I don't live in the spotlight. You know that. We spent time together and no one bothered us. No cameras to be seen anywhere."

"But for how long. How long do I get to spend time with Dave?"

"What are you saying?"

"The world wants Ridge."

"You've been around The Crows—"

"Enough to know that when I was in London, it was nice to be me. Not part of the Crow clan or Stella's little sister. Just me."

"And you're not you with me?"

She hems, then whispers, "I am." Gathering strength, she exhales a breath. "I know how this story goes—"

"Then tell me because I don't."

"Everyone wants a piece of you—"

"What do you want?"

"I don't want to be another burden in your life." She could never be a burden to me. *She's my light.* But it's typical that she doesn't realize it, always worried about me. *Selfless.*

"You're not, Meadow. You're the opposite for me. With you, I get to be me." I rub my temple, knowing we're back to square one, or maybe I read the signs wrong and we've been here all along.

"I don't want to lose myself along the way."

And there it is. Her fears summed up. "I would never want that either."

"You asked me about us being off track. I've been thinking a lot about it, about us. I might not be what you need right now. I hate saying that because we do have a good time when we're together and I don't want to hurt you."

It's my turn to step up and share that truth that's simmering under the surface between us. "We can pretend we're only friends, but we both know it's more than that. I'm trying my best to navigate these waters with you, but now you're saying you want to date other people?"

"I like the time we spend together. It's easy, but it comes

with complicated feelings I don't have time to untangle. I like you—"

"You like me," I repeat the words, incredulously. I almost don't know what to say. Almost. "Okay."

"It's not you, Dave."

"Then why does it feel like it's exactly fucking me?"

"I hate hurting you."

"You're not hurting me, sweetheart." *No, you're telling me I'll never be enough. Story of my fucking life.* "You're opening my eyes." She doesn't need this in her life, and I don't need to keep wondering where the fuck we stand. She's worried she'll hurt me . . . *Let her go, Carson. Let her go.*

She's made herself clear. It's time I listen. "I think it's best if we do our own thing. You do you. I'll do me."

"What does that mean?"

"It means you find what you need. I'm not that for you. I'll do the same. And maybe we'll both find that happiness that seems to find others so easily."

A short pause turns into an awkward silence. Sales 101. First one to talk loses.

She finally says, "I want you to know something."

I fucking hate goodbyes.

Meadow and I shouldn't be doing this. *But what the fuck can I do?* As much as I couldn't read her before—what we were, what we are—I know this goodbye doesn't feel right.

"I'll always be a haven when you need it. I'm here for you." *Except now.*

This is not what I expected to hear. I don't know the ins and outs of what we are to each other. My instincts tell me we still have unfinished business, but tonight I need the reprieve.

She says, "I'm glad you made it back safe and sound." Because she does care, more than she wants to acknowledge for some reason. "It's late, so I'm going to bed."

Hacking right through that bush. "I'm not sure when we'll talk next."

The statement makes her pause. The SUV comes to a stop in a sea of red taillights. Traffic. Fuck. I'm so ready for this day to be over.

Meadow says, "Take care of yourself, okay?"

"I will. You too, all right?"

"Good night, Dave."

"Bye, Meadow."

I slam the phone down on the seat next to me. Fuck. Fuck. "Fuck!"

The driver's attention hits me in the mirror. "Everything okay?"

"No." I turn my gaze out the window, a sickness churning in my gut. Wishing time to fly by, I'm unsettled in the back of this SUV. I need out. It takes another hour.

When I reach the house, I punch in the other code and the door releases with a click. I lock up the house and set the alarm. Grabbing a bottle of water from the fridge, I head upstairs and dump my bag on the floor.

On the nightstand is a little basket of goodies—another bottle of water, a mini Jack Daniels, granola bars, and M & Ms. I sit on the bed and read the note.

Glad to have you back.

See you in the morning.

H.

A light knock on the door gets my attention. "Come in."

The door opens just enough to reveal Jet holding the baby in his arms. "Hey. I wanted to check on you."

"For you or for Hannah?" I say in a piss-ass fucking mood. I can't take it out on him, though. Jet's doing me a favor.

"She'd kick my ass if I didn't, and this little one was up anyway." Violet's asleep in his arms, so I don't know what he's talking about.

"She's trained you well."

A tired smile crosses his face. "Hannah or Violet?"

"Both."

We chuckle. "You're probably right. How's your mom?"

"Sleeping a lot. I visited with some of the family while there, but I'm glad to be back."

"Get some rest. The next leg of the tour is intense. We need you rested and ready."

Glancing toward the baby, I say, "You too."

"I'm tired, but I'm happy to give up a few hours of sleep to be able to do this. I miss her when I'm gone."

"She's getting big."

Even though he's looking down at her, I can see the pride in his eyes. Just before he leaves, he says, "I'll see you in the morning."

"Hey, thanks for letting me stay here."

"Anytime, man."

The door is closed, and I lie down. Too much of the day weighs me down. I left out the part about my mom being too out of it from the meds to even know I was there. I left out the part where I was sitting by her side holding her hand and some relatives I barely know asked for my autograph. I didn't mention that my dad took me off her visitor's list because my presence is a *distraction* he claims she doesn't need. Fuck him.

Fuck the world.

Meadow's a hard habit to break, and I come so close to calling her back. Holding the phone in my hand, my grip tightens as I will myself not to follow through. After everything earlier, calling her again would make things *too serious*. Meadow said she'd be my haven, but even she can't shield me from this pain.

14

Ridge

THE CONNECTION WAS INSTANTANEOUS. It was as if no one else existed the moment I laid eyes on her in that crowded bar.

Rivers is so damn preoccupied with Stella that he is almost oblivious to the hottie next to her. I'm given a beer and a shot as a consolation prize while he treks through the bar on a mission.

Our friend's band is on stage and mentioned a Meadow with Rivers's ex. Seems a few people know her name. By looking at her, I want to know more. I down the shot and set the glass down on the bar before heading down to where Rivers went.

Before I get there, Rivers is following Stella through the crowded place. Meadow watches but doesn't seem happy. Do I go, or do I stay?

I'm clapped on the back before a decision is made. "Fucking hell. Dave Carson in the flesh."

I know the voice. It's someone I've avoided many times over the years until he inserted himself in my life last year in some big ego-driven show to stake his claims on Hannah.

Hunter Hix is the kind of guy you can't give an inch or he's moving in and taking over your bedroom. The Crow Brothers' success and fame is probably not an easy pill to swallow. But neither was finding out he was fucking my longtime girlfriend.

With my eyes on his filthy hand that's resting and pressing down on my shoulder, I knock it off when I turn around. "Hix. When'd you get released?"

"That's not funny, fucker."

Maybe not to him, but it's true. Robbing the bar where you just played a gig was not his brightest idea. That's what fucking desperation will do.

I chuckle because my comment was still funny as fuck to me. "Did Shannon wait for you, or did you meet a new girlfriend behind bars?"

From the side, I'm shoved into a group of guys, spilling their beers. "What the fuck?" I right myself, charging forward before he has a chance to react. Grabbing him by the throat, I walk him backward through the crowd, which parts for me like the goddamn Red Sea, until his back hits the wall. "If you ever fucking touch me again, I will break your fucking arms and every fucking finger you have. You won't be able to play guitar or play with the balls of the guy who made you his bitch." His throat is pinned by my hand, so I don't really expect a response. He'd be wise not to even try.

Security flanks me. "Let him go, Carson."

I release him and wipe my hand on my jeans. Taking a step back, I give him enough room to slink his sorry ass out of here. Hunter holds his throat and hacks up a lung. With a red face, he tries to level me with a look. "That'd be better fate than being a little bitch for the Crows. Fucking losers. Go play your pop on the radio, you fucking pussy."

"Pussy. Something you don't get much of these days. Assault falls as a violation of your parole, fucker. So who's the little bitch now?" I'd say I heard what he said next, but I was too busy walking away. I'm not interested in him enough to muster any *more fucks to give. I had better business to tend to. The little beaut who originally caught my eye.*

By the time I reach where she and her sister were sitting, she's gone. "Fuck." Now that I give a fuck about. I look around but don't see her. Fuck.

I drag the pillow beside me over my eyes. The one thing about being at Jet and Hannah's is they understand the crazy hours. Blackout curtains keep the day outside while I try to figure out if dreaming of the night I met Meadow is a subliminal message or a symptom of being caught up in a woman who isn't caught up in me. Desire versus logic.

I need to stop thinking about her, definitely stop dreaming of her, and let her figure her shit out while I figure out mine. C'mon, brain. Go back to sleep.

I grab my phone to look at the time. I didn't get in until after one in the morning. Five hours isn't enough. Rubbing over my face, the pricks of a week's worth of stubble stabs the palms of my hands. Another thing to take care of when I get up.

Willing my body to relax, I focus on my muscles and sinking back into the mattress. My breathing deepens and steadies as green eyes return to haunt my dreams.

"Shit!" I jump a fuckin' mile to the other side of the bed. Fuck. "What are you doing, Alfie?"

"Seeing who was in here?"

"You can't just sneak up on people like that, especially when they're sleeping."

"Sorry, Ridge."

I retrieve my thumping heart from the other side of the room and take a breath to calm down. "It's fine—"

Hannah gasps from the doorway. "Oh my God. Alfie, what are you doing in here?"

"I wanted to know who was here," he says so innocently while walking to her. "It's Ridge. Did you know he was here?"

"Yes. I did. He got in late last night." She holds a hand up to me while the other is over her mouth still in horror. "I'm sorry."

"It's okay," I say. "Hey Alf, I'll be down soon, bud. Save me a seat for breakfast."

He squeezes out around Hannah, who says, "I'm so sorry. I'll talk with him."

"Don't worry. It's his house, not mine." I'm about to get up but wait just in case I have another morning visitor under the blanket. "I'm getting up. I'll be down shortly."

"I'll have coffee ready."

"I'm going to need it," I reply, rubbing my eyes, trying to rid myself of the sleep that feels ingrained into my bones at this point in the tour.

"How's your mom doing?"

"There was a lot going on, so I didn't get to spend much time with her."

"I'm sorry. Will you visit her again soon?"

"I think I should. Right now, everyone is swarming around, so she has no peace. No privacy."

"I'm sorry."

"I guess too many people caring about you is a good problem to have."

She nods, sympathy in her eyes. "I'll see you downstairs."

The door closes, and I take a shower. After getting dressed, I run a hand through my hair. It's getting long, starting to hang over my eyes. Since I'm too lazy to put goop in it to make it stay in place, I need to get it cut soon.

When I finally make my way downstairs, Jet is eating cereal at the table. "You look like shit," he says.

"Back at ya, brother." He does too. "Those late nights are catching up. Be careful or you're going to lose your sex symbol status."

He even laughs at that one. He also flips me off, but I'm good with it.

Glancing behind him, I see Hannah bouncing the baby on her knees on the back patio. "My wife can't keep her hands off me, so I'm okay with looking like shit if she likes the way I look."

"And here I thought a baby would slow things down in the sex department."

"Maybe it does for some," he muses, running a hand over his head. His hair's growing out too.

I walk past him. "TMI, and we both look like shit. What is it called when chicks talk about taking care of themselves?"

Jet lowers his voice, and says, "Masturbation."

"No, and don't ever talk to me about that," I reply, disgust scrunching my nose. "When women say they need a bath and—"

The door closes behind me. Coming inside, Hannah says, "Self-care?"

"Yeah," I reply, snapping my fingers. "That's it. We need some self-care."

"I thought that's why we got married?" Tulsa asks, coming in the front door.

"Not what we're talking about," I say. Slapping our hands together, we do a slow slide back and wiggle our fingers. We both laugh, having perfected the handshake. Rubbing my hand over my head, I look up when I see my bangs flying over my forehead. "Shaggy. I need a haircut. Your brother does, too."

Tulsa rubs over his short hair. It's longer than a military

induction cut but not by much. "Nikki shaved mine. I was willing to take it all off. She put her foot down."

"Because she owns your ass."

With a tight mouth and no fight in him, he nods. "Truth, man. Truth."

I move from the breakfast room into the kitchen where Hannah is pulling a mug from the cabinet with Violet bundled around her. "Here you go."

Moving to give her a hug, she wraps her arms around my middle, and whispers, "How are you doing?"

"I'm good." Moving to the side, I bend down until I'm eye level with Violet, who's cooing with a big smile and bright eyes. "Who's a little lady? Who's the cutest baby?" When I scrunch my face, she giggles.

"She likes you," Hannah says, leaning against the counter next to me.

"I like her." I tap Violet on the nose. Jet and Tulsa walk away, so I take the opportunity to catch up with my friend.

Standing back up, I nudge Hannah. I feel like every time I see her, she looks happier than the time before if that's possible. And although I'm no baby expert, Hannah and Jet's baby is the cutest I've ever seen. Dark hair, almost jet-black like her daddy and blue eyes like her mama. "She smiles a lot. She has your disposition."

"She's a happy baby. She has a dad who can't get enough of her and a brother that tells anyone who will listen that his best friend likes too much pink." Leaning in conspiratorially, she says, "Sometimes when he comes home from the road, I catch him waking Violet up in the night just to spend a few extra hours with her. She always gives it away the next day when she's cranky, but it's so sweet that I don't say anything."

Remembering last night when he stopped by, I ask, "Does he know you know?"

"No. I don't want him to ever stop having those

moments that are just his. We can make up for the lost sleep with naps."

Wrapping an arm around Hannah's shoulders, we admire her baby together. "And a mom who anyone would be lucky to have."

Teasing, she double taps my ribs with her elbow. "Look at you being all charming."

"What?" I shrug, taking the mug to the coffee machine. "I'm always charming."

"Speaking of charming, did you spend any time with a certain someone while you were in Austin?"

One day I'll learn to control my instant reactions to certain topics. Today is not that day. She must pick up on something because she says, "That good, huh?"

"Worse."

"I'm sorry."

I laugh. "You don't have to be sorry about anything. Not my mom and not my—"

"Not your love life?"

"Love is a little strong."

Looking around as if part of a covert operation, she leans in, covers Violet's ears, and whispers, "Sex life?"

"No, not doing this with you."

"You can talk to Jet if you'd feel more comfortable."

Now I just laugh and keep laughing because this has gotten so out of hand I'm not sure where to go with it.

Fortunately, like his guitar playing skills, Jet has perfect timing when he comes around the corner. Jet is every bit the rock star. Cool demeanor. Owns a room with his mere presence. By the way Hannah spoke of his appearance when they first started dating, he's apparently "drool-worthy."

He's not much older than me, having me beat only by a year, but our lives couldn't be more different. First of all, he married my best friend. Now I don't get to see her as much.

Before that, they fought for custody of his son, Alfie. It's all a jumble now. But to top off their year of greatness, baby Violet came along.

Hannah and I have been through a lot together. Her asshole ex, my former best friend and the lead singer of our band, was fucking my girlfriend while we all toured. We gave some damn good years up to those losers but found each other along the way. We may be close, but we never hooked up, valuing the friendship we found.

Jet's eyes come alive when he sees his wife. Stopping to kiss his baby on the way, he's gentle with Hannah, touching her face before kissing her. There's no lack of love in this house, and Hannah deserves it. He's not in a hurry or worried about the days ticking by too fast. He takes his time because he has that on his side. *Lucky bastard.*

Turning to me, he says, "Rivers is here. We're going down to the studio," and then leaves.

"Kay."

When the coast is clear, Hannah says, "I'm not telling you anything you don't know already, but it's not always easy even if it's meant to be. Jet and I are prime examples of that. We had to fight to be together. Sometimes it just comes down to who's willing to go the extra mile."

Thinking about all the couples who surround me these days, no one had it easy. Maybe Tulsa and Nikki, but I feel like they went through some stuff that we're not all aware of. "I used to think it was supposed to be easier if it's meant to be."

"Sometimes, I guess. Everyone's different. I don't think you should force anything. If the attraction is there, the relationship will hopefully come naturally."

I push off the counter and touch Violet's tiny toes

because they're so friggin' small. "If I keep talking about my feelings all the time, shut me up. I'm tired of myself at this point."

"Talking's not bad. Lack of action is."

"Okay. Okay. Got it. If I love her, don't let her slip away."

Her mouth falls open. "You love her? You *love* Meadow?"

"What? No. I said like. Wait, I didn't say anything about Meadow."

She's still staring at me—silently, so I start rambling to fill in the blanks of what I guess she's thinking. "I do *like* Meadow, but that's it. We're not anything."

Still nothing from her. She shifts the fabric and adjusts Violet onto her hip. Violet seems to want something else and fusses. Hannah strokes her head and then kisses her, calming her instantly. The magic of a mom kiss. Her attention comes back to me. "You said love, Dave."

My hands fly up. "I haven't even had coffee yet. My brain's not functioning properly. I thought we were talking in generalities."

"That you're talking about love at all says a lot, so you can play this off however you want, but unlike your brain, your heart is fully functioning."

I roll my eyes. The little action reminds me of Meadow, and I smile. *Shit.* Do I love Meadow Fellowes? How is that possible? We basically ended it last night . . . not basically. She's frustrating to no end, indecisive when it comes to what she wants—from her food orders to her clothes. She's all over the place, deciding things on whims and spur-of-the-moment emotions. She's also fifteen hundred miles away.

Nothing about us makes sense.

Love? That's not possible. "Nope. Nope. Nope."

Hannah's brow is pinched in the center, so I assume I sound as nutty as I feel. *Fuck.* "Forget I said anything. I need to head down to the studio." She's not saying what she's really thinking, but I can read it all over her face, so I add, "You can stop smiling like a fool now."

"What can I say? I'm a fool for a great love story."

Although I don't give Hannah any satisfaction on the topic, I can admit, I'm also a sucker for a happy ever after. But in this instance, where I've been offered a haven and not a future, I'm not sure it's in the cards for Meadow and me. Given how I'd do anything for her, though, *maybe* that's what love is.

Considering I removed the options from the dating table last night, I think it's best if I let things lie. Not forever, but for now.

15

Ridge

"Married. Married. Married. Single." The DJ points to each of us like we're playing a game of duck, duck, goose.

Rivers says, "I'm engaged."

The rest of us know it's going to happen before it does. The radio DJ leans on her hand, making eyes at him. "So there's a chance for the right woman to come along and steal your heart before you walk down that aisle?"

I'm fucking offended for him. He should have never spoken up, drawing her attention to his personal life. Tulsa is the comedian in the group, always there with a smile and joke to cheer everyone up, so it comes as a surprise to hear him use an unfamiliar firm, slightly raised voice when he says, "He's marrying the right woman, the woman who already owns the ring. The marriage is tradition and legalities, but trust me, my brother's already married in all the ways that matter."

She seems a bit taken aback by his tone. "I didn't mean to imply—"

Jet sighs. "We know what you meant to imply, but you also disrespected his fiancée."

"He's engaged but not married. Noted for the listeners. Another Crow bites the dust." Tapping the desk, she adds, "Thanks for being here, guys."

Her headphones are dumped on the desk, and she says, "Our listeners like the single rock star angle, so we pursue it when we can. I'm married, but no one knows. It doesn't jive with the persona. It's all in fun."

No, it's not okay. No placating or making her feel better. She crossed a line, but it's admirable how the brothers not only stand up for each other but everyone who's important to them, their wives and kids the most.

When the DJ leaves the sound booth, Rivers hits my chest. "How'd you manage to dodge that bullet? You're the actual single one here."

"I lay low, and my last name's not Crow."

"Lucky fucker. Stella's gonna be pissed when she hears that shit."

When we walk out of the room, Rochelle is waiting. "I don't care if she is married. She crossed a line and can fuck off."

Jet laughs. "Tell us how you really feel."

"I've been in this business a long time." Her hands go out to stop us, and she lowers her voice so no one else can hear her. "Being on this side of a relationship with someone famous has taught me that people are unscrupulous when it comes to their personal pursuits. I wear a Teflon suit most days, but when I think of Stella, I remember being in her shoes. This life, being in the spotlight because she fell in love with someone who's famous, is hard. Just remember every time someone disrespects your family, they disrespect you." She starts walking, and we follow in silence.

I think half from fear. Half from wanting to hear her.

She's fired up.

Rochelle's a little thing, similar to Meadow. Both come up about yay high to me, but you don't fuck with them when they're mad. Rochelle stops again before we reach reception, right in front of the station manager's open office door. "She'll know better than to mess with your families next time. That level of disrespect will not be tolerated." She follows with a rub to her right temple.

The door opens, and the radio's general manager spends the next ten minutes explaining how that program goes down with listeners.

Excuses.

That Rochelle sees right through. These guys have lost any future rights to us now. *And they know it.*

Rochelle respectfully explains that we were here to promote an album, not our personal lives. When she left, we left.

In the parking garage, she carries her purse but has her phone held firmly in the other. "Great show. You're done for the day."

Our business manager kicks every other business manager's ass in the music industry. No wonder The Resistance listens to everything she says. That, or they're afraid to piss her off as well.

———————

With my head resting back, I stare up at the wood beams running across the white wood ceiling. Hannah flops down next to me on the couch. "What has you so deep in thought?"

I spread my arm wide on the back of the couch behind

her and bring her to my side just as Jet walks by. "Hey. Hey. My wife is my life. Hands off."

Holding up my hands in surrender, I laugh. "I saw her first."

"I married her. I'm not going to say first because we're forever. Right, baby?" He sets five beers and a Yoo-Hoo down on the table between us.

Hannah replies, "Forever with you."

Sitting down, Jet looks up as Tulsa and Nikki come from the backyard. Nikki carries the baby to Hannah, and says, "I want one just like Violet. I love her."

Last year, Tulsa would have broken out in a bad rash of commitment-phobia, but since he met Nikki, he seems to have calmed in so many ways. He still has a big and very loud personality, but he doesn't even bat an eye when he hears his wife talk about having a baby. *Interesting.*

Jet stands. "I'll take her. I'm trying to force Hannah to take a night off. I'm even trying to tempt her with a beer."

I bump into Hannah, and whisper, "Take a night off."

"I'll take an hour or two off, but no beer for me. I'm still breastfeeding."

"I know we're best friends, but that's a little much for me."

When she laughs, she lights up the whole room. Even though we're all exhausted from the day of interviews, it's hard to be grumpy around her. Despite my best efforts, I find myself smiling. I knew whoever won her heart would score in life. "He's lucky to have you."

"I'm the lucky one." Her eyes never leave Jet as he sits down again with the baby, making her appear smaller in his arms. He's a big dude. Not that I'm small at six foot two, but damn, those Crow brothers are big.

As if Tulsa, the youngest Crow, can read my mind, he asks, "You workin' out lately, Ridge?"

"I've slacked the past week. I'll be hitting it again tomorrow."

"Text me. I'll meet up."

Nikki settles on his lap in the chair and touches his nose. "What if I have plans for you?"

"You'll be too tired tomorrow."

"From what?" she asks.

"Tonight."

She laughs, but when he whispers in her ear, all traces of her smile disappear. "Promise?"

"I can guaran-fuckin'-tee it, darlin'."

She kisses him, and then says, "I have no doubt."

Normally, I'd laugh or just ignore them. They've been married just over a year, so I get the hands all over bit, but today their intimacy is hitting a raw nerve with me. I stand, grabbing a cold bottle of beer while trashing my empty on the way out to the backyard.

Hannah touches my hand as I walk by, causing me to look back, and asks, "You doing okay?"

"No," I grumble under my breath. Stella is coming inside when I walk out. Rivers strumming his guitar as the sun sets. "It's cold tonight."

He looks up. "The fire's warm."

I pick up an acoustic guitar from a chair and sit on the other side of the fire pit. After two long swallows of beer, I put the bottle on the ground next to my feet and start strumming along. He's playing one of the newer songs we wrote around March, six months back. "That's a sad fucking song, man."

He chuckles, and although he looks up, his fingers find every note. "You were a sad fucking man when you wrote it." His hand goes palm flat against the strings. "So what's going on with you, my single friend?" A smile creeps in as he mocks that the DJ didn't called me out.

"That's a sad song for another day."

"Today's the day, my man." That's something I've heard him say before. Losing his mom the way he did made him realize that you had to live every day as if it was the last. *Today's the day.*

"My mom's sick. Dad's giving me shit about not being home."

"Jet told me about your mom. Fuck."

"Yeah. Exactly."

"Sorry, man."

"Me too."

"And Meadow?"

"What about Meadow?" His eyes stay steady on me, not giving me an inch of wiggle room when it comes to expecting an answer. I'm too tired to play this off. "What can I say, man? She's in Austin. I'm here. I wanted more; she said she just wants to be friends. It's just fucked."

"The song you wrote . . . You were shit then, and you're even worse now."

"Our story is tragic. From lovers to friends to lovers to . . . nothin'."

This time, he scoffs and shakes his head. Looking me square in the eyes, he says, "I know tragic. You two not getting your shit together is stupid and stubborn. Not fucking tragic."

Fuck. Stella almost died. I remember the fear, the worry he went through. "I'm sorry. I'm an asshole."

Setting the guitar down, he stands. "You're not an asshole, so stop acting like one. Either go after her or move the fuck on, but don't waste your time caught in the middle. You'll either make a move, or you won't. You're tired all the fucking time. Did you ever think it's because you're not actually dealing with all the shit on your mind?"

Rivers is hard to piss off. Sure, he's moody and more

introverted than his brothers, but he's steadfast and solid in character. He also may not have approved of Meadow and me in the beginning, or maybe it was more that he didn't particularly like the idea of us, but he never stepped in the way of what was happening naturally.

"All the damn time."

"You need to sort out your personal life. I'm not telling you how to go about it, but the more you let it poison your veins, the more it will damage you. Trust me, I know. I've been there. I suffered for too many damn years, considering I had the chance to change things all along."

His words settle in under my skin. If I think about it, really listen to what's going on inside me, I can feel the truth. I feel more disconnected from Meadow than when she was halfway around the world.

Hannah comes outside, and Rivers seems to calm, both of them sitting down around the fire pit.

She holds her hands out to warm and watches the flames flicker. When her eyes are leaning toward gray, she has a lot on her mind.

"What has you worried, Han? These Crow brothers annoying you?"

Rivers snorts and gives me the bird. "I'll leave you two to talk."

When we're alone, I keep my eyes down on the guitar as I pluck a few notes. She says, "You're avoiding the question from earlier."

"See? Now that's the issue. I'm not avoiding the question. I'm avoiding the topic you're circling around."

"Meadow?"

"Meadow."

"So you love/like her?"

"There's nothing left to say. She's in Austin, focusing on school. I'm here or wherever the band needs me. You know better than anyone that sometimes the life of a professional musician isn't conducive to building a life with someone else."

"I call bullshit. Something else is going on. I'm not saying she has to take the fame and love it. She's not a groupie. Based on Stella, I feel like Meadow's intentions are good. But you're a great guy. There's no reason for her not to want to try."

I lean forward, resting on my forearms. "Did you ever feel absorbed into Jet's life? Like you lost yourself?"

"I *am* absorbed into his life just as he is into mine. That's love."

"Meadow says she wants to stand on her own two feet. So if she feels like she's sacrificing herself to be with me, I'm willing to back off." I meet her concerned grays again. "I did back off. We're pausing things." I told her I was done, but I know I'm not. *Not yet.*

She sits up, her feet moving back to the ground. She taps my leg. "I just want you to be happy. If you're meant to be, you'll find your way back to each other. My romantic side reminds me she's only twenty-one, Dave, but she's not had it easy. But equally, she's not someone who plays games, so to me, maybe she really does just need time to sort through some things. To stand on her own so she knows she can before being a partner to someone else."

"*I'll come back.*" She came back . . . like she said. *Time.* She wants time . . . I'm giving her that. I say, "Guess we'll see."

Following her inside, Stella tells us, "Jet's reading to Violet and said he'll put her to bed right after."

I hear the swoon in her voice, but then Tulsa says, "Bastard's making us look bad."

Alfie's eyes go wide as apple pies. "You owe me a dollar, Uncle Tulsa."

Nikki's laughter carries from the kitchen. "Yes, pay up."

"What?" Tulsa exclaims. "Last week, it was fifty cents."

With a shrug, Alfie says, "Inflation, man." He turns to me. "You owe me two dollars for the swear jar this morning, Ridge."

Little shit. "You snuck into my bedroom and scared the shit out of me. Fuck." I roll my eyes and pull out my wallet. "I'm just going to give you a five and get a credit."

"Wise," the kids says like he's Don Corleone.

Tulsa slaps a buck into his other hand. "C'mere. I want to tell you how you can turn that money into sweet, sweet honey."

"What do you mean?"

Coming into the living room and settling on the arm of Tulsa's chair, Nikki ruffles his hair. "Yes, Uncle Tulsa, what do you mean?"

"So you know how I told you to kill 'em with kindness last week?"

Alfie nods, complete attention focused on Tulsa, who says, "This week's life advice is not about catching flies with honey, but catching honies by being fly. Get out your note-book. You're gonna wanna take notes, Alfie, my man."

Hannah jumps from her seat near the fireplace, clapping her hands. "Okay, bedtime, Alfie."

I laugh with Nikki and Tulsa, but out of the corner of my eye, I see Stella in the kitchen and can't help thinking about Meadow. Hannah's right. They're not the sort of women who play games.

Hannah sneaks upstairs while I sit and watch this family who's accepted me as one of their own. Thinking about what Rivers said and then what Hannah seemed to echo, and it seems for now I have to accept she's not my girl. I'm not desperate to be married off like the guys, but I do want love in my future. I thought it was with Meadow, but maybe I was wrong.

Next month, I'll see Meadow at the wedding, and even though that seems too long away, maybe it's the time we both need. I took her offer of a haven to heart, but now I need to find what will make me happy.

16

Meadow

AT SOME POINT, surely she'll slow down. Darcy's arms fly into the air, and she hops off the barstool. "I love this song." Grabbing my arms, she says, "Let's dance."

I'm dragged from the stool, landing on my feet, but as I'm pulled through the crowd, I resist. "No, Darce. I'm so tired. It's after two, and I'm about to fall asleep."

She stops, and with a huge grin, she starts dancing around me. We didn't even make it to the dance floor, but she's oblivious. "Dance with me, Mead. Come on now."

I hold my arms up and give her jazz hands. She gets me back right and proper, as she would say, by ass bumping me so hard that I fly to the side and into the arms of a stranger. A strong, tall, dark, and very handsome stranger. "I, I'm sorry," I stutter. "Thank you."

"It's my pleasure," he says, helping me to right myself. He's still touching me, the bare skin of my upper arms hot under his palms.

"It's your pleasure to catch me?"

He has a rugged jaw, model sharp, light eyes, and a tailored jacket over a well-cut shirt. Everything about him should draw me in. It's as if he was created from a dream I once had as a kid.

I step back, willing his hands to leave my body, or if they stay, wishing they weren't so soft, *without calluses.* "Absolutely." He lowers his hands but holds one out to shake mine. "I'm Kenneth. What's your name?"

Looking into the crystalline blue of his eyes, they have no depth like the ever-moody hazels I prefer. "Thanks again." I turn and with tight lips nod my head toward the exit.

Darcy knows she pushed me to an extreme when I'm ready to leave. When I hit a wall, I crash into it head first. She quick steps to my side. "He was cute."

"Don't."

Her arm comes around my shoulder. With three inches on me, I feel like a doll under her protective wing. "You're right. He was an utter wanker." She leans down, and asks, "Did you happen to get that plonker's number by chance?"

"You're the worst." I burst out laughing as I slide out from under her arm to give her a hug. "I'm so glad you're here."

"I'm glad I'm here too. I missed my Meadow and your sunshine." *Sunshine.* I don't allow my mind to drift far from this moment. I've been fighting to stay in the present since Dave told me we needed to go our own ways. Darcy. Darcy. I exhale. "Is that the car?" She looks down at her phone and points. "That's it."

We hop in and head back to my sister's house. Darcy's been here for two days, and we've had a great time, but tonight was the last hurrah for us to go out in LA. "I can't wait to go to Hawaii tomorrow."

"Fun. Sun. Hot surfers. Sex on the Beach . . . wink, wink, nudge, nudge. Yes and please. Bring it on."

Laughing, I add, "And my sister's wedding, of course."

"And those hot rockers. If I get drunk and start hitting on them, let me."

That warrants another giggle, but then I remember that Crow Bro radio interview. Stella never said a word about it. Not to Rivers. Not to me. Just held it inside, taking her lumps. As much as the guys defended her and the relationship, it was another wake-up call for her, and for me, of what life with a celebrity is like.

"Hey Darce, I know it's all fun and games, but remember they're all big time taken, and their wives may look sweet as pie, but they're not afraid to fight for their men."

Her brown hair is wild and wonderful, so much like her. With her hand against her forehead dramatically, she says, "I would never hit on a married man. You know me better than that."

"It's just a sensitive subject, and I don't want it to be the cause of any undue stress for my sister right now."

"What? Me cause undue stress? You're out of your bloody mind. I adore your sister, and I promise to be on my best behavior."

"I know you will. I just felt—"

"You just felt the need to say it. That's the responsible Meadow I know and love." When she rests her head back, she rolls it to the side to face me. "Anyway, not all of them are taken, or Ridge has done a good job keeping his relationship under wraps."

My hackles rise.

Mine.

One.

Breathe.

Two.

Breathe.

He's not mine.

He never was, it seems.

When we arrive home, we're careful to sneak in, hoping we don't wake Rivers or Stella, but by the gigglefest we're having in the kitchen, that's just not possible. Darcy tops off her glass of wine almost to the brim. "God, he's so stuffy at work. Unfun." *And she's back to talking about Carrig. This girl with alcohol . . .*

"Carrig was always stuffy from his clothes to his personality."

"Exactly. So why do I find him so incredibly sexy?" I don't even know what to say, and my mouth is too busy hanging open anyway. She leans forward as if he'll hear us talking about him, and adds, "I had sex with him."

"What? You can't just say that like it's nothing."

"Oh, it was something all right. He may be stuffy, but that's the last thing he is between the sheets."

I'm in shock. My mind is replaying all the times he wanted to take me out, and the nice things he said to me. Coming to LA, which I still think was a ruse just to see me again. What about all those times? Clearly, I read that wrong. "You used to make fun of him."

"I still do." She shrugs. "During the work hours, we still poke each other with insults. After hours, he pokes me with his—"

"Ew! No. I don't want the details." Staring at her and seeing how wide she's smiling from sharing her news, I add, "Fine. I want the details, but I don't need *all* the details."

Spreading her arms apart, she says, "He's huge."

"Okay. That would be one of the details I don't need." A boisterous laugh fills the kitchen, and I say, "Shhh."

"But for my vagina's well-being, it's an important detail. What happens if the next guy isn't built as lovely as Carrig?"

"First of all, why does everything sound posh in an English accent?"

She wiggles her eyebrows, and says, "I'd drop my pants for a hot American, so I guess we're even. Secondly?"

"Secondly, did you just call Carrig's penis lovely?"

"I did. I really did. It is too, so lovely. When the parka comes down, it's straight, not too veiny—"

"Again. Ew."

"Except for the main vein of course."

"Okay, I think we're done here."

She takes a gulp of her too full wine glass. "No, I'm not ready for bed. You must tell me everything about your love life. You must have one, considering you told that chap at the club to fuck off."

Raising my finger into the air, I correct her, "I did not tell him to fuck off. I told him thank you for catching me when you ass humped me right into him."

"You're welcome."

I miss laughing this much. I just miss this. She makes it easy to feel happy, but she also makes me miss London where I felt free from my everyday worries. The internship seemed like a vacation compared to the school assignments I've been buried under this fall.

Propping up on two hands, she cradles her chin, and eyes me up. "What are you hiding, Meadow Fellowes? I just realized I've been talking the whole time. Now it's your turn. I want to hear about all the guys who have caught your eye and landed in your bed."

I hold up a circle with my hand. "That would be a big fat zero for me."

A gasp echoes it's so loud. I shush her again, but then she says, "No one?"

"I'm trying to graduate with honors. I'm sure you remember how intense senior year was."

Darcy is a few years older, and her ambition is really about marrying the right man over a career. From a rich family who supports her every whim, I'm thinking she doesn't relate to working hard, but more working enough to get by for the time being.

Her hands become flurries in the air. "So let me get this straight. You have had no one in your bed, and you've not been in anyone else's bed since you've been back in America?"

"Sadly, you're correct."

"But wait, I'm not finished. Although I think you tried to trick me into believing otherwise, you didn't actually have sex when you were in England. Am I right?"

"With other people?"

"Oh lord, child. That's ten months. Ten months!" Darcy practically shouts in astonishment. "Has your vagina shriveled up and died?"

"Okay," I say, holding my hands up. "Stop with the dramatics."

Stella walks into the kitchen. "What are we talking about?"

Oh, my God. I shoot Darcy a glare to shut the hell up, but it's too late. "Meadow's vagina has shriveled and died. We're holding the funeral right now with a toast to the once and active role it played in her life."

I cover my face with my hands, mortified.

My sister is a teacher by trade. A badass in so many ways, but kind-hearted and leans toward the classier side of Darcy's obnoxious ways. When I spread my fingers to peek between, Stella's eyes are as wide as a teacup saucer. "Meadow."

"I know. I'm sorry for waking you up. Hopefully Rivers is still sleeping. We'll go to bed now."

"I was going to say that's a long damn time, little sis." She takes a wine glass from the cabinet and sits down across from me. "Fill her up."

Darcy tops off the glass, and asks, "What's it like to get off with a rock star?"

"Darcy," I snap, shaking my head to cut it out.

Stella spews a mouthful of wine all over the table, then snort-laughs while wiping her chin. "Oh, my! I did not see that coming."

I reply, "No one ever does when it comes to Darcy."

Our laughter dies down, and we both turn to Darce, who is waiting for an answer. I crack up again while my sister says, "The best sex ever." When her eyes close, it's clear by her expression she's remembering all the amazing things. "They know how to play your body and make it sing just like their guitar."

Swallowing the memory of Dave and me, I find my breathing deepening. Stella is absolutely right. *They know how to play your body. God, does he ever.* It makes me feel weak to miss him like I do, like I have. The month has been hard, painful in my heart, messing with my mind. Even though I wasn't attempting to move us forward when he called, his final words still stung. "*. . . find what you need. I'm not that for you. I'll do the same. And maybe we'll both find that happiness that seems to find others so easily.*" He was my happiness before I left, which was why I felt so conflicted seeing him again when I got back. But now . . . even though he asked me to come back to him, he's done. *He's gone.*

Stella says, "Ten months. That's January, Mead. *That road trip was in January.*" Under my loud shushing, she pieces it all together. "Ridge was ten months ago."

Darcy's eyes whip to mine. "Ridge? You had sex with Ridge?"

Rivers comes around the corner in low-hanging sleep pants and all his hard work on display—abs, arms, shoulders. Star tattoo with his crows. A collective sigh makes us laugh.

"What's so funny?" That makes us laugh again, even louder this time. His eyes home in on Stella. "Hey baby, come back to bed."

She sets her glass down in a hurry, and asks, "Did you miss me?"

"Yes." Nodding toward their bedroom, he says, "Let me show you how much."

I say, "I thought you were saving yourself for the wedding night?"

Rubbing her hand over his ab muscles, she's basically purring. "Impossible. Good night."

"Good night," Darcy and I say in unison as she disappears around the corner. Darcy whispers, "Lucky bitch."

"I heard that," Stella calls from the stairs. "Be jealous, ladies."

"We are," Darcy calls back.

After another drunken fit of giggles, I slump, the hour catching up with me. "I'm wiped. I think it's time for bed."

"But you leave . . ." I'm about to dash, but Darcy says, "You have some explaining to do, Miss Fellowes."

17

Meadow

THE GOSSIP COLUMN calls her a "mysterious woman." Whoever she is, I already dislike her. Is that fair? No, but it's not like we're going to be friends or anything. How does a friendship like that begin anyway? "Oh hello, I heard you slept with Dave?" Holding my hand to my chest, I imagine her tone to be more on the whiny side, "Ridge? Yes. I did him." And now she's the recipient of his phone calls. Of his friendship. Of . . . his time.

Sticking the tip of my finger in my mouth, I mock gag before I realize I'm being a bitch.

Waiting on the plane, I put my headphones on and an eye mask to block out the bright sunrays of day. I'm also avoiding. Darcy and Stella are just nice enough not to call me out on it.

When I saw that article online two weeks ago, I was flat-out jealous. I hate being jealous. I have no right to be. I had Dave, and then I lost him. Sometimes . . . all the time I think about the sacrifice I made to give myself some sort of false security. My parents' words still manage to taint even the purest things in my life.

"*Never marry a man for love, sweetie. When the love runs out, it will leave you dried up and alone.*" A thirteen-year-old doesn't know how to process that kind of information. I had no way to work through whether it was good information or her opinion, but that's what she gave me regarding love and life.

I suck in a harsh breath, and I lift my eye mask to my head. Lifting my head from the side of the plane where I was leaning, I lower my headphones around my neck and look around. Darcy says, "You missed the fun."

"Oh yeah?"

Resting her elbow on the armrest between us, she whispers, "Well, it was really me wiping the drool from the side of my mouth and then trying to pull myself up off the floor, but I think my first meeting with The Crow Brothers went well."

The name triggers my body to tense, and I sit up to get a look around the private plane. Dave is by the window a few rows away from me. I duck back down since he seems to be asleep and doesn't see me.

"Don't worry," she says, "he's been avoiding . . . I mean, sleeping like you the whole trip."

"I'm not avoiding. I'm preparing."

"Hopefully you're preparing your va-jay so he can revive it." Her hands go in the air. "Like a phoenix rising from the ash—"

"Man, what did my vagina ever do to you? Such a hard time." I laugh a little.

"It needs a hard time. A good old-fashioned fucking."

"I don't remember you being this crude. I must have blocked it out," I tease.

"You have just forgotten." She ticks off her fingers one by

one. "Men. Cocktails. Sex. Shopping. Complaining about work. Those are my five main topics of conversation. Not in that order, of course, as it varies day by day."

Adjusting my seat back, I say, "Tell me today's order. I didn't seem to get the memo, and as I mentioned before, I like to be prepared." I take a drink of my bottled water, then ask, "So you met everyone?"

"I did while you snoozed like it's no big deal that we're on a private jet with superstars."

"And?"

"And what?"

"And what happened? How did it go?"

"Well, I managed to keep my cool," she says, pushing a strand of curly hair back with the rest of her hair. It springs right back as soon as she releases it. Beautifully unruly, like her. "I don't know what came over me. They are incredibly sexy but seeing them with their wives sort of softened me. But a certain someone did catch my eye."

My chest tightens. "Ridge?"

Her mouth hangs agape while offense colors her features. "Ridge? You told me last night that you've had sex with him and how much you've missed him. You know I abide by girl code. Hos before Crow Bros." She smiles, amused by her quip.

The jealousy subsides, and I kick myself for even thinking she would do that to me. "I'm sorry."

Holding my hand between hers, she says, "No need, but something you do need to do is talk to him. You have three days to get that man back."

"Back? I can't get him back. First all—"

"Queenie, Mary, and Jane. Stop with all the first of alls, secondlys, and whatever else you do to hold yourself back from having a life. You, my friend, are a beautiful woman who is strong and independent. You don't need a man,

Meadow, but just because you don't need one doesn't mean you don't want one. It's okay to be self-reliant but still want the comfort of strong arms around you. We all need to be touched, to feel wanted, to be intimate with someone else. And this time, I'm not even referring to sex but to a closeness, a bond, even a friendship."

This softer side of my friend almost comes as a surprise. Where's the girl who's crazy, the one that kisses strangers on the street just to say she did it? Where did my crazy, anti-commitment Darcy go? I lean my head on her shoulder. "Thank you."

"For what?"

"For being the friend I need." I grin.

"Someone just woke up."

I feel a crick in my neck and rub it. "I know. I need to stretch my legs."

Releasing my hand, she bonks me on the head. "Ridge, not you, silly."

I sit up and peek over the seat, but just as I do, he looks at me. *Shit.* Leaning back, I slump into the seat and hide.

Darcy says, "Tell me this is not how the next three days are going."

"I can't tell you that exactly," I say, shrinking a little on that last part.

"Girl, you have to pull yourself together. He's a hot rock star who not only, according to you, have you had 'incredible, best of my life sex,' with, but he clearly still wants you."

My mouth twists. "Um . . . is it the way he was sleeping, or the way he's ignoring me that tipped you off?"

"Both. I know men, and his standoffishness is a sign of his interest."

"Are you drunk?" I ask, peeking between the seats to see if I can spy on him. *Shit.* Guess I can, but he can spy on me too. His hazels are browns, narrowed into hard chocolate and missing the soulfulness I'm used to. *Why do I do this to myself?* He told me he was done. *I need to accept that.* He wants to find someone else, and there's the *mysterious woman.* Ugh.

Slumping back in my seat again, I huff. This trip is going to be very interesting, to say the least. If I'm saying the least, Darcy is ready to say the most.

"Oh. My. God."

The blue ocean.

"I know, right?" Stella stands there with a huge smile on her face. "We have the whole property to ourselves."

"Property? This is a compound. A compound of awesome. I've never seen a place like this. Maybe in my dreams." With tears in my eyes, I turn to my sister. "How is this our life?"

Beachfront property.

Rivers walks up, and I throw my arms around him. "Thank you."

Taken by surprise, he asks, "For what?" His arms wrap around me, and he pats my back.

"For loving my sister and for giving us," I say, turning around and walking a few feet forward with my arms out, "this."

Ten bedrooms. Two buildings. Private property.

He laughs. "It is incredible here. All of us have come a long way. How amazing is it that we get to share it together?"

Stella snuggles against his side. "I love you," she whispers. His words are whispered just for her to hear followed by a kiss to the head.

While a few others come to stand with us as we face the ocean, I notice Dave's absence. I've felt it since I last saw him, but now as I look around at Tulsa and Nikki, Stella and Rivers, and Jet and Hannah, I feel more alone than ever.

Dave works his way down the path with Tommy in tow. As they walk across the beach, my heart begins to thump, reminding me I'm alive. I take a deep breath, inhaling the sweet floral scent of paradise. Darcy swings her arm over my shoulders, and then says, "Now that is a view."

"You're talking about Ridge, aren't you?"

"I sure am." She swats my ass as she walks away. "Come on. Mai tais are being served on the lanai. Why do I feel so fancy saying that?"

"You're already the fanciest girl I know."

"Why thank you, darling." She gives me a wave over her head.

I stay a moment longer . . . admiring the view. She's right. He's quite a sight. When I turn to head back to the main house, everyone is already gone. Not sure how long I stared at Dave out there, but my face heats just from seeing him again.

Paradise.

The party planner reads from her clipboard. "And you will walk with Ridge."

I look up at the sound of his name to find her, Stella, Hannah, Nikki, and Darcy staring at me. "What about Ridge?"

Nikki's laughter fills the air as she comes over to me. "We're going to be walking with our husbands, so Ridge will walk you down the aisle. Or if you like to lead, you can walk him down the aisle."

I stand from the wicker chair. "But I'm maid of honor," I foolishly announce as if they don't know.

Marisol, the party planner, steps forward. "Right. So you'll walk down the aisle together, and then take your respective places at the altar. He will take the fourth spot down from Rivers. You will be next to your sister."

The planner moves on like she didn't just sentence me to visitation with an ex. *Ex* is a little strong. By how much time of mine he's consuming, it would probably be safe to call him a *current*.

Stella says, "It will be okay. It's like a five-second walk."

I see Hannah watching me, and though there's no judgment on her face, I feel like I've offended her. She and Dave are good friends. How much has she heard about me? Or do guys not talk about relationship stuff?

Refusing to be the cause of any discourse on my sister's special day, I'll do whatever I'm told to do to make things go smooth. As for Dave, who knows?

18

Ridge

THREE DAYS in paradise to relax and let my mind forget my worries. Four days until Austin. Five days until Japan.

Fuck. Just when I thought I could relax, I realize I can't. At least not much. I've been sitting in this chair for an hour while the party planner goes over what each of our roles are going to be and how to fulfill them with the "zest they need."

Alfie makes his way down the aisle with the pillow and fake rings and then sits and waits. The kid is usually full of funny business, but it seems he takes his part in the wedding very seriously.

I've been able to tune most of it out until the planner, I think her name is Marisol, calls my name. "You'll be with Meadow."

"What do you mean?"

Tapping the end of her pen against the clipboard in her hands, she replies, "It only makes sense to have the other gentlemen walk with their wives. Since Meadow is Stella's maid of honor, she'll take her rightful place next to her. When you part, I'll need you to come stand right here."

I get up and take the spot where she's pointing. Alfie says, "Funny how things work out."

What the hell? Is this kid inside my brain? Does he even understand what he's saying? "What worked out funny?"

"My mom used to tell me she wanted me to go to Hawaii and get lei'd."

I don't know whether I should crack up or tell Hannah. First, I try to clear things up by asking, "Get a lei, Alfie?"

"Yes, that's what I said." Alfie looks frustrated. Tell me about it, kid.

"We can get you a lei, for you or her?"

"For her. She always wanted to come here." Looking up at Marisol, the drill sergeant is busy, so I sit next to him. "She's here in spirit."

"She is?" He's not crying, but he's a little upset.

Remembering what my mom always told me, "*Even tough guys need hugs*," I bring him in for a hug. "She's always with you in your heart, Alf." Maybe selfishly, I needed one too. Hearing about his mom reminds me of mine. Two months since she found out she was sick. Two months of nonstop testing. Two months and we're left with the pain of knowing we're helpless. "*Treatments won't work . . . no real options . . . keep her comfortable.*"

"Aunt Nikki called this place heaven. Is this what heaven is like?"

"Let's hope so."

When Jet comes up the aisle, he stops, gives me a nod, and then taps Alfie. "Hey, buddy."

"Hi, Daddy." When Jet bends down, Alfie moves into his arms, and Jet picks him up. Jet maneuvers him onto his back and bounces him, which makes the kid laugh. The moment for him passed, but for me, it still twists my chest.

Marisol points her pen at them. "Positions."

Jet shrugs. "What? I'm in my spot."

Doh. He gets the don't mess with me face. "He needs to learn his part. Set him down."

"Set who down? Is something on my back?" Jet playfully spins pretending not to know Alfie's there. The giggles are loud, and the bond between them tight. "Rivers? Do you see anything on back?"

"Just that monkey."

"Whoa! There's a monkey on my back?" Sweeping him down, he holds Alfie upside down to even louder laughter.

When the drill sergeant starts tapping her foot, Jet rights the kid, and asks, "You want to go fishing with me later? Just you and me?"

"Yes," Alfie says, fist-pumping the air.

"Deal. We'll let Hannah and Violet have some girl time."

"Yeah, with all their pink. Blurgh."

"Yeah," Jet adds, popping a bicep for Alfie who mimics. "We like to belch and pump iron, eat pizza on the couch, the color black and—"

"Blue."

Trying to keep a straight face, Jet says, "And blue. And green. Yellow."

"Orange. Turquoise. Purple and red."

"Yes! We like all the colors except pink."

Alfie is breaking down in a fit of giggles. Jet's a great dad. That kid is lucky to have someone who spends time with him and loves him unconditionally. It's good to see Alfie so worry free.

Marisol marches down the aisle right behind Tulsa, then she yells, "Ladies, please join us."

My chest tightens as soon as I see her. *Meadow Soleil.* Her name might mean the sun, but she's always been the sunshine to my rainy-day heart. It's hard to keep my distance and not talk to her or touch each other the way we were meant to. It's hard not to think about her or try to convince myself she's not the one for me. I know better. But until she does . . . I clamp my jaw, the muscles clenching. I narrow my eyes and try to harden my heart for the onslaught as Marisol pairs us up.

Meadow's gaze remains down, her chin tilted with it. Sadness should never be seen on her beautiful face, but there it is, breaking my heart. Marisol wraps Meadow's arm around mine as if Meadow doesn't have the strength. The heat of her skin against mine is intoxicating. The smell of her perfume seeking out the spaces inside me that had been shaded in darkness. Every nerve ending sparks as my body feels alive for the first time in forever.

Fuck it.

I cover her hand with mine, and when she looks up into my eyes, I struggle to be mean, to look at her like I don't care. I do. I fucking care about her. "Hello, sunshine."

The sun rises in her eyes, and that fire ignites. "Hi," she replies with a carefree smile. I know she carries so many worries inside her, but it seems that maybe I lift her spirits just as she lifts mine.

"And go!" Marisol directs us.

Walking arm in arm down the short aisle, we don't say anything, but so much is felt—my heart pounding, my blood rushing, adrenaline spiking just from having her near me again. She's a high I don't want to lose, and the fix is exhilarating.

We reach Rivers, and her arm slips out from mine, but I catch her hand, causing her to look back. "I wasn't ready to let go."

"Dav—"

Marisol breaks our hands apart, and says, "We've got to keep things moving please." She spins Meadow by the shoulders away from me and moves her into place. Snapping her fingers at me, she points at the far other side. "Down there please. Thank you for understanding."

I go where I'm told to be, stop, and look up. Hannah, Jet, Nikki, and Tulsa are standing at the other side of the outdoor covered space with smirks on their faces. Looking a little more to the right, Stella stands with a heart-on-her-sleeve smile—supportive and kind—happy for me or her sister or both. Just happy.

Reaching over, I give Rivers a low five, which he slaps right back. The other couples make their way down the aisle, and when everyone is in place, Rivers looks at us and then at the thirteen empty chairs in front of us. Darcy, Meadow's friend, is sitting with a wide cat ate the canary grin in the fourteenth. I have no idea where Laird, Tommy, and Shane wandered off to. As soon as Stella joins him, he asks, "What are we doing?"

"What do you mean?" Stella asks, her hands held in his.

"This. Why are we doing all this?"

"The wedding?"

"I'm trying to help you get married," Marisol snaps as her pen hits the clipboard. "We're almost done with the rehearsal."

He shakes his head, ignoring the planner. "The guest list is so small, Stel. What do you say we just let everyone attend and enjoy it instead?"

She looks back at her bridesmaids with concern and then back at him. "They bought dresses."

Touching her shoulder, Meadow says, "We can still wear them. We want whatever makes you two happy."

Rivers adds, "We almost have more people in the wedding than attending. What do you guys say?"

Alfie fist-pumps again. Stella asks him, "You don't want to be our ring bearer?"

"Do I have to wear the suit?"

She laughs. "No."

"Then tell me the time and place and I'll be there."

Nikki steps forward, and says, "I think it's romantic that you want it to be just the two of you."

Stella's gaze goes to Hannah, who says, "I agree. It's only about you and Rivers."

When her sister turns to her, Meadow hugs her. "We're right here for you either way. Do what makes your heart happy."

"Okay." She turns back and waves her arm. "Screw the formalities. Everyone is relieved of their wedding duties." Pointing at Alfie, she winks. "Except for you. Will you still be a part of the wedding?"

"I do."

She taps his nose. "Little charmer."

Rivers lowers his voice, and says to her, "It's only about being with you. That's all I want."

"Me too. Our family will all be here. That's what matters." She turns to Marisol and says, "Change of plan."

As they walk back down the aisle, Marisol fusses about food and other things. Stella nods, reassuring her it will all be okay. I stand idly by not sure what to do. As everyone disperses, Darcy not so subtly nods toward me for Meadow then gets up and scoots out a side path.

With the two of us standing in our same spots, she asks, "Are you doing all right?"

"Fine." *Tentative.* "You?"

Hesitant. "Not so good."

My pulse quickens wanting to know how I can help her. "Want to talk about it?"

"Want to get a Mai Tai?"

I can't help but laugh. "I've not heard that one before."

"I try to keep things fresh." She shrugs with a smile on

her face, her eyes as bright green as the leaves that surround us and as full of life.

I break the invisible barrier between us when I cross it. "I—"

A text buzzes my phone buried in my pocket. I dig it out and read it. *Fuck.* When I look back up, I see the openness and warmth disappear. *Fuck.* I feel the same. I want her sunshine . . . Holding my phone up, I say, "I need to make a call."

"Don't let me keep you." She's backing away, her hands up. Her eyes glassy.

"I'm sorry. It's import—"

"No. No apologies are necessary. Don't even think twice about me, Ridge." She turns to round a corner, and she's gone. The last thing she said echoing through my head.

Ridge.

19

Meadow

"MEN ARE THE WORST," I mumble, stomping down toward the beach. Between two curved palm trees, a hammock swings back and forth in the wind, tempting me. This is what I need. A nap. After the late night and early flight, surely relaxing in a hammock will wash certain things—certain *people*—from my brain.

Spreading the thick, cream-colored knotted rope apart, I sit on the hammock carefully and then lie back. Ridge has made himself very clear—*I need to make a call. It's important. She's important*—is all I hear. "Wonder what *her* name is?"

"Lisa."

I sit up too fast, messing with my balance, and spin to a fall. Caught midway, Ridge . . . I can't call him that just because I'm mad. I know him too well for that. Dave says, "Careful or you'll fall."

That's sort of the problem. I fell for him when I should have listened to my own advice about dating and rock stars. "Too late."

Squatting down next to me like I'm the fresh catch of the day, he holds me still while I'm tangled up. "Since I have your undivided attention, I want to tell you something."

"I don't want to hear anything."

"I know you don't, but I'm going to make you listen this time."

"Let me out." I push against the ropes that hold me captive like a burrito. "This isn't funny."

"No, it's not funny. It's serious, and something that scares the shit out of you. But guess what? It scares me too, but at least I have the balls to step into the arena."

"Well, I don't have balls," I say indignant. "And this isn't *Gladiator* or a concert. This is you forcing me to listen to some story that you'll spin to cover that you're seeing someone else but treating me like I've done something wrong."

His jaw tightens, and his hazels turn an angry shade of brown. Standing up, he says, "That's what you think of me?"

"Then go ahead and free your guilt. Lay the lies on me. I'm ready, Ridge." I'm not ready at all. I want to run away from this situation before he breaks my heart all over again . . . if I could get out of this fucking hammock.

"Ridge? Is that we're doing?" He walks away. "Fuck this." *Shit. Why can't I even be a friend to this man*? Because he's let you go, Mead. But like a sucker for punishment, I try . . . try to reach out as the friend I promised him I would be if he needed. *Even if it slices my heart in the process.*

"How was your important phone call?"

"Depressing." *Oh great. So his girlfriend is ticked at him.*

And once again, my sarcasm rears her head. "Did your girlfriend break up with you?" I shout.

"Something like that. Fuck if you care." He rounds the path and disappears around the foliage.

I slam my fists against the ropes and flail back, which

sends me spinning. The hammock releases me, and I fall to the grassy ground with a hard thud. On my hands and knees, I take a deep breath before pushing up and dusting off my knees. I need to go back to my room to cry for a few minutes about the loss of the expectations of what I wanted this trip to be. Yes, I hid from him on the plane. Yes, I didn't deal with being close to him again as well as I would have liked. *But it's not because I hate him. I never could.* I wasn't honest with him or Darcy.

I did want things to work out.

Like Dave a little while ago, I wasn't ready to let go either. But I need to. *For him.* I deserve to suffer the consequences of having a foolish heart like my dad warned me.

When I reach my room, I unpack my bag and pull out my laptop before firing it up. Typing in "mysterious woman" and Ridge Carson, the original article comes up in the search along with a few others. All the photos I can find are of the same night and none of the others have details besides what I've read.

Was it a one-time thing? Or is he dating someone? If he is in a relationship, he chose not to bring her this weekend. What does that say about how serious it is? Frustration has taken me hostage. I hate that I feel so out of sorts, so out of control of my emotions. No one can get me riled up emotionally and sexually like Dave Carson.

Will I ever get over this man?

A banging on my door startles me. Darcy calls from the other side, "Come on, Meadow, dinner's started."

"I'm coming." I check my appearance once more before rolling my hands down over my hips, the bright yellow dress clinging to every curve. Slipping on my heels, I hop on one foot toward the door and then the other until they're both on.

Darcy's jaw drops open. "Now that is a dress. The hanger did not do it justice, but you sure do. If I don't find a guy, you're my first option."

I roll my eyes. "Do you have sex on your brain at all times?"

"Yes," she says with a laugh. Shutting the door, she leans against it and then looks to make sure the coast is clear. "I wasn't entirely truthful with you earlier. It's been eating me alive."

I don't know why I brace myself, my hands tightening on my clutch, but I do. "About?"

"I do like someone. Quite a lot actually."

"Ridge?"

Her forehead crinkles. "Ridge? He's hot A-F, but he's so obviously yours, honey. Girl code, remember?"

Loudly releasing the breath I was holding, I drop my head in shame. "I know. I'm sorry. Who is it that has you looking at life on the brighter side?" I try to shake this bad mood and be happy for my friend.

She whispers, "Carrig. Damn him and that handsome face. I'm a sucker for it."

"You like Carrig? Like really like him?"

"I do. Am I horrible?"

"Horrible? No. Not at all. He is very handsome and has a good heart. I think he may be exactly what you need."

"Someone steady."

"Someone steady, yes. But also, responsible and caring. I actually think he'd make a wonderful boyfriend."

"But not for you?"

"Girl code, remember?" I wink.

"Because the whole office knew he had a crush on you."

"Must not have been much of a crush if he's been dating you."

That makes her smile. "No. I guess not. So you approve?"

"You don't need my approval, but you have it. Just make sure he leaves work at the office, so he can tend to you properly." I wink.

"I'll provide a good distraction."

Giggling, I say, "I bet."

Looking me over, she says, "So Ridge it is then."

"I don't know why his name even came out of my mouth."

When she leans down her eyes connect with mine. "I do, and it's time that you get that situation sorted."

Leaning back against the smooth wood of the door, I say, "I keep screwing things up. I doubt he'll even talk to me at this point." *I used to see happiness in his eyes, especially when we were together. Now all I see is anger and regret. I hate it.*

She takes my hand and starts pulling me down the hall to the stairs. "He hasn't seen you in this dress yet."

Our seats can't be farther apart. I'm actually surprised Stella would put everyone between Dave and me like this. Fifteen seats and he's sitting at the farthest corner opposite of me. The wedding coordinator, Marisol, has the coveted seat next to him.

The worst part is that he won't even look at me. We've had our salads, and absolutely no eye contact has been made. The main course sits in front of me barely touched. I feel ill, and it's not from the food.

In the meantime, Dave's not talking much, but this wedding planner lady is getting on my last nerve. I can hear her obnoxious laughter all the way down here.

By dessert, I've lost the rest of my appetite, only picking over the fish dish earlier. The party continues afterward with a bar and music playing under the large palapa dining area. The table is cleared, and bar tables are added.

Rivers is slow dancing with Stella to Frank Sinatra, and I get my red wine topped off . . . for the third time. Darcy dances over to me, waggling her fingers to come dance with her. I'm pissy and stubborn. "No. You dance. Have fun."

Laird orders a beer and leans against the portable bar, watching everyone drink and have fun. "Is Darcy dating anyone?"

I snort. Any other time, I'd say she was free. She'd be thrilled to know he's interested in her. Nikki's brother is the epitome of a Southern California surfer with his sun-light- ened hair and golden tan. It doesn't hurt that he plays the guitar, and their band, Faris Wheel, is rising in fame and popularity as the opening band for The Crow Brothers' tour. He's everything she dreams of, so I'm almost tempted to tell him she's single. But then I remember the softness in her eyes, her heart shining through, when she confessed her real feelings for Carrig. "She is seeing someone."

"Too bad. She's hot." *She's so much more than just good looks. Men tend to overlook her huge heart to admire her great body.*

I swirl my wine around while seeing the lipstick marks on the glass. It's time for a touch up. I pull out my favorite killer shade of red and reapply using the side of the stainless- steel toaster on the bar. Catching Laird watching me and because I'm just tipsy enough to ask, I say, "We've met a few times, but you've never hit on me."

Darcy and I are total opposites in coloring and body type. She's the life of the party, and I'm starting to believe I'm more a homebody. I love the outdoors, and she loves the department stores. We just accept each other for who we are and adore one another. So if he's attracted to her, I myself—blonder, shorter, a little curvier at the hips—am probably not his physical type.

That's not the response he gives. He shrugs, and says, "Because you're Ridge's girl." I stare at him a good few seconds before he looks at me. "Did I say something wrong?"

"No. You said everything right."

He nods and sips his beer. Marisol's laughter attacks me from across the dance floor, and we both follow the sound. Dave is smiling, not the kind I get, but more the one he gives the world as Ridge. Marisol tilts her head to the side and touches his chest. Flirting, firing me up inside.

Laird says, "It's too bad what's going on with his mother. I feel for the dude."

My heart clenches. "What's going with his mother?"

Seemingly surprised that I don't know, he hesitates, but then says, "She's not doing well. Hasn't been for a few months, I think. He doesn't talk about her much, but I met Lisa last summer on tour when she visited us in San Antonio on tour."

My breath bottoms out, and a hard swallow follows. "Lisa?"

"Yeah, Lisa Carson, his mother."

"*How was your important phone call?*"

"*Depressing.*"

"*Did your girlfriend break up with you?*"

"*Something like that.*" Shit. Shit. Shit.

My heart hurts as my gaze darts to him again. This time, I catch him watching me, making me wonder how many other times he has without me knowing.

Setting my glass on the bar, I start across the dance floor.

"About time." Darcy starts clapping, and says, "Get it, girl."

His eyes latch on mine as he angles my way. When I look to his right, Marisol's eyes sharpen on me, and she steps closer to him. Yeah, that's not going to work for me.

This is the first time I'm getting a good look at him. *Holy wow*! I've seen him in everything from ripped jeans to gym shorts but seeing him rocking a suit makes me lose my cool. I'm on him, marking this man as mine. Whether he is or not tomorrow, he will be tonight.

Just as he opens his mouth, I plant mine against it and kiss him like I've wanted to for so long. With passion and bad intentions. His arms come around my lower back, bringing me in, but now he kisses with unadulterated ecstasy.

Breathless and jelly in his hands, I look up into his hazels that spark with desire. "What took you so long?"

"I took a wrong turn just outside Arizona." I kiss him again, leaving the remains of my lipstick all over his mouth. Not because I have to claim him or mark him as mine, but because he was mine all along. Just like I'm his. This time when I pull back, I say, "I do care, and I've missed you."

His body hardens against mine, and he cups my cheek. "I'm glad you found your way back."

20

Ridge

SETTING HER FREE, she begins to tug at my pants. She places a kiss on my chest as her fingers work the button and zipper. I help her out by getting naked the rest of the way while she enjoys the show.

When we're both exposed, our hearts on the line, she comes closer with a plea to her tone. "Make me forget the loneliness."

I move my hand into her hair, bring her closer to lick along her jaw, and then kiss her chin. "You'll never be lonely again, baby."

A smirk tips the right side of her lips. This time she asks, "Promise?"

"I promise." With my hand still in her hair, I walk her backward to the bed. "By making you feel so good." I kneel before her, anchoring one of her knees over my shoulder as I lean in to taste her.

Her hands hold my shoulders, but when her leg begins to wobble, I move forward to lay her on the bed. Then I put both legs over my shoulders and dive back in, licking her until her thighs clench around my head.

My dick throbs against the mattress as I bend over and tongue fuck her until she's ready for me. "I want you." Her fingers pull at my hair. So wet. So needy.

I stand, running my hand over my length a few times. "I'm not going to last." Moving her feet apart, I align myself, and push in a little at a time, allowing us both to adjust to the heat, the connection, the sensation of being one with her again.

Her breath thrusts from her lungs as her fingers curl around the blanket at her sides. Her head tilts back, warmth blooming from her center and shooting to the core of me. Deep inside, I hold still while my mind tries to find logic where there is none. I've never known this bliss with anyone else, because our attraction is carnal and unique. My breath never catches up, so I hold it, letting the sensations take over.

Being inside her again makes me understand that the lonely nights were worth it. She feels so good, too good to remain still for much longer. I pull back and push in again and then again. Soon, I'm thrusting not thinking about her needs or her release.

But she feels so fucking good I continue pushing for my own needs, my own release. When I watch her, I see how her body bends and moves, opens and accepts me, yearns for me. Like I yearn for her.

Hovering over her, I rest my arms on either side of her. "Do you like this, sunshine?"

As if she's sacrificing a part of herself, she closes her eyes, and whispers, "I do."

I do.

The vow just about kills me.

"Good." I keep fucking her, one hand anchored on the bed and the other holding her hip. Making love, we push through the tenderness that brought us together and fuck our way through the desperation and need until her body pulses around me and I'm releasing inside her.

"Oh God," comes from her lips followed by, "Dave."

Thank fuck. She doesn't see anything but the real me. I lose the steady control I was trying to hold on to, frantic to expend every last drop of energy from my body. I'm exhausted, and my mind floats free.

Time slows as our breathing regulates to match. Lying flat against the mattress, she turns her head to find me lying next to her. Looking at me through half-mast eyelids, she reaches over and touches my cheek. "I've missed you. *Dave.*"

"I've missed you so much, Meadow." *More than you could ever know.*

21

Ridge

"Tell me again why we're not doing this every fucking day of our lives?"

"That good, huh?" Although her mouth is full, she smiles, trying to keep her lips together. She's adorable, and food makes her happy. I make a mental note of that tidbit.

"Better than good."

"The donuts or the sex? I'm confused," she says, licking the corner of her mouth. We're both covered in pieces of glaze that have fallen from the sweet dough.

"The sex."

Tilting her head up, she says, "It's because it's been so long."

"No," I reply, rubbing her bare back. "It's because we're good together. We always were. One day you'll realize that chemistry like ours is hard to find." I finish off another donut, then lean in to lick sugar glaze from her chest.

"Maybe." She doesn't say more, conflicted between what she wants and what she thinks she needs. I've been there. I went with what I thought I needed—my ex—and later real-ized she wasn't what I even wanted. I learned the hard way, of course, and maybe that's the only way Meadow will learn that lesson as well.

Sometimes I wonder why I can't seem to get her out of my system. In the aftermath of sex is probably not the best time to try to see things clearly.

Meadow fills the holes that others have left behind, the voids that fame leave inside. The fame I never wanted. I wanted to be a working musician.

Answers come easy. I don't want simple. That's boring. I like Meadow's complications and her quirks. She makes me feel so much at once—unlike anyone else ever has—but at ease just as equally. Whole and at peace. In the crazy life I lead, she seems to be all I need.

I may have met Meadow when my star was already on the rise, but she never had an interest in that side of my life. Fame doesn't impress her. Money that's spent frivolously doesn't attract her.

Her breathing evens, so I close my eyes, wanting mine to find that same comfort at night. Turning off my mind, I rest my worries about what will happen tomorrow and try to savor tonight.

The bed is empty next to me when I wake up. Feels like every other morning of my life, and I hate it. "Meadow?"

She's in the doorway with her hand on her hip, messy hair, my T-shirt covering up all the good stuff . . . Well, almost all of it. She's wearing that sexy smirk that got me wound up last night. "What is it, rock star?"

"Come give me a kiss."

With a big smile, she runs and jumps on the bed next to

me. Quickly straddling me, she tilts her head to the side, and says, "Where do you want it?"

Flipping her down onto her back, I maneuver between her legs, and make sure she feels every inch of how happy I am to see her this morning. "Anywhere you might be so inclined to lay those lips, sweetheart."

Gently running her fingertips over my lips, she says, "I think I'll start here," and rises to kiss me. With her hands pushing against my chest, I fall back to the mattress, letting her control the pace and position. Leaning over me, she slides her hand under the covers. The heat of her touch engulfs another part of me. "Then I'll move down there."

When her mouth replaces her hand, I sink into the mattress, getting lost in the bliss of her kiss, quickly bringing me to teeter at the edge.

I weave my fingers into her hair when I reach the brink of orgasm. As I lift her up, her eyes meet mine, questions of why I'm stopping her filling the irises. "C'mere."

"You sure?" she asks.

"I'm sure." When she falls against my side, her hair fans across the pillow and covers my face. "I want to be inside you." I push the strands aside and roll on top of her again.

"You were," she says with the sweetest smile.

"I want to be inside you and see your eyes."

Cupping my face, she whispers, "Then what are you waiting for?"

Our clothes fly off and we're back in the same position. This time I hold my chest above her but press the tip between her legs. "Do you have to be anywhere this morning?"

I love the slow joy that works its way in to the corners of her mouth, spreading like wildfire against her slightly swollen lips. When she bites her lower one, teasing me, she stares into my eyes and tightens her arms around my neck. "I have a little time."

"I should warn you." Resting up on my elbows, I scrape across my bottom lip with my thumb, feeling so damn lucky to be here.

"About?"

"This isn't going to be rough, and I'm not going to rush. This isn't about desperation or need. This is about you and me and how every time we're together, something incredible happens. Physically. Mentally. Emotionally. We fit, Meadow. When you walk out of this room, you'll remember every inch and minute we spent together." I may not be rushing, but I'm still hot for her. I kiss her, and that kiss leads to everything more.

Any excuse to convince her to stick around has been used.

"It's Stella's wedding day. I have to be there for her."

Selfishly, I want her here for me.

Wearing one of my T-shirts that swallows her whole, she kisses me one last time. "I'll see you later, okay?"

She's asking when she never has to worry. "I'll see you later."

With her dress draped over her arm and her shoes in her hands, she opens the door and blows me a kiss. Neither of us knows what to say, so we don't. She slips out the door, and I'm left staring at the back of it, stupidly wishing it would open and she'd come back to me.

Logically, I know she can't. It's Stella's wedding day, but damn if I'm not jealous of anyone who gets to spend their day with her. Instead of moaning about her leaving, I get up and shower, then head down to the main house for food. It's been a few hours since I found donuts on the counter. The workout we did all night has left me starving and needing replenishment.

Darcy sits at the counter. "Good morning," she says with that same canary smile.

"It is a good morning." I work my way around the counter to pour a cup of coffee. Holding up the pot, I ask, "Coffee?"

"I'll take a top up."

I fill her mug and then my own. Grabbing a plate, I start loading it with food from the platters covering the long island bar—eggs, bacon, and fruit.

Sitting on a barstool, she pushes her plate away and rubs her stomach. "This is quite amazing. This place. The food. The drinks. Anything you need, you can have here."

I nod, feeling like she's going somewhere with this lead-in. "Paradise."

"You're not going to hurt her, are you?"

My gaze shoots up. Obviously, she means Meadow, but since I'm not sure where she's going with this, I play dumb. "Hurt her?"

She cocks an eyebrow, not letting me off the hook. "You know what I'm saying. Meadow acts tough, but she's soft inside. She hasn't developed her stiff upper lip."

"I hope she doesn't."

That makes Darcy smile. "Me either." The lightness lifts from her tone as she eyes me up. "We don't know each other at all, and although I've read up on you online, she's quite vulnerable to you."

Vulnerable is not something I think of when I think of Meadow. Guarded. Protective of her heart. Giving. Sensitive. Sweet. Stubborn . . . Vulnerable. She has that wall around her, but the few times I've gotten a peek on the other side, I realize she is vulnerable. "I would never hurt her."

"On purpose."

"Yes, on purpose or otherwise, if I can help it."

She stands and taps the counter. "Good."

As she walks out, I say, "Good talk. Good talk."

The door closes, and I stand there staring at my plate. I would never hurt Meadow. If anything, I've set myself up to be hurt. I'm the one who is vulnerable to that gorgeous woman.

Meadow and I have been around this block before. Not full-on, but for us both to have a little hesitancy with the excitement. When she said I could have her for the night, did she really only mean the one night?

Laird and Tommy walk in right when I'm about to toss away my food. "Brah, we're heading out for a surf. Come with?"

"Yeah, I think I will." Surfing is not something I've done but twice before when Laird convinced me to go with him in San Diego. That water was fucking cold, and you couldn't see for shit what was beneath you.

Hawaii has clear blue ocean, and the water's warm. Time to lose myself in something other than Meadow for a while.

My back is scraped up from hitting the rocks, bruises along the back of my arms. Probably not my best idea considering my body is necessary to perform and we have a show in a week's time.

Sitting on my board, my feet dangle in the water. Laird paddles up and says, "Taking a breather or waiting for a wave?"

"Breather. This is tough, man."

"A great workout. Keeps me in shape enough to play a long set on a good night."

Holding my arm up, I say, "This bitch burns."

"Ich. That looks rough. Aloe will heal that. Nature's medicine."

Sometimes I forget he's so at one with the ocean and the surf scene when he's ripping hard chords on the guitar on stage. "What happened to Tommy?"

"He and Shane threw in the towel an hour in."

"I'm throwing it in now and taking the next wave."

He looks around to find the sun. "It's almost three. Wedding's at four. We should head in. You hit it first. I'll take up the tail."

Looking around, the water can't be more flat. "Fuck. We might have to paddle in."

"Just wait a few. There are waves on the horizon. They'll be here soon." He floats next to me, sitting on top of his board, waiting. "So Meadow, huh?"

"Yeah. Meadow." I glance over at him, but don't elaborate. I'm not surprised he picked up on it really. He's observant.

"She's hot."

"She is."

"Why didn't you say anything before?"

"Not much to say."

"Seems like there was more than you pretend."

"Not pretending. Taking things slow, like a snail's pace."

I catch him looking at me. "That's cool." He says, "Wave's coming. It's now or never."

"Now or never." Taking off as fast as I can, I start paddling, and hope I don't wipe out. *Story of my life.*

22

Ridge

ALFIE MAKES his way down the aisle, looking for Hannah, who he finds sitting with Violet behind Meadow up front. The kid makes his mom proud, standing patiently next to Rivers.

When Rivers and Stella changed their minds at the last minute and went from all the stuffy traditions to what felt right for them, the location also changed. The large outdoor pavilion became only the site for the reception. The wedding was moved to the beach.

Under a clear blue sky, Jet walks down a petal path in the sand with the beautiful bride on his arm. The sound of sniffles fills the air, and I find Meadow with tears in her eyes as she watches her sister.

The skirt of the pink dress flows in the breeze, a few strands of her hair blowing across her face. I should be watching the bride or listening to what's being said, but I can't seem to take my eyes off my personal sunshine.

I was running late after surfing. Rushing over here, I

wasn't sure where to sit, so Marisol guided me to this side of the aisle and the ceremony began, so I stayed. I regret it now. The distance between Meadow and me is too far and too tenuous.

When Stella and Jet pass and everyone remains standing, I dash out the side and walk the long way around behind the other guests to stand at the end of Meadow's row. Darcy's smile is wide and knowing as if we're in on the same plan. She moves down two seats, freeing the seat next to Meadow, and I slip into the spot.

With her gaze still focused on the couple in front, Meadow angles her body, opening for me when she feels me next to her. A smile tickles her lips, but then she sniffles again, looking down as though she's embarrassed to be crying on this beautiful day. I slip my hand around hers and hold it, her softness against the roughness of mine. So much like who we are as people and the lives we lead.

Those walls she's been trying so hard to maintain protect that heart of hers, but what she doesn't realize is that I have mine on the line too. While we listen to the vows and watch the exchange of rings, I can't help but wonder about my own destiny.

A squeeze of her fingers around mine causes me to look at her, the view I really wanted all along. Touching her collarbone, I run my finger over her shoulder and down her arm until we're holding hands again. I could get lost in her again, but I won't make this about us. We have time.

Rivers kisses his wife, and the crowd goes wild. Even though it's not a show for the fans in attendance, I imagine it's still the most important time he's ever stood center stage. Stella's never looked happier, and Rivers looks as if he just won the fucking lottery.

He sweeps her off her feet and carries her down the aisle. She tosses her bouquet over her head, and it lands at Meadow's feet. No one makes a move, so I nudge Meadow, and say, "I'm not saying I'm superstitious or anything, but I think you're supposed to pick it up."

Looking up at me with the flowers in hands, she asks, "Superstition or tradition?"

"Same thing, right?"

"Kind of." She holds her nose to a deep pink flower and closes her eyes.

Marisol comes down the aisle, directing us to the reception. I got a dirty look when I left my seat earlier, but what Marisol thinks of me is none of my business. Now Meadow, on the other hand . . . I give a whole lot of fucks when it comes to her.

Holding my arm out, Meadow takes it. Darcy has walked ahead, joining the rest of the guests that include all the members of The Resistance and their significant others, Rivers's brothers and their families, Tommy, and the members of Faris Wheel. The Resistance has a show in New York tomorrow, but detoured out of their way to be here for this special day. Three bands, but one when it comes to family.

Just outside the pavilion, I stop Meadow from going in before she gets swept away into the party. The myriad of colors that makes up her hair—blond and light brown, natural reds, and the darker strands that never seem to catch the light are highlighted by the sun as it sets into the ocean—is pulled back with loose strands that hang down, framing her pretty face. She steals my breath, like I'm realizing she's stolen my heart.

Seems no matter how much time has passed, Meadow Soleil stays with me—if not physically, then in spirit. Standing here with her, looking in her lively green eyes under this golden Hawaiian sky, I say, "Dance with me."

Emotions flicker through her eyes, weaving their way

into her expression, but I struggle to read at such a fast pace. The tips of her fingers reach my cheek, and I lean into her touch. "I'd be honored."

I take the bouquet and set it aside before holding her hand in the air and rest my other on her hip. We start to sway just as the music from the reception begins. "My mother used to dance with me. Just like this. She told me I needed to know how to dance so one day I could dance with the woman I . . ."

I don't know if she doesn't mind me finishing to protect her or to give me the relief, but we both know what I was going to say. Moving against me, she wraps her arm around my neck and holds me closer. "Your mother is . . . she's not doing well?"

"Damn. I didn't see that coming." Fuck these tears that want to come. I look toward the sun, hoping to burn them away. Exhaling a deep breath, they go back to wherever I've been holding them deep inside, and I choose to look in her eyes instead. "How do you know about her?"

"Laird mentioned it as though I already knew. As though everyone already knew. But you didn't tell me."

"You had a lot on your plate already, your own problems to deal with. You didn't need mine."

"What if I want them? What if I want to be the one you share these things with?" I don't know when we stopped dancing, but we've been standing long enough for me to notice the stillness. She begins to pace away from me. "But this can't be about us. Not today." Whipping back around, she asks, "How is your mother? And how are you? That's what matters. And Stella and Rivers since it's their day. But me, don't think twice about me." She rushes back into my arms. "I want to be here for you."

"I'm not sure where to start." *It's a lot all at once.*

"What can I do for you?"

"Meadow, I don't want to talk about my mom. We have three days away, and if this is all I get with you, I don't want to waste a minute."

She glances over her shoulder and then says, "We should go then. They'll be back soon."

"They?"

A sweet smile appears on her pretty face. "Stella and Rivers. We should be there when they are introduced."

"Huh? Introduced to who?"

"No," she says, shaking her head. "When they're announced as husband and wife."

"Oh."

She takes my hand and grabs the bouquet again. We walk down the path and into the pavilion. Quickly turning to me, she says, "We don't have to stay long, but I need to be here when she arrives."

"Yes, of course. That's why we're here."

Rubbing the top of my hand, she says, "I'm sorry about your mom. I don't want to push, but if you want to talk about it, we can."

I wrap an arm around her shoulders and kiss her head. Talking about my mom won't change anything, and although I want to share my pain with Meadow, I know today's not that day. "Another time. Let's just enjoy the night."

Everyone has been eating and drinking, celebrating on this beautiful night.

Darcy sits across from us, and says, "Your sister looks sex-drunk."

Meadow looks around. "My sister's here?"

The newlyweds finally walk in looking very much as Darcy described. I laugh. "Good for them."

Rushing around the table, Meadow runs to her sister. "You're here. Congratulations, Mrs. Crow." She sways to the side, drunk in a different way than her sister. She hugs Rivers and then turns back to me.

While everyone else greets the happy couple, I can't take my eyes off the former maid of honor. Her friend pulls her onto the dance floor, and the music is turned up.

"She's fucking hot."

I shoot a glare across the table where Laird sat down. "What the fuck, man?"

"Meadow's hot too," he says, laughing, "but I was talking about *her* friend."

Relief washes over me. "I thought I was going to have to fucking punch you."

"I think you're in deep, dude. That must be some sweet cherry juice."

Cherry. I look back to find Meadow in the crowd. "Get some fuckin' manners, Faris." I laugh. "The sweetest cherry juice I've ever had." I get up to go get my girl. Sure, I've had a few beers, and she's a couple of glasses into the party, but something feels right for the first time in forever.

I slip my arms around her waist and pick her up, spinning her in my arms. I kiss the underside of her jaw, and she begins to laugh. When her arms come around me and she holds me close, I say, "I want to be with you."

Cherry cheeks meet sweet pink lips as her face brightens. She lifts up on her toes to kiss my neck. "Right now?"

"Always."

Running a finger down the center of my nose. "Be careful there, rock star. The minister's only a call away."

"I'm starting to like you drunk."

"You don't like me sober?"

"Too much." I kiss the tip of her finger. "I like you too much, Meadow."

"Is there such a thing as too much?" Her head rolls to the

side as she looks me in the eyes. "You're still holding me, by the way."

"I know. I like you like this."

"Trapped?" She giggles and hiccups. "Like in that hammock?"

"That wasn't as much fun." I lower her until her feet reach the ground. "But it had to be done."

Holding me by the face, she says, "I'm sorry I wasn't listening."

"It would help if I would have been more open and told you."

"It's not about your words. It's about your heart. I promise to hear what it tells me instead of only listening to the beats." When our lips meet, it's not just the physical contact but the words she doesn't have to say that are felt.

She cares more than she can say, and I'll take it. "Are you ready?"

"My whole life."

23

Meadow

RIDGE IS a bad boy with a charming smile. When aimed right at me, how is a good girl supposed to survive?

Ridge is all wrong for me.

He's famous.

Lives in LA.

And has probably slept with a billion women, including me.

If I'm going to be in a relationship, it's going to be with someone I can go to bed with each night and wake up next to in the morning.

As for Dave . . . I can make an exception.

I let my gaze roll over each ab muscle I was licking last night and linger on his face. I feel so much for him all at once that it scares me. That's what it all boils down to. *Fear.*

Fear of the unknown.

Fear of letting people down.

Fear of what will become of me.

Fear of everything.

I used to be brave, or maybe it was blind stupidity.

I remember how handsome Dave looked with the last bit of sunlight sneaking in the car as we drove through the desert.

Strong, but always careful when it comes to me. He really has been more patient than I deserve. His determination is attractive like his face, and swoony like his body. Delectable like his lips. I've never been more horny than when I'm with him.

"Surely, it's not natural to want sex this much."

It's him. He does this to me.

I just know it is, but I can't lose my better judgment because we're so good between the sheets. The road trip only brought out my fears because I'm not frivolous in my normal, boring everyday life. But with him, he makes me want to throw caution to the wind, so I did. It was freeing to just be, to feel like me for a few days.

No expectations.

No pressure.

No weighted thoughts arising from my upbringing.

How many other women does he do that to? Endless. He should be with someone who comes with less baggage. Someone who is light, spontaneous, fun. *But he seems to want me.*

I snuggle back against his side and wrap my arm over his stomach. *Mine.*

"Go to sleep, Meadow. Save your worries for another day." A kiss is placed on the top of my head while a yawn comes without warning.

Guess I didn't realize how tired I've been. The music is still playing, the property alive with laughter and singing, but I'm happiest in his arms. I kiss him on the ribs. "I'm glad I'm here."

"So am I."

The room is still dark, night lingering a little longer as if it knows we need the extra hours. When I find the bed empty beside me, I sit up slowly and look for Dave. The balcony door is cracked open, letting the moonlight slip in.

His body is a work of art—built biceps, broad shoulders, tall with strength built into his legs, and that ass. I've started collecting quarters in hopes of bouncing them off him one day. Wonder if he'll let me.

My lower body clenches, craving him again. I prefer the fullness to the emptiness without him. In all ways, it seems. My feet land on the wood floors, and I pad to the doorway, grabbing his discarded shirt on the way. I only bother with a few buttons before stopping to inhale his scent from the shirt. Everything about him draws me in. He's my personal aphrodisiac. Wanting the real thing more, I peek out and take in his full glory. He's wearing only boxer briefs, and a thrill of giddiness rushes through me because he's all mine.

Leaning against the railing, he turns when he hears me. "Did I wake you?"

I embrace him from behind, holding him in my arms and inhaling the real thing this time. Covering my hands with his, he brings one to his lips and kisses it. Resting my cheek against his back, I poke his side. "No, but I didn't like waking up without you, Carson."

I love the way his body moves when he chuckles. Angling my body between him and the railing, I look up at him, admiring his rugged good looks—the stubble that shadows his jaw, his nose that's straight but has a slight bump that looks earned through a fight or two, and those eyes that always see the real me even when I tried to hide behind a façade. "I like you missing me, Fellowes."

Leaning down, he runs his nose along the length of my neck. "God, you smell deliciously divine."

"I smell like sex and you."

"Like I said, sweetheart, divine." His tongue drags against my skin, and then he nibbles on my earlobe, firing off goose bumps all over my skin. "Never shower, okay?"

A giggle escapes, but soon, I close my eyes because he feels too good. My body grinds against his leg that wedged between mine. "Come back to bed."

"Turn around instead," he whispers against my neck.

I release a panting breath, feeling so needy already. Only he has ever done this to me, and I feel no shame in wanting him like I do—for being what he needs and taking my fair share. He encourages it. Sex with him isn't about him or me; it's about who we become when we're together, when we become one.

I do what he says and turn in his arms. His tone is firmer, not as kind as usual, but needy like me. "Hold strong for me."

As I grip the wood railing, the back of the shirt is lifted, letting air blow across my bare skin. His hands slink under the white cotton and up the front of my body until he's holding my breasts in each hand. His erection presses against the seam of my cheeks, and I suck in a jagged breath.

His body rocks against mine a few times to tease with foreplay, but I'm already so ready for him that I moan. Closing my eyes, I let the sensations of him running his body along mine take over. The tip of him puts pressure at my entrance, and he kisses my neck. He fills my soul as his body fills me, making me whole once again.

"You feel amazing," is breathed against my skin, and then my hair is swept aside so he can kiss my neck again. My body is full, but I yearn for more.

As I drop my head forward, the palm of his hand pushes

to bend me forward a bit more. The power of his thrust gets stronger, and I hold the railing even tighter. "Faster, babe."

He aims to please, so slow and steady turns fast and frantic. His hands leave my body and bump up next to mine as he cages me in and fucks me from behind. My breathing becomes shallow, but I manage to say, "Oh God, yes, you feel so good."

A hint of laughter fills the air, and Dave stops moving with his body still attached to mine. I hold my breath as Johnny and Holli stop to kiss on the path. They're not in a hurry, but I am. Dave covers my backside with his body, the heat scorching me, and whispers, "Breathe, baby."

I relax, feeling safe in the confines of his arms.

Holli jumps up on Johnny's back and they wander down the rest of the path to their building.

I ask, "Did they see us?"

"No. Those two only have eyes for each other, and they're two sheets to the wind. They didn't even look up." He pulls out and takes my hand. "I'm not willing to take the risk again, though." Inside, he asks, "How do you want it?"

"You were doing pretty good before."

"Pretty good? Fuck if that's not a challenge I'm willing to take. I don't do anything half-ass." His eyes are set on mine as he cups my face. "I love looking at this gorgeous face, but I want you from behind."

A tingle rushes my veins, and I climb onto the bed. "Don't leave me waiting."

The stretch that burns feels so good when he enters me again. I lose my breath and give in all over again. A hand reaches around, and two deft fingers play my clit like his guitar, sending me over the edge just before he joins me.

It doesn't take much, and I'm too turned on to last any longer. Little quakes tremor through my body, and then his control is shaken, and he comes along with me.

When he's given me everything he has, we lie on the bed together, his body on mine. I like the weight of him on me, so when he rolls to the side, he leaves me feeling bereft. His arms open wide, and he looks exhausted. "Fuckin' hell, Meadow."

"You definitely never do me half-ass. That was full ass if I ever felt it." I laugh at my lame joke, but the best part is he laughs too.

After a few minutes of basking in the afterglow, he turns to me and runs the back of his hand over my cheek. "I could get used to this."

Moving closer, I kiss his shoulder and then maneuver a little more on top of him and kiss that crow tattoo that flies over his heart. "I could too." Resting my head on his chest, I listen to the steadying beat of his heart.

"Are you hungry?"

"I've built up an appetite." My eyes remain closed, but a smile pops into place.

"I'll go to the main house and get us some food."

"I'm too sleepy to eat, and I don't want you to leave me." Before he has a chance to get out of bed, I tighten my hold around him. "Stay with me."

I get a kiss to the top of my head before he lies back, relaxing on the mattress under me. "I'll stay." *Words I wish I could hear every day.* But is it just for the sex? I mean, he's a god in bed. No. *I know it's more.* I've never felt such a strong connection with someone other than Stella. And if I'm really honest with myself, that's what I yearn for. Connection . . . every day. Dave can't promise to be that everyday man in my life because of his job. The question is, can I accept that? Because I think I've met my soul's mate.

But, he makes me believe in the possibility. His arms wrap around me, and with a modicum of peace in my heart, we fall asleep.

24

Meadow

JET AND HANNAH are sitting with the kids on the beach just as the top of the sun reaches the sky. The property faces west, so they're not there to catch the sunrise. I can't tell what they're doing. I'm too far to hear anything, but they don't even seem to be talking much.

So I continue to watch—them, the ocean waves as they crash, the clouds burning away—the beginning of the day.

Arms that make me feel safe in a world of uncertainty wrap around me, and I'm kissed just below the ear, evoking my smile. Resting his chin on my shoulder, he sees the little family on the beach and watches with me. "C'mon," he says.

I stop in my room to slip on a bikini and a cover-up while he puts on his board shorts. Together, we walk down to the beach that feels like it was created for our personal use.

Being the last morning, other people are starting to meander out of their rooms. The alcohol was flowing at the reception, but the majesty of this early morning is too hard to resist.

Rochelle and Dex come down the stairs behind us. Greetings are exchanged but not much else. I think it's safe to say that we'll be using the trip back to recover. They take a path to the right, holding hands. I've heard stories of her being a ballbuster, but after watching her with the drummer of The Resistance, all I see is a woman in love. I can't get started on the way he looks at her. It makes my heart ache for a love like theirs.

Sneaking a peek at Dave, I see the makings of it. My natural instinct is to retreat, to find the comfort of solitude. Become untouchable. But I fight it. I fight the inclination to pull away, to give in to the words that tricked my mind into believing I'm choosing to be alone.

I'm not.

I don't want to be alone.

I hold Dave's hand tighter because maybe if I let him in, he can save me.

"Meadow . . . Meadow? Baby?"

I open my eyes to find we're off the path near the hammock where we had our fight the other day. "What?"

"Where'd you go, sunshine?"

I glance around, confused by the question. "I'm right here."

Rubbing my temple, he says, "No, where'd you go in here? You disappeared on me."

Is he ready? To be exposed to the things I've tried so hard to hide? He says he wants this, wants us, and even though this scares the crap out of me, I take a deep breath and decide it's time. It's time I let him see the truth.

"My mother sat me down the day she walked out on my father and me and Stella." I want to push him away, tell him to run, but he's looking at me like I'm giving him the pieces of me he needs. "She told me never to marry a man for love. That when the love runs out, it will leave me dried up and alone. Dried up," I repeat the last part just for me. This time, his hand tightens around mine, and he takes my other and kisses it so gently I want to weep.

Lowering my gaze to the connection, I continue to say all the things I was supposed to keep hidden inside. "I was thirteen. Thirteen." I laugh humorlessly. "That's the impression she gifted me of love and life, that and weeks of nightmares that I would die alone in the desert. She didn't want me enough to stay. Stella was one foot out the door already, ready to be with Rivers. And my dad . . . my dad used to come into my room drunk, wake me up, and tell me never to rely on anyone because they'll only hurt me in the end, just as he'd been hurt. I won't even get into the names he called me when he confused me for my mother in his drunken stupor."

"I'm sorry, Meadow. That's fucked up, though. You know that, right?"

"I want to know that. I want to prove them wrong like Stella did last night."

"She did. She also wouldn't have left you there if she knew," he says, shaking his head.

"She didn't. How could I be the one to ruin the happiness she had found, to be the one to tell her it would never last because love doesn't work like that? Love is fun but turns into cruelty."

"You don't believe that. I know you don't."

"You don't want to believe that about me, but what if their words worked? What if I can't find a logical way through them?"

"Then you lead with your heart."

"You make me want to believe, babe, but what happens when we return to our lives?"

"You fight, Meadow. You'll not only fight for yourself, but you'll fight for us. Promise me." The intensity of his eyes on me makes me want to give him what he wants, but which promise do I keep? "My dad made me promise that I would only rely on myself, get my degree to support myself, and if I was unlucky enough to fall in love, I would protect my foolish heart along with my assets."

I didn't notice one hand escaped his hold and was fisting at my side, my knuckles burning from the inside. But my other fingers have intertwined with his; our hands bonded physically like my heart has emotionally. "I'll fight. When doubts creep in, I'll call."

"When you're alone and need me, I'll be there, Meadow, but you have to tell me. You have to talk to me."

"I promise."

"So we're going to do this? Try this relationship thing out?" he asks, not pressuring and not desperate, just putting the ball in my court to decide.

How can I deny this man anything he wants? I can't, just like I'm tired of denying him for myself. "Looks like it." I bring his hand to my mouth and kiss each of his knuckles and then the top. "Slow but steady."

The smile on his face beats any sunrise I've ever seen. I kiss him just to get a taste of heaven. Johnny and Holli stop on the path nearby. She has leis wrapped around her arm, followed by Kaz and Lara, who have even more. Johnny says, "We're going to say a few words for the ones we've lost."

Nikki and Tulsa are holding their leis in their hands when they walk up. Nikki says, "Come on, guys. Alfie's waiting."

We each get a lei before we reach the beach. When Hannah sees all of us there, she starts to cry. Jet takes the baby, and then Hannah kneels in front of Alfie. "Cassie always wanted to come to Hawaii."

"I wish she were here," he says, dropping his head down. "But I feel bad because I don't want you to feel sad."

"You thinking about your mother, wishing she were here doesn't hurt me Alfie. You being sad or feeling guilty does. You can love her and still love me." Hannah covers her heart. "She's inside my heart just as she's inside yours."

Jet rubs the top of his head. "Hey, buddy. She can't be here in body, but she's with us in spirit. We thought since the waves were rolling in, I could take you out on the board and we could send a lei out to sea in her honor."

"Really?"

"Yes, we get to go swimming."

"Sure," he says, smiling.

Off to the side, there are ten or fifteen boards leaning against a fallen tree. Jet sets Violet down and takes Alfie's hand. Looking at Johnny, then at Rochelle, he says, "I was thinking we could honor Cory as well."

Derrick, The Resistance's guitarist, along with Kaz, the other, are the first ones to move. They kiss their wives, who then join Hannah on the blankets spread out on the beach. Nikki takes my hand. "Will you wait with me?"

I start to leave but turn back and kiss Ridge. "Be safe, okay. I saw how the ocean won yesterday. I want you back in one piece today."

"I have more reason to fight today."

"Me too."

Holli makes sure they all have leis before they grab a board and start paddling out. Alfie sits in front of Jet as he paddles away. Tommy, Laird, and Shane leaving right after.

Darcy sits next to me just as Stella and Rivers show up. They kiss before she comes and lies down behind me, propped up on an elbow. I want to talk to her, ask her all about the wedded bliss, but this doesn't seem to be the time.

Rivers runs with a board into the ocean and heads out with Dex, who kisses Rochelle once more. They're all fit; having to perform at the level they do keeps them in shape.

The added workouts sculpt their godly bodies. The calmer waters are way offshore, but they seem to find a satisfactory space too far for us to see much other than them lined up in a row, sitting on their boards.

Cassie wasn't a surfer, and from my understanding, Cory wasn't either, but the ceremony seems to still fit for honoring them between heaven and earth. I don't know why I start to cry. I'm sure I'm just tired, but hearing the wind through the trees and the crashing ocean waves, Violet making the sweetest little babbling sounds, and seeing these men who would do anything for each other and their families, including me—emotion gets caught in my throat.

Holli and Rochelle stand with their feet in the water, arms wrapped around each other while the rest of us sit and watch, feeling the heaviness of the moment, this moment when we're all one.

My sister rests her head on my shoulder, and I whisper, "I told him about Mom and Dad."

Even though she knows what I'm referring to from living through it, surprise brightens her sage-colored eyes. "And?" *I feel safe. Adored. Cherished.*

"I think he loves me."

Tears fill her eyes just as quickly as they fill mine. "And you?"

"I think I love him too."

25

Meadow

WHAT IF?

I've posed that question to myself many times over the past year. I didn't know what my sister had truly done to protect me. She always shouldered the burden of responsibility, allowing me to fly free as much as possible. But finding out how she sacrificed herself to give me a chance to live life as it should be has shaken me to the core.

In high school, I used to act first and face the repercussions later just to push the boundaries. I'd get drunk and make out with any cute guy who looked my way, trying to forget the pain I hid inside.

By college, I wanted to find love, or what I thought was love. Bad attention and toxic relationships do not equal love, and I found this out the hard way. A string of pointless dates, some sending red flags to get out before I got in too deep. Others, I fell in to like a rock in shallow water—hard and fast.

I've tried love before, and all it did was prove my parents were right.

But when I look at Dave's hand tangled with mine between our seats, I smile. Physically, we were electric from the moment we met, and that current still flows strong between us if not even stronger.

Being in a relationship with him makes me feel vulnerable. We all handle pain in different ways, and I buried mine. But Dave isn't just a good time even though he was at first. It was safe to keep my feelings boxed that way.

This isn't about a second chance for us but giving us the first real chance we never got. Attraction has always been a pull between us, but he makes me laugh. Whether we're watching a movie, talking, cooking, or even just eating Ding Dongs, he makes me happy just being together. I've been my own damn obstacle. With an open heart and optimism paving the way, I'm going to fight for us, just as I promised him.

He deserves that, and so do I.

Holli walks down the aisle of the private plane and sits across from me. Dave has his headphones on and is sleeping, trying to catch up on some of the sleep we lost last night. "Hey," she says, tapping my knee. "We didn't get to talk much."

"No," I reply, feeling my face heat. Although she's done nothing but be nice since we met last year at Jet's house, I find her terribly intimidating. It's not her fault. It's me. She's just so beautiful, and although we dress similarly in casual clothes, she has a refined elegance about her. I think she's around thirty but is also worldly for her age.

I hope I can be like her one day.

With a bottle of water in her hand, she glances at Dave and then back at me. "I've never seen him look so happy. Have you dated long?"

"A while, but it's been more like a secret between us."

"I love that." Her eyes sparkle with life, happiness, interest. "I wanted to apologize for last night. Dalton and I . . ." I love that she calls her husband a special name. Sort of like how I call Ridge Dave, and he calls me Meadow Soleil, sunshine, and even cherry cheeks. "We didn't see you until . . . well, we left as soon as we did, but I still want to apologize."

Kill.

Me.

Now.

My cheeks flame fire hot as my heart races. "Um, I—"

"Nothing to be embarrassed by. We didn't 'see' anything, but when we realized, well, I'm sorry." Leaning forward, she adds, "Dalton and I are the worst. I'm surprised we don't have more kids."

That reminds me.

I dig through my purse to get a birth control pill.

Holli stands, holding the back of the seat to balance, and says, "Next time you're in LA, we should get the girls together and do some shopping or hang out."

"I'd like that," I say, trying not to freak out that the famous Holliday Hughes Outlaw wants to hang out with me.

"Great. Oh and he looks great on you too." Her mouth drops open, and she laughs. "That's not what I meant to say. Happiness looks good on you too."

I laugh. "Guess you would know either way."

"Guess so." Still laughing, she moves to the couches at the front of the plane and sits on her husband's lap. No other couple seems to captivate the papers like her and her famous lead singing husband, but they are so down to earth, they make you forget about that side of their lives.

Resting my hand on Dave's forearm, I begin to believe that despite his fame maybe things can be normal between us as well. I take the pill and chase it down with a sip of water.

Darcy caught a different flight back to England, so I don't get to share everything that's gone down, but I'll definitely be calling her when I'm back in Austin.

My back hurts from being in the same position for so long, so I slip out of my seat, careful not to wake Dave, and walk to the front where recliners are near the couches. Sitting next to Hannah, I look down into the portable crib at Violet sleeping. I can't help but touch one of her little hands, though I'm careful not to wake her.

Hannah's voice is soft when she speaks. "She's so tired. The time difference has thrown her off, which means we're all off schedule."

I say, "She's beautiful." Hannah tucks her hair behind her ear. "Like you."

"Thank you, Meadow."

"She's very much a Crow as well and reminds me of Jet's mother. Louisa was beautiful, inside and out."

Tears form in her eyes. "That's a beautiful thing to say. Jet will love to hear it."

My eyes well with tears as I look at this precious little sleeping being. I wipe under an eye and laugh. "I'm not sure why I'm suddenly all emotional."

"A lot has changed over the past year for you. Weddings always make me cry too."

"Yeah," I reply, gulping down my wayward emotions. "The wedding."

"The guy."

That makes me laugh in the lightest of ways. "Yes, the guy."

"I'm happy for you and Dave."

"You are?" As one of his closest friends, her opinion of me matters.

"You have such a big heart, Meadow. I've seen it in how

you are with your sister and heard from Jet, Tulsa, and Rivers how genuine, kind, and considerate you are. You have quite the fan club."

"They used to look out for me."

"I've heard some stories. They think very highly of you and your sister and care a lot about you both. I also feel like I know you better through your sister." Violet fusses, moving around, but doesn't wake up. Alfie comes from the back and sits down in the chair with me as though we're good old friends.

With her eyes on Alfie, Hannah says, "Speaking of genes, the Crow genes are strong." Hannah laughs and rubs his head. "Here's another one who hasn't gotten enough sleep."

"I'm wide-awake."

"You were last night too." He doesn't pick up on her sarcasm, but I do. "School is going to be rough if you don't sleep well tonight. I think you should go to bed early."

He looks up at me. "We're stuck learning eight hours a day, then they send more stuff home to torture us." He huffs, and even though he's Jet's son, I see a lot of Tulsa in that kid's expression.

Violet starts to cry, so I ask, "Can I help with anything?"

Touching my arm, she smiles. "You're so sweet for offering, but we'll be fine." She leans down and picks her up, holding her in her arms.

Alfie moves my hair from the side of my face and says, "You look like Aunt Stella."

My head jolts back, and my eyebrows pop up. "*Aunt* Stella." So weird to think of her like that, but the kid is right on both counts.

"Your hair is darker. Is it real?"

"My hair?" Running my fingers through the ends, I reply, "My hair is real."

"What is the real color?"

"This color. Maybe a little lighter in summer."

Shrugging as though I'm the crazy person who started this conversation, he says, "You're weird, and I like weird."

"We're both from Austin."

In unison, we say, "Keep Austin weird," then crack up laughing.

Jet comes over to Hannah. "Want me to take her?"

"We're all good."

Focusing on his son, he says, "Hey Alfie, your mom says you have homework that's due tomorrow. Get to it, buddy."

When he gets up, I do too. My emotions continue to get the best of me, and I hug my honorary big brother. "What you did for Alfie this morning was really touching." Jet's big bear hug arms come around me. Not to be left out, Alfie squeezes between us and wraps his arms around me as well, so I lower mine to include him too.

Stepping back, I get a good look at the man he's become. Like my sister, the burdens that used to weigh him down seem to be gone. His worries left in another lifetime. We turn away from the others, and I say, "Hannah's amazing."

His smile grows, and he nods. "She is."

Alfie eyes me with narrowed lids and a flat tightened mouth. "Aunt Stella is married to Uncle Rivers."

"Yes, she is," I say.

"Uncle Tulsa met Aunt Nikki on tour last year."

"I heard."

"My dad found me through Hannah." A light seems to shine, and his eyes come alive. "Ridge."

"What about Ridge?"

"Mom said you make him happy."

It's impossible not to enjoy this conversation. "He makes me happy."

His body slams into mine. "You're family, Meadow. Are you my aunt?"

"I'm not sure how that works, but we are family."

He hugs me again and says, "We hug family."

I lower down and hug him again. With my forehead on his shoulder, I whisper, "That's right. We hug family."

Then he dashes to the back of the plane. "Well, okay then. There's that."

"Meadow, come on." I see him peeking around the corner behind a seat and waving me over. "Let's surprise him."

"He already knows I'm here."

"Uncle Ridge?" he says.

Uncle? This kid is the cutest. I think everyone's family when it comes to him. He shakes Dave.

"Oh shit." I cover my mouth, realizing I've used a swear word in front of an eight-year-old. "Sorry."

"You owe me a buck."

"I'll pay ya later." Thumbing toward the back of the plane, I say, "Now scram, kid, before you get in anymore trouble."

He hightails it past me to a seat next to Jet. I try to figure out what I should do other than standing here like a weirdo. I put my arm across the top of two seats and stand like I have to pee. "What are you doing there, cherry cheeks?"

Our eyes meet—his hazels to my greens—and nothing's felt more right. I push off and fall into the seat next to him. Before he can speak, I lift the dividing armrest and move to curl up in his arms. "I missed you, rock star."

"I've only been asleep."

"I'm saying it now because I want to see how you look at me, memorize it, and recall the way you have flecks of gold around the green center, that your pupils widen when you're turned on and your eyes are on me, and watch that tongue glide over your lips like you're ready just from the sight of me."

"I am ready. I'm always ready for you."

"By tonight, I'll be in Austin and you'll be back in LA. When will I see you next?"

"Starting next week, we have three shows and a billion interviews in Australia and New Zealand."

I love the way his hand rubs my hip, holding me while taking advantage of the position. "I have midterm exams in November." We both appear to come to the same realization at the same time. "Thanksgiving."

"No, too far away," he says abruptly. "I'll come see you when I return to the same hemisphere."

"I'd like that. Your mom. Is that something you want to talk about?"

"No," he repeats. "But I know you're curious, and I should tell you."

"You don't have to." I slip off his lap and back into the seat next to him.

"I want you to know because you're important to me, like she is. I just don't like to spend what little time I have with you feeling down."

I do wonder about her and how serious it sounds, but how can I push when it's the last thing he needs right now? I rest my head on his arm, which he moves to wrap around me. Kissing my head, he adds, "Soon, okay?"

I nod, letting it go, though I worry how bad it must be for him not to want to discuss it at all. Strangely, I'm not hurt about his choice here. If there was one thing I learned from having three Crow boys as brothers, it's that men do not naturally open up about things that concern them. They internally process before they speak. So, this isn't rejection from Dave. This is his processing, and I'm good with that. *Good with him.*

When the private plane lands, I'm put in a car to take me to the next airport. As tired as Dave seems, he rides with me. Leaning his head back on the seat, he says, "This is the first time we've been alone in a long time."

"We were alone in the room."

"But still surrounded by so many people just a stone's throw away."

Eyeing the driver in the front of the SUV, I say, "We're not so alone now."

The privacy glass rolls up, and Dave moves closer. "How about now?"

Charming bastard. "How much time do we have?"

"Plenty, but let's steal some more." He pushes a button and says, "Take the long way to LAX."

With a laugh, I add, "You're so bad."

"But so good for you. We've got thirty minutes."

I've never wished to get stuck in traffic before now. "Better get started then."

I've never used this entrance to LAX, but that no cop is rushing us to leave makes me happy. It gives me a few extra minutes to shed the tears that refuse to hide inside.

The pads of his thumbs are rough, but he's so gentle that I barely feel him as he runs them over the tops of my cheeks. "Don't cry, sunshine. We'll have another day."

"I want it now and weeks after that."

"A month won't do. I'm going to need you for a year just to count the colors in your eyes. Don't be fooled, green doesn't come close to covering what I see when I look at you."

"What do you see?"

"Emerald and sea, thyme and spring, waterfall and moss, ocean and earth. I can go on about all the greens that make up who you are to me." This beautiful man and his gift in words. It's no wonder he writes incredible lyrics. They're from his soul . . . a soul I'm falling in love with.

Holding my cheeks, he brings me in and kisses the top of my head as I cry against his shoulder. He whispers, "I don't do well with your tears, sweetheart. Leave me with a smile."

He continues to rub my back as I struggle to pull myself together. This time, I dry my tears and take a deep breath before sitting up. I know I look a mess, but I'll try my best to give him what he needs. A smile. "We haven't talked much about the future, mainly because of me. But I need you to know that wherever you go in the world, I want you to come back to me."

Eliciting the smile I love to see the most, the one I only see when he smiles at me, he melts me to the seat. He kisses my cheek, and with his lips still pressed to my skin, he says, "I promise."

With that promise, I turn and push the door open. The driver is standing on the curb with my suitcase. That's when I see the paparazzi behind a thin rope barrier, cameras aimed at me. The door closes, and I don't look back. I won't be able to see him anyway. The glass is tinted too dark, and the driver is already pulling away.

I drag my suitcase right past them and am led to the private check-in counter. I want to say I appreciate the red-carpet treatment I receive by association and a phone call he made, but I'd rather have him.

I already miss him. Having spent the weekend with

Dave, having had time to slowly get to know each other even more, I feel stronger in the idea of us.

We can still connect through technology. *Thank God for that. And knowing Dave, he'll probably try to get some naughty moments in those times as well.* Can't wait. I can do this. *We can do this, Fellowes. Our future counts on it.*

26

Ridge

"It's BULLSHIT, and you know it, Jet."

"I do know it, but what do you want me to do about it?"

Tommy raises his hands. "Calm the fuck down. So we're late by a couple of days. This is your fucking job, and there are plenty of other musicians who would give their dicks to have it."

Knudson, the manager in charge of this leg of our tour, gets a smarmy grin on his face. "Don't sweat it, mates. I can help find some chicks to slick your dick and plenty of candy if that's what you're looking for. Entertainment," he says, tapping the side of his nose, "during the delay."

Rivers stands, tossing his soda in the trash like he's ready to throw down. Tommy stands and steps between them. "I think the guys are good. We'll just head back to the hotel."

"Suit yourself."

When he walks out, Rivers kicks the backstage door closed. "He's an asshole and needs to be fired. Why's he calling us mates anyway? He's from the Bronx."

Tommy looks annoyed. "I have no idea but forget him. Focus on New Zealand."

I push off the wall and walk toward the door. "No sense hanging around here. Let's go."

We file into the van and stare out the windows in silence. Everyone's pissed, but what can we do? A power outage at the stadium has the generators burning out. Two are being replaced but knowing the others might not be working in time as we were only hours away from going on, the call was made to take the open spot in three days. Luckily, Aussies are forgiving.

"We could go on anyway," Tulsa says, tapping his sticks against the back of the vinyl seat. "There would be enough juice to run our instruments and a few lights, the amps. That's all we need. My platform won't rotate, but we can still produce enough sound to give the audience the show of a lifetime."

Tommy says, "They'll never let you on that stage. It's a liability."

"I don't want to disappoint Meadow." The van goes quiet, and all eyes are on me. "What?"

The guys break out in laughter. "Fuck," Tulsa says, holding his gut. "It's about fucking time, brother. Welcome to the club."

Rivers hits my back. "Damn, Ridge. Stella will be relieved to know it wasn't just a weekend thing in Hawaii."

Jet's just laughing, but Tommy says, "You're fucking kidding me with this, right? You're done for, like for good?"

Annoyed, I say, "I'm not married." But the words don't feel right. Well the word "not" is really the root of the problem.

Tommy does a double take, staring at my face. "You okay? You've gone pale as a ghost."

"Pull over."

"It's the side of the highway," the driver shouts from the front.

I inhale through my nose and exhale slowly through the mouth. "Pull the fuck over."

The van swerves, and he takes an exit we were about to pass. *It's so weird exiting off the left of the freeway.* Rivers asks, "What's wrong?"

I just shake my head. The van comes to a stop at a gas station, and I open the door as fast as I can. My heavy shoes hold me from taking off running by grounding me to a slow pace. Standing thirty or so steps away, I look up at the sky.

We're moving fast.

Meadow and me.

From nothing to everything to marriage.

What the fuck?

Tulsa's the first to make his way over. "Save your jokes. I'm not in the mood."

"Moods. Disposition. Temperament. It's weird how the psyche works. One day, you're moving on in this thing called life, soaking in every minute of the day like a sponge, and then bam, someone's put right in your way. You walk left. You walk right, but you realize it's not about moving around them to get to your destination. They *are* the destination. Nikki's my destination."

"I don't need a lecture on how love works."

"Funny you should mention love. I used to be with different girls every night. Had a grand ball of a good time. Never felt a thing for them when I walked away. I saw Nikki on that stage, and like so many other fuckers in that audience, I was mesmerized. She has this move where her hand goes behind her head and her hips move . . . well, let's just say she knows how to move. So I see her up there, and then she comes down these stairs backstage like a goddess in white. I swear to God there was a halo hanging over her head. Well, we made the contact—"

He may be rambling, but now I'm invested in the fucking story. "What 'contact' are you talking about?"

"Eye contact. She gave me a look that said more than words ever could. Months later, we're in a Vegas wedding chapel getting married."

"Where are you going with this, Tulsa?"

"Destiny and destination share a common prefix, but their meanings are different. Yet I figure they're one and the same when it comes to Nikki. As for Meadow, you've been fucking her like you care about her. If I find out you don't care about her, you're fucked."

When he walks off, I'm scratching my head while standing here trapped in a whole lot of *what the fuck was that about* thoughts.

Tommy heads my way this time, keeping a good ten feet between us. "I had higher hopes for you, man. You're losing it."

"You're talking about me staying single, aren't you? Not the band."

"Of course. You're a badass guitar player. No one can touch you right now. But you guys keep going down for the count one by one. I've been here before. The Resistance. Now The Crow Brothers. Next it will be Faris Wheel."

Walking over to him so we don't have to shout, I say, "Have you ever thought about settling down?"

"I think about it, but I'm in no position to make a life with someone else when I don't have a life of my own."

"What if it's time?"

Shoving his hand in his pockets, he rocks back on his heels. "You trying to get rid of me, Ridge?"

"No, I'm trying to figure out what the hell I'm doing."

"You might want to start by figuring out why you got sick back in the van."

I already know the answer to that, but he's already walked away.

Rivers takes his time to come over as if I need another Crow to threaten me. "Tulsa already warned me about hurting Meadow. Technically, you have too."

"I'm not here to threaten you. I'm here to tell you that she likes you."

"I like her."

"What if she loves you?"

"Then we'll be on an even playing field."

Crossing his arms over his chest, he watches the traffic drive by on the highway. "What are you doing, man?"

"Freaking out."

He chuckles but covers his mouth enough to appear he's having a coughing fit. I ask, "No threats and no words of advice? I feel like I'm getting off easy."

"You are. But I can't return to that van before telling you that I've been responsible for Stella and Meadow for a long time now. I've known Meadow since she was eleven. To say I'm protective wouldn't be doing it justice. I'm not a fool, though. She's allowed to date whoever she wants, and you're apparently who she wants. I like you and consider you one of us, so if things go south, where do we go from here?"

"I can't answer that. I like her. I . . . have stronger feelings for her, but it's new, and she's skittish to relationships, so I'm not going to push her to make everyone else more comfortable."

Seeming satisfied, he nods. "I can live with that. Good luck."

"I'm going to need it."

"I was referring to Jet."

Looking over my shoulder. "Oh."

Jet files out of the van and passes Rivers as he returns. "Get in the fucking van."

"That's all you came to say?"

"I'm hungry."

"Me too." I follow him back to the van.

Tommy is chuckling but stops to say, "You got your color back."

"I'd rather have my girl."

"Dahhhhh," the guys grumble and then start laughing at me.

Tulsa pats my shoulder. "Preachin' to the choir, brother."

"Well, if I can't have her, let's get drunk."

"You're the best guitarist."

"No, you are," I say, pushing Rivers in the arm. He falls off the back of the bench, and I stand just enough to see him land on his ass. "Damn, man. You're drunk."

"You are." He lies on the floor and then starts laughing. Lifting his head, he rubs his ass. "Fuck, that hurt."

"I'm going to bed," I say, trying to stand, but man, this room needs to stop spinning so damn fast. I use the wall to steady me as I stumble my way to my room. "Where am I staying?"

Tommy takes me by the shoulders and directs me outside the hotel room. "This way." I walk out the door and follow the lines of the carpet as they swirl down the hall. Pulling my room key from my back pocket, I hold it to unlock the door, but nothing happens. I try again, but it still doesn't work.

"Shit." I lean against the wall and try a few more times before I slide down the wall and sit on the floor. My phone falls from my pocket, and a photo of cherry cheeks shows up.

I lie down next to her, remembering how good it felt to be with her in Hawaii.

It's only been a week or so, but it feels longer. I rest my eyes for only a second. Just one second . . . Fuck. This time change is fucking with me. I try the card once more and I get green!

Bingo!

I drop the card on the table just inside the door, which closes with a loud click of the lock. Stripping my clothes off, I head for the bed and land face down. Sleep is gonna find me fast, but then a ringing pulls me back from the abyss.

"Go the fuck away."

When it keeps ringing, I realize it's my phone. Fuck. Pushing up, I stumble to find my jeans, which almost landed on the couch but not quite. I dig my phone out of the back pocket and hold it to my ear. "What?"

The ringing jacks my ear, and I jump, realizing I didn't answer the call. Pushing the button, I say, "Hello?"

"Hi?"

"Ahhh, the sweet sound of my sweet girl." I walk back into the bedroom and flop onto my back on the mattress.

"You're drunk."

"Nah, not me. I'm a boice scout."

"Boy scout, and I'm thinking you had a few drinks by how much you're slurring."

"You've slurved. I'm lonely. Why are you so far away, baby?"

"A world away. I miss you."

Grinning like a lunatic, I reach down and adjust my balls. "I miss those lips."

"What do you miss about them?"

"How they look wrapped around my dick."

The melody of her laugh relaxes me. Happy is the only

way she should ever be. "One day, I'm going to make you the happiest woman in the universe."

"How are you going to do that, rock star?"

"I don't know, but I always keep my promises."

"*Dave . . .*"

"Hello?"

"No. I need sleep."

The soft touch a female's hand wraps around my shoulder. "Ridge."

Ridge. I fucking hate when she calls me Ridge. I take the hand and pull her into bed with me. "I've told you not to call me that, sunshin—" My body jerks back, and I jump from the bed. "Who are you?"

The woman sits up with a wide smile. Smoothing her hair, she replies, "I work for the hotel, sir. I was told you weren't responding to calls or to room service."

"Why would I?" I feel the air conditioning blow across my body from the vent above. *Shit.* Where are my jeans? I walk out of the bedroom glad I wore my underwear to bed, or I have a feeling I would've been seeing my junk all over the web. I spy my jeans on the floor next to the couch in the living room. While slipping them on, I say, "I'm going to need you to leave now. You've done your job. All's good."

She appears in the doorway, her top button mysteriously popped open. Running her hands along her tight skirt, she eyes me. "Are you sure there's nothing I can do for you?"

"I'm good. See? Alive and fine."

"Anything at all? Your request is my command."

I grab my T-shirt from the floor near the door and then look back. "Nope, no commands from me." I head to the door.

"Sir?"

The tone is familiar. I've heard it too many times, usually with Ridge in place of sir, but it's the same. Not turning around, I say, "I have a girlfriend."

"Where is she?"

Another button's undone when I look back. She should really find a good tailor to fix that issue. I open the door wide and step aside. With my free hand over my heart, I reply, "In here."

Her dark eyes stay on mine as she nods. "Very well, sir."

I shut the door and exhale.

Fuck me.

Moving back into the living room, I search for my phone. I finally find it wrapped up in the covers of the bed. Checking the call log, I see the last call I made was to Meadow. Shit. I don't even remember talking to her.

I call her back, but she doesn't answer. *Fuck. Fuck. Fuck.* "Hey, um. So I had a few drinks last night. We talked. I slept. Just wanted to say hi today. Call me when you get a chance."

Hanging up, I fall back on the bed and stare up at the ceiling. My head is starting to hurt, so I guess I need to find out why room service was trying to reach me. I dial the number on the hotel phone and when they answer, the person says, "We have your breakfast ready. Would you like us to bring it back to your room or have you changed your mind?"

I drunk ordered breakfast. That's a first, and quite wise if I do say so myself. "Bring it on. Thanks."

Twenty minutes later, there's a knock on the door. "Room service."

I open it and let the delivery guy push the cart in and set up. Tipping him on his way out, he says, "Thank you, but not necessary. We don't require tips here. There's a note next to the orange juice. Someone went out of their way to make sure you're eating well today."

Glancing back at the tray, I say, "Thanks."

Okay, I didn't order the food.

So who did?

27

Meadow

"Damn it."

"Something wrong?"

I look up to find a guy standing in my personal space. Taking a step back to regain it, I hold up my phone. "I missed a call from my boyfriend. Twice." My heart squeals with glee just from saying the word out loud for the first time.

He smiles, but says, "Too bad."

"Too bad I missed his call? I know. He's in Australia, so the time and day difference are a real bitch."

"Too bad you have a boyfriend." He turns to go but looks back over his shoulder. "Maybe I'll see you around."

Highly unlikely. This campus is huge, and considering I barely noticed how attractive he was, there's no point in even remembering his face. I sit on a bench nearby and call Dave. "Hello?" he whispers into the phone.

"Hi," I whisper right back as if I'm disturbing something. "Why are we whispering?"

"Because I'm in the back of a van, and everyone can hear."

I hear the guys say, "Hi, Meadow," and grin.

"Tell them hi. So how's it going?"

"I've had better starts to the day, but the food you sent made things better."

Pressing the phone tighter to my ear, I say, "I'm glad. I thought you might not be feeling the best this morning."

"We talked last night."

"Yes, for a minute. You fell asleep on me."

"I wish I'd fallen asleep on you. Damn, I miss you, girl."

A chorus of Crows sing in the background, "Missing you, girl."

I giggle. How can I not? He took my call when he knew they'd give him a hard time. He can't say a word without being made fun of, yet he's still talking to me. "I miss you so much."

"I have to go in a minute, but the show's been delayed three days. We have Auckland and Brisbane. We're getting on a plane for New Zealand now. Then we're coming back here. So I won't be coming home as soon as I thought."

"I'll still be here."

"Do you know what it means to hear you say that?"

"What does it mean?"

"Everything."

I cradle the phone and then lean down for more privacy. "I called you my boyfriend today. I said it to someone for the first time."

"And how did that feel?"

"Almost as good as sex."

A deep growl fills the line. "I can't resist a challenge."

"I can't wait for you to take it." I bite my lip, unsure if I should ask, but I want to know. I have to learn to let him in. "Have you told anyone that you have a girlfriend?"

"The guys know."

"I mean anyone else."

"That's not information I would share with many people, so I don't think—oh, wait. I told a woman today."

Sitting up straight, I ask, "What woman?"

"The woman in my room . . . Ugh. Fuck. That sounds really bad. It's not what you think."

My mind starts reeling with images of him and female fans rolling around in bed together. "What do I think?"

"You're thinking I did something wrong, but I woke up, and she was there."

"What? Someone broke into your hotel room?"

"No. She used a key—Fuck. I'm screwing this up."

"Yes, you are. Did you let her in, or did she break in?"

"She works for the hotel. When I didn't respond to any calls or answer the door for room service, I guess they check on the guests. Or maybe because I'm a musician, they worry I'm the next victim to the legacy."

Worry fills my gut. "I don't want you to die."

"Good, because I don't want to die either."

The alarm on my phone buzzes, and I look down at the screen. With it back to my ear, I say, "I have to get to class, but everything's okay, right?"

"Everything's better than okay. It will be too late in Austin for me to call you after the show—"

"Call me anyway. Break a leg, babe."

I hang up and suck in a shaky breath. Trust. I have trust in him. Standing, I start walking up the steps toward the building for my next class. I tug on my backpack, situating it so it's more comfortable on my shoulders when my phone rings.

Still trekking across campus, I see the screen and smile before answering it. "Hey you. Long time, no talk."

"I miss you." His voice is deep, lowered with promises of dirty talk.

Even though he already told me he missed me, it feels good to hear him say it again. "I miss you, too." I stop and feel the heaviness of the emotions I've been trying to keep at bay. "I'm ready to see you again."

"Soon, I promise."

His words echoing a promise he made to me that he probably doesn't even remember making. This time when we hang up, it's not as rushed, slower as reality sets in. Just because he'll be back in the States soon doesn't mean I'll get to see him.

I tuck my phone back in the side pocket of my backpack and continue my journey because I know we'll be okay.

"Ms. Fellowes, please see me after the test," the professor says while tapping my desk in the middle of a pop quiz.

"Yes, sir."

The quiz is easy, so easy I start doubting myself, so I go over it once more before I turn it in. Other students drop their quizzes off and head for the door, but I stay. "You wanted to see me?"

"Yes," he says, steepling his fingers. "I had an interesting opportunity come across my desk yesterday. I've been thinking about the right student that would make a good fit. I think you would."

"What is it?"

He stands and comes around the desk, leaning against it and crossing his ankles. "Have you made plans for the summer?"

"No," I reply. "I'm focused on midterms right now."

"This is a rare opportunity to take an advanced step

toward managing university departments and will give you the skills to apply the work done here to other companies trying to expand. The business department needs an overhaul with fresh and innovative new ideas. Professor Longood is retiring this summer, so the board has rearranged the department in hopes of growing with the times." He chuckles and pushes his glasses up his nose. "We're about a decade or two behind. I'd like for you to consider the position. It's temporary with potential for full-time work. It's a great opportunity. If you're interested, I can email you the details."

Stunned. This is so unexpected and a lot to take in. It's only fall and not even second semester. I could have a job secured and in place before Christmas, five months before graduation. My mind is blown. "Please do. I'd love to read more about. And thank you. Thank you for thinking of me."

"You're a star student, and anyone would be lucky to have you on their team, Ms. Fellowes."

"Thank you again." I hold my backpack in my arms until I'm in the hall. Then I swing it over my shoulder and hurry out of the building to squeal again. Today is my day. I can just feel it. It's all coming together. All the hard work is finally starting to pay off, and even though I should be excited about what *I'm* achieving, it's my heart that feels the most joy. Because, I know that Dave will be just as excited for me as I am. *He'll share my joy, not try to control it or demean it. Because that's how it should be.*

The note on the delivery says, "Since we're sending food, I miss eating you but sent this instead. I'm a poet, and I know it. Send pics." I drag the tip of the scissors down the tape seam and bust it open. I grab my phone and am about to call him, but then remember he's playing a show.

Since he can't be here to enjoy them with me, I indulge with a glass of wine while taking a bath. With bubbles not covering the good parts, I snap like twenty photos and then sort them to the find the perfect one, crop it, filter it, and then put a cute frame around it that says wish you were here. Two glasses of wine down and I finally press send.

I'm not in the mood to be alone. Stella was at Holli's with the girls tonight living the Hollywood life, and it's almost six in the morning in England, so I can't chat with Darcy, and Dave is doing . . . who knows. We're so far from each other that he's living in a different day from me.

Just when I'm getting sad, my phone rings, making my heart happy again. "Hi."

"That is the single most fuckin' sexy photo I've ever seen in my life." Dave lowers his voice. "Tell me you're still in that bath eating Ding Dongs."

I take a bite, then say, "Eating right now. Wish you were here to eat them with me."

"You're killing me, cherry cheeks. I'm lonely. I'm horny. I'm hungry. This pic has everything I ever wanted—great fuckin' tits, food, and you wet all over."

"Would you like to fuck my tits?" I'm blaming the wine.

Silence.

"Dave?"

The sound of a heavy breath fills my ear, then he says, "You can't talk to me like that when I can't get to you."

I set the Ding Dong down and take a sip of wine. "I've eaten two. I'm a whore for you."

"Fuck me, Meadow. I'm heading into another interview, and now my dick is hard as steel."

My hand slinks under the warm bubbly water to calm the pulse throbbing between my legs. "How much time do you have?"

"Not enough."

"Trust me. It won't take long."

"Tommy, I need five," he says in a hurry. "Toilet." A second of silence and I can hear the noises, but then his voice comes back on with an echo. "You touching yourself, baby?"

"I am. Are you alone?"

"Yeah. How do you feel?"

"Slick. Wet. Warm. Horny."

"Shit. Do you ever get yourself off?"

"Yes. To images of you. The way you suck my nipples and the feel of your scruff as it scratches between my legs. Sometimes I use my vibrator, but I never put it inside me. Only you go there."

"That's right, baby. Only I go there. Only I kiss those lips. Only I suck those tits and get you off, except when I'm not there and then only you can do that. Tell me how it feels to have your fingers down there."

"Not calloused like yours. Not rough how I like it. Not you."

"Close your eyes and pretend they are. Rub your clit. Make yourself feel good."

"It feels good. Are you making yourself feel good?"

"Later. Do you slip inside or stay on the outside?"

"Outside," I say through a stilted breath. Setting the phone down, I put it on speaker. "Tell me what to do, Dave."

"Circles. You fall apart under circles. Firm and consistent with a little pressure on the clit."

I follow his directions, and my eyes fall closed. "Ah." Tiny moans fill the bathroom as I get closer and closer. The feeling grows, and I move my hand faster. "Getting so close."

"Dave?"

Shit. Jet's voice scares me, and I grip the edge of the tub when I sit up, knocking my phone into the water. "Shit." Fishing it out, I stand and get out in the emergency to dry it with a towel before legging it into the kitchen and dumping it in the container of rice I keep in my pantry for this sole purpose. The screen is black, and I'm left dripping wet . . . in all ways. Shoot.

I go back in the bathroom and grab the towel I dumped in my hurry and dry my body, groaning over all that just happened.

Checking on my phone once more before bed, I search for any signs of life, but there are none. I don't have the money to get a new one, so I'm going to have to email Stella tomorrow and beg, bargain, and plead my way into offering to pay her back.

The two boxes of Ding Dongs Dave shipped to me still manage to bring a smile, though. I think he's trying to get me fattened up so he can eat me . . . I can't say I have a problem with this plan.

Two glasses of red wine have my head spinning, so I take an Ibuprofen and go to bed. Not only am I left without coming, but now I also don't have a way to contact Dave. Tomorrow can only get better.

28

Meadow

I MULLED the job opportunity over for a week, not wanting to share the news with anyone until I had a good idea of where I stood with it. I knew deep down that it didn't feel right, but the chance to secure a paid position right out of college was appealing. More than appealing, though, is it's what I've wanted all along.

Or so I thought.

Things are complicated.

Stella is in California, and I naturally thought I'd be moving out there to be closer to her as the only family I'm still in touch with. But Ridge came along sweeping me off my feet when I least expected it. Dave followed through and has made me happier than I've ever been.

Two sides of the same man.

One gives me a thrill.

The other speaks to my heart.

Who will win?

I once foolishly thought I would never fall for a rock star, but then again, I hadn't met Ridge. Now that we're in a relationship, I've allowed myself to see that side of him, to enjoy it, and seeing him onstage as fans scream his name and his fingers fly across those strings—he's the sexiest man I've ever seen. It's like watching porn, but better because he's mine, and all the ways he manipulates the chords will be how he controls my body.

And the intensity, the passion with which he plays, is the same intensity he shares with me. When we talk, he's focused on me, and that in and of itself is both a comfort and a trial. *I want more of him all the time.* And then my head goes back to the gutter, thinking about what *more* with Dave is like.

Fanning myself, I turn off the video and close my laptop to prepare for landing. I check my seat belt and sit back, trying to relax. Flying still makes me nervous, even in first class. The comfort of the bigger seats and alcohol doesn't rid that niggling deep down that tells me that if people were meant to fly, they would have been born with wings.

"Here on business?" the man next to me asks.

"Yes." My palms start to sweat. I shouldn't have had two glasses of champagne, but since it was free . . . My head swims a bit, my nerves kicking in. "Sexual."

"What?"

"Oh," I start. Shit, I said that out loud. "I'm going to LA to see my boyfriend."

The man's eyes are still wide, and I think he might be grayer on top after talking to me. He snaps his newspaper and goes back to reading.

"Sorry. I get nervous on planes when I fly by myself."

I get nothing. My sexual business has thrown this man completely off. I put my headphones on, slide down in my seat, and stare out the window. In the car I ordered on the app, I sit in the back seat. The man has an accent, but I can't tell where he's from. He's been staring at me, but more out of interest than like he's stalking me. "You're going to a nice neighborhood."

"Yes, it is nice."

"Gated?"

"Yes, it's a gated house."

"Fancy. Very Hollywood."

"Very."

"I studied in Vermont before moving out here."

"Oh, yeah?"

"It's too cold there."

"I bet."

When there's a break in the conversation, I rest my head back. Waking up at five to finish packing before my classes has caught up with me. The travel makes me even more tired, but the memories of last week still keep me going.

"You can use it anytime, sunshine."

"I don't know what to say. Thank you."

"The plane ticket is for purely selfish reasons, so don't go thinking I'm a saint or anything."

I run my finger over the new phone that arrived the day after I lost mine in what I'm calling Watergate. The irony that it shares the same name as another scandal makes me laugh a little too hard every time I think about it. I lie down and set the phone on the pillow next to me, the speaker on. "The phone and now the ticket. It's too much."

"Again, purely selfish reasons. If you don't have a phone, then how will I talk to you or hear your voice?"

"I'm feeling a lot selfish myself, so I'm taking these gifts."

"And using them."

"And using them. Thank you. You're spoiling me, though. First Ding Dongs, then a phone, and now a plane ticket. No more presents, okay?"

"No, I can't promise that. I'd be lying, and I always keep my promises."

Standing at the gate at the bottom of the driveway, I take a deep breath and then push the button. "Meadow?"

"It's me," I reply, searching for the camera. When I find it in a nearby tree, I say, "Cheese."

"What a surprise! Get up here, girl."

The front door opens, and Alfie runs out and into my arms. "Meadow!"

"Hi, bud." I embrace him because we hug family.

Hannah comes outside holding Violet. "What are you doing here?"

Dragging my suitcase in one hand and holding Alfie's in the other, I say, "I wanted to surprise Dave."

Alfie jumps up and down. "Are you going to move in with him? Are you going to get married like Uncle Rivers?"

I think I just saw my life flash before my eyes. I think we need to slow this train down. "I'm just here for a visit. I wanted to surprise him and my sister, but it seems I'm surprising all of you."

As soon as we reach the front door, Alfie dashes inside with my suitcase. I hold my hands out for Violet who reaches for me with a dimpled smile. "Hi, baby girl." Adjusting her on my hip, I look into her big blue eyes. "Can you be any more gorgeous? Nope," I say, touching her nose. "You're perfect."

"How are you doing?" Hannah asks.

I give her a side hug. "Better than ever but missing my man."

"I know he's been missing you. They got back late last night and hit the studio this morning for a last-minute change. He's been in a bad mood all day."

"I heard. He was supposed to come see me this weekend, but since he's stuck here, I came to surprise him instead."

"He's going to love it." She walks inside and shuts the door behind me. Taking the baby from me, she says,

"Make yourself at home and when you're ready, he's downstairs."

"Meadow, come on." I peek around Hannah to see Alfie waving me over. "Let's surprise them." This kid is quite the character. He's so excited. His enthusiasm for life reminds me of Tulsa again. They both love a fun plan and are always up for a party.

I've reminded myself fifty times over that Dave wouldn't have bought the ticket if he didn't want me here. I was nervous that I was making a mistake by coming unannounced, but now that I'm here, I'm excited too.

Following Alfie down the stairs and farther down the hall, I stop when he stops. He whispers, "The studio is there. We have to be quiet when that light is on."

"It's off."

"Habit," he says in full volume voice, causing me to laugh. When I don't make a move, he nods toward the door. "You can go in when the light's off."

"Thanks, kid."

When he runs up the stairs, I straighten my outfit, but some of the wrinkles in my shirt are set in. The door opens, and wrinkles don't matter. Dave does. Before he can speak, I run into his arms, and say, "I missed you, rock star."

His words are muffled since his face is pressed against me, but I think I make out, "Missed you too," somehow. Turning to the side, he sucks in a few breaths, and says, "I couldn't breathe."

"Oh." I uncurl myself from his face as he holds me by the ass. "Sorry." *So not sorry.* I wrap myself around him again because my feelings for this man feel too big to contain to a simple hug.

"I like you happy to see me." Looking up at me, he lowers me just enough so our mouths are aligned.

The laughter leaves the hall, and tension takes its place.

The good kind of tension—*sexual*. His arms don't even shake from my weight, so I pull my arms around and cup his face. "I'm going to kiss you, Dave Carson."

"I'm ready, Meadow Fellowes."

I kiss him not just because I missed him, but because I want him to know how much.

Clomping down the stairs behind me is heard, and Alfie says, "If you're staying for dinner, you have to help set the table, Meadow."

I stare into Dave's eyes, surprised by Mr. Bossy Pants behind me. "He's eight, right?"

Ridge laughs. "He is and going on twenty-five."

"I'm not even twenty-five." I'm set all the way down, my feet flat on the ground.

"Don't remind me."

"Don't worry, old man. I'll take care of you when you're gray."

"That's a Beatles song, right?"

Lifting my shoulders, I drop them and shake my head. "I have no idea." I turn to look at Alfie. "You still here, kid?"

"I was told to learn about the birds and bees."

"What?" Ridge asks, moving around me. "Alfie, we'll be up in a minute to help out."

"Okay, but since you kissed her, when do her eggs hatch?"

I hide my mouth behind my hand, mumbling under my breath, "Oh my God. I can't talk about my eggs with him."

"I'm not sure I want you to talk about your eggs with me either," Dave jokes. "Hit the road, Alf."

"Fine," he says mopey, going upstairs. "Is Meadow moving in with you because I liked when you stayed here with us? There's another room where Meadow can live." His eyes move to mine. "It's next to my room. We can play pranks on Uncle Ridge."

"You're trouble," he says to Alfie.

Looking at Dave, I smile. "I guess we should pause this until later."

"That's probably best. Do you want to stay for dinner?"

"Would you hate it if we did?"

He pushes some of my hair away from my cheek. "No. I think it's good that you want to be here, but we're leaving before dessert."

"Are you insane? Dessert is the best part of the meal."

"No, you are." He takes my hand and says, "Let's go set the table."

Dave seems to know where everything is, so we set the table on the patio. When we finish, Hannah comes into the kitchen to check on the food, but when she sees the table, she says, "You didn't have to do that. That's Alfie's job."

My glare hits that sneaky kid square in the face. I point, struggling to keep a straight face. "You tricked me."

"You still owe me a dollar for swearing."

Pointing at the table, I say, "I'm calling it even."

He knows when he's lost. "That's fair."

Tulsa and Rivers come up from the studio and straight to me. Tulsa says, "Lookin' good, Meadow."

"Not too shabs yourself, Tulsa Crow."

Rivers says, "You realize you're practically brother and sister, right?"

"We can tease each other." Giggling, I add, "Anyway, we're both in relationships."

I swear on Dita Von Teese, the room goes silent. Even the oven timer stops beeping. With Rivers and Tulsa smirking out the side of their mouths, I turn to find the only eyes that will give me comfort. When I land on Dave's warm hazels, he doesn't say anything. Just gives me that smirk that makes the girls go wild when he's on stage. My bad, bad boy. I'm starting to regret that decision to stay when he makes it so tempting to take him up on the offer to have me for dessert. But this is who we are too. We are both part of a bigger family, so as much as I want time with him, I like being here with him. Seeing him relaxed and part of the same family.

Alfie breaks the silence. "What's going on? Why are we staring at Meadow?"

Hannah quickly guides him by the shoulders away, whispering, "I could really use a taste tester, buddy."

Jet doesn't bother whispering. "Hawaii kind of sealed the deal. We've had to listen to Ridge moan about not seeing you since."

Wrapping his arm around my shoulders, Tulsa turns me toward the patio. "You could've done worse, I guess." He laughs. "How can I help, Hannah?"

As everyone busies themselves to get dinner ready, I stand there still looking at Ridge. He's slow to join me, taking his sweet time to look me over as he comes to my side and kisses my cheek.

Rivers passes by with a large pot of pinto beans as he heads for the outside table. "Wish I was staying. I'm starving, and dinner smells awesome."

Hannah trails behind him with tortillas. "You should have that pretty wife of yours join us. I've made too much."

Jet adds, "Too much for an army, much less just us."

"I never know with you guys," Hannah replies just before the door closes.

Rivers replies, "Newlyweds and I've been gone more than a week. She'd kill me if I didn't come home." Turning to me, his eyes move from Ridge to me. "Where are you staying?"

With a bottle of wine and several glasses in hand, Ridge goes outside. When I don't answer right away, Rivers says, "You're always welcome to stay at our house. You have the room and the whole upstairs."

I reach over and hug him because I haven't since I

arrived, and though he's my sister's husband, he's always been a part of my family too. "Thank you."

His embrace comes with a pat on the back. "Just give us a heads-up if you're coming over. You know Stella will want to fix the room up for you."

"I'm going to stay with Ridge, but let Stella know I'll call her tomorrow."

"Okay. It's good to see you. Stella's missed you too, so make sure she sees you at least once this weekend."

"I'll try, but no promises." He starts laughing. So I add, "Quick trip."

He heads for the door when Ridge returns. "Have a good one."

Ridge takes my hand, and asks, "What did you choose to do?"

Wrapping my arms around his neck, I kiss him. "You."

29

Meadow

"The last time we were in this 4Runner, we were on the road trip," I say, the tips of my fingers tapping against the leather seat. Dinner was good, the company fun, but I've been looking forward to us leaving all night.

Ridge has been driving Rivers's old SUV when he's in town, so being back here reminds me of so many memories. Reaching over, he runs his hand along the top of my leg. I like his hands on me. "I need to tell you something, Meadow." He pulls into a hotel driveway and puts the SUV in park.

"What is it?"

My door is opened by a valet guy at the same time as his. He's greeted, "Welcome back, Mr. Fellowes."

My head whips left. "Mr. Fellowes?"

I've never seen Dave look embarrassed . . . *until now*. He whispers, "About that. I can explain. Just go with it for now."

He gets out of the car and heads to retrieve my suitcase.

"Hi," I say to the valet holding my door open for me. "Thanks."

Taking my hand, the doors slide open, and we walk into the stark white lobby of the modern hotel. "Welcome back, Mr. Fellowes," he's greeted by the desk clerk. "Will you be staying with us for the night?"

For only my ears to hear, Dave says, "I'll be right back."

"Oh no, I'm not missing this show, Mr. *Fellowes*."

He huffs and walks to the desk with me right there by his side amused by the use of my name. The desk clerk makes small chitchat with him, but to me, I've gotten about ten once-overs since I walked in the joint. "Field Fellowes. Here we go. Your regular suite is available and ready, so we'll be able to get you right in."

Intense is an understatement. If Dave doesn't blink soon, I think he'll burn a hole through the clerk's silk pocket square. Nice try at pretending it's not weird at all that he's using my name or some variation of it. He'll only be able to avoid the subject for so long, and he knows his time is running out.

As soon as he's handed the key, we head to the elevators. "Field Fellowes?" I really struggle to keep from laughing, a giggle busting out. "That's your alias?"

He doesn't seem to enjoy the topic as much as I do. Dave's expression flickers between busted and embarrassed. "Can we talk about this upstairs?"

"Sure, but just so you know, I'm going to laugh the whole way up." We step inside the elevator, and the doors close. "And if you get to be Field Fellowes, I want to be called Cliff Carson." I bust out laughing. I knew I couldn't resist.

"Hardy, har, har. Yeah. Yeah. Real funny." Keeping his eyes forward, he meets my gaze in the reflection of the silver doors. "Laugh it up, *Carson*, because once we're inside, you're going down, and by down, I mean wet and ready."

"*Sooo* dirty. You must've really missed me or my body." The doors open, and I walk off first, ready for this wetness he speaks so confidently about. Looking back over my shoulder, I wink. "C'mon, Fellowes. Don't keep me waiting."

His eyes are intense, directed at me. "Waiting?" My ass is slapped when he passes me. "Begging is more like it."

Quick-stepping behind him, I laugh again. "Begging? I don't think so."

"I know so. I'm going to have you wet and begging before midnight."

"Wanna bet?" I finally catch up with him and then jump in his path. I've thrown the baited hook in front of him. Now I wait for him to bite.

With the suitcase pulled next to him, his stance is relaxed but strong and comfortable in his own skin. His gaze dips to my feet and slowly glides back up, making sure I feel the heat of intensity with every inch he covers. Damn, he's hot. "What's the wager?"

He loves a challenge. What he doesn't realize is I do too. But I don't want to play games when it comes to him. My feelings are too strong to restrain for much longer. "My heart. Winner takes all."

His expression softens, and he presses his hand to my cheek. I tilt into it. "I wagered mine a long time ago, sweetheart."

"What happened to it?"

"I'll let you know." Pivoting, he pulls the keycard from his pocket and waves it in front of the lock. The door opens, and he says, "Home sweet home."

There's music playing when we walk in, and the blinds open automatically, revealing the view of the pool ten stories down and the Hollywood sign in the distance. Though the hotel is on a busy street, we're located on a quiet side. It's fancier than any apartment I've ever seen, but it's a hotel room. *Home sweet home.* "Incredible."

He drops his keys and wallet on the coffee table as though he's home. "I'm glad you like it." When he returns from putting my suitcase in the bedroom, he says, "The fridge is over there if you need anything, and the basket on top has some snacks."

"Thanks." Standing in front of what feels like all of LA, I stare into the inky night and watch the twinkling lights of the city.

His presence is felt before the heat of his body behind me. My hair is swept to the side, and he kisses my neck so lightly I'm not sure he did until he does it again with more pressure. This time, he wants me to know he's been there. That's going to leave a mark. I don't mind and will cherish the souvenir once I'm back in Austin.

I angle my head toward my shoulder as his breath warms my cheek. "You're here. You came for me."

"I did. Instead of telling you how much I missed you, I want to show you."

He takes hold of my hips and turns me around while his arms move to encircle my middle. "How do you plan to do that, sunshine?"

"By not getting out of that bed in the other room until it's time to leave for the airport." I wrap my arms around his neck. "What are your plans for the next two days?"

"You. Twenty-four seven."

I'm nodding before he even finishes. "Didn't you say something about wet and begging?"

A smirk that makes me want to drop my pants right here appears. "I did."

"Then what are we waiting for?"

Though his hands stay firmly wrapped around me, he

cringes. "I wanted to say sorry about stealing the name. I'm kind of partial to it, though."

"*It* or me?"

"You." My back is pressed to the expansive wall of glass, and my ass grabbed. "Have you ever had sex against a window where it feels like the whole world can watch as you fall apart?"

My belly clenches as warmth spreads between my legs. "No." I try to ignore how breathy I sound and focus on how good his hands feel on my backside.

I'm slowly turned back around, and he says, "Lights out." The room goes dark from his voice command, and the two of us are facing the world and all the little lights outside. "Stand right here, okay?"

I bite my lower lip, but I don't move as his fingers undo the top of my jeans, and he pulls them down. I step out of my flats and then out of my jeans. He remains kneeling behind me. I close my eyes as my body comes alive for him.

The backs of my knees are kissed.

My thighs.

The underside of my ass and a little bite that makes me laugh. Wherever his hot hands touch, his lips follow shortly after until he's standing again and lifting my shirt over my head.

I watch him in the reflection of the window where there's just enough light to see his eyes drinking me in. Reaching behind me, I hold him by the back of the neck while he kisses mine. His gaze slides up and meets mine again as his hands unhook my bra. "Do you trust me, Meadow Soleil?"

I do. "I trust you." My instincts read him like an open book, so I do trust this man. It's only a second before I'm spun back around. "You're mine. Only mine. I don't want to share you with the world outside."

Leading me into the bedroom, he strips for me. It's quick, and there's no great flair to it. Just a man being masculine and sexy by the way he tugs his shirt off by grabbing it over his shoulders to stepping out of his jeans as if the denim still wants to cling to his muscles to wearing those half briefs, half boxer shorts in all black that highlights the bad side of this bad boy. Jesus, he's fit.

He comes to me without a word exchanged, takes down my thong, and tossing it on his jeans. "Saving those for later."

"You're stealing my panties, so I can only assume you're going to have your dastardly way with me next?"

"Don't talk. Don't think." His fingers slip between my legs, and my head falls forward on his shoulder. "Just feel. Just enjoy."

Dropping to his knees in front of me, he begins to eat his prey. It's an aphrodisiac to watch him devour me as if I'm the most delectable thing he's ever tasted.

My body has missed the possessive touch of his hands, the determined tongue that strokes me into submission, and the way he makes my body sing just for him. The blissful torture is fast because it feels too good to last. But before I fall apart in his hands, I'm moved to the bed, and he's thrusting inside me, reaching his own peak, so we fall together into the beautiful abyss.

⸻

"Field Fellowes, huh?" I ask just after three thirty. We seem to have our best conversations in the wee hours of the morning or at least some of our most memorable.

I don't know what woke me up, or him, but here we are lying in the dark in front of the massive living room window of this big rock star-size suite. All the couch cushions are beneath us and the blankets make a nice pallet on top.

The best part is lying here with Dave and having the whole world at our feet. "You were on my mind, and I was put on the spot. I needed a name in a hurry, and Meadow was all that came to mind. I opted for the male counterpart."

"I'd like to be mad at you, but it's creative, and you're pretty damn cute, so I'll let the single white female aspect go and focus on the flattery."

Slipping his arm under my neck, he wraps it around my shoulders and rolls me his way. I find his physical strength so damn sexy. Not that I'm heavy, but I have been eating like a queen since arriving, the remains of another meal on a cart by the door.

I rub my hand over my stomach, well aware of the food baby I'm modeling but too stuffed to care. His hand finds mine, and he brings it to his mouth, kissing each of my knuckles. "I wish you could stay."

"I do too." Allowing myself to dream of a life with him, I say, "We could stay in bed all day, and you could play music for me at night. We'd order food in and never have to leave each other again."

The back of his hand grazes over my cheek until a finger finds my lip and runs the length once and then back. I don't know why my breath deepens and my heart races, or why my lips part and my chest aches. I just know that when I look at him, I feel funny inside. Words that have never been said in a certain context start gathering on the tip of my tongue ready to topple out.

I'm careful, though, so careful and not sure how to proceed. Closing my mouth, I swallow the words, letting them find their way back where they belong.

His eyes close, and his breath comes in a puff of relief, making me see that I made the right decision.

"They knew you at the front desk, recognized you, not as Ridge from The Crow Brothers, but as Mr. Fellowes who has a regular suite here. Is this your bachelor pad, where you used to bring the ladies you didn't want to bring around our friends?"

Rolling his head to the side, that roguish grin is in full effect. *Damn him.* I wiggle my thighs together like a damn cricket and attempt to look away, but my willpower has gone kaput under his sexy gaze. "I never had ladies I brought anywhere. I have you, the only woman who makes me feel I have enough even when you're not here."

"You don't have to lie to me. I won't run for the airport or freak out. You can tell me the truth."

"I just did. Don't let your imagination run to places that aren't real."

Not sure if he can see, but he's made me happy. Once again, I'm reminded of his drunken promise. *I'm going to make you the happiest woman in the universe.* "You win, Dave."

"It was easy. All I had to do was get you wet."

He's shown me how much he cares for me. Many times over. But my emotions are muddled again, conflicted between this heaven and my other responsibilities. Trying to save this feeling to carry with me always, I snuggle against him and close my eyes, hoping everything is always this good. But even I know that would be a lie. Just like families, there are no perfect love stories.

I have to tell him. "I got a job offer."

His hold on me tightens. "It's only November."

"Yeah. It came as a surprise to me too, but they want an answer soon."

His heart pounds heavy in his chest, his body hard with tension. "What will you say?"

Lifting my chin, I rest it on him, wanting to see his face. "Don't you want to hear about it?"

"Of course, I do. But ultimately, what you think is all that matters. You're incredible and intelligent. They'd be lucky to have you. How do you feel about the opportunity?"

"I'm not sure. It was sprung on me, and as you said, it's only November."

"You have my support if it's something you want, doing what you enjoy."

"I want your input."

"Okay," he says, exhaling. "Where is it?"

"Austin."

"No."

The response earns him a little laugh, but he's not laughing. "Just no?"

"You wanted my input. I want you here. Not there. Told you I'm selfish."

I rest my head back down, listening to the sound of his steady heartbeat. "I'm going to say no."

"Why?" His warm hand slides up my back and down again as if he's unaware he's doing it.

"Because I can't commit to June before we've even reached Christmas."

"Make sure you decide based on what's best for you."

When I wanted his input, I didn't realize how much hearing it would mean to me. *You're incredible and intelligent. They'd be lucky to have you.* He isn't only confirming that whatever I'll choose, he'll be there, he's also validating us, and that's everything.

I nod and then shift, turning away from him, wanting to be held. When his arm comes over me, and I'm buried in the nook of his body, I say, "Thank you."

"For what?" *For being amazing and supporting me unconditionally.*

"For listening, but also for letting me work through it." I feel at peace, so it's easy to snuggle in and relax. This man is good for me. "Good night, Dave."

His breath covers my shoulder and then his lips. One kiss. Two. Then he whispers, "Good night, Meadow."

30

Ridge

"Hey."

The sound of that sweet melody leads me to Meadow. Innocence I wish the world still had is found in her green eyes. I ask, "How long have you been awake?"

"I just woke up, but I called your name, and you didn't hear me. Lost in thought?"

Running my hand through my hair, I glance back at the city before I try to shake myself out of the sorrow of my thoughts. "Yeah. Sorry."

"You don't have to apologize. Are you all right?"

"Don't worry about me. You have enough of your own."

"You're my boyfriend, Dave. Of course, I worry about you."

"I wish you wouldn't."

"I like thinking about you, but you know what I like more? Talking to you and when you're talking to me."

"I like talking with you as well. I know I'm not saying anything new, but I wish you went to school here."

"When I'm here, I'm all here, so maybe it's just me, but I'm glad we don't have to divide our time. As much as I miss you, you see how busy I am when you visit. I feel bad when I have to study and you're left alone on the couch."

"I don't. I can play my guitar and watch you for hours."

"Now that you say it," she says, batting those long lashes at me, "I like you anyway I can get you."

I squat down next to the pallet where I've lain with her, loved her, and held her for hours. "This bed would have been the best I could have given you two years ago. Now I've locked my Rapunzel away in this castle, wanting to keep you all to myself. Your friends must hate me."

"Darcy doesn't complain since she's in England. As for others, Stella was the one I used to hang out with. My other relationships have just sort of faded away over the years. They're focusing on school like I am or caught up in their boyfriends . . . *like me*." Her eyes shift to mine. "I can't really tell people about us, so I've learned to not open up at all."

"We're not a dirty secret."

Sitting up, she wraps her arms around her knees. "I know. But as you know already, I have trust issues. So it's just easier for me to keep my circle smaller, but I'm not missing out on anything if that's what you're thinking. All anyone seems to do is go to parties, get wasted, and hook up with each other."

I've dealt with my fair share of drunken college kids while playing down on Sixth Street. "Yeah, probably best to keep that circle small." I crack half a smirk.

"I'm feeling that may not be genuine, but I get it." She laughs. "Anyway, if you're worried about me, don't be. I like it here with you."

Never wanting her to regret anything, I say, "If you want to go to parties, you can."

"I know. Just like you can. You can also talk to me about

your shows. You never seem to say much. How was Australia and New Zealand?"

"It was awesome. Seeing fans halfway across the world love our songs was incredible. But, I get up there, I perform, and I walk off. As much fun as I have up on that stage, it's the music I still connect with. I can do that anywhere." A heavy breath gets the better of me. "I used to dream of traveling. I've been everywhere, but I'm happier being here with you."

"Do you wish you could just play without touring?"

"No, I like playing for an audience. There's an energy I can't get in a studio. But the road wears on you after a while. Even if you're traveling first class."

"First class? You mean private." She clicks her tongue as she winks.

"Both are nice, but they're not you."

Getting to her knees, she looks at me for answers of a different kind. "So what you're saying is that you care about me?"

"I more than care about you."

"I love you."

Lightning strikes, reviving my heart and making it race. I drop to my knees in front of her and hold her face. "You love me?"

The smallest of nods is followed by the softest of answers, "I do. I love you." Tears fill her eyes as her heart bleeds for me.

Kissing one cheek, tasting her tears, and then the other, I kiss her all over and then her lips to which I whisper, "I love you, Meadow Soleil. I love you so much that it hurts when you go away. It hurts to talk to you with miles and states keeping us apart. It hurts so much that I closed off my heart, trying to protect it from the ache that only exists in your absence." I kiss her chin and that tiny little dimple at the top of her cheek. "I love you. I love you."

"I love you."

———

The soundtrack to *Magnolia* fills the suite just loud enough for it to waft into the bathroom. "Save Me" plays, fitting our day. I sit on the edge of the tub, next to where her feet are propped up. Rubbing the side of her ankle, I watch her as she watches me.

Messy hair stacked on top of her head allows me the privilege of seeing that beautiful swan-like curve of her neck, her shoulders glistening from the heat of the water as she soaks.

Wiping my hand down a towel, I return to the neck of my guitar and strum along to the song. The notes are simple, the rhythm easy to follow, but I like the beat.

She sets her glass down and takes her hair down. Dipping under the water, she comes up, her pretty face clean of makeup and smiling. Sparkles in her eyes that love makes shine like stars. "Come in," she says, sitting up and running her wet hand along my dry thigh.

"How badly do you want me?" I sing.

She sings to me, "Badly because we're meant to be."

I set the guitar down and slip right inside, sending water splashing over the edge of the large tub. Her laughter fades when I tug her onto my lap. Sitting high on top of me, my gorgeously soaking wet goddess smooths my hair back while staring into my eyes, and asks, "Why do you love me?"

I chuckle. I should have known it was coming. *Let's discuss our feelings.* Women love that. For her, I'll not only tell her because she asked, but because she's given me so much, opened herself like a flower blooming for me. The woman who feared intimacy is sharing herself with me. "Because you're hot."

The whack is fast, but it doesn't hurt. I still play it up, though. "Ow, my shoulder. Careful, slugger. I have to make a living with this arm, you know."

"Don't tease. Tell me."

I angle her slick body into my arms and hold her so she's warm under the water. "I did tell you, but that was just my first thought when I saw you."

"What was your second?"

"That I wanted to fuck you."

She's too slow this time. I block the shot with my forearm. "You're terrible, Dave Carson. You know that? Just awful."

"Awfully cute," I reply with a wink.

She rolls her eyes and smiles. Resting her back on the side of the tub, she clearly wants a better answer by the way she's staring at me. So I give her my best, like she deserves. "Because you gave me something you've never given anyone else."

"What's that?"

"Your heart."

I could give the hot bath the credit, but I prefer to take it for causing the heat to reach her cheeks. Leaning her head back, she says, "Sometimes I think you got me while I was young, too naïve to know what I'm missing."

"You're not missing anything out there but a bunch of heartache. Your best bet is sticking with me, baby."

"I like you sticky." She's incredibly cute, and I love that, but I think she needs me to affirm her. To show her that I see her, and what I see I love. Her parents were so fucking wrong, and I need her to know my heart is hers, now and forever.

"I love you because you might hide your fears, but your

heart is still open. I love you because when I've had a bad day, hearing your voice makes it better. But most of all, I love you because I don't have to prove myself to you. You've given me yourself and loving you is the best thing I'll ever do, Meadow Soleil. Your heart, your trust, and your support are everything to me."

Her lips are parted, her breath deepening has her hand covers her chest. "That's the most beautiful thing anyone's ever said to me."

"It shouldn't be." I could go on and on about what I love about her.

I love her because for the first time in my life, I have someone worth fighting for.

"It is," she says, smiling gently. The heat of her hand warms my cheeks as she gazes at me with watery eyes. "My heart is in your hands." Easily slipping around on my lap, she straddles me again and wraps her arms around my neck. "Don't hurt me, okay?"

"Never, but I'm asking the same of you."

"You're too tough to be hurt."

"I'm too tough to be hurt by anyone but you."

I love her for always seeing me as Dave, the same guy I was before the fame, and the same guy I get to be when we're together. "You're the only one who can do damage that can't be undone. Protect my heart like your own."

While I rest my head back, she leans down and kisses me. "I promise. And I always keep my promises."

The woman I'm madly in love with is in love with me.

I love her bravery, her strength, her passion for life.

Life is more than good. *Life is grand.*

"My mom has cancer."

The sheets rustle, the only sound in the room when Meadow turns to face me in bed. We left the curtains open, so I can see my sleeping goddess in the moonlight.

I wait for her to say something, but I think she's waiting for me, so I continue to ramble, "This is new. Talking about it with you. I . . . *uh*. I was thinking our time together couldn't be touched by tragedy if I kept it out of our conversations, our visits, our space. But it's here, inside me, stuck to my ribs and creeping through my chest when I don't give it the attention it demands. My mind is always partially there, which is a disservice to you and this time together I was trying to protect."

"I'm sorry." She touches me on the shoulder and moves closer.

"People say that, but no one's sorrier than I am. She gave me my first guitar after I took lessons as an elective. My dad said it was a waste of money since it wouldn't lead me to a 'real' career." I laugh without humor.

"He must be proud of you now."

"I was supposed to take over the law firm."

"Your dad's a lawyer?"

"It was his dream for me to follow in his footsteps. I had to work in the mailroom during the summer in middle school and high school until my junior year."

"What happened then?"

"I joined my first band, and we weren't half bad. Booked gigs, which was a good thing since he refused to give me spending money. Back then The Crow Brothers were making their own name. We'd run into each other around town and even did a few shows on a Texas tour once."

She smiles. She always does when she hears stories about them. It's like the five years the Fellowes sisters were out of the picture, they still weren't far. Family. Time and distance don't erase a bond.

"About your mom, what options are there?"

"My cousin is helping her decide on treatments. She's leaning toward surgery."

I didn't realize how much I was holding in until I shared. After asking questions that show her honest interest, she waits patiently as I gather the words, attempting to unlock the pain a little and allow her to hold it with me.

"I don't know much about treatments or what happens, but I'll help however I can. I'm in Austin when you're not. If I can do anything—"

"I'll let you know."

"You're not going through this alone now, Dave. I'm here. I'm always here." God, her words bring more comfort to my soul than I knew I needed. I'm already in love with her, but I feel her love so boldly without her saying the words.

Girlfriend almost doesn't seem enough for what she means to me. I touch her because she's too goddamn beautiful not to. The skin behind her ear is her most ticklish, so I touch there just to see her smile again. She asks, "You never talk about that band and avoid any questions about it. Why?"

"Because my best friend slept with my girlfriend and then beat up his girlfriend when she got mad."

Her thoughts cloud her eyes, and she looks away. "That's Hannah, right? The girlfriend he beat up?"

I nod, not sure what else to say. Feels like it's all been said before.

Tipping her head back, she kisses me under my chin. "You're one of the good guys, Dave."

"If I'm so good, why is this happening to my mom? I'd trade my life for my mom's."

"She'd trade hers for you."

"She would. I had a good childhood. My dad can be an

asshole. He's a lawyer, after all, so he likes to argue his point into the ground. I learned at a young age to let him and to just keep my opinions to myself."

"Don't," she says, kissing the edge of my jaw. "I want to hear you. I want to know how you feel and what you think. Don't ever stay quiet with me."

She's offering me something that only my mother and then Hannah have given me. Giving me a safe place to vent my troubles, lay my burdens, and ease my mind. Hannah's life is so full, I don't dare bring my worries into her world. She doesn't need more piled on.

My mom . . . It didn't matter what I did as long as I was happy. I could sit with her and have coffee, tell her how hard I was struggling, but she'd point out the light in my eyes— that spark of passion—that I was still pursuing my dreams. I'd leave the coffee shop more motivated than ever to keep going, keep pushing, and to make it work. Her slipping me money wasn't bad either.

I can't tell her that she's the one I'm worried about. She knows and doesn't need to think about me worrying about her.

Looking at Meadow, I realize what she's offering me even if she doesn't. She's giving me the haven, a safe place to share the fears and concerns I keep buried inside. She's giving me more than her heart. She's giving me something so real: deep and true love.

I happily give her the same.

She's also charming me with her sweetness. "Same goes for you, sunshine." I bring her onto me, wanting to feel her body on top of mine. This isn't about sex. It's about the intimacy she's giving and the physical closeness I need. I stroke my hand over her bare back and lower, and then wrap her in my arms, holding her to me so I can feel her breath against my skin. "So now you know."

"Thank you for sharing with me."

"I was thinking I could take you to meet her and my dad next time I'm in Austin."

When I feel her smile against my chest, I know she's accepting all of me instead of just a piece of my life. "I'd like that."

———

I shush the room service guy when he pushes the tray inside the suite. Even though I shut the bedroom door, I don't want to risk waking her. Meadow needs the rest before she returns to Austin. I know for a fact she stays up to not only study but also to talk to me. I owe her a few Z's.

As soon as he's gone, I hear, "What are you up to, rock star?"

"Hungry, cherry cheeks?" And there they are, matching the blush at the base of her neck. "Nice shirt."

She tugs it away from her chest and looks down. "This old thing. Eh, I found it lying around in the bedroom." Coming toward me, she asks, "Hope you don't mind?"

"Mind? I prefer." I kiss her on the cheek as she tries to look around me at the table of goodies.

"Wow. Did you leave any food for the other guests?"

"No. What can I get you?"

Her hand slips under the hem of the shirt, lifting it up. "You're fattening me up. Are you planning to eat me later?" As soon as the question is asked, she laughs. "I didn't mean that way, but," she says, winking, "I'm happy to oblige if you're hungry. Again."

"I'm always hungry for you."

She lifts a lid to find a BLT and french fries. Mac and cheese is under another silver dome. Pecan pie and chocolate mousse are on smaller plates next to a big bowl of strawberries, blueberries, and grapes. The food all looks good and smells even better. "Considering it's midnight, I figured we've worked up quite the appetite, so I went with comfort food."

"As soon as I get back to Austin, I have to start running again."

"The hotel has a great gym. We can work out together when you're here if you want."

Running a finger under my jaw, she says, "I want. Right after I eat that mac and cheese."

As impressive as this spread is, it's not the food that gives her that faraway, star-struck look in her eyes. It's the hot tea. "It's Yogi bedtime just like you drink at home."

"How did you remember I liked that brand?"

"It has the quotes. I know you like the tea, but I told the concierge about the quotes. They did a little digging, and here it is."

She takes a sip and closes her eyes. "Does money buy you everything you can dream?"

"My mom used to tell me that dreams are free."

"I like hearing about your mom and your life before . . ." She pokes me in the side. "Before me."

"You really don't care about the fame, do you?"

"No. Enough people in the world want to be famous. I don't want to spend my life making sure the world never forgets me. I just hope that one day when I pass that I have family and friends who want to remember me."

"That's love."

"I'm feeling mushy." Lifting her foot, she rubs it against me where our legs are tangled together in the middle of the couch. "You caught me at a good hour."

"Midnight. It's the hour that Meadow Soleil Fellowes gets sentimental on me. I'll make sure to remember that."

"There are other things I want to do on you, but I think I'll start by feeding you this mac and cheese."

"I'm all yours."

"You already were, rock star."

"Good point. Feed me, woman, and then let me feast."

I shouldn't find her eye-rolls so amusing, but I do. She gives me an epic one as she gets up to straddle me, rubbing herself where I'll grow the most. "You're insatiable."

Grabbing her by the ass, I hold her down and grind myself against her. When she moans the sexiest little moan I've ever heard, I say, "Turnabout's fair play."

"Touché, Mr. Fellowes."

"You're never going to let me live that down, are you?"

"Never. It's too fun to tease."

Flipping her onto her back, I settle between her legs. "Speaking of teasing, wanna fuck?"

"You're so romantic." She pushes off me and walks toward the bedroom, leaving the shirt on the floor behind her. "You gonna keep me waiting?"

I run and lift her over my shoulder. "Not another damn second."

31

Meadow

SNEAKING out from under his arm this morning is tricky. But considering we were up late and active, he's too worn out to notice when I kiss his head and leave. He sleeps so soundly that I wonder if he always does or just when I'm around.

It's dark outside, but I stumble sleepy, and sad that I'm leaving, to the waiting car he hired to drive me to the airport in style. My sister's going to kill me that I didn't stop by and at least say hi, but maybe she'll understand since I was here less than thirty-six hours.

The gate is getting fuller by the hour, but I manage to find a spot with open seats on either side. The chair is not comfortable enough to sleep in, so I sit and stare down at a photo I took of Dave last night. He didn't know or maybe he's just gotten good at pretending people aren't snapping pics of him all the time.

My heart beats a little faster just looking at him. He's mine. All mine. And I'm his, only his, happily his girlfriend. In my peripheral vision, I spy a man in a ball cap sitting in the seat to my right. I curl in on myself to protect the photo from being seen by outsiders.

But the nosy bastard presses into my space. "Who's that?" he asks.

That voice—deep, a cadence my body knows by heart— mine. He's all mine. Peeking over and playing along, I reply, "My boyfriend."

"He's a lucky guy."

"No," I say, nudging his arm off the armrest between us before looking him straight in the eyes. "I'm the lucky one." It has to be the hour and the fact I'm exhausted because it's not normal to tear up just because my hot boyfriend shows up at the airport, right? "What are you doing here?"

"I have to tell you something."

Wow, must be important. I sit a little straighter, suddenly a little worried. "What?"

"I love you."

And I die, my heart feeling as though it's too big for my chest to contain. Screw it. The tears fall, and I lower my head to his shoulder. He didn't need to come here and tell me that. I know he loves me, and my heart couldn't be more happy. But he gave up precious sleep to be here with me. For me. *How did I get so lucky?* "I love you, too. I was just sitting here staring at your photo like some pathetic, love-sick puppy."

He doesn't mock me, but he does chuckle. "Welcome to my world." An arm comes around my neck and he pulls me to him and kisses my head. When I sit up, he continues, "The bed was empty, and the room was cold. I looked for you, but you were already gone. I may not want to say bye to you, but if I have to, I want to make sure it's a good one."

"Dave?"

"Yeah?"

"How are you sitting here at the gate with me? Only

people with tic—" My eyes go wide. "Did you buy a ticket on my flight just to come see me?"

"No. Your flight is sold out." His hand, big and comforting and rough in all the right ways, slips around mine. "I bought a ticket to Cincinnati at noon."

"I'm sure it's a lovely city."

"I hear they have a great zoo."

I love how much we laugh together. "Let me know how it is."

"I'm afraid I won't be catching that flight." Resting forward on his knees, he looks back at me. "The truth is, I didn't want you getting on a plane without seeing you once more to tell you that I love you."

"You're going to make me cry again."

"Then I'll hold you as long you want. Forever even."

I get up and settle on his lap sideways so I can look at him. "I might need longer."

"You got it."

Nestling against him, I say, "This might be the most romantic thing anyone has ever done for me."

"Might be? If this only earns me a 'might be,' then I'll have to try harder."

"You don't have to try at all. It seems to come natural to you, like playing your guitar."

"I prefer you over my guitar any day, and you know how much I love playing guitar."

"Wow. Looks like I'm on a roll."

The announcement to board interrupts us, so I squeeze him as tight as I can because I don't want to say bye. There's nothing good about leaving this man. "When I see you in three weeks," he says, "you're all mine again."

"I promise. At least until the turkey's served."

We stand. "That's fair." Holding me in his arms, I feel the tension creeping into his muscles. He kisses my head. I don't have the strength to let him go, but he's stronger than I am. I knew if I ever fell for him, I'd be the weaker of the two of us. "Don't say goodbye, okay?"

"See you at Thanksgiving." He steps back and adjusts the straps of my backpack. With my ticket in hand, I start to walk away, but he says, "Wait. I brought you something."

"What is it?"

He pulls his hand from his pocket, a gold chain wrapped around his fingers. "Just a token. I found it in Australia." When he opens his hand, a little cherry pendant dangles against his palm.

I move into his shadow, feeling so much in this space. "It's beautiful." Turning around, I ask, "Will you put on me?"

His arms go wide with an end of the necklace in each hand. He tries several times, swearing under his breath. "Damn clasp is so fucking small." I offer to help, but he mumbles, "I'm a guitarist, for fuck's sake. I can do this."

When he gets it, he smiles like a champ. I turn to show him how it looks on me and lift for a quick kiss. "You're my hero."

"Fuck that little clasp."

Sliding the cherries along the gold chain, I look down to see the pendant and smile so much just knowing he bought this with me in mind. He says, "The leaves remind me of your eyes, and the cherries remind me of your cheeks."

"I love it, but I love that you thought of me when you saw it more." I slide the pendant back and forth and then feel a lump in my throat form. I can't extend the goodbye. It already hurts too much. "See you at Thanksgiving."

I turn to the sound of silence, thinking that same lump has formed in his throat as well. Looking back once, I see him standing there with his hands in his pockets, the bill of his hat pulled down low, and his eyes on me.

He doesn't see the few cameras nearby aimed at him, but I do, realizing how much he's willing to sacrifice—his privacy, a piece of his life—to be here for me. I walk down the jet bridge and find my seat. *Three weeks. I can do that.*

Straightening my skirt, I look at Dave for reassurance. He's always good to me. Taking my hand, he says, "They're going to love you."

The time apart flew by because we talked every spare minute we had. I don't even feel like we've spent time apart. From our hours of video calls to long conversations while we lay in bed about everything from the weather to dreaming about what the future holds, to becoming so comfortable that we could lose ourselves physically while listening to each other's voice.

My heart is fuller than it's felt in years because of the man standing by my side, now wanting to introduce me to his parents.

"Is this too much?" I ask, referring to my outfit. It was one of my faves when I lived in London—chic but not too over-the-top dressy. The black skirt gathers at the waist and ends just below my knees. My gray sweater has a sweet little Peter Pan white collar, and I'm wearing new patent leather black flats. I feel pulled together and comfortable though a little short next to Dave, which is why I usually like to wear heels around him.

He rubs his thumb over the top of my hand. "You look beautiful, like always."

Guys. They don't get it. Though I can say, he wore a button-down that looks nice on him. "I'm so used to seeing you in jeans and a tee that you look fancy in your shirt. I remember how hot you were in Hawaii when you wore those suits."

"So you're saying you don't find me sexy now?"

The door opens, and a woman with a kind smile is there. "Why are you knocking? It's your home, David."

His home. I've come to think of that hotel suite in LA as his home, even my apartment when he comes to Austin. I can't help but feel a little possessive over the term home when I hear her say that.

My hand is released, and he steps up and hugs the woman. "Good to see you, Aunt Pat."

"You too, David. Your mom's been so happy knowing you were coming for Thanksgiving." She smiles at me over her shoulder. "This must be Meadow."

When Dave steps aside, she holds her arms out for me. I walk into her welcoming embrace. "Hello."

"You're just as pretty as David said you were."

My gaze meets his over his aunt's shoulder. I mouth, "Charmer."

"Come inside," his aunt says, stepping inside the foyer of the Rollingwood neighborhood home. The house is pretty and traditional in style with white walls with dark wood floors. Lived in, but pristinely clean. It's an area of town far from where I grew up. Like the Crow brothers, we had a nice enough home but didn't have money to spend frivolously. Dave clearly grew up differently.

He takes my hand and leads me into the living room where a few people around our age are hanging out. A girl stands and rushes to hug him. His hand briefly tenses around mine before he lets go. "Hey."

They're introduced as cousins, Pat's kids. He apologizes to me for being on edge, but I tell him he owes me nothing. It must be weird to leave one day as a normal guy and then come back years later famous with more money than your parents.

In the kitchen, I see his mother for the first time. I've not seen photos but one of him when he was young, but I recognize her smile. It's the same one he has. Lisa sits at the table directing her sister, Pat, and a few others. When her hazel eyes land on me, she stands and looks at my hands, one still holding her son's. "David, you snuck in."

"I did," he says, the room coming to a stop as everyone looks at us. He leads me to her but releases me to hold her. She's so small compared to him, closer to my height, but I wonder if the medical treatments have stolen more than her energy.

She has a colorful pink, red, and navy silk scarf wrapped around her head that matches the pink of her shirt. She's dressed more casually in denim capris. Holding her son's face between her hands, she says, "You're too skinny."

"I eat like a horse."

"When you eat, you mean. I have a feeling you don't take as good of care of yourself as you should." Her eyes find me almost tucked behind him. "I bet Meadow would agree with me."

"I worry about him too."

That makes her smile, large and happy. "Thank you for watching over him." She holds her hands out to me. When I take them, she says, "It is so lovely to finally meet you."

"You too." She's so kind that my heart starts to hurt, and I feel sad because this woman, Dave's absolute supporter, is terribly ill. For so long, he grieved silently and alone. I wish when I found out I would have pushed for more, to help him, to help her, to do whatever I could for them.

But I see where his quiet strength comes from.

Patting her son on the arm, she says, "She's gorgeous. Now leave her with me, and you go say hello to your father."

I'm not sure if she's protecting me while Dave breaks the ice with his dad or if she wants me to get to know me better, but I stay. Dave gives me a wink and says, "I'll be back in a minute."

She has me sit next to her just as a colander of green beans is set down on the table. "Ever snap beans?"

We get to work, taking off the ends and chatting about my schooling. She went to the University of Texas too, though she lived in a building that's been long remodeled into something new. My gaze occasionally drifts outside to the back patio where a few men are smoking cigars. But Lisa always pulls me back in with some engaging story about her college days or Dave when he was younger.

She calls him her miracle baby. Doctors said they couldn't have a child and then one day Dave decided he would make his way into this world despite the predictions. "David is named after my father. Those two were inseparable before he died. David was only ten, but they were best friends. I think my husband was a little jealous of the bond they shared." She laughs to herself.

"I've been a chatterbox." She touches my hand. "Tell me about your family."

We chat about the wedding and Hawaii. "It was so beautiful. I could smell the flowers in the air. And my sister . . ." I can still see her in my head, never looking happier. "My sister is so beautiful with a soul to match. Rivers is wonderful. They deserve all the happiness."

"I met him last year on their tour. He was very nice." Her expression flickers to curiosity. "And your parents?"

The bean snaps in half, the sound grabbing her attention as well as mine. "Sorry," I say about the broken bean in my hand. My throat feels dry as I sit in Dave's idyllic home talking to his sweet as pie mom. "My mother remarried a few years back, so I don't see her very much."

She pauses snapping the bean ends off. "That's too bad."

Just thinking of my father upsets me. What do I say? He sold his daughters to pay a debt, and my sister saved my life while almost losing hers? *Too much too soon?* "My father lives in Austin, but Stella and I don't see him anymore. It's a complicated relationship."

"All families have those. I haven't talked to David's uncle in five years. All because he said I was too old to wear a bikini during a family trip to Galveston." She laughs, then leans forward to whisper, "Really, my husband's brother has always been an asshole. I just used the bikini comment to finally have an excuse not to hang out with him. John sees his brother by himself now, and I kick back at home with a glass of wine." She touches her scarf. "Well, I used to. I still have a glass every now and then. Tonight I'll celebrate meeting you."

We drop the last of the beans into the bowl. I say, "We made fast work of that."

Covering my hand, she says, "You made the task a lot more fun." Lisa Carson is the mother I wish I had. *Kind, supportive, funny, and quick to praise. Selfless.* So much like Louisa Crow was for me for too brief a time.

Resting her chin on her hand, she stays close to me. "Tell me how he's really doing."

I glance once more out the window to find Dave's eyes on me. He waves, so I wave back, wanting him to know I'm doing fine. "He's wonderful."

32

Meadow

Life is wonderful.

Everything is coming up roses.

All the clichés fit.

Happiness is—acing your midterms and flying to LA to see your boyfriend.

We've been boyfriend and girlfriend for five blissful months, and my life cannot get any better.

"He's more than a handsome face." I roll my eyes as if his looks are my least favorite thing about him. *They're not.* I like his face—a lot actually—but I don't want to come off like a braggart.

"That's great." The man sitting next to me on the flight points at the aisle. "I just needed to use the restroom before we landed."

"Oh, sure. Sorry." I stand and let him by, ending our chat that started with him asking me if he can squeeze by and me being reminded how Dave and I were squeezed in the back of the 4Runner in the desert. "Good times," I mumble to myself, sitting back and remembering that trip.

I want to say so much, to tell him all the feelings I've been burying for months. I don't want to spend time with anyone else but him. I don't know what's come over me. I have everything I've been working for at my fingertips. I'll be leaving in two days for a dream job. But here I am wanting to stay, to be with him.

Moving on top of him again, I hadn't realized I had stopped. The gentle grip of his hands on my hips encourage me while I stare into his eyes, memorizing how even in the moonlight, they grow darker when we're together like this.

I touch his cheek and then remind myself that I have to leave.

Pull back.

Protect yourself.

I close my eyes and let myself enjoy these last few minutes we'll have with our souls as bare as our bodies.

The flight attendant taps my shoulder. "Another champagne?"

I've had three. That's probably enough. I don't want to be drunk when I see Dave tonight, or I'll be passed out and miss all the reunion fun we have planned. "No, thank you."

We've come so far . . . I have come so far in giving him my heart, something I never thought I'd give anyone. But there's just something about him. I tighten my belt around me, my nerves calming from the thought. It's becoming easier to fly knowing I'll be in his arms again soon.

I open my e-reader and start reading my book again. I'm a sucker for a rock star romance, and then I realize I'm smack dab in the middle of one.

Happiness is Dave.

When we land, I make my way to baggage only to find a man standing with a sign that has my name on it . . . well, technically, it reads: Cliff Carson. I'm pretty sure it's meant for me, though.

My phone dings with a message that Dave had an unexpected meeting come up with Johnny Outlaw and the other guys, so he sent a car to pick me up. Stopping in front of the man with the sign, I point. "I think that's for me. My boyfriend's got jokes."

My boyfriend also still makes me squeal in delight.

***

I've been in Los Angeles all of four hours and thought Dave would be back to the suite by now. After being promised a date night out, I've been sitting dressed forever, so I text him: *What's going on? Are you on your way?*

The three dots flash on the screen before disappearing again, then a message pops up: *Soon.*

Me: *That's not a time. I've been ready for almost two hours. I'm starving.*

Dave: *That's the best I can give you, sweetheart. I'll text you when we're leaving.*

Me: *You told me you'd be here.*

Dave: *We'll talk about it later.*

Me: *I'm going out.*

Dave: *Adios.*

Me: *Rude.*

"So rude." I grab my clutch, pouting, and slip on the Louboutin shoes my sister gave me for Christmas. I never get to wear them in Austin, so I made sure to grab the tight black dress I bought for Dave and to pack the shoes. Now I'm all dressed up and have nowhere to go. I spent over an hour getting dressed, trying to look drop-dead gorgeous for him, and it hurts to feel that he's blowing me off.

I popped a bottle of champagne, and I'm two glasses in

to keep me in the mood. A lot of good that did me. Now I feel a little lightheaded, and I'm getting tired. If I stay here, I'll fall asleep, so I'll let him find me in the bar downstairs.

When I enter the bar, it's bustling—great music, a few celebs hiding in the dark corners, and dim lights that create a romantic ambiance.

I feel the weight of eyes on me as I make my way to the bar. I slip onto a barstool and order a glass of champagne. Might as well stick with a good thing. I'll charge it to the room since I've been stood up.

Another hour passes and another drink has been ordered. I laughed when I was served an endive salad that consisted of one leaf with two diced grape tomatoes and a sprig of chives set on top. I thought I should get food in my stomach, but it seems I'll have to order more.

The bartender's been great about shooing away the men who keep working their way over here to talk to me. One guy asked how much I charge. I didn't know if I should take that as a compliment or be offended, but I decided not to worry since I have bigger fish to fry. Namely, Field Fellowes.

I've been checking my phone what feels like every five minutes since we texted earlier. Nothing. I'm well past mad and have been stuck in disappointment for the past thirty minutes; the night I had planned in my head ruined.

I get it. He's busy. But I flew here to be with him. I should have gotten a call or, at the very least, a text update. It's almost eleven at night, for crying out loud. One a.m. Austin time. I'd take a smoke signal at this stage.

I'm ready to throw in the towel when I get a bright and devious idea. I finish the rest of my champagne and decide to screw around with his head like he's screwing with mine.

Me: *You around? I'm horny. I was thinking anal might be fun to try.*

I wait a few seconds, cackling from the joke. But to take

it to the next level, I don't torture myself waiting for the infamous three dots. Instead, I type: *OMG! That message wasn't meant for you.*

There. And now I wait . . .

"What the fuck is this?"

I jump, startled by the commanding tone behind me, and then swivel around on my barstool to come face to face with the man himself. "Well, well, *welllll*. Look who anal dragged out of hiding."

Dave is holding his phone toward me with my message on the screen. "What the fuck do you mean this message wasn't meant for me? Who the fuck was it meant for? And for the record, I wasn't hiding. I was working."

He's sexy when he's angry. Actually, he's always sexy, but that clenching jaw does things to my nether region. He's making it really hard to play hard to get, so I stop trying and touch his chest, though I want to hump it . . . and that mouth. *God, I love that mouth.*

I drag my fingers over his mouth and let his bottom lip rebound under my attentive gaze. His eyes start to glaze with lust, and he grabs my hand. "Meadow," he says in that hot and commanding voice. I mentally dust my hands. Job well done. Go me. "Am I in trouble, Mr. Fellowes?"

"So much trouble."

My eyes dip from his to that jaw again, and I watch with rapt attention to his impatience as it clenches.

Tic.

Tic.

Sigh.

So hot.

Popping off the stool, it's time to play the game again. I pat his chest, and reply, "I've been sitting here for hours. Alone. Long, *lonely* hours. I wanted company since my date stood me up."

"I didn't stand you up. I got held up in an important meeting. There's a difference. I couldn't just walk out because we want to have dinner. This is my career."

"But I'm your girlfriend who you made a commitment to." Wait, that sounds heavy. "Made a date with. Look." I spin for him but almost lose my balance. Damn shoes, I think the bubbles are affecting my balance. "I got dressed up for you."

"And you look incredible," he says. "Edible." Pulling his wallet from his pocket, he tosses money on the bar and nods at the bartender like they're old friends. "Close her out." Turning back to me, he leans in, his lips to my ear. "So incredible that I can't wait to see how amazing you look under this dress."

Dragging my hands over his shoulders, I whisper, "Your Ding Dong ways may have won my heart, but I've been working out." Okay, it's only been three weeks, but I don't have a food baby anymore. "And just to give you a preview . . ." I drag my hands over my waist and hips.

"You win. Let's go."

"How are you going to punish me?" I raise an eyebrow. "Do we get to have anal?"

"Goddamn it, Meadow." He adjusts his package, not even caring that everyone can see, including me.

I struggle to stop from laughing, but I've got him right where I want him. Since the hotel enforces its strict paparazzi-free zone, I lay it on heavy to wrap this up with a bow. "What? Don't be so uptight, *Ridge*." Shrugging, I say, "I thought anal would be fun."

Staring down at me, his brow is furrowed like he's looking at a crazy person. "Are you drunk?"

"Maybe. What does it matter if I am or if I'm not? You didn't care until I brought up anal."

"I care because you don't seem to care that the entire bar

can hear you right now." He eyes me from head to toe and back again. "Fuck me. You can't go out in LA looking like this. You're like a lamb—"

"A lamb? Like a lamb headed for the slaughter?" My hands anchor on my hips. "Don't keep me waiting next time. Anyway, I'm not that innocent, but it seems that talk of anal embarrasses you. So you've never done it either?"

Looking around again, he says, "You're feisty right now. Are you wanting to fight? Because despite being late, I got here as soon as I could."

"Admit it, *Field*." Poking him three times in the chest and once on the chin, right in that cute little indention, I smirk. "The anal brought you here."

"Jesus H. Christ, Meadow. Keep your voice down. I was valeting the car, for your information, so I was already here. As for the anal, what do you know about it?"

"Nothing. That's why I thought it would be fun to try."

The bartender sets the change down, but Dave leaves it, taking me by the elbow to lead me away. I did this to get him sexually wound up, but it seems I'm the horny one. Even the hefty tip he left is a turn-on. Sexy as fuck and generous. *Yes* and *please*.

Everything about him is sexy as hell right now, making me forget why I was mad at him in the first place.

"Fun to try?" he replies with widening eyes. Rubbing his left temple, he shakes his head and leans in. "You don't just do it. You have to prepare."

"Seems you know a lot more about anal than I do. And I guess you have done it, considering you know so much about anal," I say, emphasizing the last word loudly for others around us to hear.

"How about saying anal a few more times?"

I hear his sarcasm and laugh. "Anal. Anal. Anal."

"Let's get you out of here before you get us thrown out or, worse, arrested."

A lady—mid-thirties, low cut shirt, friendly smile—says, "Try the anal, honey. Just make sure he lubes you up beforehand."

"Fuck me," Dave grumbles under his breath. "What the fuck is happening?"

I drape myself on him before he has a chance to drag us away. His muscles are taut, the veins in his forearms bulging, like another part of his body. "You hear that, babe. All you have to do is lube me up good and—"

"*Annnd* we're outta here." His arm comes around my waist, and he holds me close.

Protective.

Strong.

Caring.

I feel it all when we're like this, even if a ridiculous text kicked it off. "So that's a yes to *anal?*"

A group of guys laugh when we walk by. This time my hand is taken, and we weave through the tables toward the exit. "C'mon. We can't talk here."

His anger flares like his nostrils. "Are you mad because I want anal? Or are you mad because I sent a message to another guy about trying anal?"

Cutting through the lobby, he stops just as we reach the elevators. He pushes the button and glares down at me. "First of all, if you want anal, more power to you, sweetheart. Secondly, you didn't send that message to another guy. You sent it to me, and I have no doubt it was always intended for me. So if I'm deducing this whole anal situation correctly, you want anal because you think it will be fun. I'm happy to fuck you however you want to be fucked, Meadow. But what you're not going to do is play some game to fuck around with my head." He turns to face the lobby and raises his voice, "See? I can say *anal* really loud, too."

The elevator doors slide open, and he walks inside. Crossing his arms over his chest, he stares at me. "Are you coming?" he asks. I see a smile trying to peek out.

Scurrying inside next to him, I laugh, but as soon as the doors close, I ask, "Dave?"

"What?" He glances down at me.

"Does that mean anal's off the table?"

Rolling his eyes, he chuckles. "You're ridiculous. You know that, right?"

I nod as I walk into his open arms. "The power of alcohol. Anyway, I got your attention."

"You already had it, sunshine."

33

Ridge

MEADOW IS DEFINITELY TIPSY, if not drunk.

She's wild tonight.

Feisty.

Sexy.

Fantastic.

I can't take my eyes off her, though. Like at all. First, she turned up the music, blasting our band's latest album, and then she opened the curtains in the suite. Fucking hell, I'm a lucky guy. But with her almost naked and the lights on, I'm not okay with the world watching my girl.

With only a bra and a string that doesn't cover much on her lower half, she's been dancing around the living room with a glass of champagne in hand. She's only spilled twice, which is impressive, considering some of her moves. "Do you like what you see, Davey Babe?"

Davey Babe? Okay, she's definitely drunk.

I set my beer down on the side table when she comes

over to me. Her eyes are closed, her body relaxed and swaying to an easy rhythm of a slower song. Sitting on the couch, I reach forward to hold those swaying hips and pull her a little closer. When she opens her eyes, I can see the lust swimming in them. "I like what I see."

Lifting her hair off her neck, she leans back and lets it tumble down. "I like the way you look at me."

"How's that?"

The languid roll of her head forward tells me it might be time for her to go to bed. Her hands hold my shoulders, and she straddles my lap. *Simply irresistible.* My calloused guitar-playing hands against her soft skin make me even harder than I was watching her dance for me.

"Like you believe in me."

"I do believe in you, baby."

"Why?"

"Because you can't hide from me. I see how you drink your tea with just a dash of cream. How you twist your hair up in an elastic band when you study. How when you start your car, the same Crow Bros song is always playing."

"And which one is that?" The sly tip to the corner of her lips gives her away.

"The song I wrote that has my solo."

With a casual shrug put on for me, she laughs. "Maybe I'm really into a great guitar solo."

"I'm hoping you're really just into me." I get a good grip of this great ass on my lap. "Anyway, I see how you watch me sleep, and the way you look at me."

"How do I look at you?"

"Like you love me."

"You know I love you."

Draping her arms over my shoulders, she brushes her lips against mine, but I whisper, "I know."

I turn her so her back is against the arm of the couch and lean over her. Kissing her feels different these days, like somehow she's let me in. Not just in her mouth or body, but behind the wall that used to keep me out. *God, it feels like I've been waiting forever for this. For her.*

"I want you," she says, resting her head back and looking into my eyes. With her arms tightening around my neck, her breathing deepens. "I want you inside me. I want you beside me. I want you every day."

Fuck. Yes.

But she's drunk. I pinch the bridge of my nose. *Fuck.*

I lift her into my arms and start for the bedroom. "Lights off." The lights dim until they're off, the music still filling the suite. "Music off," I add, the music fading into silence.

Not even trying to help me out, she's completely relying on me to support her weight. Since I have her here, I weight curl her a few times to pump my biceps much to her amusement and mine. I like her laughter.

When I reach the end of the bed, I could toss her but decide to set her on her feet instead. "You can use the bathroom first. I'll wait."

"You don't have to wait out here. I'm not embarrassed."

I actually don't think much would embarrass her in her inebriated state, but I don't want her to think back on this and feel it. "It's fine. I'll wait unless you need help."

"I'm good," she says, waving over her head as she heads for the bathroom. As soon as she reaches the door, she slides it until it's almost closed and peeks out. "Don't miss me too much, rock star."

"Too late."

"Charmer." The door slides closed, and I sit on the end of the bed. Looking at my hands, I wonder if they're too rough to touch such beauty. Are they worthy of the silkiness of her body? Her barriers are down, and suddenly, I'm worried I'll damage her in ways that have nothing to do with her skin.

Am I to blame for my last relationship going up in flames? Did I not care enough? Was I not attentive enough? Fuck, that's why she was on tour with us—so we could spend time together. I didn't realize until after I found out the truth that she was there to spend time with the other guy she was fucking.

When Shannon told me she'd been cheating on me, I struggled to believe it. I didn't miss the signs because there were no fucking signs. I just blindly served my heart up on a platter, and she stabbed it.

Glancing toward the bathroom, I can hear Meadow humming. She sounds happy. She looks like the worries that have weighed on her are gone. It took us a year and a half to get this point, five months into us confessing our feelings and committing to make this relationship work. Here she is in LA for me.

Me.

I deserve her.

I deserve to have someone in my life who wants me for me.

I deserve this happiness.

She loves me. I don't care if the confession came on the end of a drunk tongue or in the middle of the night when real emotions shine brightest. It was my eyes she was looking into when she spoke those three words and me who she wants to be with.

I got the girl, so why does it not feel like a victory? Why do I feel like I'm waiting for the other shoe to drop?

The door slides open, and just as I suspected, her eyelids are lower than before, and her energy is waning. I meet her halfway. Holding her by the waist, I kiss her neck and then wrap what feels like my whole body around her, never wanting to let go.

I deserve her.

Gently pushing back, she cups my face. "Hey, what's going on?"

"Nothing." I put on a smile that feels forced, the first I've ever had to put on for her. "I'm just glad you're here."

Her eyes close as her lips press to mine. Things have slowed since the living room, touches more purposeful instead of fleeting. "I'm glad I'm here too." I move around her and walk to the bathroom. She says, "Don't be too long. Okay, rock star?"

"I won't keep you waiting."

I love that beautiful smile. Closing the door, I know she'll be asleep by the time I come out. She needs it. Between the late nights studying for her midterms, to traveling, and then drinking however much she had tonight, she needs the rest. As for me, maybe I'll stay up a while.

Surprised when my headphones are lifted, I jump. "Sorry," she says, putting them down around my neck.

"It's okay. Did I wake you?"

"Yes." A small upturn comes with a side of teasing. "Because you weren't in bed." Meadow sits next to me on the couch, resting her head to the side on a cushion. "What are you doing up?"

"Couldn't sleep."

"Did you try?" The words sound harsh, but her tone is soft, a genuine curiosity filling her eyes.

"No."

She sits up and takes the guitar from me. I was playing

music in my underwear, so when the guitar is moved, she sees me, taking me in as she admires my body.

Leaning it against the side of the couch, she replaces it in my lap with an arm slung over my shoulder. I remove the headphones, and she curls to the side. With her arm pulled back and tucked against me, she fits me. *A perfect fit.* We fit together so well physically.

Lying in my arms, we both stare out the window. "Why didn't you come to bed?" she whispers.

"Too much on my mind."

"Can I ease it?"

"You are right now."

I don't have to see the grin to know it's there. I can hear it in her voice. "You give me too much credit."

"I give credit where credit is due."

"You'll be tired tomorrow if you don't get some rest." Tilting her head to the side, she looks up at me. "It's two in the morning."

"Speaking of, how are you feeling?"

"I woke up with a headache, so I took an Ibuprofen and drank the water you left me." A kiss is placed on my chest. "Thank you for taking care of me."

"Are you feeling better?"

"My head's not throbbing, but a pill and water won't replace you in bed. Do you want to try to sleep?"

"No."

"Are you awake because you're thinking about your mom? Has she had any other treatment or any changes?"

"I talked to her earlier. She's as good as she can be." A nod of her head is followed by an arm hugging me.

"Okay." She pauses, but just long enough to take a deep breath and exhale. "We exchanged numbers when you took me home for Thanksgiving."

My mom didn't say anything, but it doesn't surprise me. She's very fond of Meadow.

"I'm so glad you took me to meet her, Dave. She's amazing."

"She is."

"We've texted a few times just to say hi. She wants to get coffee soon."

"She's a good woman, like you. I like the thought of you getting together. My mom doesn't tell me as much as I want to know. She thinks she's protecting me."

"She probably is. What an incredible gift that is."

My mind riffles through her words, trying to understand, and when I do, my heart hurts for her. She doesn't have a mother or a father who would protect her. I rub her skin, wanting to take away any pain she feels inside. "My mom is only one of many reasons I'm awake. Sometimes, I just struggle to stop the brain from thinking. So I grab my guitar and play."

"And then often write amazing songs with incredible solos."

I chuckle. She's good for my soul. "Thank you, sunshine." She shifts on my lap, and I'm not sure if she's going to leave or if she's getting more comfortable until she stays. "Talk to me. I want to hear your voice." Angled sideways, her cheek rests on my chest with an arm over my middle. The heat from our bodies being pressed together tempts me to take her to the bedroom. She gets me hard with a look, but when she touches me, I get anxious to fuck—side effect to being with the girl of your fantasies.

"When I was a teen, my mom was popping in and out of my life like she still cared. She'd lecture my dad on how to raise me, but the next day, she'd disappear. Every time she did that, it was like resetting the hands of pain on his shattered heart. He hated her. He loved her. He couldn't decide.

Mentally, I decided for him. She wasn't worth his time. Eventually, he wasn't worth mine."

She takes a breath, and her head shifts so she can see out the window again while she continues, "I tried for a while. I did anything to get his attention. I was so desperate for any attention, so much that I used to try to get away with stuff without anyone finding out, like sneaking out when I was a sophomore to meet senior boys after curfew."

I'm not jealous of kids from high school, but I fucking hate that she was doing that to get attention. She should have had it from her parents all along. "Did you ever get caught?"

"One night, I realized I didn't have to sneak. I could walk right out the front door because my father was too drunk to notice whether I was home. That was at the same time my mother lost her phone while traveling for almost a year."

Fucking hell. "She didn't call you for a year?"

"No, but she posted a lot of selfies that year, and when asked, she claims it was her boyfriend's phone."

"Was she lying?"

"You can see her pink phone case reflected in the sunglasses in the photos. So yeah."

"Why would she lie?"

"Because her now husband wanted her to himself."

"Where was your sister?"

"Stella was living on her own, post breakup from Rivers at the time, going to school and trying to keep her life from falling apart even more while trying to be there for me when she could."

"You haven't told anybody any of this, have you?"

"I inherited Stella's talent for putting on a pretty face and pretending everything is okay." She looks up at me and traces my jaw with her fingertip. "Unfortunately, you've had to pay the price for so long."

"The wait was worth it because I got you. You're not the

same person who used to hide your feelings. You speak your truth. Don't ever change." She can't get any closer. She's right on top of me, almost all of her touching me, but she seems to try.

"Why are you so sad, babe?"

"I'm tired. We should go to bed."

"I don't want to go to bed. I don't want you upset." Angling my chin toward her, she says, "Talk to me. Please."

I've kept this inside for so long that maybe she's right. Maybe if I tell her, it will release me from carrying this around on my own. "My mom's decided to undergo surgery. The woman who did everything for everyone else has been abandoned by most of her friends when she needs them most. I can't be there as much as she wants me to, as much as I should be."

"From the short time I've known her, I know she'd *understand* why you can't be there physically."

"She shouldn't have to. The guys backed me, willing to ditch the date." I exhale a shuddery breath. "But the venue threatened to sue if we're not there."

"She's so proud of you. She'd never want you to jeopardize what you've worked so hard for. I think you should talk to her, tell her everything you're telling me now. She'll understand. She loves you more than anything."

Meadow means well, and I know she felt the loss of Louisa's death like a daughter, but she doesn't get this. No one really gets this. *Unless they've gone through the long, frustrating hours, months, waiting for something positive. Waiting for the fucking cancer to go the fuck away.* So, I don't find the gratification I was hoping for.

Her heart's in the right place, so I can't be angry with Meadow, but I can fucking hate the cancer for trying to steal my mom away. "I think I'm tired enough to sleep now." I set her on the couch and get up.

"Hey, Dave?"

Stopping before I enter the bedroom, I look back over my shoulder. She says, "You can tell me anything. I'll always be your haven."

I acknowledge her with a nod and then enter the bedroom. She quietly follows me, and when I climb under the covers, she slides in next to me, onto my outstretched arm. I kiss her head, and say, "Night."

"Night."

34

Meadow

BRIGHT STARS DOT the clear blue night sky, and the moon is so big and bright that I can't take my eyes off the stunning sight. I ask, "How much did you spend on that sky and perfect weather?"

Dave chuckles. "It's Hollywood. Anything is possible." I take a sip of wine just as he says, "You look pretty."

"Why thank you, kind sir." I run my hand down his chest. The surprise birthday party for Holli is in full swing on the large patio of The Outlaws' LA home. LA, as in they own more than one home in the world. "You're not too shabs yourself." My glass is empty, so I turn my attention to the party inside the large house where Dave has gone for another round.

There's no hiding with all the little globe lights hanging from the trees. A party of musical legends and legends in the making fill the premises. Candles flicker in lanterns and classic rock drifts through the light breeze. When he returns, I say, "The party is amazing." He takes my empty glass in one hand and hands me a full glass of white wine with the other. "Are you trying to get me drunk?"

"I don't have to try. You do a fine job all by yourself." He laughs.

"You're a funny guy," I tease right back.

Stepping so close to him that I can smell the soap I lathered on his body earlier, he stands to his full height before me, causing a delicious shiver to course through my body.

I love our size difference. I feel safe with him, though not just physically. Toying with the gray button on his dress shirt, I keep my eyes on it, but ask, "Dave?"

"Yeah?"

"How long do you want to stay?"

An arm slinks around my waist, and he pulls me close. "You want to have your wicked way with me? Damn, girl, you can't keep your hands off me."

"If your ego wasn't taking up so much space, you'd get to feel how handsy I can be, and then you'd be ready to go too."

"*My* ego?" He laughs. "I've let you call the shots since day one of this relationship. How about you hand over the keys and let me drive for a while?"

I lift on the balls of my feet and kiss him. His hand presses to my lower back, and his head tilts to the side to take it deeper.

Our lips part and our tongues meet—warm, firm with need, possessive.

"See? I can give up contr—"

"Ew." We both stop to find Alfie staring at us.

Shaking my head, I take a step away from Dave though my whole body feels that kiss still racing through my veins. "It's not ew. Anyway, what are you doing out here spying on us, kid?"

"My dad told me to find Uncle Ridge."

Sighing, I say, "Guess you should find him."

"Come with me." He holds out his hand for me, and I happily take it.

Inside, Stella and Rivers are with his brothers, Hannah, and Nikki. We join the group, and a warm sensation blooms in my belly. This is my family. These men and these women. Alfie, and also baby Violet sleeping in a sling across Jet's body.

It's not late, but it has just gone nine. Alfie leans against me, using my arm to rest his head. I wrap it around him instead. Jet says, "Hannah and I are taking off because we need to get these kids to bed, and I need to get my wife into bed."

While everyone else chuckles, I don't. The reality that these people would do anything for me from caring about me to taking me as one of their own is turning me sentimental. Dave puts his arm over my shoulders and holds me to his side. I've not just gained brothers, but also amazing sisters.

Nikki says, "I have a fitting tomorrow. You should come with us, Meadow. A few of the girls are coming, and the designer will be there." Turning toward the group, she says, "I've been trying to get Hannah out of the house for the past month. We can get Stella to come and make a day of it."

"That will be fun. Text me tomorrow."

Dave says, "Now I'm ready. You?"

"Yep."

After our goodbyes to everyone else, we walk to the door hand in hand. He stops us just before we leave, and says, "I've been thinking about our anal conversation."

"Oh, no!" I walk ahead, swinging the door wide open. "You had your chance."

His lips twist as he follows me outside. "Not really since you were drunk."

I realize I have my hands over my ass. Dropping them to my sides, I say, "Well, I'm not drunk enough tonight." As he laughs his ass off, being very dramatic, I hang on his arm. "I don't know why you think this is so funny."

"You're funny, Meadow Soleil." Grabbing me into a tight hold, which I think he does because he sees the valet guys eyeing me up, he stakes his claim by kissing me until my knees go weak, then says, "But you know what else you are?"

"What?" I feel gooey in his arms, the strange feeling growing every day.

"Mine." He kisses me with the intention of a thousand conquerors and the lips of Brad Pitt.

Yes. Yes. Yes.

I'm so his, and the best part—*he's all mine.*

I find I'm clenching on the way back to the hotel. He starts laughing, and says, "We're not doing anal, so relax. But I will take you from behind and from the front. Most likely from the side as well."

"The side?"

He just smirks, but then says, "I want your mouth on me, and I'm going to have my mouth all over you. How does that sound?"

"Positively sinful."

My body feels blissfully sore this morning. Dave Carson is the devil in disguise. Or maybe I got his alter ego Ridge last night. Either way, it was pure heaven.

I stretch, reaching for the headboard as my toes point toward the end of the bed, enjoying the feel of my worked muscles.

Suddenly, I'm grabbed by the middle and pulled against his front. "Let's lie here all day," he says, a roughness working its way through his voice as he begins to wake.

Rolling over, it's hard to see him with the curtains closed, so I reach over and push the button. The sun burns my eyes as it floods the room, but as I adjust, the strong features of his face come into view—a jaw that's shadowed in scruff, dark lashes against the tops of his cheeks, those lips that are licked, and then the lower dragged under by his teeth. I touch his face, tempted to touch him much lower. "Good morning, rock star."

"Good morning, cherry cheeks." He seems to have all these nicknames for me, and I'm starting to follow the pattern of when he uses them.

Sunshine when he's in a lighter mood.

Cherry cheeks when he's in the mood since he's caused my cheeks to pink in the first place.

Meadow Soleil is used when he feels close, the commitment we've made to each other filling his heart.

Meadow when he demands my attention.

I love each and every one of them, just like the sides of him when he uses the terms of endearment.

Dipping a finger down his chest, I go lower. "Do you want to go to the gym to work out with me?"

Kissing my shoulder, he replies, "We can work out right here between the sheets."

I play along because I'm determined to get out of this bed today . . . I think. I do love it here, though. "Tempting. We don't even have to get dressed if we stay in." Tapping his nose, I add, "But if I don't leave now, my whole day will be gone, and I would've gotten nothing done."

"You would have gotten *me* done." His hand dives under the covers, and he readjusts before touching me between the legs. "Anyway, it's too early. What's gotten into you?"

"You. Too many times last night."

Lying back, he keeps his eyes with the happiness embedded inside trained on me. "Is there really such a thing as *too many* when it feels so fucking good?"

Much to my dismay, I toss away my plans and reach under the covers because I'm not able to resist him. Running my hand over his stomach, I feel the taut muscles clench and release, reacting to my touch. When I go lower, I take hold of his hardness, his body ready for me. "You're ridiculously impossible. I don't think one woman can satisfy your needs."

Covering my hand with his, he stops me from taking it further. "That's where you're wrong. You're the only one who satisfies me. I don't need anyone else." As I move to sit up, his eyes try to read mine. "Do I satisfy you?"

"You do." I prop myself up, resting on my hand. "We eat. We have sex. We lounge. We talk. We laugh. We eat. Always with the eating. You're making me fat and happy."

He gives me a wink and a sweet morning smile. "And the problem is?"

"I'm trying to find a routine when we're together. We have none. After all these months, I eat terribly, and I drink all the time when I'm here. LA is just a nonstop party. It takes me a week to recover after every visit. So I think it would be good for us, or even just me, to bring a little of my home routine with me."

Caressing my cheek, he says, "I like hearing you talk about a future with me."

"Speaking of the future, how long are you planning on living at this hotel? It has to be costing you a fortune, and as much as I love having the best mac and cheese in the world delivered to the door at three a.m., are you planning on staying forever?"

"Do you want to change hotels for a new scene?"

"No," I say, laughing. "It's not about me. I'm just wondering what your plans are for staying in LA." I keep my eyes on him, wanting to see every one of his reactions, if he gives me any. "I mean, you still pay rent on the place in Austin, and you never even visit it when you fly back."

"It's like paying for a storage unit until I have time to go through all the shit in there." He gets out of bed—fully naked and incredible to watch. Stone-carved abs, athletic legs, strong arms . . . great ass. His back is to me as he takes in the view of LA. "You know I bounce between houses when you're not here. I stay at Laird's place down by the beach or with Jet, sometimes with Rivers. I just haven't been ready to commit."

Dragging the sheet over me when I lie back, I ask, "To a place? To the city? To what, Dave?"

He glances back over his shoulder, not hiding any part of his body. I hope he doesn't hide what's on his mind. "It sounds dumb, but I always thought I'd buy a place when I was buying it *with* someone . . ." The way the last word drifts from his lips and fades away, it feels like the rest is left unsaid.

I'm not naïve. He doesn't mean a roommate. Excitement heats my cheeks because I want him to ask me about the potential for us living together one day. "A friend or a girl-friend? Someone like a wife?"

I need his words. I need to know what he's thinking so I understand where he's at with us. Maybe I've taken our time for granted, enjoying the present since the future holds fears I'm not ready to face.

His gaze works its way up from my body to my eyes. "Have you given any more thought to LA after graduation?"

I try not to come off as surprised. I understood the direction where we were headed. Hell, I threw some coal on the fire to help get our train here. LA is one thing, but I hadn't thought about us living together officially. We do now when we're in the same city but not sharing bills and money. I take a breath, trying to block out the words of my parents, and focus on the good that Dave and I are. So good. "I have three hundred dollars to my name, Dave. There's no way I'd be able to buy a home with you. I don't have the money to even consider that right now. I need a job and—"

"It's never been about the money. You know that."

"To *you*, the man with all the money, it doesn't matter. To *me*, it does. How am I an equal in a relationship where everything is literally given to me?" I'm inclined to hide in the bathroom until this conversation goes away, but I can't do that. Not without hurting him in the process. "I have to stand on my own two feet. I have to know I can."

"It always comes back to the same bullshit with you. I can say a million things, but you only hear one." His steps are heavy, matching his mood. I watch in shock as he begins to dress.

"What is happening? Why are you so upset?"

His eyes shoot to mine when he's standing in a pair of gym shorts. "It will never matter how much I tell you I care about you, how much I love you. All you will hear is that I want to control you, own you, or take away your dreams." Pulling a T-shirt over his head, he pops through the hole and then grabs a pair of socks and his sneakers.

By the way he's dressed, I'm thinking we're going to work out, but something tells me to wait, to stay where I am, a vibe he's exuding. A vein in his neck is prominent; the way his jaw clenches worries me. I sit all the way up, holding the sheet to my chest and dragging the cherry pendant across the chain anxiously.

Like an agitated tiger that's been caged too long, he moves across the room to stand in the doorway, and says, "You know what the saddest fucking part is?" Waiting for an answer, he blows out a harsh breath, but then loses his patience. "You don't even know what your fucking dreams are."

"I just turned twenty-two," I snap, all compassion for his bad mood gone. Turning to walk out, he stops once more, looking back knowing the next step he takes makes or breaks us. I point at my chest. "Me not knowing everything I want to do in life isn't the saddest part. You making me feel less for it is."

His head is lowered as his shoulders lose the fight he was holding on to, a grimace taking over.

Only his eyes are aimed in my direction when he says, "You never even asked me why I was late the other night."

"You had a meeting. You told me."

"Okay." Then he turns his back to me and walks away. Seconds later, the door to the suite shuts with a loud click of the lock.

Okay? I throw off the sheet and go after him. When I open the door, I peek out, hiding since I'm not wearing clothes. "Dave?" I'm greeted by an empty hallway and his echoing name.

What the hell just happened?

Moving back inside, I scramble to find my phone. When I spot it on the coffee table, I call him, but a ring in the bedroom tells me it's here with me.

Unlike him.

35

Meadow

ALL THE MOTIVATION I had to exercise and get back on the health track was left in the suite. With a glass of champagne in hand, I sit numbing myself on a purple couch in the middle of the Tonio Vittori store in Beverly Hills.

Nikki turns in front of a three-way mirror to check out her backside while wearing a pair of her signature sneakers. Squinting, I realize they literally have her signature horizontally on the back of the shoes. The lead singer of Faris Wheel has become a style icon and a brand in the last year. It's incredible when she still acts so down to earth.

Holli Hughes Outlaw was dragged into the role of stylist until the designer himself, wearing head-to-toe purple that matched his couch, pops into the showroom to assist. They're all rich and famous, so naturally, they're all besties as well. Holding his hands together in front of his face like he's praying to the fashion gods for inspiration, he says, "No. This is not the dress, my dear."

I always thought he had an Italian accent when I've seen

him on TV. Today, it's leaning more toward the boroughs of New York, though I'm no expert to know which one. And he's insisting we call him Vinnie. I'm so lost. Rich people are weird. I snicker, thinking how Alfie and I embrace our weirdness, but Hollywood types don't even realize how weird they are.

"Nikki could wear a bag, and she'd look amazing," I whisper to Hannah.

Vinnie snaps his fingers and points at me, startling me. "Yes! That's it."

"What's it?" I ask. "A bag?" I would not be surprised if it's literally a bag.

"I have the perfect design idea." Turning to Nikki, he takes her hands. "I have your measurements and know your style. Give me a week and I'll have something made in time for the awards show." They exchange a two-cheek kiss, reminding me how Dave calls me cherry cheeks.

I touch my pendant, ready to wallow in the memory of our fight this morning, or whatever that was. He was so unlike himself, and it's thrown me out of sorts, not sure if I should have left the suite and come today. The girls had plans, though, and Dave hadn't returned to the suite even an hour later.

Vinnie's attention grabs mine when he asks, "Who is this darling, and why have we not been introduced?" As he holds two fingers and his thumb to his head, his gaze seeks out the heavens, and he says, "Let me guess."

Not awkward at all. Nope, I'm just sitting here with a famous designer who thinks he's Zoltar the psychic, trying to guess who I am. Oh God. I feel the heat rising under my shirt while everyone waits for him to be willed the answer. *Is it hot in here*? I start flapping my shirt to cool off when he says, "I see suburban chic with a carefree edge of youth."

"Yep, you guessed it. That's me. Suburban chic." I laugh

because the description is hilarious. Fine, the champagne has also gone to my head.

He laughs in delight and comes to me. "I was tugging your foot." Clasping one of my hands between the two of his, he says, "I would love to design a whole line around the color of your eyes."

"I'm going to need you for a year just to count the colors in your eyes. Don't be fooled, green doesn't come close to covering what I see when I look at you."

"What do you see?"

"Emerald and sea, thyme and spring, waterfall and moss, ocean and earth. I can go on about all the greens that make up who you are to me."

Turning to Holli, Vinnie says, "She's beautiful. Model? Starlet? You must tell me."

Wait. Back up.

Let me get this straight. He's asking one of the most beautiful women in the world who I am? She has legit been named The Most Beautiful Woman in the World by magazines, and he wants to know who I am. *What crazy universe is this?*

Stella nudges me. "You're not in Austin anymore."

"No. I most definitely am not," I reply.

Holli says, "This is Meadow Fellowes. Stella's sister. She's visiting from Austin, but we're hoping to convince her to move to Los Angeles after she graduates from college."

"Beautiful and smart," he says, releasing my hand. "It's an aphrodisiac of combinations. You must have someone special in your life or a line around the block vying for your company."

I'm still feeling a bit emotional from the fight we had, so I don't know how to answer this one. I've felt sick all morning about Dave and not knowing what's going on with him. Seeing me struggle, Stella says, "My sister has never worn one of your designs. I'd like to find something special for her to wear."

"Fab!" he exclaims. "Like Nikki, Miss Meadow was born to shine. I'll sketch a few designs and send them over. If you like one, we'll make magic." He holds his hand out to her. "Come with me. I have something that will look divine on you. You'll be attending the same awards as Nikki, correct?"

"Yes," she replies, taking his hand. "But Nikki's performing and nominated. I'm only going as a plus-one."

"The most important plus-one to that handsome husband of yours."

I'm indebted to my sister for saving me. While she disappears with Vinnie and Nikki is gone to get dressed, Holli and Rochelle browse the store, leaving me sitting on the couch with Hannah.

Jet's wife.

Stella's friend.

Dave's Hannah.

One of his best friends.

As soon as the other women are out of earshot, she asks, "Are you okay?"

Okay. The word rings through my ears in Dave's voice from this morning.

"No."

"Dave called me," Hannah says, her tone treading carefully with me.

She knows him better than anyone. He's told me they've been through a lot together, but my defenses go up. *Will he tell her what he's been through with me*? "What did he say?"

"He wanted me to make sure you're all right."

I pick a piece of fluff off the couch, then look at her. "He did?" Of course, he did. That's what Dave does—takes care of everyone else while bottling up his own emotions to explode at another time, like this morning.

Her eyes tend toward gray with concern etched in her expression as she whips her hair up into a ponytail. "He said you were gone when he got back from his run." It's warm under the showroom lights, so she fans herself.

He went running? I should know this, but she does instead. "He didn't call me."

"I'm sorry. I don't mean to intrude. He was worried about you and remembered that I would see you."

"I don't know why he was upset this morning."

"He's usually a pretty straight-forward guy. He didn't say?"

Deep down I know. I know because he's shown me in subtle ways. It may not have been as blatant as blurting it out, but this morning he told me. "He wants more than I can give him right now."

"Don't take this wrong, but that doesn't sound like him."

"Well, it was. I'm in school, and I'm not here. I can't magically divide myself in two."

"And that's what he wants?" She reaches over and gently touches my hand. "I'm sorry if I've made you uncomfortable. You're not obligated to talk to me about this."

"But he brought you into it." I angle her way, resting my elbow on the back of the couch. "You're his close friend, but I consider you one of mine as well. Jet loves you. You've been a good friend to my sister, and Dave calls you one of the best, so I feel your interest comes from a good place."

"But?"

She caught that before I said it. "But Dave and I are in two different places in our lives—emotionally and physically. We live half the country apart on a regular basis. I was willing to do what needed to be done for us to be together, but I'm only letting him down. This morning, he was upset, irritated, but he wasn't mad. He was frustrated. So yes, I do know what caused it. I just feel helpless because I can't fix it at this time."

When I close my eyes to hide the tears that threaten to fall, the couch dips, and she wraps her arms around me. "I'm sorry. I don't want you to cry. I wanted you to know you can talk to me, and I'm not taking sides." Her head rests against the top of mine, and she says, "I care about him so much, but I care about you too. You're family."

We hug family.

I look back up with a lump in my throat. This time I hug her, looking to find the light in a dark situation. "You're kind and pretty. I see why that husband of yours fell so hard."

"I also feed him well," she jokes. "He's a sucker for a home-cooked meal."

"I think he's there for more than the meals."

She wipes her thumbs lightly across the apples of my cheeks. "No crying, okay? If I know Dave at all, he'll tell you how he feels. He doesn't play games. You always know where you stand with him."

"Should I call him?"

"No. Just enjoy the day and talk to him in person when you get home. I mean the hotel." She half-rolls her eyes. "He really needs to find a place to live. That hotel life must be getting old."

It's then I realize he didn't tell her the dirty details of our fight. He was truly just making sure I was all right. Standing, I hand her the glass of champagne. "Do you mind if I cut out early?"

A knowing smile spreads, erasing her worry. "Go. I'll let Stella know."

I take off because Dave and I may be in two different places, but we only have tonight to be in one.

Stuck in traffic drains away the adrenaline. Sitting in the back of this car, I want to hit the window I'm so frustrated.

I'm so tempted to call Dave that I hold my phone staring down at my favorite photo of him. Beyond his sex appeal, my heart flutters because I know his heart is good as gold.

Finally. I arrive back at the hotel, rush out of the car, and speed through the lobby. The elevator is the slowest in history, but when the doors open, I run to the end of the hall and practically bust through the suite doors. "Dave?"

My feet come to a stop in the entry, and I watch as he turns around with his hands in his pockets. His cologne drifts through the air, mingling with the smell of fresh flowers on the table next to me. He doesn't say anything when our eyes meet, so I ask, "Why were you late the other night?"

Hope lives in my heart that this is an opener and not the end.

His chin tilts down, but his hazel eyes stay fixed on me. A thumb runs over his bottom lip as he studies me before a roguish grin appears. "We're signing another two-album deal with Outlaw Records. Johnny wanted to get business out of the way before the party the next night. Rochelle drew up the negotiated deal, but the lawyers had to finalize the contract. I waited as long as I could before I told them I had to go."

"You didn't sign the contract?" I take a step.

"Not yet."

"Because you left for me?" Two more steps are covered.

Nodding, he sighs.

I take another large but tentative step closer, and ask, "Why are you so perfect?"

"I'm not, Meadow. About this morning—"

"You were right. If I'm going to talk about my dreams, I should probably figure out what they are." I stay in place.

He makes a move, coming closer. "I shouldn't have diminished them, though. You don't owe me anything. You don't owe anyone answers but yourself."

"You're wrong. I owe you a thank you for believing in me." I hate the space that still divides us, so I close it by running and jumping into his arms.

Spinning, he presses my back to the glass, and our tongues entwine. When all oxygen is swallowed and gone, we part, panting for more—more oxygen, more kissing, more of each other. Just more.

He's amazing and deserves the same. "I'm so happy for you."

"I haven't signed yet."

"But it's a done deal, a deal you earned, a deal you worked for."

"A deal that makes me want to invest in a future."

"A future? Your future, or our future?"

He chuckles. "I know a trap when I hear it. I'm zipping my lips on that one."

My feet find the floor, but my arms stay around his neck. "It's not a trap, but I want you to think about what you want. Where I see you doesn't matter, only that I get to." I hug his middle and rest my head on his chest. "I'm sorry I didn't ask about your meeting or what's going in your life."

Stroking my hair, he rests his chin on the top of my head. "You would have hated me at twenty-two. I called you out earlier, but you're one of the few people I know who has their shit together. You don't have to figure out everything right now. Fuck, I don't either." Tilting his head to the side, he moves my hair out of my eyes, and asks, "How about we stop stressing about the future and live in the present?"

It's like he's reading my mind. "Are you still my boyfriend?"

"Fuck yes, I'm your boyfriend. If I see one motherfucker come near you, I'm going to lose my fucking shit." Swear words may be flying, but I can hear the lightness in his tone. His arms tighten around me again. "We're going to live in the present as boyfriend and girlfriend because I like those fucking labels."

Straight forward, just as Hannah said. "Me too."

There's no sneaking out the next morning. I roll right on top of Dave and kiss his face until one eye opens and then the other. His arms come around me, and he says, "I'm never letting you go. You're stuck with me forever."

"There are worse places to be stuck."

"A few. Not many, but a few."

"Rock star's got jokes this morning."

"What are you talking about?" *Playful. Sexy. Fun.* It's probably best if I get out of bed before we end up here all day. He says, "I'm damn funny all the time."

Pushing up, I mean to roll to the side of him but end up rolling right off the edge of the bed. I pop up and land the ending with my arms in the air. When he stops laughing at me, his fingers form a one and zero. "Definitely a ten because you stuck that landing . . . right on your ass."

Speaking of my ass, I rub it. "That's going to leave a mark. I'd worry that someone will ask how I got carpet burned, but yeah, no one sees my ass but you."

He grabs my hand and pulls me closer. "That's the way it should be." His hand slides to my backside. "All. Mine."

"If I miss my flight, it's all yours for another day. I tried to move to a later flight two days ago, but they're all sold out."

"You're not going to hear any complaints from me about you staying an extra day."

"My graduation advisor might if I miss my meeting tomorrow."

The smirk on his face gets me drunk on the inside. He's

tequila on a girls' night when my inhibitions fall away. God, this man. That voice. The messy, sexy hair. Those eyes looking at me with moons in them. Hands. Good lord, he has great hands. But it's that mouth and those lips that make me want to mount him. "When's the latest I can leave to catch my flight?"

"You have an hour."

My lips reflect his, but I add a little wink. "That's all we need."

I kiss him before climbing on the bed and straddling his neck. Chuckling, he takes me by the hips. "May I help you?"

"Absolutely. We have thirty minutes before I need to shower to get clean."

"That means we have thirty minutes to get dirty. C'mere." He presses his head into the pillow and guides me over his face. "Nothing like breakfast in bed."

When his hot and so damn sexy mouth presses between my legs, my thighs clench, and I bear down as my head falls back. My fingers curve around the headboard to hold me upright from his delicious attention.

I barely make my flight, but I do and sleep with a smile on my face the whole way home.

36

Ridge

ON A TORONTO TARMAC, I got the news I'd been waiting for—my mom's surgery went as planned, and she's recovering. My cousin called to explain the details to me and has helped put my mind at ease. I immediately called Meadow. Knowing she went straight after class and sat in that waiting room for six hours gave me comfort in a whole other way.

"Your dad has been worried sick."

"He lives for my mom."

"He talked a lot about you while we were waiting."

This news surprises me. He barely grumbles two words when I call for updates. "Have you seen my mom?"

"No. They said only family tonight. I might be able to see her tomorrow, though. I'll have to come after two of my finals."

"Finals?"

"It's my final exam week."

"Meadow, you should be studying."

"I am. I studied here instead of at home. It's fine. I'm ready for my tests."

"Are you sure?" *If I've caused her to fail . . .*

"I'm sure. I'm heading home now."

"What about dinner?" This woman is amazing. Since she probably hasn't thought about herself or eating in hours, I'm ready to hop on an app to order her food. It's not much, but it's the only other way I can think to thank her when I should be the one there. "Can I send something your way?"

Her breath comes and goes as she walks to her car. "Believe it or not, your dad treated me to a hospital meal this evening."

My dad's never been cheap. He just uses his money as leverage to get his way with me. "That's interesting."

The sound of her door closing, fills the air, and then she says, "How are you, babe?"

"Missing you. Feeling guilty for not being there."

"Don't. Everyone understands, even your dad, but especially your mom. What is the plan tonight?"

"We have a radio interview that we're heading to straight from the airport. I need to get off the plane. Call you later?"

"Please. Before you go, remember that I love you." *She has no idea how much I needed to hear those words.*

"You too. Thanks for everything you did today."

"I was glad I was here. Now go be awesome."

"Kick ass on those tests."

"I plan to."

"Between the number of hours we're rehearsing and playing every day and the one hand five-sliding I'm doing, my hand is raw."

By the sound of her laughter, I'm thinking she's lacking

sympathy for my situation. "I'm serious," I add as if that will garner at least a flash of her tits on the screen. I'm easy, especially since it's been almost a month since I've seen them in person.

"Nashville tonight and you'll be here tomorrow. Do you think you'll survive, or will we have to amputate the limb?" She can't even keep a straight face. I'm close to asking her if she's drunk, but I see her teacup on the desk beside her with the little words of wisdom tag hanging over the edge.

"I don't know. You might have to give it a thorough exam with your tongue."

Her jaw shifts side-to-side, and then she opens wide. Tease. "All limbered up and ready to go."

Fucking hell. How am I going to last another day? I'm not. Not with that visual stuck in my head. Checking the time, I say, "Hate to cut this short."

She rolls her eyes. "I know. I know. You have to go."

"And you need to get some sleep."

"Yeah. Yeah." She always turns melancholy when it's time to hang up, and even though it shouldn't, it makes me feel good. She wants me. She wants to spend time with me however we can get it, and I've never had that before. I feel the same about her, but I also want her to know that I'll urge her to keep working toward her goals and dreams. *Always will.*

"Hey, tomorrow."

Nodding, she repeats, "Tomorrow."

Bye never feels right when we hang up these days . . . or when we say hello or strong enough for anything between. I've held my tongue, but it's hard. The woman makes me happy. "Good night."

"Good night."

I hang up and head back to the dressing room. The Crow Brothers changed my destiny. I could have been a studio musician brought in to fill in the sound for the album, brought in out of need. They didn't have to keep me or make me an official part of the band. Hannah introduced me to them, and the rest is history. My history.

There will never be a day when I want or need for anything.

Except one thing.

My girl.

I'm going to do my damnedest to get it right with her and to keep it right for us.

I walk in, letting the door close on its own behind me. Picking up my guitar, I notice the chatter and laughter has stopped. Tulsa's sitting with his sticks in hand across his lap, kicked back on the couch. Tommy and Jet hanging out around the table. Rivers tunes his guitar and messes with the knobs. Jet stands. "'Bout time."

All of them watch me as if I'm here to entertain them. "What?" I give up trying to pretend all is normal in here.

Jet fidgets with his water bottle. Rivers keeps quiet, but the look in his eyes and that cocked eyebrow speaks volumes. Tulsa says, "Good luck, brah. You're the last man standing."

"What do you mean?" *Oh.* Bopping my head to the side, I say, "There's still Tommy."

"That's low, bro," Tommy says, laughing to himself. "If I wasn't wasting my time making sure you guys don't fuck up yours, I might have a life of my own."

Jet gets up and claps Tommy on the back while we chuckle. "One day you're going to meet a woman who will make you forget all about us."

Tommy says, "I don't need to forget about you. I just need to get laid more often."

Rivers plucks at his guitar, and adds, "You need more than that, but we'll let you and the lucky woman figure that out on your own."

Drumming on the couch cushion, Tulsa stops suddenly and looks at me. "Back to Ridge, who, by the way, is having sex with our little sister."

"Nope." I start to pace. "We're not doing this."

He laughs. "We agreed not to give you shit, Ridge, but you make it so easy."

"What? 'Cuz I was talking to her on the phone?"

"No," Jets states matter-of-factly, "because of the shit-eating grin you wear *after* you talk to her on the phone."

Busted. "Whatever." But when I can't wipe that grin off my face, the room rolls in hysterics . . . at my expense. "I can't with you guys. Fuckers." I open the door to the dressing room. Fortunately, it's time to set Dave aside and let Ridge ride his high.

Tommy passes me and leads the way to the stage. I hand my guitar to a roadie. "The A string isn't sounding right. Can you fix it and bring it onto the stage by the third song in the set?"

"Done, dude." He walks away with my favorite guitar, but it's not one I need right away. At the base of the stage, I spy my rack of guitars off to the side where I stand.

We huddle, doing the same routine we always do. Just the four of us. Four guys. Four friends. Four musicians. One band.

One family.

Jet looks each of us in the eyes, then says what he always says, "We've got this, guys."

"Just doin' what we love," Rivers adds.

Tulsa nods, his cockier side written in his grin. "Nothing but a good time."

And I repeat, "Nothing but a good time."

The lights go down, and Tulsa's the first to dash to his kit, sticks in hand, ready to count us in. The three of us take our positions, a roadie handing me my Strat and then plugging me in. Taking inventory of my pedal positions and mic, I make the adjustments just as the lights hit Tulsa, and he hits his kit with power, kicking off the set.

The low hum of the crowd builds with excitement that creeps onto the stage. Anticipation fills me. It's always at this moment that my whole world converges. My mind more focused as I swallow down the good and bad, and the sad that has weighed me down.

Out here, it's my guitar, the music, and me. The energy from the fans rushes through me when the lights strike. The beginning of the first song virtually deafens me to the band or the instruments, even with an earpiece hidden in my ear.

But I play.

I play through the screams.

I play through the cheers.

With my soul on fire, I play. Stepping up to the mic, I back Jet up and sing as well. By the end of the fifth song, we step back and convene in front of the kit. Our gripes or concerns aired while a roadie runs across the stage to clean up the underwear and gifts thrown there.

Finishing a bottle of water, I throw the empty to the side and get ready for the solo that starts the next song. I fucking love this song, but I can't help seeing Meadow's pretty face on the fans below. She's come to two shows, and both times she was under the watchful eyes of security. I understand Jet's worry over Hannah and Rivers not wanting Stella at every show. I get it now.

So much can go wrong so fast and what would I be able to do? It still doesn't take away the desire to see her there, smiling up at me, watching while I play this song for her.

As soon as the song ends, I whip the strap off over my head and hand my guitar to the handler. Jogging down the steps behind Tulsa, Jet and Rivers tail us. Tommy's already waiting outside the door and follows us inside the dressing room.

The door closes and we all do our own thing, using the time to recover our muscles, or hydrating to keep going, even jumping to keep the energy high. We play hard, the tempo held strong for almost two hours, giving the audience every dollar's worth and more. I'm tossed another bottle of water and grab my phone from my bag. Sitting on the arm of the worn-out couch, I pop an Advil and lean my head against the wall, resting my sore right arm, and call my girl.

Tommy shouts, "Five minutes."

That shit-eating grin returns as soon as I hear her sweet voice, "Hello?"

My heart still races from adrenaline, but we'll go out and play some of our slower songs before we end on our hits. That gives me a moment to breathe. "Hey, what are you doing?"

She laughs, and I can imagine probably rolling her eyes as well. "Eh, just cleaning up since I'm having company this weekend."

"Oh yeah? Who's coming?"

"Both of us if we're lucky."

"Doesn't take luck to get off with you."

"Not necessarily romantic, but there's still a charm about it. But let's get to the heart of the matter. Aren't you in the middle of a concert?"

"Yeah, three minutes before we return for the encore."

"But you're calling me?" *How could I not?*

"I always call you."

"I like this habit you've formed, Mr. Fellowes."

Damn. I'm never going to live that down. Chuckling, I add, "Not all habits are bad for you. You're one of my better ones."

"Aww, there you go again, charming the panties right off me."

"Hold that thought until tomorrow."

Tommy shouts, "Two minutes."

Even she can hear him. "Go be awesome for all those adoring fans. Then you can perform a solo on me . . . *for me*," she says, correcting herself at the end.

That's the kind of Freudian slip I approve of. I lower my voice and hunch down so only she can hear me. "I do, you know. Every time I sing that song, it's for you. I can't fucking wait to see you tomorrow."

"Not more than me. I love you, rock star."

"Love you."

The door opens, and Tommy shuffles out. "You're on in one minute. Get your asses out there and show them who The Crow Brothers really are."

We do too.

After closing out the encore, we file into the SUV. As soon as the doors close, I ask, "When's the plane leaving for Austin?"

37

Meadow

A MILLION THOUGHTS race through my mind. Is my lipstick worn off, is my eyeliner smudged, does he notice the spaghetti stains on my T-shirt, or the big bruise on the side of my leg I got for cutting the island corner too close?

I could worry about my hair, but I know it's a catastrophe.

As if he'll never learn, Dave still looks at me like I hung the moon, and says, "You gonna invite me in?"

Tightening the bun on top of my head, I grab him by the shirt and tug him inside. "Get in here, rock star, and kiss me."

His bag is dropped and the door kicked closed as he takes my face between his hands and kisses me like a man in need of water. My knees weaken under the passion this man has for me. Leaving me breathless, he pulls back, and says, "You are so fucking gorgeous and taste even better."

There's nothing normal about how I react to him—my

mind going blank, my body edging forward, closer to him—and my heart beating faster in my chest. "Marinara."

With humor in his eyes, he asks, "What?"

"I had spaghetti."

With a chuckle, he kisses both sides of my mouth. "I like spaghetti. Save me any?"

"Nope. I ate it all." I drop my head forward, laughing, realizing what a mess I'm making of this reunion. "I would have saved you some if I'd known you were coming." Pushing him back with a smile on my face, I pout. "You should have told me. I'm a complete mess. I would have gotten ready for you."

"You don't have to get ready for me. I like you like this. Messy little sunshine."

I move back into his arms, already missing those arms and the strong beat of his heart. Squeezing him as tight as I can, I say, "You're here."

"I couldn't wait until tomorrow. I caught a private flight. I expected you to be asleep. It's almost two in the morning."

"I was waiting for your call. You always call after a show. I was starting to worry."

"Sorry. I wanted to surprise you."

"You did, all right."

"Are you mad?"

"God, no." I wave him off as I hurry into the kitchen to hide the empty box of Ding Dongs and push my dishes into the sink. "I get more time with you. How could I ever be mad?" I catch my reflection in the side of the shiny stainless-steel toaster and gasp. "I'll be right back."

Rushing into the bedroom, I head straight for the bathroom, practically ripping off my shirt and tossing it on the floor. I scrub the remnants of my dinner from my chin and quickly brush my teeth.

A knock on the door causes me to pause. "Meadow, it's

me. You're beautiful. I'd rather see you with food stuck to your face then stare at the back of this door. Will you come out?"

I push my makeup bag to the side and give up the fight because he's right. He flew all night to see me after playing a huge concert. Turning around, I open the door and lean against the counter. "You really do love me, don't you?"

He comes in with that sexy smirk on those kissable lips and runs those big hands over my waist, then settles on my hips. "I do love you, Meadow Soleil. But you love me more."

Tilting my head, I give him my best smirk right back. I run my fingers over his shirt, and ask, "How do you figure that?"

"You left me the last Ding Dong."

"What? No, I didn't. I finished off the box. A little midnight snack."

"Man," he starts, pretending to be offended. "I found one still in there, but now I hear it wasn't meant for me. Cruel. Just cruel. First, no spaghetti. Now, no dessert. I'm hungry. What do you suggest I eat?"

Easy answer. *Me.*

"*Andrea Andrews.*"

Looking around, I try to spot Dave or Stella, but the stadium is too big, and I have no idea where they're sitting. I receive a text from him: *You know what love is? Love is wanting to see the sunrise in your green oceans.*

I snicker to myself, my neighbor looking at me like I'm crazy. I am. Crazy in love with that man in the stands, wherever he is. Me: *You know what love is? Love is a box of Ding Dongs.*

.

.

.

"*Kim Carters.*"

I relax back, knowing it's going to be a while, and send him another text. Me: *Love is both of us thinking we're the lucky one.*

Dave: *Love is sitting in a stadium full of people to watch your girlfriend graduate.*

Giggling, I read it over and over, thinking about him hiding from fans in plain sight. *For me.* He's doing it all for me.

.

.

.

"*Leonard Downey.*"

Grabbing my phone from the small purse under my graduation robe, I check it. There's a message with their location. My row is asked to stand and we're led to the side of the stage, so I look for them once more. But there are too many people here for graduation to find *my* people.

.

.

.

"Meadow Fellowes."

I walk across the stage when my name is announced. Shake hands. Take my diploma. Smile for the camera. I release the breath I was holding when I reach the edge of the stage.

This is the moment I've waited for, the payoff for all my hard work and the hours and years dedicated to my studies. Through tears and pain, I fought for this, and I've earned every glorious moment. I, Meadow Soleil Fellowes, am now the proud recipient of a Business in Marketing degree. Watch out, world. I'm coming for you.

I'm tempted to keep walking right out of here. We've been stuck here for over two hours already, and I'm ready to go and spend time with everyone. I walk back with my row and file back in, hoping this ends soon or I'll leave anyway.

The last name is called an hour later. *Thank God.*

Hats fly into the air, and I immediately work my way through the crazy crowd to find my family. I search through thousands of people, hurrying through reuniting families in the direction where they said they were. But when I reach the edge of the celebration, the stadium ahead is empty.

My shoulders sag, wondering how I'm ever going to find them in this mass of chaos. I turn around and check my phone once more.

Me: *Love is sitting through four hours of a graduation ceremony when all I want to do is celebrate with you.*

Dave: *It's not too late to celebrate.*

Me: *Where are you?*

Dave: *Look up.*

Twenty feet in front of me with a Crow Bros. hat pulled down low in the front, stands what I love most—my own personal rock star in the flesh. I run, wanting to hug him, to cover him in my love, to drown in a sea of all the emotions that fill me. He catches me in his arms and spins us around. With those pillowy lips against my ear, he says, "Love is finding the love of your life in a crowd of ten thousand because she's the only one who exists to me."

Love of his life?

My head drops to his shoulder as my tears fall. "I love you."

"I'm so proud of you. Congrats, graduate."

As soon as my feet hit the ground, I hear, "Meadow?"

My sister.

I turn to see Stella running toward me with Rivers behind her. Not too far behind him is Tulsa carrying Alfie on his back, and Jet with Hannah. "How is everyone here? They'll be seen."

"They wouldn't miss this."

Stella crashes into me and hugs me so tight, I beg for air. Squeezing my cheeks, she says, "You did it, little sis. Congratulations."

An arm comes around my head as Rivers hugs me. "Way to go, Meadow."

By the time Tulsa reaches us, Alfie has been set down and is already in my arms. "Hey, little dude. Thanks for being here."

"It was really boring, but Uncle Tulsa promised me a Frosty if I was good."

Tulsa gives me a side hug and a proud smile. "You've done good, Meadow. Congratulations."

Patting his arm, I reply, "Thanks. Thanks for being here. This is such a surprise."

Alfie says, "Dad said he had to come. I earned three bucks from that conversation."

"Ha. Ha. Ha." Tulsa grabs Alfie by the back of the shirt, pretending he's mad, and then leans down eye level with him. "You're a quick learner." High fiving him, he says, "If you can't be nice—"

"Be funny," Alfie finishes, cracking the two of them up. "Nailed it."

"You guys are ridiculous."

Hannah reaches me first and embraces me. "Congratulations. We're so happy for you."

Jet takes over after her. I'm lost in his bear hug, feeling the love. "This is a great accomplishment, and you've made us all proud."

"Thank you."

Stella says, "We should probably separate again. We're starting to get attention."

Hannah takes Alfie's hand. "We need to head back to California. Rochelle's watching Violet."

"Wait. You flew here for the graduation and are leaving right now?"

"We wanted to be here for you just as you've been there for everyone else."

Dave rubs my back, and then says, "They insisted."

"You guys are going to make me cry again."

Hannah touches my wrist. "Don't cry. Go celebrate and enjoy your special day."

One more hug is exchanged before they leave, Tulsa in tow with the other Crows. Stella and Rivers stay with us, but before we leave, Dave says, "Do you have a minute?"

"Sure. What's up?"

"Come over here." He takes my hand and leads me toward a section of seats near the stage.

I start crying as soon as I see her. Lisa Carson sits next to her husband. I rush to her and am gentle when I give her a hug. Kneeling in front of her, I ask, "Why are you here? You should be resting and recovering."

Touching my cheek, she smiles. "This is an important day for you and David, so it's important to us."

His dad says, "This is the closest we might ever get unless this band thing goes south."

I feel Dave bristle next to me, and my heart breaks. Even here, in front of me, with possibly other witnesses around us, he still shoots his arrows at his son. And it makes me angry.

I want to ignore him like Dave does, but I can't. "I'm not sure why you feel you need to say this here at my graduation or anywhere."

"Meadow, don't. It doesn't—"

"No, Dave. This should be said." I stand and with my eyes still directed at his father, I say, "Your son is an exceptionally talented singer, songwriter, and musician. He'll never be a lawyer as that has never been *his* dream. He is fulfilling *his* dream, though, and outstandingly. He's loyal, strong, selfless, and kind. I love him, and it has nothing to do with his career choice, so I have no clue why you can't feel the same when he's your own flesh and blood."

"Look here, young lady. You shouldn't—"

Lisa's small sob catches his attention, and I see the instant change in him as he looks at her with a tenderness I am stunned by.

This man is just as capable of loving wholeheartedly like his son. It's in her eyes, and it's in his for us to witness. After a quiet, wordless conversation, he nods at her and strokes her cheek. "Seems like David's found a woman like you, Lisa. Fearless. One with backbone."

"Yes, he has."

His father turns to Dave, and I can't say there is pride in his gaze—baby steps and all—but I don't see judgment or disappointment. His father's hand runs along his wife's shoulder, and he says, "Your mom helped me download your two albums the other night."

"Really?" Dave seems surprised.

"You're not a lawyer. You're a band man. Your mom always loved music, so if you take after her, I'd say we all win."

His mom's hand covers her husband's hand and Dave takes mine, then asks, "What did you think of the music?"

I guess, like me, he still fights for that glimmer of acceptance, something that will bring pride to his dad's eyes. I almost hold my breath, but his dad answers too fast, "They're good. I liked seeing your name on there. Showed my partners at the firm and anyone else who would listen." He steps forward and hugs his son. "I'm proud of you, but I'm more proud of the man you've become." Clapping his back, his father beams with pride. "A chip off the ole block, I say."

I think Dave's too stunned to react, so I do. "I think you probably have more in common than you realize. Maybe you can find some common ground over a cup of tea."

Dave laughs. "Or coffee."

His dad agrees. "See? We're finding common ground already."

Lisa says, "This is better than Christmas." When her eyes find me, she mouths, "Thank you."

38

Ridge

I NEVER THOUGHT I'd see the day that Nielsen David Carson would change his mind in regards to me after making it up years ago. But my girl held him accountable and broke through his stubborn views to make him see the light for the first time where it concerns me.

My girl did that. For me. For him. For our future. "You didn't have to go to bat for me, Meadow."

"I did. That what's family does for each other, even when it comes to ornery family members."

She's right. She never ceases to blow my mind with her big heart.

Though it's been a great day, I feel like I've been waiting for tonight since I woke up. The sound of her sister and the others fill the living room. Behind a closed bedroom door, I set the box on the bed and wait.

Dragging her fingers along the dresser, she stops, sets her glass of champagne down, and steps out of her heels one by one. "What is it?"

"Open it."

"I'm nervous."

"It's not an engagement ring or anything. I'm smart enough to know not to tie you down."

Walking barefoot over to me, she sits on my lap, and says, "You can tie me down one day."

"I'll hold you to that." *But I want forever.*

She takes the box and tugs the ribbon with a big smile on her face. "What'd ya get me, rock star?"

"Something I've wanted to give you for a long time now. I was just waiting for the right time."

Lifting the lid, she asks, "Now's the right time?"

"Like no other."

The smile softens, but there's no less happiness invested. Pulling the paper from the box, she opens it and reads, "Redo." Her eyes meet mine. "What would you like to redo?"

"The road trip."

"You want me to go on a road trip with you again?" When she tilts her head, her hair falls to one side, tempting me with a view of her graceful neck.

"Through the desert. Austin to LA."

An arm comes around my shoulders and she leans back to get a better view. "You sure you want to do that? It didn't turn out so great the last time."

"That's why we deserve a redo."

"We do, don't we?" Standing up, she takes a sip of her champagne. "When do we leave?"

Four days later, and fifteen hours into the road trip, I find the place where we went wrong last time. Pulling off the highway, I take the detour and park far enough off the highway not to be seen overnight. We're not in a hurry, but it's been a long day, and I'm getting tired. The memory of us together last time we were here has carried me this far.

Her gaze is glued out the window, and she smiles. "There are a billion stars out there." Playfully pushing my arm, she adds, "And one in here."

She mocks the celebrity thing lovingly, but I'm reminded how she never talks about money either. Eventually, we'll have to address it. There is nothing normal about the money I've made or how our lives will be changed. I also overheard her tell her sister on the phone once that she had enough to survive. Two hundred dollars.

The girl is going to survive off two hundred bucks until after graduation. *For how long*? Even if she starts a job tomorrow, she won't get paid for weeks or upward of a month. Thank God Stella and Rivers are paying the bills, or she'd be out on the streets.

She pokes me again, and that brings me back to how great the past eight months have been. I say, "You're the only star I see."

"You always did have a way with words."

The door is opened, and she's out of the SUV, spinning under the stars. I cut the engine and turn out the lights before joining her. "You did that last time. We also danced in the moonlight." I hold out my hand. "Will you dance with me, Meadow Soleil?"

Taking my hand, she squeaks when I spin her in. I hold her tight, right against me. "Where do we go from here?"

"You wanted a redo. I want to give it to you." She pulls me back to the 4Runner that I owe Rivers for letting me borrow again.

"I thought college students were supposed to be able to hold their liquor."

Three hours later into the wee hours of the night, she's not holding her liquor at all. "I'm tired and tipsy, thinking I can fall asleep right here under the stars if we don't go to bed soon."

"Come on, let's get settled in the back before you fall asleep on me."

"I like being on you."

"And you call me insatiable." I stand, then lean down to help her up.

When she pops up, she says, "You're the rock star of boozing it up. I see where I went wrong now."

"I see what you did there. Good one."

"I have plenty more where that came from. You should hang out with me more."

"Be careful what you wish for."

She snorts. "Was I wishing?"

Walking her back to the SUV, I reply, "I'm good at reading between the lines."

We crawl into the back of the 4Runner, and I lie on my back. Meadow climbs up and relaxes on her side, holding me while I hold her. We can hear the wind whistling through the cracked open window with a backdrop of insects singing.

While her fingertips run along my bare chest, her breath warms my neck. Just when I close my eyes, she whispers, "I got a job offer."

I'm now wide-awake. She can feel the beat of my heart, so I try to regulate it from beating out of my chest in a panic. "Really? That's great." When I trust myself to sound normal, I say, "Tell me about it."

"It's in London."

Fuck. Closing my eyes, I catch my arm tightening around her, never wanting to let her go. "What will you be doing?"

"Marketing. For the firm where I did my internship."

"You liked it there?"

"I did."

I turn enough to bury my nose into her hair and inhale. *Please don't leave me.* "There's nothing in Austin?"

"The job came to me."

I just got you back. "What do you like about it?"

"It's a good opportunity. I'd be working for a highly respected international investment firm. I know some of the staff already, and that makes the transition a little easier. What do you think?"

"Is this your only option?"

"The pay is good, considering I'm a new graduate. Do you think I should take it?"

I kiss her head. She's put me in a spot that either makes me the bad guy or the hero. I'd rather be the hero of her story than a regret she once made. "You need to follow your gut."

"What if I can't decide?" *Then stay. Stay with me.*

"Only you'll know if it's the right or wrong thing to do. It will come to you."

When her body relaxes again, she kisses my shoulder. "Thank you."

I listen for her breathing to calm like her body. When she falls asleep, I don't. I can't, just like I can't lose her. Not again.

But how do I stop her without being an asshole?

I can hold her here, guilt her into staying if she decides to go. I'm not sure she'll choose London. She went once because she had to. Now it's a choice she'll be making.

Shifting, her leg comes over mine. When she settles back into her slumber, I think about the two ways this can play out. Either way, I lose.

If I support her, I lose her.

If she stays, she'll hate me, and I'll lose her.

That means there's only one way this can go. I have to support her, no matter what.

The tips of her fingers come to life, running across my chest. Her hand slips around the side of my neck, and she moves on top of me. With sleepy eyes and a sleepier voice, she whispers, "I want to make love."

She's on top of me, leaning over me, bare breasts, soft hips, and pink lips that need to be kissed until they're swollen. Aphrodite come to life. "We've already made it." I run my finger over her collarbone and lower, pressing my hand to her chest. "It's in here."

A languid smile spreads, and she lifts up to slide down on top of me. She will never feel less than incredible, her heat fighting the chill in the SUV. "Babe," she says, her head falling back as her long hair hangs down, hiding too much of her from my view.

I push one side of her hair so it's over her back and watch her. Watch her move with intention. She's not just chasing an orgasm. She's doing what she said she would. She's making love, creating it with me.

Love. I love her so much that I can't waste a second worrying about what might happen. I have to make her feel loved, cherished. To show her that I believe in her.

Turning her over, I take over, wanting her to feel the love she created inside me. Her hair is splayed across the pallet, a lust in her eyes when she says, "Kiss me, babe."

I kiss her for her and me, for us. I kiss and thrust until she bites my lip and falls apart beneath me. My own releases surges through me, and I grunt against the base of her neck until my body is depleted, left only with the remains of what I hope can be rebuilt with the love we made.

She holds me, her arms encircling me, but I know I'm too heavy to stay for long. I place a kiss on her head and then move off her. Keeping my eyes closed, I rest against the side of her shoulder. This time she kisses my head, and says, "You always keep your promises."

I'm not sure where she's going with this, but I say, "I do."

"Promise me you'll always love me." I can hear her need, the insecurities that she's allowing to come between us.

Fuck.

Though it's the truth, this honesty hurts because it feels more like an ending than words with a future. "I will."

39

Ridge

Under a golden sunrise, I grab a shirt and pull it on over my head before popping open the door. I slide out and take my jeans with me, putting them on as she looks back.

"You're awake?" she asks, coming back to the vehicle, and unabashedly watching me as I dress.

"I am." The hour or so I got of sleep wasn't worth shit.

Stopping a few feet away, she smiles. "I prefer you naked." She's sunshine. Mine. My fucking sunshine.

Keep it casual. Make her want to stay. *Make her choose you.* "You're stealing my lines, sweetheart." With my fly still hanging open, I go to her, closing the gap and kiss her, not giving one damn about morning breath or onlookers from the nearby highway.

Her hands slip under my shirt and flatten against my back. If I'm not mistaken, she seems to be holding on to me this morning. It gives me comfort. She feels like I do. She's going to stay. I close my eyes, wanting to hold her forever.

She whispers, "I've been thinking about what you said last night."

I kiss her temple and then her cheek on my way to her ear where I whisper, "Oh yeah. Which part?" *Play dumb.* I know which part, but as much as she wants to talk about it, I don't. It's inevitable, though, and has to be done. She pulls back just enough for our gazes to meet, the sunrays reflecting in her eyes. Gorgeous. "You're prettier than any desert sunrise and more beautiful than an ocean sunset."

Shyness takes over her delicate features and her hair with a million incandescent shades of blond are highlighted by the sunlight. The palms of her hands find my chest and rest under my shirt. "You say the sweetest things."

Kissing me on the chin, she then lifts higher and kisses my lips but lingers. Keep kissing me. As long as we're connected physically, the rest will follow. But the mood shifts, the air getting wind of the changes ahead, and I look at her. That's when I see it—all those fears she's been trying to overcome coming back. I know what I'm willing to do to make her happy, to give her the life where she doesn't live under the thumb of fear, but the sunlight of happiness. I have to sacrifice myself to be the support she needs. I push forward when all I want to do is pull back. "What were you thinking about?"

"I'm going to take the job."

Stealing a look at her with no makeup and her hair pulled up messily on top of her head, a sweatshirt that she stole from me last night when she got cold, and her fitted pants, I fail to notice the beauty of the landscape. She's all I see. All I ever want to see.

Swallowing my needs, I ask, "You'll be doing marketing?"

"Yes," she says, seeming to brighten. Taking my hand, she smiles so sweet, something I'm going to miss in my world. "You were listening."

"Of course, I was." My tone is curt, my heart speaking for me. "I care what you have to say."

"I didn't mean to imply—"

"I know. I didn't mean to snap at you." I just want to hold her as long as I can, so I don't need the compliment. *I need her.* "Is this for now or . . ." Debating if I want to say it, my gut tells me to ask because I might not get another chance. "Forever?"

"I don't know. I just know I want to accept their offer. It will be great on my résumé, and then I can apply back in the States—"

There's no taking my eyes off her. Like an interrogator, I need any small detail she'll give me from her body language to her words. "What about us?"

I hear a shaky sigh before she walks away. Her shoulders drop as she stares at the sunrise. "What do you want to do?"

"What do *I* want? I want you to stay."

Looking at me over her shoulder, she asks, "In Austin?"

"On the same fucking continent." I can't contain my anger. "Goddamn it, Meadow, I love you."

She's not even surprised. I'm sure she's been waiting for me to blow up so she can rebuild that fucking wall to keep me out. "I love you, too. So much."

"Then don't leave me."

A fire flares to life in her eyes, one I haven't seen in a while. She turns all the way around with her arms crossed over her chest. "Don't leave you? You live in a hotel in California part time, spare bedrooms the other times, and on the road the rest. You can be anywhere. Anywhere, Dave." Her demeanor changes, that flair still there but tinged in excitement. She rushes to me, my shirt twisted in her hands as she holds me close. "You can be based anywhere. You can come to London. You can be with me."

Taking her by the wrists, I pull them down slowly until

she releases me. "I can't. You know I can't." But I can do one thing for her. I can let her go, so she knows I'll never hold her back. *Even if it means she'll find everything she wants in London and forgets she once needed me.*

Fuck. *Fuck.*

When I step back, she steps closer. "Dave—"

"Remember how good we are together because the rest of the world will tear us down. We'll only have the memories." Her struggle to figure out her next step is evident. I don't want to be the cause of any pain. I once promised her friend I'd never hurt her, and I won't go back on that. "Listen to me, Meadow. You're drowning in what you think the world wants from you, expects of you. You've forgotten that you're in the driver's seat of your own life. Only *you* get to determine your future. Fuck society. Fuck your parents. Fuck it all, including me."

Her decision is catching up with her heart, her emotions wavering through her words. "I know you're right. I know, but I love you."

"You still need to do what's best for you."

"I have to try. I have to do something on my own to know I can. But this is also an opportunity that I don't feel I can pass up. It's good money, great experience."

"In another country from me."

"We're good—"

"So good that you're leaving."

"This isn't a breakup."

"Sure feels like it."

"You don't want me living with doubts—"

"Doubts I didn't cause. Your fucked-up parents did, but I get to pay the price, don't I?" I wish I could shut my fucking mouth, but my anger consumes me.

"This is why I've worked so hard the past four years, to earn a degree that can support me." Catching herself, she grapples for anything to hang onto, even if for one more day. "You support me emotionally, but I need to know if everything goes away, I can survive. I may never get this opportunity again." *If everything goes away . . . And there it is.*

She reaches out to touch me, and I let her, but we both know that our connection isn't enough anymore.

"We should go." I head back to the 4Runner, finally letting the cold bitterness seep into my once warm heart. "I'm sure you have a flight to catch."

"Stop. Please. Please don't walk away from me."

Stopping with the keys in hand, I turn back. "I never did. It's always *you* who left me."

"That's not fair."

"It may not be fair, but it's true. You're doing it again."

"You know what? Life isn't fair. I learned that early on. Guess it's time you did."

"You think I don't know life isn't fair? My mom is fighting for her life. You think that's fair?"

Anger leaves her chest in a hard breath. "That's not what I meant." Rushing to catch me when I walk to the driver's side, she grabs a hold of the back of my shirt. "I'm sorry. I'm sorry, Dave."

"So am I." I open the door and look at her through the glass. "Get in. We should make LA by sunset."

I turn the key, but the engine doesn't start. Fuck me. I try again and then once more after shifting the gears. "Fuck!" I slam my hands down on the steering wheel. "Piece of shit."

Popping the door open, I say, "Fucking SUV won't start."

"Do you want me to try?"

I scoff. "Yeah, that'll work," I reply, sarcastically, hopping out, and stepping aside. While she climbs in, I cross my arms and wait.

She tries a few times, but then stops. "Didn't work."

"No shit," I mumble, pulling my phone from my pocket.

"You're being an asshole."

I shrug. "So? What does it matter?"

"That's like saying *I* don't matter."

I rub my left temple. "Are you being for real right now? You're all that fucking mattered to me, and it's not enough for you."

"Mattered?"

Sighing, I try to calm down. "You're going to do what you need to do, Meadow, and I'm not going to stop you. If I do, you'll hate me."

"You're pretty high on that list right now."

This time I walk to her, the dust rising under my feet. "But one day, you won't hate me." Tilting her chin up, I add, "That's all I can ask."

With tears in her eyes, she shakes her head. "You can ask so much of me." Her hands are on me again, palm to heart. "Please, Dave, just ask."

Like her, I'm stubborn and have to learn the hard way. I won't ask because I don't think that's truly what she wants from me. I'm fucking proud of her for being accepted for a role she's perfect for. And she deserves this. Deserves to give this her everything, and I won't fucking ask her to not try. Because she should try.

But as noble as that sounds, I'm fucking angry. Angry that a job in the States didn't come up. I wonder what will become of us but then become angry with my own self-ishness.

I look down at my phone and find the number I need. Putting the phone to my ear, I plug the other so I can hear, walk away, and make the arrangements.

I find her leaning against the back bumper when I hang up. I rest my arm against the side of the 4Runner. "A car will be here in a little while."

She opens the back of the SUV. "We should get our stuff

ready." Climbing in, I let her pack, choosing to hang out at the front and watch that sunrise we drove out here to see.

I thought things would be different this time, that maybe we were finally meant to be, but she's right. Like last time, I won't be the one to hold her back from achieving her dreams, even if her dreams are standing on her own two feet.

Why can't she do that with me, or at least in the fucking States? I hated her being so far away in Austin, but it was easy enough to go see her. LA to London is a whole other ball game.

A text message gives me a five-minute warning. "The car is almost here."

She peeks out and then drags her bag to the edge. I reach in and take it, setting it down on the ground. She crawls up front and grabs her purse, then comes out the door up there. When the car pulls up behind us, I greet the driver and give him a hundred-dollar tip to drive safely.

When Meadow is settled in the back seat, the driver gets in. Her eyes track me as I walk back of the SUV. I close the door and then make eye contact with the driver. I text him once more before I reach the car, making sure he understands. I receive a visual acknowledgment—one nod and a tightened expression. Meadow slides across the seat, but when I open the door, I don't get in. "Text me when you get to LA."

"What?"

"There's a tow truck coming for the SUV. I'm going to stick with it. Rivers will kill me if I don't." It's not a lie. He loves this 4Runner.

Her mouth is open, but she can't seem to process the reality of what is happening. "I'll stay with you."

I shut the door, but the driver cracks the window. "Please," she begs with tears in her eyes. "No. I don't want to leave without you. Please come with me, Dave." I step back as the doors lock and the driver starts driving away.

It's bordering on kidnapping to force her to go, but it's for her best, even if it kills me in the process.

She's tugging at the door, but even when she gets it unlocked, the car is going too fast to change our fate. Just as the car reaches the highway, she has stopped fighting. Acceptance coming over her face as she looks back.

My phone rings. When I answer, she says, "You should have said bye even if it wasn't a good one."

I want to slow things down or turn back the clock even. I want to relive the last year with her again just to hear her laugh, see her smile, kiss her without worrying about time ticking down. I want a third chance to get us right the next time.

"I love you, Meadow Soleil. Remember that always, okay?"

The sound of her tears fills the line. I close my eyes, hating this goodbye more than the last.

She says, "I love you," and then hangs up.

My body loses strength and slumps against the vehicle. Dropping my head into my hands, I lean forward, not knowing how to get her out of my head, much less my heart.

Tires come to a stop on the highway not ten yards away, and my gaze slides up to discover her standing there. A mirage in the desert. *Please be real.* I push off, never wanting a wish to come true more than now. The gravel crunches under her shoes as she runs into my arms.

I lift her into the air, and our lips lock together. When the kisses slow and our mouths part, our eyes open. "You're here," I say so dumbly, but with hope filling my chest.

Worrying her lip, she glances away. "What happens if I can't handle it?"

Hope vanishes, and my stoic strength comes back into

play. I must give her this. For her, I have to make her go. "What happens if you can?"

"This isn't goodbye, so I don't want to say it."

I set her down and wipe her tears away. "We won't then. I'll see you later, sunshine." I kiss those cherry cheeks that aren't pink from love, but sadness.

"Promise me that this isn't it?" I hate that she's begging me. I feel like an asshole. But how do I promise her something I don't know is true?

For me, it's not the new beginning I want with her, but it's not an ending to our story. "We'll both be busy the next few weeks. The band and the South American tour, the new production schedule . . . You, packing up your life and leaving." But looking into her beautiful eyes, I let my heart speak for me. "I promise."

A sense of relief washes over her and with the smallest of nods, her arms return to her sides. After giving the driver a quick glare, the tension he caused disappears when I turn back to her. "I paid him a good tip to drive you safely back to LA. How much did you pay him to return?"

"Everything I had left."

Wanting to keep her here, I shove my hands in my pockets and watch her back away to return to the car. A breeze blows her blond hair in the air, messy and beautiful. *Like we were.* "Was it worth it?"

"Every penny."

40

Meadow

"I don't understand, Meadow." Darcy sits across from me after making us tea. Leaning forward on her teal velvet chair, she goes on, "I saw you two together in Hawaii, listened to endless hours of you saying how amazing Ridge is, but here you are in London, dressed like a slumper on my couch."

Tucking my legs under me on the fuchsia couch, I ask, "What's a slumper?"

"It's like a sloppy jumper. Look at your posture." Darcy's hands are in the air as if there's no hope for me. *Maybe she's right.* She adds, "Anywho, you're changing the subject."

"What's the subject?"

"Nice try. You and that amazing man you left in LA. So explain again why you're here and he's there?"

"Because I've lived my whole life needing to do something for myself. When I'm there, I'm my parents' disappointment, or Stella's little sister. Rivers's sister-in-law, or a student. Now that I've graduated, I need to be more than Ridge Carson's girlfriend."

She huffs, blowing a section of fallen curls away from her face. Wearing a silk shirt and pleated skirt, she holds her teacup and saucer in hand. Her casual wear is making me feel very slumper comparatively. She's so elegant even when her hair is giving her the struggles us mere mortals deal with on a daily basis.

I tug at my alma mater's sweatshirt and try to hide my slouchy socks under me a little more.

Standing up, she says, "Well then, it's been three weeks. I'm not letting you sit around and pout any longer."

"I'm not pouting." I've so been pouting, but I can't help it. I've doubted my decision while getting the work permit paperwork together. I questioned myself while packing up my apartment. I almost didn't step on the plane to fly here. Even after all the weeks gone by, my doubts haven't lessened.

She says, "There's really only one thing left to do."

"What's that?"

"Girls' night." She takes my hand and drags me off the couch.

I barely have time to set my teacup down before my ass hits the floor. "Ouch!"

Clapping, she says, "Come on, girl. We only have a few hours, and by how you appear, we'll need every second."

"I don't want to go out," I say, pouting on her expensive rug.

"Too bad. A fresh start means a new start, not carrying your problems like baggage around the world with you." Her voice fades when she enters her bedroom, but she peeks back out. "Now!"

Rolling my eyes, I get up. Maybe she's right . . . she'd be thrilled if I ever admitted it. "Where are we going?" I whine as I head for the bedroom where I now live, again.

Ridge

A squirrel outside the window has been chucking nuts at another squirrel hanging out on the fence. Normally, I'd be amazed, but even nut chucking squirrels can't take my mind off my sunshine. "It's another gray day."

"Maybe you should call her," my mom says.

I look back at her curled up on the couch. "She's probably jet-lagged and tired from the move."

"She'd still probably like to know you're thinking of her."

Rubbing the back of my neck, I feel uneasy in my own skin these days. "I don't know if I'd be a burden to her or—"

"Or a blessing? Go with the latter. She loves you."

"Did she tell you that?"

"She didn't have to. Just like you don't have to tell me the obvious." I sit next to her and then flop back to stare at the ceiling. Her hand rests on my forearm. "She'll come back."

Rolling my head to the side, I ask, "How do you know?"

"Because I saw how she looked at you."

"Like you love me." Remembering the conversation I had with her warrants a smile, and I give in to it.

My mom says, "She may have made the decision to go, but it wasn't easy to leave you. I know it's hard on you, but I can bet it's just as hard on her too."

"How long do I wait?"

"As long as your heart tells you to wait."

"My heart's not speaking to me these days."

Her smile is so good to see. She pats my arm. "It will when the time is right."

"I hate the guessing game."

"Me too." I move closer, and she moves over. Holding my mom, I try to give her comfort as she always did for me. "But it will be worth it in the end."

"How do you always hold on to hope?"

"I don't. I just try to have faith." Time is almost up, but I'd do anything to spend more time with her. "Your dad will be home to drive you to the airport soon. Are you packed?"

"Yes. Thanks for washing my clothes."

She moves back over, resting on the arm of the couch, but her smile remains. "It made me useful again."

That's just it.

With her.

For Meadow.

It was never about me. Sure, I can bury Meadow into the shadow of my career, fitting her into my life without her experiencing any of her own. It might be fun for a while, but that would leave her empty inside. It wouldn't matter what I did, or what I can provide. Nothing will make her see what we can be until she sees herself as her own person fulfilling her own dreams.

She told me what she needed, and if standing on her own two feet means I have to wait, then I think I can. Pushing off the couch, I kiss my mom on the head. "I need to get my bag. Thanks for being here for me."

Before I head upstairs, she says, "Always believe in the possibility."

I nod, remembering her saying that to me my whole life, but for the first time, it has meaning.

Meadow

Four texts in four weeks.

I guess Dave and I are doing better than we did last time. Some contact is better than none. I can tell from the awkwardness of the exchanges that he has no better idea how to navigate this change than I do.

It's not fair to tell him, but I miss him terribly. I used to think we were great sex and chemistry. Now that those aren't blurring my thoughts, I realize how much a part of me he has become. His laughter, humoring me over my bad jokes, late-night calls after he performed, checking on me after a test to see how I did. Listening to me vent about my parents, and then how alone I sometimes felt with my sister gone.

He knows me, and I know him and how he wakes up early to run an extra mile or two after binging on snacks with me. When he goes to Jet's house, he makes sure to check on Hannah, his friend, just to see how she's doing. That when his mother and I had coffee before I left, she brought his yearbook from high school to show me how he used to run on the track team. He'd never admit it now, but he won regionals.

He prefers movies to a night on the town, that he uses an alias with my name because he misses me. And that he doesn't much care for the nickname Ridge but likes the anonymity it brings. He's a Carson and not a Crow, and I love him so much that it's sometimes painful.

Pushing off my desk, I roll my chair back. I need fresh air, a distraction from my own thoughts. When I walk out of my office, the rest of the office has cleared. Checking my watch, I realize it's after five. *Damn it.* I've lost another day dreaming of how I used to spend mine, thinking about Dave.

"You bastard. You're a complete wanker," Darcy shouts from down the hall.

I run to her. "What's wrong?"

"I knew it." She points inside Carrig's office, and I follow only to find Lola from HR climbing to her feet while Carrig rushes to pull up his pants. Darcy slams the door closed and storms toward her cubicle. "I knew I should have never trusted that rat bastard. He belongs in the sewage with that cheating whore." I struggle to keep up in the high heels I'm wearing, but her rant reaches far enough for me to hear. "She just got back from her honeymoon last week." Whipping around, she says, "We should talk to her husband. He's quite the catch, but she threw him back."

With my finger in the air, I say, "No, I don't think we should get involved in that." I finally reach her, but she takes off again. "Darcy? Wait." Grabbing her purse from the top drawer of her desk, she's tight-lipped. "Are you okay?"

"I'm fine. It was my mistake for letting my emotions get in the way. You've been right all along, Meadow. Who needs feelings when they only get in the way? We're better off being independent, not needing anyone."

"That's not really what I said—"

She waves me off as she treks toward my office. "But it's what you meant, and I'm agreeing with you. Who needs love when you'll only get hurt? Fuck him. Get your bag, we're going to get wasted."

I don't want to get wasted—because I think I *believe* in love now—but I owe her a night out after all the times she listened to me complain.

Ridge

We come off stage and I grab a towel to wipe away the sweat. I'm tossed a beer and down it like water. My muscles are drained and tight, so I round out my shoulder a few times before grabbing my bag and following the guys to the bus.

Three cities in three days.

Someone, I'm glaring at Tulsa, thought it would be fun to travel old school. Well, as old school as a jacked-up, fully stocked, locked-and-loaded tour bus can be. With a whiskey and Coke in hand, the adventure continues as we drive through the night to the last tour stop.

The first pothole sends drinks splashing over the edge of the cups onto our laps. Delirious from the wild show we just played, we crack up. We're all too tired to give a shit about jeans and sweaty T-shirts.

I begin to reminisce about the old days and that shitty van I used to sleep in. "We were packed in like sardines. Chaotic Circus was the dumbest fucking name ever, but we landed good gigs. The five of us were broke, drunk on a good night, and smelled to high heaven. But we had good times together . . . until they went bad."

Finishing off the rest of the drink that didn't spill, I then add, "I've said it, but thanks for bringing me into the band. I was lost for a few years there, not having a home band that I could count on. Being a fill-in musician was never in my plans."

Rivers claps my back. "We're the ones who scored a badass guitarist dropped right in our laps. We know talent when we hear it. You always did outshine your old band."

"Thanks."

The Crow brothers share their own war stories of the early days—Tulsa was only fifteen when they started out. At nineteen, Jet had to get him home right after the show or their mom would ground Tulsa. Jet says, "The problem wasn't getting him home. The problem was getting him home without a groupie in tow." Shaking his head, he kicks the boot of his youngest brother. "Such a little shit, even then."

Chuckling, Tulsa's kicked back in a captain's chair. "It all worked out in the end. Look at us now, Ma."

A moment of silence is heeded, allowing my thoughts to wander across the great pond. *Four weeks without her.* I liked that encore break call, the habit, and her voice. Sometimes I hold the phone in my hand but then remind myself of the time difference and never push the button.

It was only a matter of time before my mind drifted back to the road trip. I have my pick of which trip. They both ended the same—me losing the girl—but lying in the back or looking up at the stars, time and distance has started to give me a new perspective. It's become easier to remember the good, not just the bad.

Rivers says, "I bought Stella a car."

This is new information. The two of them have held on to their old cars like they held on to a memory they didn't want to forget. Curious, I ask, "Why now?"

"She was never a safe beige sedan to me."

I sit up, repeating his words, "Safe. Beige. Sedan." Visions of evergreen and trees, grass and the sea. "She was never a hotel suite or an apartment in the sky. She's a home, a haven wrapped in a lullaby."

From the built-in dining booth, Jet adjusts, resting forward on the table. "What's that?"

"Meadow."

Meadow

"I miss you." Cradling the phone to my ear under my covers, my tears bleed into the sheets. I should have hung up when I got his voicemail, but my heart hurts so deeply that I gave in and decide to tell him. "I thought I would feel—"

"Are you awake?" My door swings open, and Darcy falls on the mattress next to me, the call disconnected, just as Dave and I are. The sheets are pulled back just as I hide my phone under the pillow and try to wipe my eyes. "Are you crying?"

"I'm tired. Go to bed."

"I can't sleep." She rolls onto her back and stares up. The room is dark but not dark enough for us to hide our inner thoughts. "I didn't love Carrig. He's a wanker. But I liked him when he wasn't being a wanker."

I'm a terrible friend. Here I am, caught up in my own upset when my friend needs me. I move closer, resting my head on her shoulder. "You deserved better than him. You're beautiful and vibrant, the life of the party, and you make a killer Cosmo. Fuck him."

"Fuck Lola. Just because you can doesn't mean you should. God, I can only imagine the fans you had to beat off Ridge."

Lying back, I stare up at the ceiling too. "I used to worry about that."

"Used to?" she asks, looking at me.

That's when I realize that I only had that fear in the beginning. Once Dave and I were together, it just disappeared. "His actions spoke louder than words ever could," I say to myself as the revelation materializes. Sitting up, I look at her. "He wouldn't do that to me. He wouldn't cheat. I knew it, so I didn't worry about that."

"He sounds perfect. Are you sure you weren't just blinded by love?"

"Blinded? No." A laugh bubbles up. "I loved, *love* him with my eyes wide open like my heart. We took things so slow that we knew exactly what we were getting into."

"I'm confused. Let me ask you again, Meadow. Why are you here?"

Why am I here again? I can still hear my dad's voice in my head. *Never rely on anyone because they'll only hurt you in the end, like I've been hurt. Don't be a fool like me. Protect your heart. Protect your assets.* "My assets," I mutter, getting up out of bed and pacing. "I have nothing, and he still wanted me." He wanted me because he loved me. He wants nothing but me. "I thought I had to build a fortune, build a life, build myself from the ground up to feel whole." Smacking my forehead, I see how clear it is now. "But I'm empty without him."

"What are you going to do?"

Ridge

"I don't know, man. My gut says go." With my knee bouncing, I wait for him to finish his drink. When he does, he finally sits back, and says, "But it's a long way, and I have to be in bed by eight."

"Good point," I reply. *What the fuck am I doing?* It's a sad fucking day when I'm looking for advice from anyone who will give it.

Alfie sets his juice box on the counter, and says, "Mom, should Ridge go to England to get Meadow?"

I knew I couldn't trust a nine-year-old to keep a secret. "Damn it, Alf. You said you wouldn't tell."

A jar stuffed full of money and labeled Swear Jar appears with Hannah. As I dig out some cash to add to the stash, I don't dare make eye contact with my friend. I know what she'll say.

And she says it anyway, "Yes. You should have gone a month ago when she left or, even better, stopped her from getting on that plane."

I try to shove two bucks, getting credit for the next curse word, in the jar, but it's too stuffed. "You're going to need a bigger jar, Alfie."

He runs around to a cabinet under the bar and opens the door. "Holy shit." Three rows of full jars fill the cabinet. He grabs an empty jar and puts it in front of me. "I think you're going to need a jar of your own."

Hannah laughs. "I think he'll be able to pay for his own tuition at this rate."

I drop my money into the new jar. He snatches it away, and says, "Uncle Tulsa says I need to invest in Corvettes. Chicks love Corvettes."

"When did he become girl crazy?"

Shaking her head, Hannah says, "Tulsa's started writing a book with him called Alfie's Tips and Quips – For the Fly Guy on The Grow. I'm having a talk with him when he comes over tomorrow."

Chuckling, I say, "They might be onto something here. Maybe you should ride it out and see where it goes."

"Um. No. As for you, go get the girl."

"What if she's happy there? What if she doesn't want to come back? What if . . . she doesn't want me?" There. I've put it out there. I blow out a big breath, the confession lying on the marble between us.

"What if she does?"

"Good point," I reply, repeating my earlier answer to her son.

Shoving me in the arm, she asks, "What are you waiting for? I checked the schedule, and you have nothing for the next week."

"We have rehearsal."

"No." Her eyes roll up. "Well, yes. But you can miss it, and you know it."

I stand and start to pace. "What if—"

"What if? What if? What if? There are a billion what-ifs you can ask, but you won't know anything until you ask the only person who has the answers."

"Meadow."

"Meadow," she repeats softly. Coming over to me, Hannah hugs me. "I love you, Dave, so I want you to have the same happiness I've found, to feel love like you deserve, to love like I know you can." Stepping back, she adds, "Instead of asking yourself what if, ask yourself why not."

Meadow

What am I doing?

Am I doing the right thing?

I've wrestled with this so much over the past five weeks that I just have to trust my gut. Taking the fancy pen that Carrig gave me, I spin it between my fingers and read the engraving again—Well done, Fellowes.

Screw him for screwing over my friend. I scribble my signature and march down the hall. I drop my resignation on Lola's desk, along with the fancy, too-expensive pen and leave without another word. She calls my name, but I let the door shut behind me, cutting her off.

I may be fucking up my future, but it sure doesn't feel like it. I grab my purse and take the elevator down. Cutting through the lobby, I give the security guard a wave, and say, "Cheerio."

He just stares at me as I go. Outside, my partner in crime waits at the curb in her Audi convertible. "Need a ride?"

Tossing my purse in the back next to my suitcase, I say, "To Heathrow."

Ridge

Rivers pulls up to the curb at LAX in his fresh off the show-room floor Toyota 4Runner. "It's a nice SUV. You gonna loan it to me for a road trip?"

"Fuck no." He rubs the dash like it's his woman. "She's too fine for you, but you can have my old one. I think I'm ready to part with it."

"Nah. I'm good, man."

"Oh yeah?"

"Better than ever." A lot has changed in the past few weeks. I'm hoping for the best.

An hour later, I board the plane. The flight attendant comes to my seat and says, "Welcome aboard British Airways. May I get you anything to make your journey to London more comfortable?"

"Nope. I'm good. I'm about to have all I need."

"About?"

"Long story."

She smiles kindly. "Well, I hope it has a happy ending."

"So do I."

Meadow

Dragging my suitcase behind me, I'm so happy to be back in California, my heart beating out of my chest with excitement. My sister squeals with glee.

I run into her arms. "I missed you so much."

"I'm so glad you're back."

Releasing a long breath like the weight of my troubles is lifting, I say, "So am I."

She slides against her new red Tesla and smiles. "Isn't she gorgeous?"

"Gorgeous."

"Watch this." The back doors go up, and my mouth drops open. "They're called Falcon Wings. Great for now. I told Rivers that when we have children, we have to get something more kid friendly."

"That's the coolest thing I've ever seen." We walk to the back to load the suitcase in. "About time too."

"Are you excited to see Ridge?"

"So excited. I should have never left."

"At least now you know."

"Yep. The only regret I have is going."

"But now you're back." She hugs me just as my phone rings.

My eyes go wide, and I giggle, too happy to contain it. "It's him." Answering it, I try to keep my voice even so I don't ruin the surprise. "Hello?"

Ridge: Ten Minutes Prior

Standing on a stoop in the middle of London, surely I must have heard wrong, so I ask again, "What do you mean she's not here?"

"I'll come down."

Her friend, Darcy, comes down in a dash. The door to her building swings open, and I'm greeted with a confused look on her face. "Why are you here?"

"I'm here for Meadow. Good to see you too."

"I'm sorry. Hi, Ridge. I'm just so confused."

"So am I. Want to fill me in?"

"Meadow's not here."

"So you said. Where is she? Do you mind if I wait for her to come back? I want to surprise her."

Darcy opens the door. "Come in, but I think it's you who's going to be surprised."

"Why is that?"

"You'll see." When we reach her flat, she opens the door and lets me in. As soon as I drop my bag, she says, "I think you should call her."

"Okay," I reply skeptically. Pulling my phone from my pocket, I find her number as Darcy grabs two beers from the fridge.

While I wait for the call to go through, she hands one to me. "You're going to need this."

"Hello?" Hearing her sweet voice calms the nerves that had become raw while she's been gone.

"Hey." Smooth. Real smooth.

"Hi."

"What are you doing right now?"

She giggles. "Nothing. What about you?"

"Um . . ." I look at Darcy and then to the bottle in my hand. "Having a beer. Are you home?"

"Ummmm . . . Yes. I'm finally home."

Furrowing my brow, now I'm thoroughly confused. I glance at Darcy, who shrugs. Holding the phone against my chest, I ask Darcy, "She's not here, is she?"

"No."

I put the phone back to my ear just as she asks, "Where are you? At the hotel?"

"No. I'm in London."

"What?" She yells so loud that I have to hold the phone away from my ear. "What do you mean you're in London? You can't be in London."

"Why not?" My eyes find Darcy again who's shaking her head. With my head held down, I say, "Shit. Let me guess. You're in LA?"

"Yes. I'm in LA and driving to see you."

I move to the couch and sit down. "Unfortunately, you're not going to find me unless you're about to walk through the door of your apartment."

"You're in my flat? With Darcy? Why didn't she tell me?"

"I just arrived."

Her voice trembles. "So did I. Oh Dave, what are we doing when we can't even reunion right?"

No. No. "Don't cry. We both just had the same idea."

"At the same time." She sucks in a jagged breath, but then her tone steadies. "You're right. If that's not a sign that we're meant to be, I don't know what is. Wait, you were coming for me, right?"

"I was," I reply with a quiet laugh. "I came to tell you that I love you—"

"And I can't live without you." She sounds happy. I'll take that over sad any damn day of the week. "You flew all the way there for me?"

"Yep. You flew back to LA to be with me?"

"Yep. Well, this is not how our story was supposed to go."

"I have an idea."

"What is it?"

I stand up under the power of an idea. "Meet me in Austin."

"I'll be there."

41

Meadow

IT'S HUMID IN AUSTIN. The sun can't seem to break through the clouds, but it won't ruin my mood. Even the airline losing my luggage won't dampen it. Exhaustion will, though, so I check into the Omni Hotel and settle in to sleep. I want to be good and rested by the time my boyfriend arrives because I don't plan to get much sleep after that.

I hop in the shower, brush my teeth with a toothbrush the hotel provided me, and wash my face before checking my phone one last time when I climb in bed. After texting him my room number and that he has a key under Field Fellowes waiting at the front desk, I rest my head.

Not sure how I'm going to sleep when I'm so excited to be starting my life with him, but I close my eyes anyway, determined to be awake when he gets here.

Rolling to the side, I keep my eyes closed despite the tingling at my neck. "Hello, sunshine," is whispered in my ear, and like my body, my mind is roused awake.

In the dark room, my eyes adjust quickly as they fall on my love. My grin is not quick, but fitting and genuine in the morning hours. His hands slide down my side, and I wrap my arms around his neck. "What took you so long?"

"I got here as fast as I could." He kisses me, and it's a lot like my smile, lingering and warm. "I missed you so damn much."

Holding his face between my hands, I take him in, wanting to stare into his soulful eyes forever. "I'm sorry for leaving."

He sits back shaking his head. "Don't be. You're here because you want to be, not for me, but for you. That's all I ever wanted."

"I did what I thought I was supposed to do instead of trusting my heart." I push up, the sheet slipping down. I'm quick to catch it, not wanting to speed past this moment too fast. He needs to know I'm here because I know what I want, not because I feel pressured or guilt. I feel love in the most basic form—innocent and pure.

Real love.

"It's still dark out. Just after four. I'm going to shower and clean up before climbing into bed with you. You smell too good to dirty with travel."

"I don't care. I want you."

His hand caresses my cheek, and he kisses my forehead. "I care. It won't take long, but don't wait up. We have forever."

The bed rises when he gets up, and I watch as he digs through his bag. When he heads into the bathroom, I try to stay awake, but the sound of the shower lulls me back to sleep on the words of *we have forever*.

The soft sound of slumber wakes me up, and I smile. Dave. *My Dave.* Even though I want to look at him, watch him sleep, and kiss on him, I don't move because I love his warmth wrapped around me, spooning me from behind.

I'm careful and reach slowly for my phone to check the time. I'm in no hurry to do anything today other than the man holding me captive in his strong arms. 7:53 a.m. It's too early to worry about the hours wasting away. I spent the entire day yesterday traveling to be right here in his arms, so I close my eyes and go back to sleep.

My breasts are squeezed, my neck kissed and sucked, a wet trail left in the wake to my shoulder. His body is warm and moving against my backside. Rough fingers find their way between my legs, and I shift, blooming open. Running slick through my wetness, my body stirs with my mind. "I want to feel you inside me," I whisper, keeping the day at bay a little longer as we come together.

Fingers are replaced, and he enters me slow but steady; the stretch I've missed as he fills my body, the fullness that allows me to breathe for the first time we've been together since the desert. Our souls connect as our bodies do, a way we've always been able to bond when the words don't come.

Reaching over my shoulder, I hold his head, needing those wet kisses and gentle sucks, wanting as much of him touching me, taking me, filling me as I can greedily get.

When our movements become rushed, too ragged to continue, he pulls back and turns me so I'm on my back. "I want to see you, watch your face, look into your eyes when you finally give in."

"I want that." I love the sound of our bodies moving together, fighting for a release. With hands anchored on either side of my head, he pushes in and pulls out, eyes on me the whole time. I meet his thrusts, driving forth for my own needs, and when it becomes too much, I hold on as we start falling over that cliff.

"Fuck, Meadow," comes at the end of an exasperated moan as if he came before he wanted.

I love it. I love that I make him feel too good to hold on. But then I'm closing my eyes and chasing the stars in the darkness. My nails sink into his skin as my whole body tenses and becomes his once again.

We lie in the love we made, our breathing too harsh to say sweet things. They're not needed anyway. I only need him, so I hold him to me, welcoming his weight bearing down on me.

My jaw is kissed and, just as we started, my neck gently sucked before he finds my ear and tugs my lobe between his teeth. "You. Are. Incredible." He rolls to the side and rests his head on the pillow.

I can feel his gaze on me, so I look over to find his smile matching mine. "I love you."

He kisses my skin, and my body burns for him again. He says, "I love you."

"So we're in Austin again."

He waggles his eyebrows. "The scene of the crime."

"If you're wanting to redo the first night we met, I'm nixing this idea. We are absolutely terrible at redoes. I'm calling them re-don'ts when it comes to us."

His laughter fills the air. "No more redoes. I promise. As for us, where do we go from here?"

"I was thinking LA."

Although he had to know it was coming, the answer still seems to surprise him. "Not Austin?"

"Nope."

"Not London?"

"Though I love it there, like Austin, you're not in either of those places, so no."

"Why LA? We were living in a hotel room, and I was in spare rooms before." His arm slides under me, and he moves me so easily into the sanctuary of his body.

"You're in LA, but if you were in New York or Chicago, Miami, or even Timbuktu, I'd want to be there because it's not about the place. It's about you. You're my home. *My* safe place, your love my shelter, your support the roof. I can weather anything when I'm with you."

A smirk that's been itching to come out finally shines on that handsome face of his. "There you go stealing my lines again, charmer."

I giggle. "You stole my heart, so I guess we're even."

As our laughter dies down, he says, "I have a few things I need to take care of while I'm here. You don't have to come, but I feel like I need to wrap up my life here once and for all before making a commitment to live somewhere else."

I turn over and face him. Still so happy to be back in his arms, I rest my hand on him and kiss his chest. "What do you need to do?"

"I'd like to visit my mom before we fly back."

"I'd like to see her."

"And I guess it's time to let that apartment go."

Sitting up, I rest on my hand and look at him. "Really?"

"Like you, it's time for me to make some moves, and I'm ready."

"I'll help however I can, but first, I need clothes."

"Umm . . ." I stand in the doorway of his old apartment in a little complex hidden by a run-down shopping center. "Wow." I scratch my head in disbelief, staring at the mess.

"I said don't judge." He looks back from the other side of the studio apartment. "You also said you would help however you can."

Boxes are stacked against the wall, trash bags full of clothes are piled in the middle of the room, and old shoes tossed about. "I'm not even sure where to start." I pull an old Chaotic Circus shirt from a bag, and say, "I prefer The Crow Brothers on you."

His gaze darts up, and then he laughs. "Most definitely."

Looking at the dishes in the kitchen, he asks, "The dumpster?"

I step over wadded up sheet music and a tipped over cat-scratching post. "Did you have a cat? And tell me it didn't die because you stopped coming here."

He laughs while grabbing a box of trash bags from under the counter. "No. It belonged to a guy who stayed here once for a month. The cat found a new home, and I kicked him out for not paying rent."

"Thank God." It doesn't smell, which is good, but dang, boys are messy. "I'm thinking trash."

"Yeah, most likely."

Two hours later, a truck arrives and starts taking the old clothes, minus a few shirts he saved, the furniture, bed, and dishes to a nearby donation center. Most of the remaining stuff we haul down to the trash, except for two boxes. "What's in here?"

"Kid's stuff—a few toys, photos—that kind of thing my parents gave me when I moved out."

I pull out a photo of Dave from high school. "You play golf?"

"Used to. Lettered in it."

I knew about the track team, which makes sense because

he runs for exercise, but golf? I like these insights into his life, but this one still surprises me. "How un-Ridge-like of you."

"But very David Carson of me." He winks at me. "I grew up playing golf with my mom and dad. We had dinner at the club at least once a week. When I found music, I felt like I'd found something just for me. I guess the rest is history."

I run my finger over the paper, admiring how handsome he was even then. "Did you ever have an awkward growth stage?"

"Not sure." He makes a face while clearing out the cabinets of cans of food.

"You're handsome. I would've totally had a crush on you."

That draws his attention. "Oh, yeah?"

"Totally." I set the photo back in the box and look around. "Well, it's official. The place is ready to go. Are you ready to leave and give notice?"

When he doesn't answer right away, I find him contemplative, his stance steady, but a million things seem to be on his mind. I go stand in front of him and lean against the counter. "Are you all right?"

"I'm fine. It's just weird." He looks over my head at the small space. "I stopped coming in the past year, but I always knew it was still here. It just blows my mind that this was my whole life at one time."

Wrapping my arms around his middle, I say, "Change is scary. I know firsthand, and so do you, but it's time to let go of this period in your life and embrace this next stage."

He holds me and nods against the top of my head. "I'm not sad. We have so much to look forward to. It's time to let go of the past and start living in the present while planning for the future. You, the band, that's my whole life."

My heart clenches from the sweetness. "What plans do you have?"

"I have a few surprises still up my sleeve."

Giddiness bubbles up inside me because, like him, I cannot wait to start our life together.

After showering back at the hotel, I slip on another pair of jeans and a silky tank top I bought this morning. "This is going to have to do until my luggage arrives."

"Mom won't care. She's just happy we're coming to see them."

Holding my phone up to show him, I say, "No messages or updates on the suitcase. I only bought concealer and mascara this morning hoping I'd have my makeup bag back. Fortunately, my fave lipstick is in my purse. Hope you don't mind bold red lips."

He pulls a shirt over his head and glances at me. "I like when your lips are bold."

"Cheeky."

When he rolls his eyes, I laugh. I love that I'm rubbing off on him. He asks, "How long until your British-isms wear off this time?"

"I hear the snark. I might hold on to them just to torture you, love." I let my voice lilt up at the end just to add to my point. "I'm giving them one more day to deliver my luggage before I start throwing a fit."

"It's all replaceable."

In the bathroom, I drop my head, sucker punched. "Damn it. Darcy just gave me a new Vivian Westwood dress and my Louboutin heels were in there."

Standing in the doorway, unfortunately dressed, he leans against it, and says, "It's. All. Replaceable. So don't stress. If they find it—great. If they don't, we can buy all new stuff." He kisses my cheek before sitting on the edge of the tub.

I start putting on lipstick while he watches. Turning toward him, I ask, "How do I look?"

"You're making it hard to leave this room."

"Good." I kick out my hip and walk with a wiggle out of the bathroom.

By the end of the meal, I'm stuffed and about to bust the button on my jeans, but when I look next to me, I'm relieved to see Dave isn't faring much better by how he's rubbing his stomach. Italian food. "I'll be working this off for a week."

Dave says, "I'm so tired from traveling that this pasta is gonna knock me out for the night."

His mom laughs, smiling with pride just from looking at her son. "When do you fly back to LA?"

Dave glances at me and then reaches over to hold my hand—on top of the table for all to see. He does his best to blend in like any other patron of the restaurant, but with his movie star good looks and the charisma he exudes, he still gets unwanted attention. "We're in no hurry. Once I'm back, I'll be back in the studio. We want some time together just the two of us."

His dad asks, "Why did you decide to meet in Austin?"

"Why did we?" I ask, leaving it to him to reply.

Dave says, "Neutral territory. As much as I knew the decisions we had made, I wanted to make sure Meadow made them where she would feel comfortable."

Leaning forward, I tease, "And he wanted me to help him finally clean out his apartment." That garners a good laugh, but I think we're all tired at this point. His mom is still following her treatments, but she looks better than ever with more energy and a smile that isn't put on for anyone. It just shines from the inside.

We hug them goodbye, but his mom whispers, "Take care of him."

I intend to with my entire heart and life on the line. I will love this man with all I have to give. "I will."

"You ready?" Dave asks.

"My whole life."

"I tend to talk a lot on flights," I warn him. "It's a nervous habit. I blurt things out like they're everyone's business."

Dave chuckles, and his hand tightens around mine. "You have nothing to be nervous about, but if you do want to talk, I like listening to you."

"You had me at Ding Dongs, so the rest is just gravy you're laying on me at this point."

"I'm happy to lay on you. Ever hear of the mile-high club?"

After sleeping in, eating, talking about everything, laughing, making love, and making the most of this reunion for over a week, I purse my lips and narrow my eyes at him. "I have, but you better not be a member."

"No, but we can initiate each other if you want."

"It's a tempting offer until I think of how small and gross the bathrooms on planes are."

"Good point."

I suck in a hard breath, my hand going over my heart. "Speaking of sex—"

His head whips to the sides to see if anyone heard. "Meadow, you're so loud." His laughter makes me laugh.

I grab my bag from the floor reflexively, but stop myself from digging through it. "Sorry, that's my nerves." My tone turns frantic. "I just realized something." Oh my God. Do I tell him now? On a plane? Or wait?

"What?" When I don't answer, he sits Forward and asks, "What's wrong?"

"My pills." My gaze goes up as I try to remember the last time I took one. "Dave, I have to tell you something."

"Okay."

My hand covers my mouth and the realization sets in.

He leans in, panic written in his eyes. "What is it? Tell me, Meadow."

I slowly look his way, feeling sick to my stomach from what I've done. "I . . . I stopped taking my pills in London."

"What do you mean?"

"I mean I stopped taking my pills in London. I ran out of them and needed to get a refill over there, but didn't."

"Why not?"

"Because I wasn't going to have sex with anyone, so I figured I'd give my body a break."

The same realization I had dawns on him. "You're not on the pill?"

"No. I guess I fell out of my pill routine and I'm so used to being with you without using anything else that I didn't even think about it." Tears fill my eyes while a lump clogs my throat.

In a lowered voice, he says, "We've had sex like ten times in the past week."

"I know. That's why I've been so distracted."

"Shit. What are we going to do?"

The pilot comes over the intercom. "Buckle up and prepare for takeoff."

42

Ridge

"So now we know you can't shout that you're pregnant on a full flight without everyone around us hearing. It's sort of like yelling anal in a crowded bar. These are a few things we should just keep between the two of us."

"Got it. I'll try to be better, but—" She can't seem to stop from laughing "It was funny."

"Glad you're in good spirits."

She rifles through the drugstore bag and then looks up displeased. "How many tests did you buy?"

"Five."

"Five boxes, but each has two tests." Pulling out a pack of Ding Dongs, she says, "You do love me. You bought a lot of those too."

"Well, you might be eating for—"

Pointing a finger in my face, she threatens, "Don't you say it."

I take that finger and kiss the tip. "No matter what happens, remember we're in this together."

In the back seat of this SUV, she rests back. "I know I should be freaking out, but I'm not." Exhaling, she sets the bag on the floorboard. "But there's nothing I can do in the back of a Suburban."

Her calm eases me. I'm not freaking out, but I'm not sure what to think. I haven't even had a chance to give her the gift. "Except eat a Ding Dong."

"True," she says, unwrapping one. "Bite?"

I take it and sit back. We're due to Rivers and Stella's soon, choosing to stay there instead of the hotel suite. Meadow's idea of starting new, and she said we'll look for a new place tomorrow. I have a surprise first, and when I look out the window, we're getting close.

Angling toward her, I take her hand, causing her to turn to look at me suddenly. She asks, "What's up?" sensing my anxiousness.

"I have something for you."

The SUV comes to a stop. I push the remote, and tell the driver, "It's fine. Go on up." The gate opens, and we drive up to the house.

Meadow runs her cherry pendant back and forth on the chain while looking out the window in curiosity. "This isn't Stella's house." Our eyes meet, and she asks, "Where are we?"

Shit. I didn't expect to be so nervous. "No, it's ours."

Looking back at the house, her mouth opens, and then her eyes fill with tears, the glassy surfaces reflecting the light that's coming in. "What do you mean it's ours?"

I nod toward the house, and then pop the door to get out. "Come on. Let me show you around." Moving around the back of the vehicle, I reach her door and help her out.

She takes my hand as I lead her toward the front door. "What do you think of the outside?"

"It's the most amazing house I've ever seen." She stops before we reach the porch and looks up.

"It's modern in architecture, but the front's not the best part. I like the privacy it provides to the street if anyone looks over the gate."

"I like that too, but I love the clean lines. It reminds me of my apartment in that way."

"I thought the same. I kept that in mind when I was looking."

Squeezing my hand, she asks, "You thought of me?" her voice getting raspy.

"Always." Pulling her close again, we move onto the porch, and I open the front door. "Let's go inside."

Holding the door open, she comes in and I hear her suck in a large breath. "Dave?" she says, glancing back at me over her shoulder. "This can't be ours."

I shut the door and follow her further inside the empty home. With my hand on her lower back, I guide her to the wall of windows that overlooks what appears to be all of LA. "I've had the offer accepted and put a deposit down. It's ours if you want it."

"It's not only my decision; it's ours together."

"I love this house because I can see us living here."

Turning into me, she starts to cry against my chest. I hold her and kiss her head. "So you're not mad at me?"

She laughs through her tears. "Mad? How can I be mad? You picked out a house for us, one that I can tell you had me in mind. I'm not mad, Dave. I'm the happiest woman in the world right now just like you promised."

I try to have faith. My mom's words come back to me. "I bought this house in good faith, the same faith I held on to for us." *Always believe in the possibility.* "I always believed in you, but to know you believe in us means everything to me."

She lifts up and kisses my chin. "You're an amazing man." Her happy bubbles over. "I want the tour. Start with the bedroom."

That's my girl right there.

After giving her a tour of the kitchen and master bedroom, I show her the last two bedrooms. "The house is only a three bedroom, but we can always move when we need more space."

I steal a glimpse of her eyes, catching her peeking up at me. Stepping into the bedroom closest to the master, I say, "I'm not sure what you're plans are for these rooms, but if we need a . . ." I blow out a breath as the reality of what could be hits me. "A baby room, this one gets nice light."

Her hand covers her stomach, but the smile on her face reaches her eyes. "You did all this for me?"

"No, I did it for us."

"But you didn't know I was coming back until two days ago."

"You're right, but I went to you, and if that meant staying in London, I'd let this house go and put down roots wherever you were in the world."

"What about the band?"

"I would earn a lot of frequent flier miles."

She releases a happy sigh looking out the window. Turning around, she rests on the windowsill. "How will I ever give you something as amazing as this?" She still has no clue that she is my world. Her heart, her soul, her mind . . . her body. I had no idea this was how good it could actually feel, that I'd know this level of love, but thank fuck I do. *How will she ever give me something as amazing as this*? My beautiful sunshine.

"You already did," I reply, settling between her legs. I cup her face and lean down to kiss her. "I got you."

When we return to the living room, our bags are just inside the door. She rushes to the door and opens it. "The SUV is gone. I don't want to leave, but we told Stella we'd be there by now. We're late."

"Good thing we live nearby."

"We do?" Her green eyes shine with excitement.

"Figured like Rivers, I'd like to be home instead of commuting across LA."

Still peeking outside, she asks, "Why is there a black Range Rover and silver sports car in the driveway?"

Spinning the keys around my finger, I say, "Want to go for a ride in your new car?"

"Holy crap! You did not do that." Running outside, she drags her hand along the spoiler of the sports car. "Can I drive?"

Wait . . . "The Range Rover, right?"

Hugging the Porsche, she closes her eyes, enjoying my car a little too much. "Is this my graduation gift because I just fell in love for the second time in my life. Toss me the keys to my new car."

My hand tightens around the keys. *Damn.* I think I just lost out on my new car. I special ordered that loaded Carrera GT, a car I've wanted since I laid eyes on it. But I don't have the heart to tell her differently. "Here you go. She's," I say, whimpering, "all yours."

She runs in and grabs something from inside with her purse, then runs by and snatches the keys. Jumping in the driver's seat, she says, "Come on. Let's go."

Shit. I really did lose it, but no way in hell am I taking it away now.

I fold down into the sexiest car I've ever seen and buckle in. She starts the car, but we don't go anywhere. I watch as she plays with the gear shift, not moving it, but tinkering with it. "You don't know how to drive a stick shift, do you?"

Too stubborn to admit the truth, she replies, "I'm a quick learner."

Thirty minutes later, we've barely reversed twenty feet. There's no way she'll be able to turn it around without taking down a tree or two and a large cement planter. After I've been cringing while she grinds the gears, she flexes her fingers around the steering wheel, and says, "Fine. You win. I'll take the Rover." She cuts the engine and gets out. "But I'm still driving."

I park the Porsche and then come around and get in the Rover where she's waiting on me. As soon as she backs out and turns around in the driveway, she says, "I'm going to learn how to drive a stick shift and then it's all mine, right?"

"It's yours whenever you want it, baby."

The gate opens, and she asks, "Which way to Stella's?"

I look right. "That way." She turns onto the street and drives, but I add, "Stop."

Startled, she slams on her brakes. "Geez Louise, you scared the crap out of me, babe. What is it?"

"We're here."

"What do you mean?" Leaning forward, she looks out the windshield. "Oh my God. You did not."

"I did." I pop my imaginary collar.

"You bought the house next door? To my sister?"

"I did. Lucky we love it, huh?"

"I love you."

"I know. Now go. We're already late."

The melody of her laughter fills the new SUV, making me the happiest man in the world.

Three hours later, the whole gang is sitting in chairs in the backyard. Stella says, "We can install a gate in the wall over there so we can cut through."

"We can do that, right, babe?" Meadow asks, such comfort in her body language. She's talked about the house and car, me, and even hinted at the major change coming our way.

Pacing the bathroom upstairs, she says, "Three minutes and then we'll know."

"C'mere."

She comes to me, where I've been waiting on the bed in the guest room where we were supposed to stay, and sits on my lap. "What if—"

"No what-ifs. Only why not."

"You're okay if I'm pregnant?"

"It may not be what we chose to do at this exact moment in time, but maybe it's part of the master plan for our lives."

Her arms loop around my neck. "How are you so wonderful?"

"I'm nervous because it will be a big change, but there's nothing I would change about us, so whatever happens, we'll deal with it."

"You wouldn't even redo the desert redo?"

"Nope. If that didn't happen, I wouldn't have you."

She kisses me, and then says, "It's been five minutes."

I stand, her feet landing on the floor. Before we go to look at the results of the test in the bathroom, I add, "It doesn't matter what it says. I love you, and you love me. Together there are no wrongs or rights, mistakes or accidents. Whatever it says, we're together, and we'll face everything together from here on out."

"I love you."

"I love you." *I feel her nerves, so I bring her hand to mouth and kiss it. "Ready?"*

"Never more."

Just as I take a big gulp of my beer, Alfie runs outside and announces, "Dad, someone's pregnant."

Beer is spewed everywhere, but not just by me, but by Rivers too. Eyes dart from one person to the next while

Hannah runs to Alfie and takes the test from his hands. "Where did you get that?"

"It was in the trashcan."

"Ew. Don't take things out of the trash."

Everyone is dead silent, until a quiet murmur sweeps across the group. Tulsa leans over toward Nikki, and says, "Tell them, darlin'," just as Rivers says, "Should we say something?" and Meadow says, "Oh my God," all at the same time.

My heart stops beating in my chest, and my eyes go wide in astonishment. Meadow stands up and points at her sister. "Are you pregnant?"

Stella bursts into tears. "I am."

Meadow can't stop saying oh my God as she runs to her sister, and they embrace each other, both now crying. Then she turns to Nikki. "Are you pregnant?"

Nikki nods, and the women go to her, sobbing to each other. Hannah joins in with tears streaming down her face. I set my beer down and shake Rivers's hand. "Congrats, man. That's awesome."

"Thanks."

Tulsa hugs his brother, and they congratulate each other while Jet joins in the hug fest. Alfie is jumping up and down, singing a song about having cousins when Meadow comes to me. I tuck her under my arm while she's still crying and kiss her head. "Do you want to say anything?"

Stella screams out, "Oh my God," just like her sister.

Oops.

Meadow's hand covers her stomach, but she's beaming. She's not mad at me and squeezes her arms around me quickly before the women are hugging her again.

Jet stands with his arms over his chest, shaking his head, but with a big ole grin on his face. "Well fuck me. This is amazing."

Alfie pulls a pad and pen from his pocket, and says, "I'm adding to the tally."

After another round of celebration, I say, "Looks like the second generation is on its way."

43

Meadow

TWO MONTHS LATER . . .

"How are you doing?" Dave whispers for my ears alone.

I can't stand any closer to him. If I could, I would. I didn't expect to feel so nervous on the red carpet, but I never realized how many paparazzi cram into such a small space to take photos.

I'm careful not to bite my lip, ruining my lipstick like Nikki advised. I keep my shoulders back like Stella reminded me to do. Head forward on my neck. Rochelle said it would feel unnatural, but I'll be happier with the pics. Wearing a Vittori original with makeup done by Holli's team, who made my eye color pop, I try to not squint when the flashes go off, blinding me.

Holli told me I'll be the belle of the ball and taught me to stand to show off my great figure. I won't have it for much longer, so I kick my hip out and anchor my hand on my hip while holding Dave's arm with the other.

A reporter stands in front of the group, asking questions. When she asks who I'm wearing, I mention Vinnie and say, "Nikki Faris shoes." I angle my heel so they get a good shot.

Nikki's band is performing tonight like The Crow Brothers to an audience full of legends, including The Resistance. It feels like the whole gang's here. Faris Wheel ahead of us on the carpet and The Resistance behind us.

The reporter says, "Ridge, your fans have been dying for an update. Any news on the marriage front?"

Dave glances at me but leans in and replies, "Some things we're keeping to ourselves."

Anal and *we're pregnant* come to mind, making me giggle out of nowhere. I don't even care because I'm too happy to worry what the rest of the world thinks of me.

Doesn't matter how popular you are, you're old news when another band shows up on a music awards red carpet. As the crowd goes wild for Johnny Outlaw, Holli sends me a little wave.

I return a smile just before we're shuffled along. Dave takes my hand and leads me inside. "I'm done out there. Unless it's about the music, I'm not giving them any part of us."

He's always strived to keep his life private from the media, but now that we're public and I'm secretly pregnant, he's become super protective. He makes me feel safe and cared for. I couldn't ask for more.

Stella once told me she chose Rivers over an ocean view. I've come to understand what she meant. I met Ridge on a wild night in Austin. I fell in lust with him the moment I laid eyes on him.

But Dave was unexpected. He didn't just put all my fears at ease; he taught me what real love is.

When Dave slips his arm around my waist and he holds me close, I breathe easier knowing I'm exactly where I'm meant to be. I snuggle against him and whisper, "Love is being with the man of your dreams."

"How do you feel about husband?"

I run my hands over his shoulders. "I feel very strongly about husband *and* wife."

"I didn't want to scare you with all the other changes."

"Being with you forever doesn't scare me. The thought of living a life without you does."

He kisses the apple of my cheek. "I've lived life without you. It's not living."

We hang back when the others start to go in. He takes my hand and leads me to a corner for privacy. Cupping my cheek, he says, "I never thought I'd feel this way about someone, much less be blessed enough to have someone feel this way about me. You're in my veins, sunshine, shining your light from the inside. You're ridiculously stubborn, but you usually come around to my side. You're smart and determined, and so goddamn gorgeous that sometimes I just stare at you because how can I not? But as much as I think you're pretty and intelligent, it's your soul and the way it connects with mine that drew me in." When he kisses me, I hold him, feeling emotional not just from his words but the way he's looking at me like I hung the moon makes me swoon.

"You're everything I never knew I could have—kind, loving, supportive, and giving. You love me with your entire being like I love you. We're not just a match made in heaven, we were made for eternity."

"You're stealing my lines, sweetheart."

Even though he's already brought tears to my eyes, I cock an eyebrow. "I'm hoping you're saving the best for last."

Chuckling, he says, "I am. Are you ready for it?"

"So ready. Lay it on me, Mr. Fellowes."

He double-checks over his shoulder with a roguish grin. When his eyes land back on mine, my heart's still fully lodged in my throat, waiting for him to say the words I've been dying to hear, he says, "It's coming. I promise, but this isn't the time. The show's starting."

This time, I laugh, which takes the edge off the moment and leaves us in the mixed-up bliss. He's right. The middle of an auditorium lobby when he's about to perform is probably not the best time or place. But I love that he felt it enough to try.

Our lips meet once more, and then he says, "It's a promise you can count on."

Very true. The man always keeps his word.

"And I am counting on it." Taking his hand, I tug toward the group who's waiting. Impatiently, I might add. "Let's go, rock star. You have awards to win."

Coming in fast, he practically sweeps me off my feet in his rush to take hold of me. With a strong arm around me, I remain steady. Steady, something that I cherish in all aspects of my life these days. Other than Stella, I could never rely on anyone, but he's more than proved himself time and time again. So the final question may not have been asked, but I do. *I do. I do.*

I thought he had to prepare. Buy a ring. Pick the setting. Plan the words he wanted to say.

I was wrong.

He was ready.

As we make love surrounded by gold awards for Album of the Year, Best Song, Top Rock Group, and two others, Dave is buried inside me—emotionally and physically. When he stops moving, he looks at me beneath him, and says, "The night I saw you, talked to you, and kissed you—the night we first met, I knew you were the one I was meant to meet, to love, to honor for the rest of my life. This world had no meaning until you gave me the green that brought me to life. Vivid. Bright. Intense. Brilliant. Light. You gave me what I never knew I needed until you walked into my life with sunshine and cherry cheeks and smiled at me."

His body moves effortlessly as he continues to look at me, admire me, love me with all he has to give—body, heart, and soul. Touching his cheek, I want him to talk, to hear what he wants to say. But my body craves his and begs for release. My head tips back, and his delectable lips take to my neck—kissing, sucking, owning—sending me into a fast release. When he chases mine, he falls over the same cliff and then plops down next to me to recover.

With uneven breaths filling the air of our personal sanctuary, he props himself up on an elbow and takes the hand I had resting across my chest. Kissing each finger and then my palm, he reaches under his pillow and pulls a small velvet box out.

"I never want to spend another moment without you. But neither of us is that naïve. I'll have to tour and travel, but when you can, I want you with me. And when you can't, you'll always be inside me. No more detours. I love you, Meadow Soleil Fellowes, so I beg of you to make me the happiest man and become my wife."

Choked up with tears threatening to fall, I whisper, "You shoot straight to the heart, Dave Carson."

"I know what I want—I want to spend this life with you. Will you marry me?"

"I want that too." I sit up while he slips an emerald cut diamond ring onto my finger. I don't let the worry of how much he spent sink in. From the house to the bank accounts, he's already added my name. I've not looked at any numbers, but knowing how much he trusts me, I don't have to. What's his is mine, and what's mine is his. Equals, as it should be. It's a strength I've found in our partnership and in our love. Not reliance, but because together, we are stronger.

We kiss, and my bottom lip is plucked when we pull back. He says, "Say it, sunshine."

Happily ever always. "I'll marry you, rock star."

Four Months Later

Sometimes life comes full circle at the most unexpected times, times we may not be prepared for or maybe we are . . .

"You look beautiful, Stella. Your bump is so adorable."

She turns sideways and tilts her head, analyzing her changing body in the full-length mirror. "Are you sure?"

"Positive. I wouldn't let you wear something that didn't look good. But I'll be honest, you look annoyingly good in everything." Standing up, I walk over to the mirror and turn sideways, rubbing over my own growing belly. "I have about five minutes until I'm back in that bathroom vomiting. Please tell me it gets better."

"I'm only a month ahead, so I can't give you wise advice, and as you know, my pregnancy hasn't been too bad. I think you're having a boy."

My mouth drops open. "I don't know anything about boys other than they're messy."

She laughs, holding her belly. "At least you can afford help to clean up after them."

"Jeez, thanks."

A gasp is heard, and we both turn toward the sound. Standing not ten feet away from us in the middle of the Beverly Hills Vittori store is our mother. Not looking like she's aged a day since we last saw her years ago, a smile tinges her eyes but doesn't move a muscle in her face.

I don't recognize the man whose arm she's clinging to. It's not the one she left our father for and not the one who insisted she cut ties with us. It's a much older man in a navy jacket and white pants as if he's just stepped off his yacht.

Vinnie breaks the silent standoff when he comes out with a purple dress draped over his arms. "I think this one will be stunning, Stella." His gaze darts around the room, taking in the scene, and he asks, "What is happening?"

I reply, "That's our mother."

This time, he gasps. Bending toward my ear, he shields his mouth with his hand and asks, "The mother that left. She just walked in?"

"Apparently, and she can hear you."

"Well, that's a weird coincidence. Oh, I just realized this is not the dress I meant to bring out. I'll be right back." He turns on his heel and hightails it back out of the main show-room. I'm pretty sure he's not coming back.

Daphne Fello—actually, I'm not sure what her name is anymore—slowly wades through the years of pain she caused us while looking at each of us like she's seeing herself in a mirror. Unlike the pain, we can't hide our looks away. We do resemble her on the outside, but our insides are of our own making, filled with the love of family.

She releases the man and holds her arms out. "My beautiful—" She catches herself and glances at the man next to her. "It's good to see you."

Neither of us makes a move. The lack of response seems to throw her off guard, but then her gaze lowers to the stomachs we have a protective hand over, and she sighs in disappointment. "If nothing else, I thought you would have learned—"

Holding my hands up, I have to stop her from saying

another word. I will not allow her poison to infect another second or part of my life or Stella's. "We did learn. We learned to love despite the hate we were taught. We learned to appreciate family, and if you're lucky, that includes friends."

Stella says, "We learned to love ourselves instead of being ashamed of our past." She smiles and rubs her belly. "But most of all, we learned the power of true love, and the magic that creates." She turns away from her, this time admiring herself in the mirror. "This is the dress. Rivers will love it on me, and that's all that matters."

"I agree," I reply, keeping my eyes on my sister.

Wordlessly, our mother stands just a few feet away but doesn't move. She only stares at us almost like she doesn't even recognize us. I understand her reaction. We're not the same girls she once knew. We're the women who rose from the ashes of our pain, the pain she set in motion, and we are thriving.

But my heart still aches. I bite my lip to keep from saying anything more. I don't owe her anything, not even my words. We weren't the ones who left. She left us, tossing us and her relationship with us away for a better opportunity, for financial gain.

Stella and I watch as our mother begins to slink out of the store, but she stops before she reaches the door, and says, "I travel. It's hard to keep in touch. I don't have email—"

My big sister says, "It's okay." Her eyes never deviate away from me. I'm not sure if she's responding to our mother or comforting me. Either way, there's a sense of finality.

Like Stella, I don't have a hard heart. We'd welcome her back into our lives if she were genuine and actually cared. Clearly, she's not there yet.

I don't need her to make a disingenuous effort. I have family who do care for me. I have family who love me and who I love in return.

Stepping up beside my sister, I embrace *her* . . . because we hug family.

EPILOGUE

Ridge

Six Months Later . . .

I dropped my bag by the door and carefully reset the alarm. Scrubbing a hand over my face, I make my way to the kitchen guided by moonlight exposing the vast view.

Starving, I open the fridge and find a plate labeled Rock Star sitting on the shelf. My wife's got jokes. I pull the plate out and unwrap it. She's also become quite the cook. Or maybe she always was, but we were stuck in a rut of ordering out and eating junk food. She worries about my health, wanting to grow old and gray with me.

I set the plate in the microwave and get that going while getting a glass of water.

"Hey, you," she whispers from the corner of the kitchen.

My heart always stops for a few beats when I see her— my angel, my goddess, my personal Aphrodite. As always, she revives me with a smile. My gaze drops lower to our sweet baby girl, Willow, cradled in her mother's arms.

The microwave beeps, but I go to my girls. Kissing Meadow, I then whisper, "I missed you."

"We missed you, too."

Trained well, I pump antibacterial gel on my hands and rub them together before tapping her little nose lightly. Willow doesn't stir. She's like me and appreciates her sleep.

Meadow places Willow in my arms, and at two months old, she's still the tiniest thing I've ever seen, much less held. She seems even smaller in my arms compared to Meadow's. But I hold her as carefully as I can, choking up every time I have this honor. The only other time I get affected like this is when I watch Willow snuggled securely in my mom's arms. To see her healthy again, growing stronger, and holding my daughter . . . it's a miracle.

Meadow tucks a corner of her blanket in, admiring what our love created. "I don't think Lisa set her down today except when your dad was holding her. He's such a softie when it comes to her, like he is with your mom."

Both of them have become wonderful parents to Meadow, stepping in and loving her unconditionally . . . as if that wasn't possible. But as grandparents? They dote. They love. They are proud. As for my dad, he's come to three of our concerts since Meadow's graduation. *Another miracle.*

"I feel like I have to sneak time with her in the middle of the night." Her laughter is light, so she doesn't wake Willow. "What a lucky little girl to be surrounded by so much love." *I'm the lucky one.* She looks up at me, and asks, "How was the show?"

"Good."

"And the flight?"

I glance up at her and smile. "I'm glad to be home."

"Me too." She kisses my bicep as she moves around and

gets my plate out of the microwave. "I'm sure you're tired. Go sit. I'll warm this up for you."

Remembering the boxes in my bag, I say, "I have something for you. I'll go get it."

The microwave is the only sound in the house as I walk back to my bag and dig out two turquoise boxes. When I return to the kitchen, I set them on the marble counter. She eyes them, but waits for the microwave to finish before saying, "You know I don't need gifts. I have more than I could ever need, and my life is like living a dream because of you and Willow."

"I like to buy you things. It's never about the money. Just saw it and thought of you." I lean against the counter and look down at the baby who's sleeping soundly. "If it helps, it wasn't expensive, and I bought a matching one for our daughter to have some day."

"Now you've made me curious."

Quietly, she takes one in hand and analyzes it. "Open it," I say. She is the worst to spoil because she legit doesn't want for anything. So everything has to be a surprise. The payoff is that she's always so grateful, and I reap the rewards.

The box is opened, and tissue hides the gift inside. When that's removed, she smiles. "This is a compact?"

"It is. I once saw you use a toaster to check your makeup. I thought this was handier."

Her expression is one of love, one I've earned one kiss and day at a time. "You remember everything." For almost being two in the morning, her smile could rival the midday sun. "It's beautiful. Thank you." She comes to me and kisses my jaw before leaning her head on my shoulder. With her arm around my back and mine wrapped around her, together we watch the baby sleep.

I made a promise when I said my vows, and I'll spend the remainder of my days holding myself accountable to this perfect woman and the best gift she ever gave me. Her smile and this little girl in my arms are whom I live for, who I love more than anything in this world. They are where my heart makes its home while I protect theirs with my soul.

We started in love and grew from there. Meadow Soleil is mine, and I'm hers. So the silver compact might not cost a lot, but as I hold my family, my entire world in my arms, the engraving reflects what she's brought to my life. "Hello, sunshine."

The End.

If you loved spending time with Ridge/Dave, make sure to meet his bandmates in their own full length novels.

Jet - Now Available
Tulsa - Now Available
Rivers - Now Available

Meet the all the members of The Resistance in their series, Hard to Resist, which kicks off with Johnny Outlaw's story - **The Resistance - Now Available**

To receive goodies, including free books, release news, sales, steals, insider scoop, deals, giveaways, adventures, and more, sign up here: http://bit.ly/2TheScoop

To receive a free book now, TEXT "slscott" to 77948

ON A PERSONAL NOTE

I travel a different journey with every book I publish. Sometimes they are straightforward and sometimes they are winding roads. This story didn't come easy. There are subtleties that were important in creating these unique characters and story. And I loved the route I chose to take. I hope you did as well.

Quick thanks you to my family who lose so much time with me and I them when writing. They are my biggest cheerleaders and I could not follow my dreams if I didn't have them by my side. Love you, family. XOX

Thank you to my readers. You are my ROCK STARS!

To my incredible team readers: Lynsey Johnson and Andrea Johnston - Thank You! You are the best. Thank you!

My editing team is amazing. Thank you Marion, Marla, Jenny, and Kristen. You are awesome!

Thank you to Adriana for picking up the phone, even if it's the 10th time that day. ;)

Thank you to Devyn and Kim for helping me pursue my dreams.

XO,
S.

ABOUT THE AUTHOR

To keep up to date with her writing and more, her website is www.slscottauthor.com to receive her newsletter with all of her publishing adventures and giveaways, sign up for her newsletter: http://bit.ly/2TheScoop

Instagram: S.L.Scott

If you love audiobooks, make sure to find S.L. Scott titles available on your favorite retailers.

For more information, please visit
www.slscottauthor.com

ALSO BY S.L. SCOTT

To keep up to date with her writing and more, her website is
www.slscottauthor.com

To receive the Scott Scoop about all of her publishing adventures,
free books, giveaways, steals and more, sign up here:
http://bit.ly/2TheScoop

Join S.L.'s Facebook group: S.L. Scott Books

Audiobooks on Audible - CLICK HERE

The Crow Brothers

Spark

Tulsa

Rivers

Ridge

Hard to Resist Series

The Resistance

The Reckoning

The Redemption

The Revolution

The Rebellion

The Kingwood Duet

SAVAGE

SAVIOR

SACRED

SOLACE

Talk to Me Duet

Sweet Talk

Dirty Talk

Welcome to Paradise Series

Good Vibrations

Good Intentions

Good Sensations

Happy Endings

Welcome to Paradise Series

From the Inside Out Series

Scorned

Jealousy

Dylan

Austin

From the Inside Out Compilation

Stand Alone Books

Everest

Missing Grace

Until I Met You

Drunk on Love

Copyright © S.L. Scott 2018

The right of S.L. Scott to be identified as the author of this work has been asserted by her under the Copyright Amendment (Moral Rights) Act 2000

This work is copyright. Apart from any use as permitted under the Copyright Act 1968, no part may be reproduced, copied, scanned, stored in a retrieval system, recorded or transmitted, in any form or by any means, without the prior written permission of the publisher.

This book is a work of fiction. Names, characters, places and incidents are either a product of the author's imagination or are used fictitiously. Any resemblance to actual people living or dead, events or locales is entirely coincidental.

ISBN: 978-1-940071-75-6

Cover Design: RBA Designs

Marion Archer of Making Manuscripts

Jenny Sims of Editing4Indies

Marla Esposito of Proofing Style

Proofreader: Kristen Johnson

Team Readers: Lynsey Johnson and Andrea Johnston